THE REINHOLD CHRONICLES
THE THREE THRONES

THE REINHOLD CHRONICLES
THE THREE THRONES

BO BURNETTE

The Reinhold Chronicles: The Three Thrones
Copyright © 2018 Bo Burnette
Published by Tabbystone Press

Tabbystone Press

Cover design by Damonza.
Arrow logo by Kendall Schlender.
Map by Kelsey Halverson.

ISBN-13: 978-1-7325924-0-7
ISBN-10: 1-7325924-0-3

First Edition
Printed and bound in the United States
Also available in eBook editions

To Kelsey and Dylan—
for all the adventures behind
and the ones to come

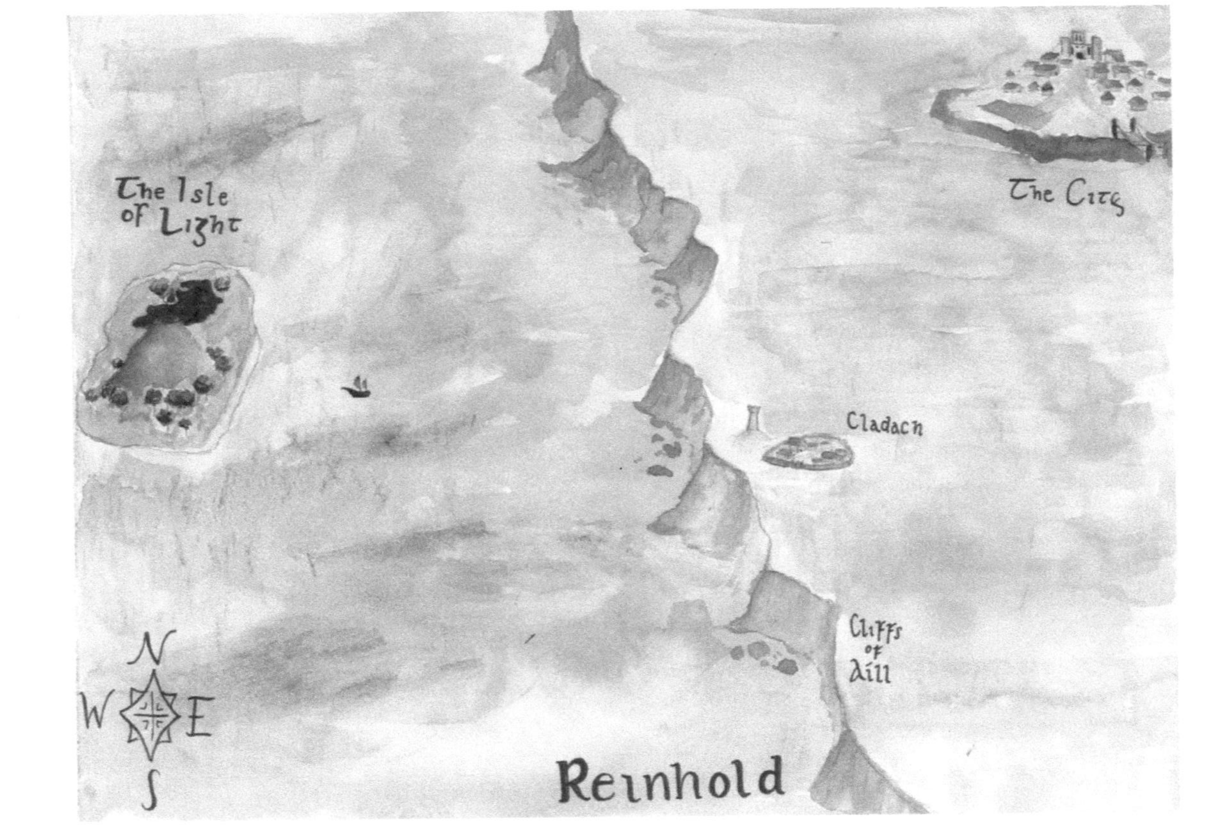

The Isle
of Light
The City
Cladach
Cliffs
of
Aill
N
W   E
S
Reinhold

A princess on a gilded throne
Clothed in silken raiment
A queenly look is in her eye
And grace is on her forehead

CHAPTER ONE: ORLIANNA

ORLIANNA STARED OUT AT THE BLOODSTAINED HORIZON. ALL AROUND HER, red fingers of the sunset reached down and disappeared in the distance as the western sky dipped into darkness.

She tensed and kept striding across the bridge. Perhaps she should have lingered and admired the view. Yet somehow the sanguine sky seemed an omen of danger—of death. She hurried on along the bridge.

Below, the river meandered through the city, its narrow second branch diverging to section off the wide peninsula ahead. The library loomed just across the bridge, its glass walls gleaming in the dying light. Orlianna shivered—but not because of the wintry chill. Colder fears plagued the depths of her mind.

She'd come here every day since Harrison left for Anmór.

Now, he'd been gone for well over a month, and she'd heard nothing. The silence had roared in her ears each day as she stared out the mouth of the cliff-lined bay. Supposing something had happened to him? Supposing the situation with Anmór had drifted one step closer to war?

She closed her eyes, but she saw more red. More blood. She hated the color, despite the fact that it dripped down her head in long tresses. Why did it have to haunt even the skies above her? Was God so cruel as to plague her with her deepest fears? If Harrison died, she died with him.

She opened her eyes. Harrison *would* return—alive and well and bearing good news. She tramped the last few paces across the open-sided bridge. The light had all but disappeared now, revealing the flicker of torches within the glass library. She hesitated at the wide double doors. Had the city guards forgotten to extinguish the lights? Or did someone else seek sanctuary here, so late at night?

She tugged open the wooden doors.

They clanked shut behind her. She inhaled the scent of smoke and ancient paper. Shelves spanned the walls on either side. The intricate floor held a map of Ikarra. Orlianna stepped over the tiles that symbolized her own city of Cahair.

The wide wall at the far back of the room was one vast, curved window. It overlooked the peninsula—and the ruins beyond—and the sea beyond that. Darkness beamed in through the windows, but a tall form clotted the very center in thicker shadows.

Orlianna caught her breath.

He turned.

"You're back." She ran across the marble floor.

Harrison wrapped his strong arms around her, his greying beard rubbing against her forehead. "Yes. I'm back."

She stared up into his eyes—or his eye. One had been lost in battle years ago and now held a glass replica. She focused on his good eye. "How did you get here so quickly without my hearing of it?"

He smiled. "The ship got caught up at the harbor entrance—imports and inspections and whatnot. They let me off by the old ruins and I walked the rest of the way. I had to see my princess."

Orlianna turned to stare out the window, toward where the ruins lay at the peninsula's edge overlooking the water. "What news from Anmór?"

Harrison stepped away. "No news, I suppose."

"You suppose?"

"I don't mean there's nothing to report. But in a way, there isn't a ruddy thing. Anmór is as cold and courtly as usual. But their silence is eerie. Something is lurking under the surface."

Orlianna's heart thrummed beneath her snug silken bodice. Supposing Merwin—or even worse, Merna—had grown suspicious of Ikarra's own silence? Supposing they had heard rumors...

"Do you think they've guessed?"

Harrison shook his head. "They would be more weaseling if they had." He grasped her hand. "Don't worry. The birds of Ikarra are safe."

She slipped her hand from his and stepped to the window, pressing her palms against the glass. "Praise the Lord for that. We've spent too long on them to have them discovered now."

He sighed behind her. That meant he had something difficult to share—something that took a while to decide how to say. She turned and scrutinized his face.

Torchlight cast shadows across his lowered brows and ridged forehead. "Orlianna, there is something else. Something beyond anything I expected when I went as ambassador to Anmór."

She tilted her head forward.

"Rather, I *thought* I was going as ambassador to Anmór. Things ended up going rather awry in a most curious way." He pressed his chin into his hand. "Brace yourself."

"You know I'm always ready for anything."

"Very well." He smirked. "The clan of Reinhold has been found."

She reached for the pendant around her neck, forming a habitual fist around it. "Reinhold? But they disappeared long ago."

"Turns out we've all believed a lie—a myth. They have built a kingdom across the sea in the wild lands. And, while I was in Anmór, their princess and her posse reemerged into the society of the three clans."

She scoured the darkness outside, mulling his words. If this was true—if Reinhold had been reborn—then they were truly three clans again. No longer was the world a duality of Ikarrans and Anmórians.

And that meant the ancient prophecy—the one about the three thrones—could come true. It was always said that one day, rulers from the three clans would bring peace. Until now, though, she'd never considered it to be possible.

Harrison leaned forward to catch her eye. "I spoke with their princess briefly, but afterwards I heard much more about her through…several less than savory sources. Some I paid for a good deal in cards and ale and wasted time. But I heard many things about her and her clan. She seems to have quite a story. Even in her short stay, rumors began to grow about Arliss, the princess with the fiery arrows."

"*Arliss.*" Orlianna stared out at the eastern darkness. An old longing rose in her chest, and for the first time in many years she didn't suppress it. The mysterious lands across the sea had always beckoned to her. Now she could feel it crescendoing in her chest—that thirst for adventure which she had once nurtured.

And she knew what she had to do, what she *would* do.

"I'm going to Reinhold."

Harrison seemed to expect this declaration. "Your grandmother will not approve of your going."

Orlianna's spirits sank back to earth. She gritted her teeth. Of course she wouldn't. Maeve didn't approve of *anything* Orlianna did these days. She'd always told her to squelch her wishes for exploration when she was younger. These new developments with Reinhold would do nothing but produce another of their heated quarrels.

She cocked her head. "My grandmother does not have to know."

"She knows everything—she has eyes and ears everywhere. She'll be three steps ahead of you before you can even board a ship."

She turned to him. "Then you stay here and buy me time. Only reveal I'm leaving when it's too late for her to stop me."

Harrison's eyebrows curved. "To openly defy Maeve? That could be considered treason. There's no need to start a civil war."

"Maeve is not the queen anymore."

"But you're not the queen yet, my little darling."

There was no need to remind her. She crossed her arms. Did his fifteen years superiority give him leave to say whatever he liked? But he was right. She *wasn't* the queen of Ikarra—not yet. But one day she would be. If she could unite not only the two clans, but the three…

Maeve would have no choice but to allow her to claim the throne. The people would finally follow her as their sovereign. And she could restore the land, rebuild the ruins, and prevent the war which lurked at every turn.

She looked out again across the sea, past the ruins, to where she knew the northern stretches of the Reinholdian land must lay.

"I must go to Reinhold and bring their princess back. We can renew the ancient friendships. We can restore the gifts to their proper owners." She fingered her pendant. "The three thrones can be filled once again."

CHAPTER TWO: ASHES

ARLISS STOOD IN THE MIDST OF THE RUINED HOUSE AND let the wild wind toss her hair wherever it liked. She filled her lungs. It was a spring wind—still hanging onto winter's chill, but promising life and warmth nonetheless.

She exhaled. Life and warmth had become precious commodities in Reinhold's stark, cold death. Thane's attack had razed their lives back to their starting point. The ruins which ran the length of the city's tiers about her had creaked and crumbled as the months wore on. Stone walls collapsed. Charred roofs caved in.

The wind coughed a sprinkling of ash into her eyes. She blinked and brushed away the sharp specks of pain.

More ashes floated into her vision. She whirled, shielding her eyes as the air filled with ash.

"Philip!" she shouted in his direction.

He was occupied with shaking the far wall and didn't hear her.

She tromped across the splintered floor of his old house and tapped his shoulder. "Dearest?"

Philip turned and coughed. "Yes?"

"You're getting ashes in my eyes."

He shook the wall one more time. A beam crackled free. A small box dropped into his hands.

He grinned. "Sorry. I had to find this, though. I thought it'd been burned."

She ran a finger over the dark wood. "What is it?"

He popped the lid open. "Just a few treasures."

She peered in and examined the contents: a piece of green silk, a charred arrowhead, and three copper coins.

He rubbed the silk between his fingers. "Do you remember this?"

"It's one of the armbands from my gown at the party in Anmór." That *had* been quite a party—what with Merna sneaking around and trying to assassinate them. "I loved that dress. Pity I only got to wear it once."

"A pity, indeed." He plucked out the arrowhead. "And this?"

"Is it…oh…an *arrowhead*, by any wild chance?"

"Not just any arrowhead. It's from your first fiery arrow."

"Oh." She looked down. Had he treasured these things so long? She'd almost forgotten about them. "What about the coins?"

Now it was his turn to smirk. "I won these from Erik in a bet a year and a half ago. A bet that I would dance with you at your birthday ball."

She stepped closer and pressed her head against his shoulder. "I'm glad you won the bet."

"So am I. Have you decided on a date for the wedding yet?"

"Father says the new chapel will be finished in a few months."

Philip pressed his chin into the top of her head. "I want it to be now."

She chuckled. "How about this—I promise we will be married by midsummer?"

"I will hold you to it."

She sighed against his chest. "I wish the whole city was already rebuilt. I want to raise our children here. I want to explore every inch of this realm with them—no matter how dangerous it may be. And I want to do it in peace, with you."

"It won't be easy, you know. We will never take this land for granted, because we had to fight for it. But our children—they will have to be taught."

"I'm ready for anything, as long as it's with you."

She savored the silence a moment.

"If there's a wedding to plan," Philip said presently, "shouldn't a coronation follow?"

Arliss sucked air through her teeth. He did have to bring this up again, didn't he? Just when they were having a golden moment. "You're too hasty about this coronation business."

"You're too hesitant."

"My parents are alive and well. I don't see why we should be ousting them from their thrones just yet."

Philip pulled her even closer. "Your father is ready for us to be king and queen. He's told me so."

"There's just one problem. I'm not ready to be queen."

"Hmm," was all Philip replied. He kissed the top of her head and ran his hand down her hair. Then he froze.

Near-noiseless footsteps pattered through what had once been the doorway.

"We have a visitor." Philip's voice resonated in her head against his chest. "We must be sensible now."

"When are we ever sensible?" Arliss asked.

"Rarely." Orlando stepped across a pile of blackened wood. "In fact, I think I could count on one hand the number of times you've been sensible."

Arliss let go of Philip and faced Orlando. "As if *you* were ever a reasonable sort."

Orlando raised his hands. "I never claimed to be!"

She laughed. "What are you doing this morning?"

His face turned grave. "Nothing. I came looking for you two. There wasn't much else to do."

Philip snorted. "They're building a city out there. Surely you could find a job of some sort."

Orlando shrugged. "One would think so. But somehow I don't seem to be the favorite face among your people."

His words stung Arliss deep within her heart. *Her* people. Not *their* people. So he still couldn't see himself as one of them.

The fingers of her draw hand curled and tensed. The new city was going to be vast—surrounding and containing the old one. Perhaps one day the wreckage could be cleared and a new castle built, one which would be so grand it covered all three tiers of the hill. But not just yet. For now, her father Kenton focused on building homes for the bereaved citizens of Reinhold.

"If you want a job," she said, "I can get you one. Royal powers, you know."

"I don't want to be where I'm not wanted."

"You *are* wanted, Orlando! This is your home."

"I could never be at home here in Reinhold."

She bit her tongue to stop the words. He'd nearly said this so many times, but having him speak it so bluntly sealed it in her mind. He was not one of them, and he would never be.

Philip closed the lid of his box. "We forgive you for what you've done. We want you to call this your home."

"I know you forgive me. But there are darker things I've done—deeper in my past than I wish to recount. Some things are too horrible to be forgiven."

Arliss shook her head. "Anything can be forgiven. Christ wasn't crucified for some of it. He died for it all."

Orlando closed his eyes and ran his fingers through his ash-blond hair. "I wish I could believe that."

Philip clasped Arliss's hand and pulled her past Orlando and through the doorway. Outside, the sun tried vainly to warm the windy morning. It shimmered on stone—not so much the sooty rock of the old city, but of the fresh-hewn slabs which lay in piles all around the old moat.

Even from here on the bottom tier, Arliss could see that the building progressed quickly. But from higher up—from the very top of the hill—

She glanced up to where her beloved castle once stood. The bare hillside now held nothing but a dark, lonely figure, her brown hair whipping around her head. She stood like a statue, and if it wasn't for her hair, Arliss might not have noticed her at all.

Philip eyed Orlando. "I wish he could see the truth."

"It will take more than my words to change his heart. His healing is meant for someone else."

"He's free but not healed. His heart has been broken in so many ways—too many."

Arliss nodded toward where Ilayda stood upon the heights. "His isn't the only broken heart around here."

Ilayda's arms trembled as she unfolded them and let her fingers curl at her sides. How long had she been standing here? It had to be near midday already. Time trickled past up here, as unaware of her as she was of it. The air felt thin and cool and free—unlike the thick, confusing atmosphere of the new city. Mortar and sweat and axes and splinters.

She shuddered. And people, people, everywhere she looked. Not that they were all bad. But it seemed whenever she dared to walk through the city's progress, she just happened to run into *him*.

Arliss, Philip, and Orlando were leaping the old moat and starting through the new thoroughfare. They were probably looking for the king. They wouldn't find him there—he was overseeing the thatching of roofs on the opposite side of the city. He and her father Adam, as well as many young men and women, had been at work since dawn. Although Ilayda's family lived in Cladach, where her father was governor, they were constantly helping Kenton rebuild the main city.

She started forward to the edge of the crowning slab of rock. She'd been up here long enough. And, after all, *he* was probably helping thatch roofs on the other end of the city. So no danger of a run-in this morning.

The creaking wooden sled still lay at the tier's edge where she'd left it. She positioned it at the hilltop's edge, sat on it, gripped the worn edges, and shoved off with her feet.

Wind screeched in her ears and blinded her vision as the sled scraped down the incline.

She'd worn this downhill path to a smooth slide in the past few months. She'd gotten Erik to arrange a few boards and supporting stones across the moat at the bottom for a smoother ending.

The sled stuttered across the bridge at the bottom of the hill. It skidded to a halt and spat her up to her feet. She kept going, jumping up and grabbing the attached rope.

She dragged the sled behind her as the clang of hammers pounded into her ears. This was to be the new city's main street. Already it bustled with Reinholdians running to and fro on errands. Children clambered atop stones which marked the road's wide borders. A few stray chickens completed the look.

She stopped to let two men with a log spanned over their shoulders pass. Where'd Arliss gone? She'd just come this way. There weren't too many places to hide. Not yet. Frames of buildings lined the road, but only one building—the king's current headquarters—boasted the luxury of a roof and walls.

She jerked up her skirt with one hand and yanked the sled with the other. Maybe Arliss had gone to fetch something for the king.

She reached the gray stone building and pressed her hand against the doorframe.

Brallaghan stepped out into the street and nearly knocked her over.

Her pulse warbled out of control. She dropped the sled's leash and stepped backward.

His mouth opened and closed as he thumbed through a stack of parchments. "Ilayda."

"Brallaghan." She choked on the name.

He glanced down at his boots. "Do you need something from in here?"

She shook her head. "I'm just looking for Arliss."

"Oh."

She bit her lower lip. Did this have to last any longer? Didn't he realize that it would be less awkward for him to simply leave, rather than trying to talk to her? She had nothing to say to him.

His eyebrows curled with a mix of emotions which she couldn't read. "I hope…I mean—" he reached for her arm. "I only wish to say—"

She swatted his arm away, refusing to look at him. "Don't. It won't help either of us." What did he think he could do to mend their rift? Nothing. There was nothing.

He nodded and booted down the street, his tall frame vanishing out of sight.

She tried to normalize her breathing, to restrain the tears. It had been four months. Did it still have to hurt so deeply?

Someone touched her shoulder. Arliss, accompanied by Philip and Orlando.

Arliss stroked Ilayda's cheek, tucking her hair behind her ear. "Time will heal your wounds."

"I wish it could." Ilayda closed her eyes and pressed her cheek into Arliss's warm palm. "Do you think I could ever be whole again?"

Arliss started to answer when the hammer of horse hooves crescendoed down the road toward them.

Erik jerked his charger's reins and trotted around the group once before clamping to a halt. He panted hard, his dark hair as sticky with sweat as his horse's hide was streaked with foam.

Ilayda wiped away her remaining tears. "Someone's been riding hard."

Erik nodded, his eyes bright. "Arliss, you have to come to Cladach—immediately."

Arliss arched an eyebrow. "Do explain."

"We spotted a ship far off, heading straight for our bay."

Ilayda glanced from Erik to Arliss and back again. Strange ships showing up in Reinhold rarely meant well.

Erik held up a hand. "This ship flew a black flag—the flag of the dragon."

"The flag of Anmór?" Arliss demanded. "This could be an attack. We need to call out the guards, prepare the archers—"

Erik interrupted. "The ship is flying the Anmórian flag, but it isn't an Anmórian ship. Arliss, It's your ship."

BO BURNETTE/18

CHAPTER THREE:
THE COMING OF RÍON

ARLISS DIDN'T SLOW KIRRAS'S GALLOP TO A TROT UNTIL SHE was halfway down the main road of Cladach, the seaside city.

Erik rode just ahead of her, scattering the people on the road. "Make way for the princess!"

Good thing Philip wasn't in front. Otherwise, he'd probably be calling, "Make way for the queen!" Did he really think she was ready for such a role? Or was he simply itching to be king himself?

Behind her, Philip, Orlando, and Ilayda all clambered down the city's cobblestones on their own mounts. Orlando rode like a true horseman—supple and poised. Philip rode…well, rather like she expected from the carpenter's apprentice who fancied himself future king of Reinhold. Ilayda rode like a sack of potatoes.

Erik reached the cliff's edge and reined his charger to a halt. Arliss pulled Kirras up beside him. The day was perfectly clear, even by the sea. Only the vaguest wisps of mist drifted over the water's clear surface. The green clifftops dropped into a mile of pale sand which spread across the bay.

And there, anchored in the middle of the bay, floated a small ship bearing the flag of Anmór.

The Sea Swan looked the same as when she'd last seen it, drifting down the river from her city and back to this very sea. Ríon had departed almost as soon as the battle was over, with hardly so much as a goodbye to her. She knew he hadn't spoken a word to Orlando.

Ríon had said then that he wanted to get back to his realm before his mother—Queen Merna—became suspicious. But if that was the case, why was he coming back? Or was it a trap? Perhaps Merna had taken the ship and sailed it back here as a disguise.

Kirras stamped her hooves against the cliffs. Arliss slipped off her back and stroked the mare. "Don't worry, girl. I'm sure we'll be all right."

Kirras nuzzled Arliss's hair with her gingery snout.

Arliss patted her before stepping away and leaving the horses with the guards who'd just run from the city gates. She rushed down the drop-off to the beach. The wind threatened to make her skirts take flight about her. She'd considered wearing a longer dress this morning, but she hadn't been planning on a trip to the seaside. This one would do nicely, what with wind and waves and sand.

The others hurried behind her. Philip matched her pace. "Why do you think they're here?"

"What if it's not them?" she countered. "Merna might have found out everything. This could be the first phase of an assault."

"If so, this isn't the subtlest way."

"I don't think Merna cares a bloody thing about subtlety."

Philip pointed. "Look—it's him."

Surely enough, Ríon stood at the prow of a longboat that speared across the water toward the beach. Behind him, Clare's unmistakable golden-brown waves nearly dipped into the water as she leaned over the side, letting her hand skim the gentle waves.

So it wasn't a trap. Unless, of course, their friends had turned against them. Arliss relaxed her tight muscles. They were Anmórians, but not traitors. Ríon and Clare had fought and killed against Thane's army. She'd trust them with her life.

Clare saw Arliss first. Her face brightened, and she leapt up, rocking the longboat. She waved.

Ríon had already seen her. He must have been staring at her the whole time.

Arliss held his gaze as she reached the base of the hill and his boat scraped up onto the sand.

"Why are you here?" Arliss couldn't stop the question from slipping her mouth.

Ríon jumped out of the boat and landed with a crunch on the sand. "It's good to see you, too, Arliss." He grabbed the prow and jerked the boat further up on the sand. He wore a a muted red tunic over a loose, white shirt.

Philip offered a hand to Clare and helped her off. She grabbed him in a hug, then turned to Arliss.

"It seems so long since we last saw you!" Clare wrapped her arms around Arliss. Her dress was black, but the red edging matched Ríon's tunic. "I've been longin' to come back here ever since."

Ríon folded his arms. "I, for one, haven't had such a longing. I saw too much death and bloodshed here."

Arliss dipped her chin in acknowledgement. "Without you, the battle would have been lost."

"The battle," Ríon said, "is not over."

Gooseflesh prickled the back of Arliss's arms. "Is that why you are here? To bring a declaration of war?"

He shook his head. "To bring a message. A warning. But not a declaration."

Philip spoke. "If you're bringing a message, who's it from?"

Ríon didn't answer. Arliss studied his blank face for a hint, then looked to Clare for explanation.

Clare's jaw hardened, her brows tight. "From someone who did not deserve our services."

"Then why are you here?" Arliss repeated.

Clare scuffed a foot through the sand. "Because the message itself could change the three realms."

The three realms: Reinhold, Anmór, and Ikarra. She still had not visited Ikarra. But she wanted to—almost as much as she wanted to explore her own land. Sir Harrison's promise still burned in her memory. Maybe the old friendship between the clans truly could be renewed.

Arliss ran her hand down the knife sheath at her side. "What is the message?"

Ríon eyed her knife, not her face. "It's long. And I'm to share it with the king and queen of Reinhold only."

"Anything you have to share, you can share with me."

Ríon glanced over Arliss's shoulder.

She turned. Ilayda and Erik had approached—with Orlando right behind them.

She whirled on Ríon. "If this is something against Orlando—"

"It isn't. But we have orders to deliver the message not just to you, but to the king and queen."

"Orders from whom?"

Ríon swallowed. "My mother."

Arliss narrowed her eyes. Since when did Ríon give two coppers what his mother thought? They detested each other, unless something had changed since her own visit to Anmór. Merna and Merwin treated their son like an outcast and a vagabond.

She turned and stalked back up the hill, her hair flying in the breeze. They'd better follow. If not, she couldn't waste her time gabbing about messages she was not allowed to hear.

She grabbed Kirras's reins from a guard at the top of the hill. "Find two more horses for our guests."

The guard nodded. "Should I send word ahead of you to the king and queen?"

"No," Arliss swung into the saddle, sand scraping off her boots as she poked them into the stirrups. "The rest will take a bit to get saddled and ready. I'll go myself."

She squeezed her calves into Kirras's sides and barreled down the streets of Cladach toward her home city.

The landscape beneath Kirras's hooves shifted from grassy plains to rocky fields. Arliss's throat constricted as she looked to where her city stood—or used to stand. Once, the majestic tower would have glistened in the sun.

Now, there was nothing but a flat hilltop.

She squinted. The city was still a good two bowshots away. Nearer to her, jutting out of the plain, bulged the round shape of a dirt mound. She slowed Kirras's gallop as she passed it.

Eamon's death still stung as much as it had four months ago. Every time she passed this spot, she could almost feel the sting of snow in her eyes, his dying breath on her forehead. And always, always, his promise burned in her mind. She had promised to never stop fighting the evil of Anmór.

Wasn't the fight over, though? Thane was dead, his warmongering influence gone. Perhaps Ríon was here because Merna wanted to negotiate peace. If the same thing could happen through Harrison of Ikarra…

They'd have no need to keep fighting. She and Philip could marry and rebuild their lives. And when she felt quite ready, they'd succeed her parents as rulers of Reinhold. That could be many years yet.

She rounded Eamon's grave and spurred Kirras back into a gallop as she neared the new city's outskirts. It would take too much time to ride all the way around, dodging construction. She'd ride straight down the thoroughfare, up the hill, and over the old city.

She rode through where gates would eventually bar the way.

Brallaghan rushed from the king's headquarters to her right, and she swerved to avoid trampling him. "What's the hurry?"

"Visitors." Arliss clamped the reins between her fingers. "Ríon and Clare. Make things ready."

She vaulted off without another word. Kirras leapt the moat and cantered up the hill, jostling Arliss as she scampered over uneven stone. Arliss paused on the hilltop and looked back. Far below and behind her, a cluster of dark shapes streaked across the plains.

Of all the insolent rogues—

Her mother stood at the base of the hill, waiting.

Arliss tugged up at the reins and whispered into Kirras's ear, "Faster. And don't forget the moat."

The horse understood. Muscles knotting with anticipation, Kirras reared up and bounded the last few feet toward the other side of the circular moat.

Time froze. Arliss soared through the air—wind rushing—heart drumming. They were flying. Wind filled Arliss's open mouth and tasted bright as citrus, as the sun itself.

Then Kirras's hooves clamped the ground again. Force shot up Arliss's spine. She tried to maintain her seat, but her momentum refused to cooperate. She gave up and dismounted, slipping a leg over Kirras's neck.

She stumbled to the ground right in front of her mother.

Elowyn clapped. "Quite a show."

Arliss winced. "It felt like flying."

"You were flying, for a moment."

Arliss tossed her hair out of her eyes. "I want that feeling again."

"And what brings you flying here so quickly?"

Arliss's spirits sank into the dirt. "We have company. Ríon and Clare have come with a message from Merna."

Elowyn's eyes darkened. "What message?"

"I wasn't allowed to hear it, apparently. Not without you and father present."

Elowyn whirled away, her rust-colored dress twirling slightly. "We must find your father."

Arliss grabbed Kirras's reins and hurried alongside her mother. "Mother, something's not right. I can see it in Ríon's eyes. Whatever he has to share, it isn't good."

"I know. I sensed that the moment you spoke his name."

"What do you think he has to share?" Surely her mother knew. She seemed to know and predict everything.

Elowyn sighed. "I am not omniscient, Arliss."

Arliss grasped her hand. "Surely you have some premonition."

"Did Ríon say anything to you?"

"Only that...the battle is not over."

"No." Elowyn went rigid. Arliss turned to her, but her mother wasn't looking at her. Her eyes glazed over. Something had come over her—something dark and horrible. One of her visions. "No, it is not over. The battle is only just beginning. Death wields its greatest weapon: war."

Arliss took her mother's other hand and squeezed it.

Elowyn's eyelids fluttered. She shuddered out a breath. "Death wields its greatest weapon…"

Arliss looked to her left as six horses and riders rounded the city. "War."

BO BURNETTE/26

BO BURNETTE/26

Chapter Four:
The Clans Converge

ORLANDO LET THE CLOAK FLAP WHEREVER IT WISHED AS HE hiked up the steep ascent to the top of the former city. The wind was inconsistent—one moment raging, the next quiet. Right now it was trying to tear his cloak off.

He stole another glance ahead of him. Ríon gripped Clare's hand as they walked up to the council. That was his brother. Well, half-brother. What difference did it make? A brother was a brother.

He'd hardly spoken a word to Ríon his whole life. They'd crisscrossed paths in opposite directions on opposite missions, never once guessing their connection.

He could hardly blame Ríon for shunning him. He'd done so many things he regretted. They all raged in the back of his mind, sometimes taking over his thoughts on dark, cold nights.

Couldn't Ríon forgive him now, though? He had changed. And they were *brothers*.

Orlando sighed and clamped his eyes shut. He would never be a Reinholdian, that was true. But try as he might, he could never imagine himself as an Anmórian. And Ríon was, after all, the heir to the throne. Why should he love the half-brother, the half-heir?

Philip drew his sword and held it at arm's length, letting it cast the sun's light across the group gathered in a circle around him. Then he tossed his weapon into the central pile. It already held so many others: Arliss's bow, Orlando's twin knives, Erik's longbow, Ilayda's arrow knives, Ríon's sword, and Clare's stiletto. Usually this seemed a harmless, ancient ceremony. Yet the glint in Ríon's eyes hinted at something darker.

Kenton and Elowyn had come straight to the council, so they had no weapons to drop in the ceremonial pile. They seated themselves on the opposite side of the circle from Philip.

The chairs had been dragged up the hill and arranged on the flat surface, spaced around the edge like the spikes of a crown. This had once been the castle tower. Now, only a faint circle indicated what had once stood there. Beside the council circle, the remnants of Elowyn's garden wisped in the breeze.

Philip sat and surveyed the group. Lord Brédan and Brallaghan had come. So had Lord Adam and Lady Elisabeth, who sat on either side of their daughter Ilayda. Very good. It would be better to have many councilors to hear whatever the message was.

Arliss sat beside Philip.

Orlando cast a wary glance at Ríon, then sat next to Arliss.

Ríon stomped around the circle and sat as far from Orlando as he could. Clare hesitantly followed.

Philip propped his elbows on his knees and set his chin on his fists. "Well."

Kenton swept a hand toward Ríon. "I am not the one with a message. Let the visitor speak."

Ríon stood and cocked his head, lank hair falling to his shoulders. "Thank you for calling this meeting so quickly, King Kenton. It's good to be back in Reinhold."

Philip's arms tightened. Not two hours earlier, he'd been claiming he hated returning to this land. That had changed quickly, hadn't it?

Arliss must've sensed it, too. She cast Philip a suspicious glance which fell back on Ríon. "Is it? I thought this was a land of death and bloodshed."

Ríon stared at her. "It will be, if you don't listen to me."

Philip scooted further down his chair. "We're listening."

"My mother Merna sends her greetings to you. She regrets that your meeting in Anmór was so brief and—" Ríon glanced at Arliss. "—misunderstood."

Arliss laughed. "She tried to assassinate me. She stabbed me in the leg. She chased us—including *you*, Ríon—out of the city. I hope your memory isn't that weak."

"It isn't," Clare said. "But Merna said what she said. Let him finish."

Had Merna bought them both out? Philip leaned back and crossed his arms over his chest.

Ríon continued. "Merna regrets doing anything to cause animosity between our clans. She wants peace between us, and she's asked me to be the propitiator of that peace."

Now Philip laughed. He couldn't help it. It was all too ridiculous. "Your mother regrets causing animosity between us? She started the whole blasted war by aiding Thane."

"That's debatable. Your war with Thane started long before she got involved. And as for your other notions, my mother was never the mastermind behind this."

Kenton waved a fist through the air. "Thane did not act alone. He could not have done all he did without substantial aid from an outside source."

Arliss nodded. "He's right. Merna was backing him up from the beginning."

Clare set her jaw. "I'm afraid Ríon's right. Merna's support for Thane has been…recent. And shallow, at most. Otherwise she couldn't have done it without our noticing."

"But you did notice," Ilayda pointed out.

Clare shifted to face Ilayda. "Aye. But that was because Thane started amassing forces and trying to hunt you down. Merna may have given him safety, and a few squadrons and chariots, but that is all."

Philip twisted in his seat. Even in the breeze, the afternoon sun sent drops of sweat down his back. Was Clare right? Could Thane really have been self-sufficient? Or was Thane aided by someone else? Someone stronger. Darker.

Elowyn spoke. "You fought for Reinhold against Thane. What is more, you fought without hesitation. Tell me, why are you turning against us now?"

Ríon slitted his eyes. "I'm not turning against you."

Elowyn rose from her seat. "If you have joined with Merna, you are no longer on our side."

Ríon motioned around the top of the hill. "I'm not on the side of one clan. I'm on the side of peace." He pointed to Arliss. "You seem to draw conflict like a beacon wherever you go."

Philip pushed to his feet and repeated a phrase Arliss had once used. "Lack of conflict equals lack of conviction."

"I think what *you're* lacking is perspective," Ríon shot back. "Do you want war? If so, you're no better than Thane."

Arliss stood. "Do *you* want Merna to have her way in all the realms? If so, you're as bad as Thane—a reprobate and a traitor."

Ríon stalked closer to Arliss and Philip. "Don't talk to me of traitors when you harbor one in your midst."

Philip glanced at Orlando. The spy tensed, but didn't move but for the wind blowing his burgundy cloak about his heels.

Ríon smirked at Philip. "If you want to know about Merna, why not ask one who's spent all his life as her prized possession?"

Philip turned back to Ríon. It took every muscle in his body fighting against itself to stop from punching him square in the face.

Heat boiled in Arliss's chest as she came within two paces of Ríon. "Have you come that low? And to think I would have died for you once!"

Ríon's expression cracked. "To lose your respect is a great insult indeed."

"It's an insult you deserve." Arliss clenched her teeth. "I won't let you cut your own brother down with your words."

Elowyn still stood. "Arliss, bring this council to order."

Arliss glowered at her mother. Were they all playing at this game—edging her on to playing the role of queen? She faced Rίon. "Sit down and finish delivering your message, before I lower my opinion of you even more."

Rίon still stood. "I won't. Because I am afraid for you, Arliss. For all of you." He gestured around the circle. "Your country is young. You're naive."

Elowyn chuckled. "And what advice would the older, wiser clans have for us?"

"Be wary. This isn't just about Anmόr. The clan of Ikarra knows about you now, too. And they want to seize your land as their own territory."

"How do you know this?"

"My mother is the sister of the former queen of Ikarra. She has told her that the mood of the Ikarran people is sour toward you Reinholdians."

Arliss shook her head. "It's a lie. I spoke with Harrison of Ikarra, and he assured me quite the opposite."

"One person," Rίon insisted, "does not represent the entire opinion of a people."

"How true." Clare rose, pulling her golden-brown curls over one shoulder. "And let me assure you that Rίon's representation of Merna is just his perspective. Now let me give you mine."

Rίon placed his palm against her shoulder. "Don't do this."

She shook free. "They need to know the truth."

"What truth?" Arliss asked.

"That no matter what Merna says, she wants Reinhold as another jewel in her crown. She wants its land. She wants its gifts. Ikarra is just an excuse." Clare's jaw jutted out. "And if it came to war, I would never fight on Merna's side."

Rίon backed toward the pile of weapons. "It won't come to war. That's what I'm trying to tell you! Listen!"

Erik spoke for the first time. "As long as you speak Merna's words, I can't believe a thing you say."

"Why does it matter where the words come from, if they are

peace? My mother wants peace. She wants unity!" Ríon bent suspiciously near the pile.

Arliss edged to the center of the hilltop. If it came to this, she had to stop Ríon. "How can you trust her?"

"How can I trust *you*?"

Arliss ducked to the ground, grappled for her knife, and jumped to face Ríon. "You don't trust me."

He pulled his sword from the pile and pointed it at her. "Not anymore."

Everyone around the circle leapt to their feet.

Arliss scraped her knife down the length of Ríon's blade. "I want you to trust me."

He arced his blade closer. It touched her hair, pressing it to her neck and sending chills down her back. "I feel the same."

"So why can't we?"

"Because you have chosen the side that will lead to war. To death. And I can't bear to see any more of that."

Arliss gasped. Was he really saying all of this? He made a living out of fighting. But then again, he wasn't a warrior who ventured out to find war. He was a vigilante who stopped the battles before they began.

She stared into Ríon's dark eyes. He was just like her, in a way. He wanted to marry Clare and live in peace, just like she wanted to marry Philip and rebuild her life. But unlike her, he wasn't willing to fight for that peace.

Elowyn appeared in between them and pushed them away from each other by their shoulders. "Peace—all of us!"

Arliss glanced around. Everyone else had retrieved their weapons. It looked like the beginning of a battle. She looked to Ríon.

He sheathed his sword, then strapped it back around his waist. She did the same with her own weapons. Everyone else quickly followed suit.

Her breath felt like water in her lungs. If a simple message—a warning—nearly sent these few into conflict, what would happen when the clans converged on a wider scale?

Ríon was right about one thing. The battle had only just begun.

Bo Burnette/34

CHAPTER FIVE: RUNNING AWAY

ARLISS BREATHED IN THE SWEETNESS OF BUDDING LASAIRBLÁTH MINGLED WITH the rich scent of alder trees. They were all around her, surrounding the forest path, bursting upward with fresh life. She and Philip had kept this path through the woods clear of trees and brambles, but Lasairbláth couldn't be contained. It sprawled around everywhere and covered the forest floor like a blanket of snow.

Clare exhaled beside her. "It's beautiful. So wild—so secluded."

"Is there anything like it in Anmór?" Arliss asked.

"Yes, in the western outlands. But I haven't traveled there since I was a girl. I'm too busy…"

"Fighting?"

Clare exhaled. "It's a war that never starts and never ends."

"Ríon seems to think it could end." Arliss looked up ahead, where Ríon and Philip walked together. Further up, Orlando stayed near Erik and Ilayda. Brallaghan hadn't come. He hardly ever did anymore, and Arliss missed his company. But she would rather sacrifice his than Ilayda's.

Clare stared ahead. "He's right, it could. But to end, the war has to start first."

"So you think it will come to that?"

"Merna wants your land. She wants your gifts. And Ikarra, it seems, wants the same thing. You're caught in the middle."

Arliss swallowed. She trusted Clare, but somehow these words against Ikarra seemed wrong—false. She didn't have peace with them.

Ríon turned and looked at her, then gave a little jerk of his head. So he wanted to talk to her, did he? She'd plant her boot in his stomach if he said one more rotten thing about Orlando.

She turned to Clare. "Excuse me." She traipsed up the path to join Ríon. As if on cue, Philip slipped back to flank Clare.

Ríon rubbed his palm over his sword's pommel. "You know what this is?"

"It's the sword of Anmór."

"Yes."

"I always wondered, where are the other clans' gifts? I've spent so much time worrying about Reinhold's that I never thought about yours."

"My mother wears the crown. The ring they gave as a gift to me. I promptly gave it to Clare."

"And what about the missing gifts of Reinhold? Does Merna have those as well?"

"The secret gifts? I haven't a clue."

She eyed him. He was speaking the truth. His eyes alone betrayed that. But she couldn't help but being suspicious. Gally himself had confirmed that the secret gifts existed: a vial, a sphere, and a pendant. She'd found the vial beneath the waterfall which tumbled only a few minutes' walk from where they were. But the sphere and the pendant…

She didn't know where they were, much less what they could do.

Ríon fisted his hand around the pommel. "I—I don't think I came across the way I intended to at the council."

"I should hope not." She smirked. "Words are like magic. You have to be careful how you use them."

"I'm not very good with words sometimes." He glanced sideways at her.

"My parents think you've turned against us."

Ríon groaned. "You'll have to explain to them what I really meant."

"I'm not sure *I* understand what you really meant."

They had come to where the front wall of Thane's fortress once stood. Arliss kept walking down the rock-lined road, motioning Ríon to follow.

He stared up at the darkening sky above the mountainous peaks. "My parents want peace with your land. They helped Thane, yes, but Thane is gone. Perhaps they're being ingenuine, but I can only tell you what they told me. Merna wants to build a friendship—a buffer—in case Ikarra tries to come after both our clans."

"So we're a means to an end."

"A means to preventing an end."

"And you agree with her."

It wasn't a question, but he took it as such. "Not with her person, or her methods, but with her outcome. It's the outcome that matters, isn't it?"

She weighed this. Did it matter how they achieved peace—as long as they did achieve it? How could one's intentions play no role? An outcome wasn't an isolated event. It was the final link of a chain.

Ríon blew a sigh through his lips. "I made Merna tell me everything about Orlando. And she did. Not just about our brotherhood, but about how she'd tried to cover it up. How she found Orlando and had him trained under Thane—isolated from the court his whole life. She did everything she could to prevent his birth from becoming known. It fed her hate of my father."

Ahead, Orlando stood by the waterfall's pinnacle with Erik and Ilayda. "It doesn't need to feed any more hate, though. You can make up for lost years with him."

Ríon whirled to the side of the path and slammed his fist into a boundary stone. "Lost years? As if I owed him anything! If anything, he has a lifetime to repay to me—a lifetime I've spent trying to undo his evil."

Arliss pressed her hand into the stone and leaned into it. "How can you say that? He's changed."

"I don't know him. I never have. Now that I know the truth, I feel I know him even less."

Her face flushed with heat. "He's your brother, Ríon! You said you left right after the battle to avoid your mother's suspicion, but I suspect you left to get away from him. You're afraid to face him."

Ríon motioned toward where Orlando stood. Blood streaked his fist from striking the stone. "Do you think I'm the only one who's afraid? He's avoided me from the moment I arrived."

She reached out for his bloody hand and lowered it. "You can't run away from who you are your whole life. From who he is."

He shook his head. "He's done worse things than you can imagine. He's a stain on the Anmórian line. Indeed—*he's* the one who can't run away all his life."

Orlando rushed down the sandy incline so fast he thought he'd stumble onto his face. They were leaving—might have already left. The ship was still in the bay, of course, but what if Ríon and Clare had already boarded?

The morning sun pierced through a smattering of wispy clouds. He reached the bottom of the hill, and half his fears vanished as he looked across the beach. Clare squatted in the sand, chatting with Arliss and Ilayda.

So *she* hadn't left yet. But of course, that wasn't what he was afraid of. He had spoken with Clare at length the evening before— during the king's feast, and at Arliss's tea later in the evening. Clare accepted him as if they hadn't been lifelong enemies.

Ríon had not spoken a word to him.

He could not leave things like this. He had to find his brother and speak to him before he left for good. But where was he? The whole court had gathered by the sea, plus half the town of Cladach. Somehow Ríon wasn't among their number.

A strong hand clamped down on Orlando's shoulder.

He spun, grabbing the forearm and jerking it to the side. He thrust his own arm under and around his assailant's biceps. His hands met, completing the loop he'd created.

Ríon grunted. "I wasn't trying to startle you."

Orlando held the loop. One movement, and he could snap Ríon's arm if he wanted to. "You did."

"I just wanted to say goodbye."

Orlando released Ríon and staggered backward. No hate...no ulterior motives...just a simple farewell? He gaped.

Ríon grasped Orlando's arm. "Farewell. Stay out of trouble."

Orlando almost smiled. "Can't promise that."

"I know. Still, don't get yourself killed. And don't trust anyone you aren't sure of."

"Who shouldn't I be sure of?"

Ríon leaned closer. "Arliss. Philip. Any of them. And especially, don't trust the Ikarrans." He glanced around as if to make sure no one was too near. "They want your ring."

Orlando looked down at his right hand. "Why would they want the ring of Reinhold?"

Ríon shrugged. "I don't know. Merna told me."

"Who told her?"

"I haven't the faintest idea." Ríon sucked in his lips. "Be careful."

Then he stepped away.

Arliss stood at the fringe of the receding tide, her bare forearms clamped across her chest, watching Ríon's ship—*her* ship— disappear into the west. He'd insisted they could not stay longer than a day.

For her part, she regretted it. Despite his sharp manner at yesterday's council, he had warmed as the evening wore on. She'd enjoyed every moment of the late-night tea upon the hill—except that Orlando and Ríon didn't speak a word to each other, and Ilayda and Brallaghan sat at opposite sides of the circle. All the same, she wished they would linger in Reinhold.

Merna needed them back, apparently. With her private forces destroyed—and her purported change of heart—she wanted to assimilate Ríon's band into her personal guard. Clare had spoken of this transition with fierce irritation.

Arliss released her folded arms and sighed. The wind clawed through the sand and sprayed it up onto her bare skin like tiny darts.

The spray of sand stopped as Kenton came to stand beside her, his hands clasped behind his back. "I was surprised to see them gone so soon."

She frowned. "He was insistent."

"I think he's afraid. Like the rest of us, he realizes the times are changing. Being in a strange land with his half-brother so close fans the flames of his fear."

"Perhaps so." She switched her gaze from the distant ship to the far north. "Do you think he's right about Ikarra?"

"I do not know. I have never met an Ikarran. They always helped our clan in the past when we lived on the mainland, generations ago. They fostered us like an older brother. But that was a long time ago."

She burrowed her bare feet into the sand. "I can't get Sir Harrison's words out of my head. He made me a promise, and no matter what Ríon says—"

"Don't think about what Ríon says." Kenton tilted his bearded chin toward her. "What does Arliss say? Ask God. Search your own heart. You know the answer already."

She closed her eyes. "Harrison spoke the truth."

"What else?"

"Ríon spoke the truth as well."

"Thus?"

She wrinkled her brow. "Ikarra is our friend. But like all the realms, there is evil lurking. If we don't fight against it, it will devour us."

Kenton draped an arm around her shoulders. She filled her lungs with salt air and leaned into him. His beard brushed her forehead. Sometime in the past few months, gray had overtaken it. His wild hair still shone golden—like hers—but he was starting to look...not *old,* but aging. He wasn't the young king she remembered from her childhood.

He held her a moment longer, then turned away. "I'm going back to the city. There's a lot of work to do." He eyed her, his forehead creasing. "Stay here in Cladach. Watch the seas."

"Why?"

"Because your mother desires it. She feels something is coming to Reinhold—and may come soon." He chuckled. "And I have my reasons as well. I want you to guide this seaside city. Prepare them for the new methods of commerce and trading which the new capital will bring."

"You mean, act like I'm the queen."

He shrugged. "I suppose you might put it that way."

"I'm *not* the queen."

"Not yet. But I won't be king forever. I'm going to start stepping back, letting you lead. You're ready."

She nodded as she watched him leave. But deep in her heart, she knew that she was not ready.

BO BURNETTE/42

BO BURNETTE/42

CHAPTER SIX:
THE STORIES CROSS

HOT ENERGY COURSED THROUGH ARLISS'S LIMBS AS SHE DUCKED
TO avoid Orlando's jab. She grabbed his outstretched arm.

He pivoted, circling his arms around her. He noosed her own
arm into her neck.

She sputtered, tucked her leg, and jabbed it into his groin. He'd
been training her long enough that she at least knew when to do
that.

His grip loosened just enough for her to slide free. She scrambled
to the other side of the great hall.

Orlando reached for the twin knives sheathed on either side of
his jerkin's chest. "Shall we speed things up a bit?"

She drew her own single knife—longer than her hand, and
slightly curved at the end. "After you."

He grinned, and the knives flashed like lightning. He whirled
toward her, flipping his right-hand knife into a backhanded grip.
The other knife he plunged toward her.

She slashed into his left-hand blade just as his other fist slammed
into her side. She buckled. He twisted his right hand and curled it
around her shoulder, pressing the blade's flat against her neck.

She grunted, struggling to hold down his other knife with hers.

Barely panting, he stared into her eyes. "Give up?"

"You must not know me very well."

His arm rippled. He torqued every ounce of strength into his left
knife. Pressure darted up her arm, forcing it upward.

She gritted her teeth and grabbed the arm hooked around her

shoulder. The metal against her neck only pressed harder.

He smirked. "You're deadlocked. At least, at this level of your training. A more experienced fighter would be able to get out."

So he was going to resort to taunting, was he? She licked her dry lips. "You're the master, aren't you? Tell me how to get out."

"Don't just think about your knives, or even your arms. Use your whole body. An enemy can defeat you simply because you don't use all your resources."

She stared at his face. What more of her body could she use?

Then she saw the answer was staring right back at her.

She slammed her head into Orlando's.

Red jagged into her vision. His arm slipped free of her shoulder, and one of his knives clattered to the floor. They both staggered away from each other, grabbing their foreheads.

She looked up. "Did I do that right?"

He glared, but the corners of his mouth twitched upward. "Just about."

She sheathed her knife and walked through the hall. Until recently, it had been packed with refugees from the old city. Squashed in like fish in a storehouse, pallets and belongings scattered across the floor. Now, though, people were moving back to the new city. Some even decided to build permanent homes in Cladach. For once, she and Orlando could practice indoors—away from people's prying eyes. She hated feeling like everyone was critiquing her.

Orlando picked up his dropped knife and sheathed them both. "You seen Philip this morning?"

Unlike Ilayda and the rest, Philip had stayed here in Cladach, but she hadn't so much as glimpsed him. "He's been out by the cliffs, overseeing the shipbuilding."

"How many are finished?"

"None. But Father hopes to have four ships completed this summer."

"And what's he planning to do with them then? Your father's never been the exploring type, from what you've said."

"Perhaps he's changing. And I think he felt a true fleet was necessary in light of everything that's happened. We need to be able to travel and to defend ourselves, easily."

Orlando strode toward one of the tall windows. "You had a ship already. You shouldn't have given it away."

She folded her arms. "Ríon deserved it for the service he rendered us."

"Did he?" He turned. The light from the window illuminated half his face and left the rest in shadow.

A loud crack sounded out as Philip burst through the door, slamming it all the way into the wall. "Arliss! Come out here!"

Sharp fear spiked her heart's race, but she kept her breath steady. Philip's voice didn't hold danger or even fear. He sounded curious, even excited.

She hurried to the door, her skirt swishing just below her knees. "What is it?"

Philip's eyes lit up with all their colors shining. "Another ship."

Orlando left his place by the window. "They're back already?"

Philip shook his head. "It's not the dragon flag, nor our own."

Arliss shoved past him and into the street. He jogged alongside her as she hurried down the smooth cobblestones toward the cliffs. "Then *what flag* is it?"

"A unicorn," he panted, "with a golden horn."

Arliss kept running, but her heart felt like it had stopped. She knew that flag. She'd seen it pictured in the book called *Finscéal agus Stair na Trí Clans*. A magnificent unicorn, its gold horn circling upward, leapt across an emerald background.

She reached the cliff edge and saw the ship.

It bore the flag of Ikarra.

Orlianna sat on a smooth boulder and stared out at the waves which cast themselves upon the seashore. This beach was so peaceful—so unlike the wild breakers which rushed up against the ruined tower of Ikarra at high tide. Four wooden skeletons, their curved beams arching all along the sand, framed what would soon be ships.

Her own ship waited expectantly in the bay. It would take a while before Garrick would be ready to unload all the crew and cargo. In the meantime, she could sit and savor the salt air.

Where were all the people? She'd glimpsed the fringes of some sort of settlement on the cliffs when the ship was half a league off. Now, the sheer height of the cliffs prevented her from seeing anything.

She scanned the sandy descent which bisected the middle of the cliffs. Nothing. No one.

She took in the ocean once more. These Reinholdians—if they truly existed—had found a glorious spot indeed to call home.

But did they exist? Perhaps Harrison had been mistaken or lied to. Merna was just the sort of person to imagine long-lost countries to reappear just for the convenience of having something to fight about.

Orlianna bit down on her tongue. She despised Merna. It was a pity to be related to her, even if it was just by marriage. She was a fool, ten times less wise than her sister Maeve, and a hundred times more irritating.

Not that Orlianna *didn't* despise her grandmother, in a way. But Maeve was simply a strict, constricting leader. Merna was a snake and a witch. More than that, she was the mother of that accursed outlaw Ríon.

Orlianna clawed at the boulder beneath her. If ever she met Ríon, she'd rip his throat out with her bare hands for what he'd done. He deserved it. He was a murderer.

She sensed a hand reaching towards her.

She whirled, jumping off the rock. She whipped out her short stiletto.

The newcomer withdrew her hand. The girl was pretty—beautiful, even. Golden waves of hair framed an oval face with bright blue eyes and full lips. She stood a few inches shorter than

Orlianna—but of course, Orlianna was tall for a woman. The stranger had a bow strung about her torso, and a full quiver hung at her side.

Orlianna hesitated. So this was a Reinholdian—the first Reinholdian to ever meet an Ikarran for nigh seventy years. What should she say?

The golden-haired stranger spoke first. "Welcome to Reinhold. I'm Arliss. Princess Arliss."

So this was the princess—the one with the fiery arrows. Orlianna bowed slightly. "It is an honor to meet you, Arliss."

"Who—who are you?" Arliss asked.

Orlianna smoothed out her tangled hair and took a deep breath. "I am Princess Orlianna of Ikarra, and I come to renew the friendship between our clans."

BO BURNETTE/48

CHAPTER SEVEN:
AN INVITATION

"ORLIANNA." ARLISS MURMURED THE NAME AS SHE EXAMINED THE PERSON it went with.

She was tall, pale, and dressed plainly—a green frock with a tan linen overlay. A belt hugged her hips and held an array of weapons and tools. Eyes as green as springtime and deep as death stared back at her. But most interesting was her red hair—not a carroty red, nor pale like straw. Her hair was redder than blood and just as thick.

"Orlianna," Arliss repeated.

All at once her time in Anmór became so vivid she could almost feel Merna breathing down her neck. Harrison had mentioned this name. It had sparked something in her spirit then. The same spark ignited now.

"Yes." Orlianna fingered the curious-looking pendant around her neck. "That is my name."

Arliss brushed a strand of hair aside. "You must excuse me. But I've been longing to meet you for some time—even if I did forget your name. Harrison told me, I just forgot."

Orlianna curved an eyebrow. "Harrison talked about me?"

"Yes! He said he'd give you my regards."

Orlianna leaned her head back and laughed, and her red tresses shook. "He gave them, indeed. And now I'm here to give them back." She stepped away from the boulder. "How did you cross paths with Harrison in Anmór?"

Arliss fell suddenly quiet. She'd only just met this princess.

Could she trust her with her story? Her meeting with Harrison wasn't an isolated episode. It was a stop on a much larger journey.

She smiled. "It's a rather long story."

"Good. I love stories. But, perhaps later?"

"I'll tell you everything later." *If* she could trust her. If she could determine who she really was.

Orlianna glanced around. "Where is everyone?"

"Pardon me." Arliss jumped toward the ascent to the clifftops. Where were her manners, her senses? She had to make a good impression. "Come. I must introduce you to a few people at once." She pointed at the ship which lazed in the bay. "Did you sail here by yourself?"

Orlianna laughed again—deep and musical. "Goodness, no. My crew are still making things secure after the voyage. They will be ashore in a moment. Then *I* will be the one with introductions to make."

"I look forward to it." She motioned for Orlianna to follow her up the hill.

Arliss said nothing on the way up. What *did* one say to a guest like this? They probably had similar things to talk about. They were both familiar with Anmór. They were both princesses. But did Ikarra have the same enmity with Anmór that Reinhold had? Did a princess of Ikarra do similar things to one of Reinhold? She couldn't say.

Philip and Orlando waited at the top of the hill. They gaped when they saw Orlianna. Orlando shoved his hands in his pockets and let his burgundy cloak stream out behind him.

Arliss climbed the last few steps up the hill. "Philip, Orlando— there's someone I want you to meet. My new friend, Princess Orlianna of Ikarra."

Orlianna swept a full curtsey. "What a pleasure to meet gentlemen of the Reinholdian court."

Court gentlemen, indeed. Arliss chuckled.

Philip smirked.

Orlando reddened.

Orlianna finished her curtsey and glanced around. "Oh dear. It seems I've said something wrong?"

Philip grinned. "Neither of us are exactly gentlemen of the court."

"Then what are you?"

"By trade, I've been a farmer and a carpenter's apprentice. More recently, I'm a knight. And most importantly, I'm engaged to Arliss."

"You chose well, Sir Philip."

Arliss's cheeks grew hot. In the five minutes they'd been acquainted, she felt Orlianna could see right through her soul. Even she didn't know herself to be this confident.

Orlianna turned to Orlando. "And what do you call yourself?"

Orlando looked to Arliss for help, his face tight. "Well…"

Arliss tensed. Few people knew who Orlando *really* was.

Orlianna's brows arched. "You don't know who you are?"

Arliss cleared her throat. "He is a new knight of Reinhold—and my personal teacher."

"Ah." Orlianna widened her eyes. "And is she a good pupil?"

Orlando relaxed. "Sometimes."

Arliss stepped through tall grasses toward the rear gates of Cladach. "Come. We must find you refreshment."

Orlianna waved her hand. "No need. The ocean air's been refreshment enough. For now, I need to speak to the king and queen as soon as possible."

Arliss strode for the gates. Didn't everyone want an audience with her parents, but not her? Maybe being queen had some perks. Well, this one perk, at most.

Philip booted to the edge of the cliffs, his steps casting sand over the edge. "What about your ship?"

"They can follow behind me. I've set my mind to this, though, and I'm afraid I will not be stopped." Orlianna hurried to catch up with Arliss. "I have an important message to deliver."

Arliss almost groaned. Another of these bloody messages! She'd had enough of surprise visitors from other realms who wanted to bring secret messages to her parents. "What kind of message is it, pray tell?"

Orlianna's smile spread across her face without revealing her teeth. "An invitation."

Ilayda gripped her skirts and rushed to the far side of the city. It sounded like half a dozen horses—riding hard and approaching fast—bore down on her.

Why would Arliss be coming home so soon? King Kenton had said just this morning that she was in charge of Cladach for the time. *That* mustn't have lasted long. Some job she was doing of being in charge.

Boots pounded the new stone road behind her. Unlike Cladach's roads, this one wasn't cobblestone. Kenton had insisted on hewing smooth stone slabs to fit together as the capital's roads.

And there he was—the king himself, gaining on her quickly. He rushed through skeletons of new buildings. Ilayda slowed her pace as he reached her.

"Horses?" Kenton panted. "Arliss?"

Ilayda nodded. "And company, from the sound of it."

Kenton tightened his lips and kept moving.

The road branched to the right and connected with the main thoroughfare where she'd run into Brallaghan earlier that week. Hopefully that wouldn't happen again.

Her hopes squashed into the stones the moment she rushed onto the main road. Everyone in the city seemed to have heard the horses' approach. Bodies packed the street from doorway to doorway.

Ilayda shoved someone's shoulder. "Make way for the king!"

A few people around her parted, but most of them didn't hear her. They pointed, murmuring, as four horses bounded across the nearing horizon.

She kept shoving. "Make way! The king is coming through!"

Kenton elbowed his way in front of her and nodded his appreciation. The crowd finally bisected to let the two of them to the front. Ilayda gaped at the cloud of grass and dirt the horses kicked up as they rode.

Brallaghan appeared beside her and jostled her shoulder. "It's Arliss."

"Obviously." Her heart thumped, but she kept staring ahead. "Who else could it be?"

"Philip, naturally." He squinted into the dust. "Orlando, too, it looks like."

But there was someone else. Orlando's burgundy cape wasn't the only shade of red to flash steadily toward them. There was another shade—brighter, stronger, wilder.

The riders slowed. The dust cleared. And the new shade of red crisped into vision.

It was someone's hair.

Ilayda squinted to make sure she'd seen correctly, but there could be no doubt now. The four riders reached the street's end and dismounted.

Arliss jumped off and ran to her father, her face shining.

Philip dismounted and grabbed the wayward reins of Arliss's mount.

Orlando leapt down and glanced behind him. He extended his hand to the newcomer.

A tall young woman with flaming red hair accepted his palm, but she clearly didn't need it. She dismounted with an air of practice and refinement. Yet there was something wild in her nature—something nonchalant and saucy in the way she strode down the street toward Kenton.

Arliss glanced at the stranger. "May I introduce you?"

The crowd fell into silence.

"I can introduce myself, Arliss, but thank you." She drew herself up to her full height and faced Kenton. "I thank you for your daughter's kindness and hospitality, King Kenton of Reinhold. It is a pleasure to meet you. I am Princess Orlianna, ambassador from the clan of Ikarra."

Kenton stepped forward. "Ikarra? Is this possible?"

"It is. And I intend to renew the old friendship between us." Her gaze landed on Ilayda, and she smiled. "I am sure we have much in common, though the years have shaped us differently."

Kenton bowed and took Orlianna's hands. "You are welcome here, lady. I must ask you your purpose in coming across the seas in such a dangerous time."

Orlianna's eyes darkened. "It is dangerous indeed, but the danger hides in the shadows—for now."

The bottom of Ilayda's stomach twisted.

Orlianna continued. "You're right, though. I would not have come so urgently without a purpose. I am here as an ambassador. My mission is to bring back Reinholdian ambassadors with me when I leave."

A murmur rippled through the crowd.

Ilayda's heart jumped up into her throat. A journey across the sea? To Ikarra? It sounded frightening. Impossible, even.

But it would get her away from Brallaghan—far away, myths and legends away.

Kenton's grim voice brought her imagination back to earth. "You have come to ask me to leave my kingdom on such a voyage?"

"No, my lord. Not if you do not wish to. I have come to ask your daughter."

Kenton glanced at Arliss, then back at Orlianna. "I must talk with you alone."

Ilayda hoped that "you" included herself.

Arliss struggled to keep a steady pace as she trotted to the royal headquarters. She knew her father was right behind her, but she refused to look. He'd be curious and confused—even angry—and he'd be full of questions she couldn't answer. Did he expect her to know everything about Ikarra? As if she'd—

She forced herself to stop. He had every right to be curious, just like she did.

She waited for him to catch up. Orlianna and the rest had adjourned to prepare themselves for the council (Orlianna had called it "refreshing" herself). She had, after all, been on a ship for quite some time. And Ilayda and Erik had been helping with construction, so they weren't exactly in regal attire. But they'd all be here in a moment, and she probably still wouldn't be ready for the council.

Kenton cleared his throat beside her. "I thought I told you to stay in Cladach."

Her arms tensed. "Surely this takes precedence over that?"

"Riding across the plains with a stranger is more important than guarding your own people?"

They'd reached the headquarters at the head of the main road. She stopped and pressed her palm against the brick. "Father, she's the first Ikarran to ever visit Reinhold! I couldn't just say, 'Sorry, but I don't have time to listen to you, I'm busy doing my parents' job. Good day to ya!' What would she have thought?"

Kenton gripped her shoulders. "You left the city unguarded and open to attack from her crew. We know nothing of these Ikarrans or their loyalties. Did you not think she could be lying?"

The bottom of her heart turned to ice. It *was* foolish—extremely so. And she hadn't even given it a second thought. She'd ridden off without so much as instructions to the city guards. Orlianna's crew could be ransacking the city as they spoke.

She sighed. "I'm sorry."

He released her shoulders. "I know. And I do not think she is hostile. But we have no way of knowing. You must be more careful in your rule. A queen always guards her own."

Heat knotted in her chest. "I am not the queen."

"You will be one day."

"One day is a long way off. You and Mother aren't old."

"We aren't young either," he said. "In truth, we don't have to pass for you to take the throne. Many rulers have stepped down before old age to allow the new generation to take charge."

Arliss unlatched the door of the headquarters. She had no reason and no desire to become queen. Being princess was good enough for her. And she wasn't even eighteen yet! What was her father thinking?

He entered, and the door banged shut behind him.

It reopened almost instantly, and councillors and friends started to fill the wide room. Philip. Erik. Ilayda. Elowyn. Brédan. Adam. Elisabeth. Orlando. Thus far it seemed much the same crowd that had gathered on the hill with Ríon and Clare—although Brallaghan was missing.

Finally, Orlianna herself entered and gave a low bow.

Orlianna surveyed the room as everyone took their seats—some in chairs on the right, some on a bench along the left wall, and the king at a desk in the back. The room was simple and sparsely furnished—but the chairs, the king's desk, even the doorframe: the carpentry on all of them was immaculate and carven. A glance at Sir Philip's callused hands said he was the craftsman behind it all.

So this was the court of Reinhold? Surely this couldn't be the entire council.

Kenton introduced everyone, then motioned to the only empty chair—next to Arliss by one of the long right windows. "Please, sit."

"Is this all of you?"

His muscled neck rippled. "All who are coming."

She swept her skirt beneath her and sat. Imagine if the Council of Lords was this small! They'd spend less time yammering and more time deciding. Ten voices were preferable to a hundred any day. And ten hearts would be easy to persuade—especially when her grandmother wasn't among them. If she could sway fifty Ikarran nobles to support her transportation improvements, how difficult could it be to convince Reinholdian ambassadors?

For she *had* to convince them. Usually this was Harrison's job—visiting cities and speaking peace to everyone. How she longed for him to be here with her! He'd have the Reinholdians throwing themselves on her ship in an instant.

Kenton spread his hands across his desk. "I assume your trip was charming."

Ah, so the usual formalities, even in these wild lands. She should have expected it.

"No, not charming at all, but quite thrilling. Stuck in a wooden tub for two weeks, getting drenched with seawater and living off half-decent food."

"Two weeks?" Arliss turned to her. "Ikarra lies only two weeks' journey from us?"

"Yes, of course. You've been to Anmór, haven't you?"

Arliss stiffened, her manner suddenly guarded. "Indeed I have. But if you are so near us…"

Philip leaned forward to look Orlianna in the eye. "I believe Arliss is asking why you haven't been to Reinhold in so long. If we're so close, why are we isolated?"

"A fair question. Explorers from all three clans did come, once, but they deemed it unsuitable for living. Ever since, it's been abandoned and ignored by Anmór and Ikarra simply because we supposed we had better things to do. Some even made up stories to scare people away from here." Orlianna sighed. "How wrong we were."

Arliss directed her voice across the room. "Is this true?"

Orlianna followed her gaze to Orlando. Why was she asking *him* to verify her word? Why would he know more than any of the rest of them?

Orlando folded his arms. "Yes. Reinhold is as much of a legend to us as we were to you."

"*We?*" Orlianna raised her eyebrows at Arliss. This deserved an explanation. "Is he not one of you?"

"Oh—" Arliss's eyes widened. "He—he is one of us."

Orlianna glanced back and forth at them. "And?"

Silence. Neither Arliss nor Orlando spoke.

Kenton slid his chair back. It squawked along the wooden floor. "Please, allow us to consider the topic at hand—why you are here, Princess Orlianna."

Orlianna leaned back into the chair's chiseled wood. Was Orlando an expatriate Ikarran? Or even an Anmórian? That would explain his accent, his awkward mien.

She brought her gaze back to Kenton. "You may leave off 'princess' to save time in the future. And I believe I already told you all why I am here, though I can say it louder if no one was listening. I am quite good at speaking loudly when I need to."

Ilayda giggled. She was the only one.

Kenton leaned so far across his desk she thought he would fall over the other side. "You indicated you want to take my daughter back with you to your land."

"That is my wish, sir."

"And you expect me to let her go—a young woman not yet eighteen—with a pack of strangers?"

"We are not a pack of wolves, waiting to kill and eat her. We are a family. Reinhold and Ikarra were friends once, you know. We watched over you like an older brother."

Arliss inhaled sharply.

"I don't want her to come alone, either," Orlianna said. "As many as she wishes to bring are welcome."

Kenton stood and booted around his desk. "Orlianna, I'm not sure if you are aware, but Reinhold has been in the middle of some controversial conflicts lately."

She slipped her hand down her neck to her pendant. "I've heard rumors."

"There have been battles fought here. Lives lost. And all of them because other realms have meddled in our business."

Was he accusing her and her people? She grabbed the wooden chair's arms. "Excuse me, but Ikarra has done nothing to you. I don't know what Anmór has been involved in, but you can't blame us for their iniquity."

Lord Adam spoke from the far corner. "If you knew everything that had happened because of Anmór, you would understand Kenton's hesitance."

"Perhaps you could tell me. You could tell us your story as we tell you ours. And we could weave our stories together."

The challenge hung in the air, but no one answered it.

Then Arliss rose. "I will go back with you, if my father allows it. It is time to renew our bond."

Philip stood. "Where she goes, so do I."

Erik pushed himself up. "If Philip goes, I go."

Ilayda jumped up. "And me. You can't leave me behind."

The lord named Adam snatched her arm. Orlianna wrinkled her brow. Oh, of course—she was his daughter.

Adam shook his head. "No. You cannot go gallivanting across the ocean to some place we don't even know."

Ilayda jerked her arm free. "You can't do this to me."

Lady Elisabeth looked ready to both leap up and fall over. "Ilayda! Stop this nonsense."

"It's not nonsense! If Arliss goes to Ikarra, I *am* going." Ilayda looked pleadingly at Orlianna. "Please."

Adam glared at Orlianna. "It's too dangerous."

Kenton strode swiftly between them. "He's right. It is very dangerous." He stopped before Orlianna's chair and stared at her. Fear swam in his blue eyes. "I cannot give you an answer yet. Give me time to think."

"Please, think. Pray. I am patient," Orlianna replied.

But inside, she could feel a burning excitement—bursting and bubbling up in her chest—that she could not wait to bring Arliss and her company back to Ikarra.

BO BURNETTE/60

CHAPTER EIGHT: THE FLAME KINDLES

"I hope my father's manner wasn't overbearing." Arliss pressed her hands into the log seat and inhaled the scent of burning wood.

Her father was just being cautious—and rightly so, although Orlianna's crew seemed peaceable. They were lodging the night in Cladach, where Arliss and the rest would ride the next morning.

So Kenton's suspicions were wrong. But what if his demeanor scared Orlianna away? What if she changed her mind about the voyage?

Arliss laughed hesitantly. "I hope he hasn't frightened you off."

Orlianna stared into the fire. It sparked her eyes and made her hair look like real flames. "Not at all. Your father is a good man—steadfast and careful. The three realms would do well to have more such men."

The tension in Arliss's shoulders melted. "Thank you."

"I wouldn't say it if I didn't mean it." Orlianna glanced at her. "I never do."

All around the wide hilltop, Arliss's friends were gathered about the fire. Ilayda sat in silent shadows, scribbling furiously in her notebook. Through the fire, Erik and Orlando scrubbed at their various knives, polishing and sharpening. The fire flicked this way and that, sometimes obscuring her view of Orlando and his cloak completely.

Arliss picked up a stray twig that lay by her feet. "I would leave with you tomorrow if I could."

"I know."

She threw the twig into the fire. "The realms are dangerous, yes, and I know that, but I'm not afraid of what may come."

"And what *may* come?" Orlianna grasped the back of her own neck and stared up at the stars. "What does Arliss say?"

Arliss bit her lip. "You aren't the first visitor from another realm this week."

Orlianna's body jerked taut. She stared at Arliss. "Someone from Anmór? Whom?"

Her throat felt dry. Should she tell her? Harrison had hinted that Ikarra and Anmór didn't get along well. Anmór was their enemy—but Ríon himself was not. At least, not yet.

Orlianna pressed harder. "Please, you must tell me who came here. This could change everything."

Arliss stared at the flames. Her twig crackled and disintegrated into ash. "Prince Ríon."

"Ríon!" Orlianna choked. "He came *here?*"

"Yes."

"To attack? Did he try to assault you in Anmór, too?"

Arliss hated the direction this conversation was traveling. "No. He isn't like that. He helped us—more than you could believe. He traveled here simply to deliver a message."

Orlianna lowered her voice. "What message?"

"It was for Reinholdian royalty alone."

"So you don't trust me." Orlianna stiffened. "I'm not surprised. And I don't blame you, if you keep friendship with the likes of Ríon."

Arliss wanted to scream. Orlianna had to know everything—about Thane, Merna, Ríon, Clare, Gally, and all the rest—and she had to know it soon, or things would grow uglier and more confusing.

"What was the message?" Orlianna grasped Arliss's hand. "You must trust me. This could be a matter of life and death."

The western wind huffed across the hilltop. Arliss closed her eyes against the sting of smoke. "You're right. This is life and death.

Peace and war." She opened her eyes and looked at Orlianna. "That's what Ríon said. Anmór is like a snake, poised and ready to strike."

"So they intend to go to war after all."

"They already have." Philip strode from the shadows and sat on the log beside Arliss. He was wearing a long tunic, the front of it only fastened halfway up. The loose cloth flapped in the breeze, and Arliss wondered how he wasn't cold.

Orlianna arched her eyebrows. "You have quite a story to tell me. You already promised to tell me how you met Harrison. I can't help but feel this is part of the same tale."

Arliss nodded. "All our stories are connected. Someday I'll have to make sense of them all…tie them all together. I know they are more connected than we know."

Orlianna smiled. "All good stories are. But for now, you can tell me your story."

"Maybe another time." Philip eased himself onto the log beside Arliss. "They've finished preparing your lodgings. The king sent me to tell you."

Orlianna's lips pursed slightly.

Philip motioned behind himself encouragingly. "It's a new place. Just finished today, in fact." He grinned. "You're to be the first to spend the night in a proper home in this new city."

"Am I, now?" Orlianna stood and motioned around the hilltop. "I'm not blind. It may be dark, but I can see what happened here. This city was attacked—and destroyed. The ashes mean extensive igneous warfare. The destruction was clearly wrought by catapults. And there were chariot ruts scarring the plains all the way here."

Arliss exhaled, staring. Orlianna seemed to be as much a detective and military analyst as she was a princess. At this rate, she would know the whole story before they told her.

"All right," Arliss said. "I'll tell you tomorrow over breakfast."

"With tea?"

"Certainly."

Orlianna dipped her head and swished around to leave. "I look forward to it."

Arliss leaned her head back into Philip's chest as she watched Orlianna descend the hill.

Philip slipped his arm around Arliss and pressed her against him. It had been a gloriously sunny day, but the nights still loomed with lingering chill.

He huffed out a breath. Arliss had quite a choice to make. And it would be hers, in the end. No matter how worried Kenton was, he would leave the decision to her—because he wanted her to take responsibility.

Arliss shivered and slipped her right hand into his encircling left. "You're cold."

He grasped her fingers. "You're warm."

"I don't feel warm. The more I think about Ikarra, about Anmór…"

"The more your head wants to explode?"

"Precisely. And Orlianna isn't helping anything."

Philip cocked his head. "I think she is."

"How so?"

"She's offering you a way to figure this out. To solve it. If you go with her, you can put an end to all this confusion. You can figure out how to balance relations between the clans. You can—"

"Stop." She pressed her hand into his chest. "This is exactly what I don't need to hear."

He leaned away from her enough to look her in the eye. "I think you do. You're confused because Ríon, Orlianna, your father—they're all telling you different things. And you respect them all."

Her muscles unknotted slightly at the thought. "You're right."

"As usual, right?" He grinned.

"Right." She sat up straight, slipping her right hand out of his left. She quickly grasped it again, resting their hands in between them on the log. "So who do you agree with—my father, or

Orlianna?"

"I think Kenton's right. This is dangerous. Ikarra lies right next to Anmór. At least, they did in all the old legends. If Merna finds out you're there, she might attack."

"I want to go. I need to go."

"I know that. I'm just telling you the truth." He took her hand in both of his. This was this, then. Once she set her mind to a quest, it would happen. He unfolded her three draw fingers. "If you go, I am with you, no matter what may happen."

She stared into the fire. "I don't want to do this again—to go off on an adventure without you really agreeing with me. I did that once, and I almost lost you. I won't go without your agreement."

So she was thinking of that, too.

He smiled. "I don't think we can really disagree anymore, Arliss. You're too much a part of me."

She simply closed her eyes.

He tensed. "You don't agree with me?"

"No, I do. And that's what I'm afraid of. That I have grown so close to you that I'm afraid of losing you." She looked up at him. The firelight revealed tears hiding in the corners of her eyes. "This mission will either bring peace or war."

"Or both. War brings peace."

"War brings death."

He knew she was thinking of Eamon. "You will not die. You're going to be the queen, and I'm going to be the king. No matter what happens—peace, war, whatever. I promise."

She didn't say anything. She could have looked away. She *should* have looked away. But she did not.

He touched his forehead to hers. "I would kiss you."

Her lips trembled. "It's not time yet."

"When will it be time?"

She smiled. "When we are married, of course."

"What about when you become queen?"

"You have my permission to kiss me then as well."

"Will I always have to ask permission?"

"No. But on special occasions, you may kiss me especially well, if you like."

He stroked her cheek and let his hand fall to her shoulder. "When you are crowned queen, I will give you such a kiss as has not been given in the history of the three clans."

Arliss forced her stiff eyelids open. They felt sealed, as if with wax.

She rolled onto her back. Her muscles knotted in irritation. She stretched, and her hand brushed against the dewy mossiness of a log.

She opened her eyes wide. A newborn sun flooded down onto the hilltop. So she'd fallen asleep here? Of all the places—

She stumbled to her feet. The remains of last night's fire crumbled in a circle of chalky ash. Everyone else had gone in the night and left her lying here.

Today was the day, then. The day she had to tell Orlianna the whole story about Thane and everything. The day she had to convince her father to let her go to Ikarra.

Her heart drummed as she started down the hill. She wanted to go to Ikarra. Wanted it so bad her chest physically ached. She began to sing to distract herself.

"A princess on a gilded throne, clothed in simple raiment."

She released her skirts and took a running start, bounding across the moat. Orlianna was walking down the street between unfinished buildings—a market to the left, houses to the right.

Arliss slowed to meet her. "A queenly look is in her eye, and grace is on her forehead."

Orlianna smiled weakly as Arliss approached. Had she been sleeping? No—she looked far too alert and focused. Then again, she probably woke up that way. Still, she seemed stiff. Shocked, even.

"Good morning," Arliss offered.

Orlianna nodded. "What were you singing?"

"It's an old favorite of mine." Heat flooded her cheeks. "Some seem to think it's talking about me."

"I know the song." Orlianna looked west, her body rigid. "I know it well. And the moment Harrison told me about you, I thought of that song—that princess on her carven throne."

"Why?"

"Because there is a legend in our land—a prophecy, if you will—which says that only a great queen can rise up and unite the three clans."

"The song is about a princess."

"What do princesses become?"

Arliss bit her tongue. She tried to focus on anything else. She opened her mouth and filled her lungs with fresh morning air. Dust scratched her throat. The crescendo of voices and chiming hammers from the marketplace contrasted with the clunk of boards from houses on the other side of the road.

They were standing in the middle of one of many new streets. This one served as the main road for the city's eastern side—a sister to the true thoroughfare which led in on the western side. This road would eventually spread its hands to a church and market on one side, homes and craftshops on the other.

Orlianna motioned to the wide, new bridge that ran perpendicular to the road. "Shall we walk?"

Arliss swallowed, but followed Orlianna to the bridge. She still hadn't gotten used to it. Habit—and playful urge—still forced her to leap the moat instead of using the sloping bridge.

Was this to be their talk? So much for tea. So much for formality.

Orlianna folded her arms behind her back. "I am sorry if I seem stiff to you this morning. My world has just expanded."

"How so?" Arliss asked. "I haven't told you my story yet."

"Your father did."

Arliss halted. "He did *what?*"

"Told me everything. If his story had come from anyone else, I would have deemed it impossible. But there was too much truth in his eyes." Orlianna kept walking. "Besides, it matches all too well with what I know."

Her father was so steadfast, yet he never stopped surprising her. He'd saved her the difficulty of telling Orlianna herself.

So she knew everything. That leveled their conversation a good bit. Arliss now had no superior angle, but at least she didn't have to speak in guarded riddles.

"So what did you say to my father?"

Orlianna finally stopped. "I had little to say to him. I wanted to stop my ears at the accounts of Thane's atrocities and Merna's collusion."

Arliss hesitated at the bottom of the bridge's arch over the river. If her father had told the whole story, he hadn't left out Orlando. But she didn't want to find out. It felt too sensitive a subject, too close and raw to touch. She stared out at the river which threaded beneath the bridge.

Orlianna stepped closer. "Your father will not stop you from coming with me now."

"I suppose I ought to thank you."

"Perhaps." Orlianna smiled. "I think he sees that I can answer your questions if you come to Ikarra. He has so many questions about the story he just told me. And he wants those questions answered. He's afraid of war as much as you are."

Arliss clenched her fists. "I'm not afraid."

"Everyone is afraid." Orlianna reached for her necklace and dropped her voice to a whisper. "Even I have fears."

Arliss eyed the silver chain with its heavy pendant. "You don't seem afraid."

"If only you knew." Orlianna's lips twisted in some dark cousin of a smile. "You don't understand how much I need you to come with me. My grandmother…she doesn't believe I can be queen. If I can singlehandedly restore relations with Reinhold, though, she might."

So she wasn't the only one who was having to act as if she were queen. "Your grandmother is the queen?"

Orlianna stepped to the bridge's edge and clawed at the handrail. "*No*."

Arliss stepped back. She spoke her next words more carefully. "And you…want to be queen?" She left the rest unspoken—that Orlianna wanted to be the queen to unite the three clans.

"I do." Her response was confirmation enough.

Arliss looked up the hill to where her home once shimmered in the sun. "I, too, want to bring unity to our realms. Reinhold's time of hiding is done. Ikarra needs to know the truth."

Orlianna suddenly lifted her chin and looked behind Arliss.

Arliss turned.

Kenton stood, his tunic dusty, his hands streaked with muddy scars, his blue eyes fierce. "I want to talk to you. Alone."

Orlianna shot Arliss a glance before dipping a curtsey and striding off the bridge.

Arliss edged to the top of the bridge's arch. Her father stomped up to her.

He huffed. "Well, I've made a fool of myself. I told that confounded princess everything."

She smirked. "How foolish of you. Now you've promised her I can go. What *will* you do with yourself?"

He choked on his laugh. "I like to tell myself I will go on rebuilding, trusting that you are safe and well. But I know deep in my heart that I will torture myself with worry every day you will be gone."

Arliss grasped his arm. "Father, I go as an ambassador to council, not a warrior to battle."

"I want you to come back."

"I will come back." She wove her arms around his back. "Why are you afraid of my going?"

"The danger. The unknown." His chin touched her head. "My heart stirs within me."

"My heart stirs within me as well. And it tells me that I must go to Ikarra." She took his hands and held them to her lips. "Philip will look after me."

"And who will look after Philip?"

"Me, of course." She kissed his hands. Pained lines crisscrossed his forehead. "Father, we are in God's hands. I don't need to know exactly how my chapter fits into this story. Yet if I don't go with Orlianna now, I may never know how this story really goes."

"I can guess. Anmór will want to finish what Thane started. They will come with war and vengeance." A bead of sweat dripped down his brow. "If you do this, you may die."

"If I do not do this, we may all die."

"You sound just like your mother." He squeezed her hands. "You'll have to be both her and me if you go."

And for once, being queen sounded like a good thing—as long as it involved going to Ikarra.

CHAPTER NINE:
IKARRA'S CALL

THE MOMENT THE CARRIAGE CLATTERED ONTO CLADACH'S COBBLESTONES, ORLANDO LEAPT out and dashed for the cliffs. He had to see the Ikarrans' ship again, had to assure himself it was real, that Orlianna wasn't a phantom. He hadn't seen her at all that day, as she'd taken an earlier carriage with Arliss and Philip.

The cliffs spread out before him, stretching away into fog on the right and left. He stepped closer, the toes of his boots aligning with the cliff's edge. Rock shaved straight down for two hundred feet before disappearing into sandy earth.

On the beach, Philip and Arliss chatted with a fair-haired stranger. Beyond them, the raw ocean threw itself upon the beach before recoiling its waves back. They swirled around a magnificent oceancraft.

He sighed. So it was real. And that meant Ikarra was waiting.

Acid twisted his empty stomach. He'd never liked Ikarra—too many suspicious people, ready to accuse him for every thing he did and didn't do. But perhaps that was just because Thane had never gotten along with anyone from Ikarra. Thane had only associated with Anmór. Why should *he* do any different?

But things were different now. And if Arliss went to Ikarra, he had to go with her, no matter what Ríon said. As likely as not, Ríon was mistaken about the Ikarrans wanting his ring. What could they want with it—really? It was just a piece of jewelry.

"You're Anmórian." Orlianna's voice pierced the midmorning stillness.

Orlando whirled, his cape swishing. He drew a knife out of habit.

She held up a hand. "I didn't mean to startle you."

What *did* she mean, then—sneaking up on him and stating his secrets? He glared and kept the knife level. "What difference does it make if I am Anmórian?"

"I only mean there was no reason for you not to tell me in the first place. There are Anmórians whom I despise, but it's not because of their race. I'm not xenophobic."

Whatever *that* meant. Orlando shrugged. "Of course you're not afraid of spies. You seem to be one yourself—sneaking up on me."

Her brow tightened. "Afraid of spies? That isn't what xenophobic means."

His cheeks felt like they were on fire.

"And thank you for the compliment to my espionage skills. I do pride myself on my ability to sneak up on others."

Well, this was getting lovely, wasn't it? He had to save face somehow.

He tilted the knife back and forth. "Sneaking is one thing. Fighting is another."

"Sir Orlando, I can fight in any circumstance, using any weapon. Sword, bow, knife, axe, anything."

He smirked. "You can leave off the 'Sir' next time, to save time."

She stared levelly ahead, but her red lips twitched. "A clever one we have here! Don't think I don't know when you're mocking me."

"I'm not mocking you." If he'd gotten her this riled, he might as well go all the way. He pulled out his other knife. "I'm goading you."

"I do not use my skills lightly."

"You mean you don't practice?"

"I have no need."

From anyone else, this would have sounded prideful, but there was nothing but truth in her green eyes. He lowered his blades. "How disappointing. I'd love to practice my skills on you."

She seemed to find more in his words than he meant. "I am a

princess. You will do nothing of the sort."

He felt his cheeks burning. "I meant no disrespect."

Her expression stayed stern, but she jerked her head at him. "Come. Arliss and Philip have already met my crew. You'd best make a good impression if you're to spend two weeks on a ship with them."

He hesitated. Ríon had warned him against the Ikarrans. But somehow he couldn't help but follow her.

She started the descent between the cliffs. "You are coming, I presume?"

It took all Orlianna's focus not to glance back at Orlando as they descended the hill. She glued her hands at her sides and fixed her gaze on Arliss and Philip. They stood beside Garrick, laughing and talking as if they'd always been friends. Very good. It was always good for a crew to like their captain.

Orlando maintained a distance of a few paces behind her. Was he afraid of her? She bit down on her lips to restrain her smile. After his comment about *practicing his skills on her*—the nerve of it—he would do well to be afraid. He said he wanted to see her skills. Once he'd seen them, though, she doubted he'd want to see them again.

It wasn't the right time, anyway. Not until the heat and rush of battle flooded her skull, until the thrill tingled down to the tips of her fingers—then, and only then, could she truly fight to her uttermost.

And that had only truly happened once.

She shuddered and quickened her pace. She'd promised herself not to think about it, but her thoughts refused to listen. They pierced the back of her mind like so many arrows.

Why did she have to think about death? She looked around the beach as the ground beneath her shifted from grass into sand. This place was full of life. She didn't need to bring thoughts of death to it.

But she couldn't change what happened to her brother, any more than she could change her mother's death. They were both gone. No amount of thinking about them could change that. And she certainly couldn't absolve Ríon of his sins.

Arliss looked up and waved as Orlianna crunched over the beach—unlike the rocky sand of Ikarra, this sand was finer than sugar and smoother than silk. She tried to smile back. The cliffs loomed above. She stepped over their shadowy boundary and into the sunlight near Arliss.

Orlando loitered back in the shadows, the cliffs behind him framing his burgundy silhouette.

Orlianna nodded at Garrick. "I see you've met my captain. Do you like him well enough?"

Arliss nodded. "I could think of worse people to spend two weeks under."

Garrick's wide eyes got even wider. "Well now, I may be the captain, but I know my place. My dear Orli's in charge here."

Orlianna rolled her eyes.

"Orli?" Arliss laughed.

"He has a new nickname every day, it seems," Orlianna explained. "That one is an old favorite of his."

Arliss snuck her a questioning glance.

Did she think Garrick was her lover? Orlianna shook her head slightly.

Arliss raised an eyebrow. She clearly wasn't convinced.

Orlianna gazed out at her ship. No matter how much he tried, Garrick would never turn their friendship into something more than it had always been. Their years weren't so different—his thirty, hers twenty-five—but she could never romanticize him. He was simply Garrick—nothing more, nothing less.

Surely he understood that. Surely he saw that she was above romance, that she had no time for it. After all, her closest friend was Harrison, a forty-year-old ambassador. What could Garrick *really* expect?

She smoothed down hairs that wisped rebelliously in the wind. "I find it hard to admit anyone being my equal in much of anything. But Garrick is such an accomplished seaman, I couldn't have asked anyone else."

That, and the fact that anyone else would have turned her in to her grandmother, and they wouldn't have left Ikarra in the first place. Orlianna had many allies, but few of those allies were willing to go against Maeve. They all remembered when *she* was queen of Ikarra—and they still revered her.

Garrick bowed slightly. "Orli exaggerates. She could captain this boat as well as I could. You just wait and see—once we leave land, she'll be itching for the helm."

Arliss sighed and stepped away from the group. "Once we leave land. How strange that will be."

"You've left this land before." Orlianna followed her to the water's edge.

"This is different. I didn't think I'd be leaving Reinhold then. I never imagined I'd visit Anmór. This time, I know what I'm getting myself into."

Philip laughed. "You do?"

Arliss narrowed her eyes in his direction. "More or less. We're going to Ikarra to help her" —she nodded at Orlianna— "stop a war."

Orlianna folded her arms across her chest. "From your father's story, it seems the war has already started. If Merna and Ríon are colluding, this could mean much ill for all."

Arliss trudged up to Orlianna, her eyes raging inches away. "Ríon is not our enemy. He wants to stop this war as much as I do."

Orlianna laughed bitterly. Arliss didn't even know half the truth. "Do you not know what Ríon has done? The sins he's committed?"

Arliss glanced nervously toward Orlando. "He has done nothing but help me."

"Ríon of Anmór is a murderer." Orlianna curled her fingers as the past raged in her lungs. "I believe I told you I am an only child—the heir to the throne?"

"Yes." Arliss froze.

Orlando tensed, halfway in the shadows.

"How is Ríon a murderer?"

Orlianna couldn't stop the drops that streaked her cheeks as she lifted her voice. Tears flooded her closed eyes as her mind grabbed at the memories: the catacombs, the flames, the weapons flashing like lightning, death rolling in like a thunderstorm. She hadn't seen Ríon that day for the darkness. But she had seen the evil his hand had dealt.

She turned and faced Arliss. "Ríon killed my brother."

Arliss gasped for air and found she couldn't breathe. Was this what it felt like to be shot in the heart with an arrow—your breath suddenly expunged from punctured lungs? To have your heart stopped in a single moment?

She tried to utter words. They refused to obey.

Ríon—a murderer? And of Orlianna's brother, of all people. It didn't seem possible.

Yet Orlianna stood there two paces away, her eyes dripping with sorrow that could not be anything but real. Arliss knew that sorrow. She'd felt it in her own eyes enough times to recognize it in someone else's. Like herself, Orlianna had a brother once. And also like herself, death had stolen him away far too soon.

"I'm sorry," Arliss finally managed.

Orlianna bowed her head. "It isn't your fault. You didn't know the things he's done."

The tide rolled in. It washed over Arliss's bare toes as she struggled to reconcile the thoughts in her heart. Ríon—and Clare, of course—had done nothing but good to her. They'd helped her to safety in Anmór. They'd fought against Thane, turning the tide of battle at the last moment. And they had come less than a week earlier with a warning.

They had her trust. How could Orlianna expect her to reject them now? She had no reason to trust Orlianna, beyond her connections to Harrison. And even Harrison had done little to warrant her confidence. They'd offered her only words and promises thus far. Even if they intended to keep them, they hadn't yet been tested.

"I cannot believe he would do such a thing," Arliss said. "But I also cannot disbelieve you. I don't know what to think."

Orlianna folded her arms. "I can only tell you the truth. I was there the day it happened. My grandmother, Maeve, testifies to it with vigor. And even Merna admits her son's treachery."

Philip snorted. "Merna has always been quick to do that. Until recently, she's hated him. And she still does, for all we know."

Orlianna whirled toward him. "Do you accuse me of being a liar?"

"Certainly not." Philip's arms tensed, but he held his ground. "And I don't wish to pain you. But did you *see* him kill your brother?"

"No," Orlianna whispered. "But his band was there. They fought us, deep in the heart of the mountainous catacombs. I may not have seen Ríon, but I saw the work of his hands. I saw my brother lying dead on the ground where he left him. And I heard his last words."

Arliss's heart felt like it was being wrung like a towel. "What were those words?"

"He said, 'The Prince of Anmór did this.' And I have learned that you should never doubt the words of a dying man." She tottered, and Arliss worried she would collapsed in the shallow water. "This was six years ago. I was only nineteen at the time, and he twenty-three." She trembled once more.

Garrick splashed through the fringes of the waves. "Come, you need to sit down."

She shook her head. "I'm fine."

But she let him guide her up the hill nonetheless.

Arliss glanced after them. Orlando lingered in the shadows. His face was twisted with grief. She understood. She, too, felt the sorrow, the conflict, deep in the pit of her chest.

Philip pressed her shoulder. "This gets more and more complicated, doesn't it? Anmór and Ikarra are not friendly with each other, if this is true."

"If Merna has propagated this story—no matter how false it may be—I doubt Anmór claims any connection to it at all. Ríon is an outlaw."

"You know what we're getting ourselves into?"

She stepped further out, letting Philip's hand drop away. The waves tumbled up and splashed against the hem of her linen dress. "Five minutes ago I said I did. Now, I'm not certain."

She stood there and let her feet sink into the wet sand as the water drifted higher and higher up her shins. She closed her eyes and felt the water of a thousand worlds swirl around her.

"If we go, we'll have to postpone our wedding."

She caught her breath. She hadn't thought of that, in all the excitement and revelations of the past few days. It was true, though. Who knew how long the expedition to Ikarra might take? She had no confirmation of when they would return.

It was fine. They had waited many months. What were a few more?

She looked at Philip. The thirsting edge in his eyes told her that a few more months were a serious thing indeed.

The bottom of her soaked skirt floated about her knees. She stepped further out and let the ocean trickle up her clothes in branching rivulets. "Then we must postpone it. Ikarra is calling to me. And I know it's calling to you, too."

CHAPTER TEN: DEPARTURE

THE SUN HAD ALREADY STARTED TO COOK THE SHIMMERING SAND as Ilayda scampered across the beach. Everywhere she looked, people were moving, working, rushing, splashing, casting up sand. The voyage last autumn to the Isle of Light had been nothing compared to this one.

For one thing, Orlianna's ship was twice the size of theirs. For another, the beach had been nothing but naked sand. Now, it boasted four ship skeletons which grew steadily more substantial each day.

Ilayda filled her lungs with rich salt air. Where had the time gone? It seemed Orlianna had only just arrived. Now, not five days later, they were leaving. Kenton had saddled her ship with provisions and prayed a blessing over the voyage the evening before.

And within an hour, Ilayda's feet would leave Reinholdian land.

She stole a furtive glance around. No sign of Brallaghan. Maybe she could get away without so much as a word to him.

Then she saw him, his long legs pumping as he jogged down the hill. The flame red tunic of his guard uniform beamed in the sun as he rushed down the incline, nearing her every moment. She wanted to run.

But he wasn't heading for her.

He was heading straight for Arliss.

Arliss's pulse throbbed with excitement as she watched the movement of the crowd that danced around her—some carrying barrels of fresh water to the ship, others rowing across the waves to load the royal trunks onto the vessel. Most, though, were simply there for the show of it all. And it was quite a show.

Orlianna stood with Kenton at the base of the hill, pointing people this way and that. She wore a handsome maroon gown with sheer sleeves that fluttered in the breeze. Her hair was pulled to the side and arranged over one shoulder in a long braid.

Arliss grabbed up her own hair where it hung, sticky, against the back of her neck. Reinhold was getting warm. If it was like this in April, how much more by summer? Ikarra would be refreshingly cool, to be sure, with its northern atmosphere.

She stared out at the ship again. Her feet itched, and not because of the sand that had seeped into her boots. Her whole body yearned to depart so strongly that she could feel her insides being dragged forward.

Someone behind her cleared his throat.

She turned. Brallaghan stood there, dapper as ever in his guard uniform. A sword hung about his waist and a knapsack around his back. His face was sad—even desperate.

"Arliss," he managed. "We've always been friends."

She nodded. They had—their whole lives. Yet recently she had felt further and further from him. She couldn't help what had happened with Ilayda, and it *wasn't* all Brallaghan's fault. But that changed nothing in the inevitable rift between them.

"I want to come with you. I'm the child of a lord. I have as much right as any of the rest of them."

She bit her lip. He was right. The rest of them—Philip, Erik, and Orlando—were not royalty. Besides herself, only Ilayda was.

She'd dreaded this conversation the past few days. Amidst preparations and the feast last night, she'd almost forgotten Brallaghan. She'd almost forgotten Ilayda's heartbreak, too. And now it slapped her across the face and demanded her attention.

She inhaled to her full height. "You know I can't do this to

Ilayda."

"What about to *me*?" he demanded. "Can you do this to me?"

"Ilayda is coming with me." Arliss held his gaze. "I will not leave her here. And to have you come with us would cause her nothing but grief."

He stare went to Ilayda. "I want to forgive her. I want to be friends again, if only because I want to be friends with *you* again, too."

So he, too, felt they were no longer friends. She rubbed her hand up the polished wood of her quiver. "Brallaghan, I can't do this. She's not ready to forgive you yet. I wish she was. But she has to heal. If you come, her wounds may break open beyond healing."

He shook his head. "You're walking straight into a war. I'm a guard—a fighter. If it comes to fighting, what good will Ilayda be?"

"We're going to end a war, not join one." She arched her eyebrows. "I will not talk about this any more."

He spun on a clipped heel and disappeared in the masses.

Arliss finally noticed Ilayda had moved and stood not far away. She must have heard the whole thing.

Ilayda sighed. "Thank you."

Chaos flowed around Orlianna—through her—and spiked her heart to double its usual pace. They were leaving. She was going back to Ikarra. And the Reinholdians were coming with her.

She folded her arms, then let them drop at her sides. Why should she be tense? She didn't give twopence what Maeve thought, or what Maeve would do. Her grandmother wasn't dangerous.

But she was. Her power was old, digging down to the very roots of Ikarra. And even if the people did not all love her, they feared her. Who knew what she would do when Orlianna came floating up the city's bay with five Reinholdians in tow.

Kenton cleared his throat and pointed to her ship with two fingers. "You are almost ready, Prin—I mean, Orlianna."

She bit the corners of her mouth to stop her smile. "It would seem so."

She looked down the beach in either direction. The skeletal ships were no more than a valley of dry bones, it seemed. But they would find sinew and skin soon enough.

She glanced at Kenton. "You yourself are almost ready, I think."

He raised his eyebrows. "You mean the ships?

"Your small fleet will be ready to go to war within months."

"We do not plan to go to war."

"The hunter does not plan to use his bow for battle. It happens nonetheless."

Kenton stepped around, squared his shoulders, and faced her. "I know you're doing this for your people, and for all the three clans. But there is more in your heart, is there not? You want to prove yourself to your people. To your grandmother."

Orlianna's fingers froze. "So Arliss told you?"

"Arliss tells me many things."

What conclusions might he have jumped to now? She narrowed her eyes. "I suppose you think me a self-centered manipulator."

He shook his head. "I think you're trying to do too many things at once. Prevent war, unite the three clans, become the queen of Ikarra—it's quite a list."

"And you would try to stop me?"

"No." Lines trenched his forehead as he pulled something from behind his back. "I would help you if you would help me."

The item in his hand was an ancient dagger—long and straight and in a rotting sheath of black leather. The back of her throat dried out.

He balanced it across his palms between them. "If you become queen of Ikarra, you can bring balance to the clans. In the few days I've known you, I have seen that. But I need you to do something else for me. I cannot bring peace to the realms. Elowyn cannot bring peace to the realms. Our place is here. But Arliss—" He looked to where his daughter stood expectantly by the shore. "—*she* can. But until she takes up the mantle of monarch, she carries no authority. No confidence."

"So you want me to force her into becoming queen?"

He placed the dagger in her hands. "This dagger belonged to Thane. According to the inscription, he was given it by the king of Anmór."

"Merwin," Orlianna whispered.

"I want you to have it. And every time you look at it, remember your promise."

She curled her fingers around the scarred leather.

Kenton turned and walked toward his daughter.

Orlianna paused. She had made no promise. If Arliss was to become queen, she had to discover it for herself.

Even upon the whispering sand amidst the chaos of preparation, Arliss could recognize her mother's floating footsteps.

Elowyn's footsteps stopped. "I think you already know what I'm about to say."

Arliss didn't turn. The stationary ship stared back at her. "How do you know that?"

Elowyn came closer and took Arliss's hands in her own. Her mother's hands felt cold, and her voice wavered. "You are perceptive, Arliss, beyond most people. What many do not notice, you see. And more than that, you realize its importance."

Arliss swallowed, unable to say anything. It was flattering to be so complimented—and she couldn't deny the truth of her mother's words—but she knew her mother had much more to say.

Elowyn squeezed Arliss's fingers white. "I have a task for you during your trip."

Here it was coming again. Become queen. Embrace your role. Take up the crown of Reinhold. She'd heard it from her father with varying (and sometimes unvarying) phrasing more the past week than she wished to count. She knotted her brow. Red pressure crowded her head as she prepared a rebuttal.

Her mother sighed. "You will inevitably meet people from Anmór during your trip. We know now from Ríon that Merna was not the only one involved in Thane's villainy. Perhaps he supported himself, but I suspect something darker."

Arliss's chest rose and fell with constrained breaths. What task was her mother prescribing?

"I want you to find out the truth about Thane—about our whole story. For my sake. And not just for mine, but for Eamon's."

Pain grabbed Arliss's heart and squeezed. She closed her eyes, but the sunlight burned through her eyelids and she saw nothing but blood. She hadn't had time to eat anything that morning, and now her empty stomach twisted like a wet rag. Eamon's death had been dealt by Thane, but the weight—the responsibility—draped heavily across her own shoulders.

Elowyn's squeeze calmed her senses. "And not for his alone, but also…"

Arliss turned her head. Her mother wept silently, the tears dripping down her face.

Grief wrenched Elowyn's face. "…for Nathanael."

The pain and nausea jerked at Arliss's body again. She was responsible for both her uncles' deaths. She had been close enough to witness both. And she hadn't been able to stop either of them.

Arliss pulled her mother's hands to her chest. "I promise you, I will find out the truth."

Elowyn kissed Arliss's forehead.

Kenton's strong arms wrapped around them both.

Arliss tensed with her hands stuck at her sides. She dug the toe of her boot into the sand as Kenton squeezed his family together. The warmth of her father's arms against her back, her mother's chest against her own, melted the tension in her fingers. She let them relax all the way.

After several moments Kenton let his arms drop. "I suppose it's time for you to be off."

"Yes," Arliss said. "I've been waiting for this for so long—my whole life, really. Ever since I read about the mythical lands of

Ikarra and Anmór, I wanted to visit them. Now it's finally come, and…"

"You don't want to leave?" Philip appeared, finishing her sentence as he slipped his arm around Elowyn's shoulder.

She nodded. He always finished her own sentences better than she herself could. She rolled her heel around in the silky grains of beach.

"It's frightening," she said. "I'm going somewhere no one in Reinhold has been before. And with everything I've been told—by Ríon, by Orlianna—I don't know what to think."

Would she find out the origins of Thane's attacks? Would she discover the missing gifts of Reinhold? Those elusive items, a pendant and a sphere, evaded her at every turn. She'd found some of their gifts in Anmór. Who was to say they wouldn't find more in Ikarra?

She exhaled. "Are you sure it's safe?"

Elowyn turned her head and regarded Arliss. "Am I sure *what* is safe?"

She shook her head at her own silliness. How often did her mind rush ahead of everyone else—even herself? She had to slow down. "Taking the gifts with us. It's quite risky."

Kenton studied Arliss. "The gifts were created long ago to bring peace between the clans. You may need them now more than ever. More than anything."

She'd given Ilayda the vial. It would be safe in her careful hands. The crown she'd hidden deep in her own satchel, beneath all her other belongings. And, of course, Orlando still silently guarded the ring of Reinhold.

Philip placed his hand on the sword of Reinhold which swung at his side. He edged closer to the lapping waves. "Arliss, it's time."

He was right. In the midst of their conversation, the final longboat of stores had emptied its contents onto the ship. Now it headed back to shore for its final load of passengers.

Arliss stared at the straining necks and rippling arms of the Ikarran oarsmen as they plowed through the water toward her.

This was it. She was leaving home. And unlike last time, she wasn't going to be dragged off to another realm unknowingly. She was doing this with every drop of her blood, every thought in her head.

Orlianna strode up beside them as the longboat skidded onto the beach. "Are you ready?"

Arliss stepped toward the boat, then jerked to a stop. She looked over her shoulder at her parents. "I will think of you every day."

"So will we." Kenton pressed his fist to his lips and opened his hand toward her.

Arliss returned the gesture. "Pray for me—that your princess may have a queenly look in her eye and grace on her forehead. Heaven knows I'll need it."

Elowyn spread her hands wide in blessing, the brown sleeves of her dress flapping behind her. "You know well the third verse of the song, Arliss—a princess on a gilded throne, clothed in silken raiment. When a princess sits on a gilded throne, do you know what she is? A queen."

Arliss nodded.

Philip touched her hand, pulling her gently toward the boat.

She dipped her head. "I will try my best."

"Farewell," Kenton said. "And Godspeed."

Arliss stepped into the boat and gripped the high stern. They cast off, and the land melted away into wobbling water beneath her feet.

Her voyage had begun.

Orlianna stood atop the crow's nest, her back against the pillar of wood. On the deck, Garrick readied the helm as the crew tugged up the anchor and flared the sails. Arliss and her company crowded the poop deck, straining for the last glimpse of their land.

She smiled and spread her arms wide. The sun seemed so close, so warm this high up. She closed her eyes and let her body soak in the flaming light.

The ship far below her jerked. Garrick gave a shout. The sails flapped limply just below her as the crew cast them wide.

Orlianna opened her eyes and stared out at the Reinholdian cliffs. No wind at the beginning of a voyage was considered an ill omen. If nature itself was against them, had God cursed their voyage? Perhaps she would return to Ikarra to find Maeve waiting with chains and shackles.

No matter what happened, she was going back to Harrison. He would listen as she unfolded her journey, introduced her new friends, and revealed to him everything about Thane and Merna and Reinhold. He would hear and hold her as he always did. Unless someone had found out his role in her disappearance…

The breeze caught her hair up and tossed it. It ruffled her sheer sleeves. It pressed the front of her dress flat against her legs.

The sails inflated. The crew cheered. And the ship lurched onward, picking up speed as the east wind breathed it to life.

Orlianna spread her hands wide, wider. And for once, Maeve didn't matter. Her past grief didn't matter. The weight of war and peace didn't matter. She was the wind. She was the sun. She was joy.

And Reinhold was coming to Ikarra.

BO BURNETTE/88

CHAPTER ELEVEN: THE WATER'S MENACE

PHILIP CROSSED HIS ARMS TIGHT ACROSS HIS CHEST. HE STOOD at the prow, staring out into a murky sky. Two days into this voyage, and they'd seen little sea and even littler sky. Everything had dipped into gray. The clouds hung thick, like foaming ocean waves hung in the sky to dry.

He exhaled against his arms. The sea was still—too still. Anyone or anything could sneak up on them in this fog.

He turned and made for the helm, forcing his arms to swing at his sides. They still knotted up with tension.

Garrick had one hand on the helm, the other on his hip. He nodded at Philip then stared back into the surrounding gray.

"Know where we are?" Philip came to stand beside the massive wooden wheel.

Garrick's eyebrow twitched. "Is that a question? You're speaking to the finest seaman in the realms."

Philip nodded, but silently he disagreed. No offense to Garrick, but that honor went to Eamon, and Eamon alone.

"Even fog can't stop me. 'Specially not with this." Garrick lifted a clear, rectangular stone. It was bright as sun and clear as water. "You ever seen a sunstone?"

Philip squinted. "What does it do?"

"'Tis a bit complicated. But it shows me where to go—rather, tells me where the sun is." He tilted the glassy stone back and forth and held it to his eye. "To answer your question, though, we're passing around the eastern lee of the Isle of Light."

That was strange. If old maps—and Orlianna's new ones—were true, then it would save time to go around the western side and shoot up the coastline to Ikarra. This was no shortcut.

"Why are we taking the long way?" Philip asked.

Garrick paused, peering over Philip's shoulder. He dipped his head.

Orlianna tromped up the stairs to the elevated helm deck. "Sir Philip, I would like to speak with you in the stateroom."

"Now?" Philip rested his hand on his sword's pommel.

"Arliss and the rest are already gathered. So yes, now." She tossed her red hair, whirled away, and stalked back down the stairs and across the deck. The opaque glass doors to her stateroom slammed into place behind her.

Garrick shrugged.

Philip started down the stairs. As he did, the boat seemed to shift slightly beneath him.

He turned and tried to catch Garrick's eye, but the captain wasn't looking. He stared down at the boards beneath his boots. Had the boat really jerked?

Perhaps it was just his imagination.

Arliss glanced up from the map on the table as Orlianna shoved the double doors open and entered the stateroom.

A moment later, Philip opened one of the black glass doors and slipped inside. Excellent. Orlianna had been holding back these past few minutes. Now that they were all here, she could really say what had to be said.

"Good morning." Arliss stroked her finger across the map of the realms. "We've been waiting for you."

Philip shoved his hands in his pockets. "I wouldn't have kept you waiting if I'd known."

Orlianna waved her hand at him. "No need to apologize. Some of us just woke up."

Arliss glanced at Ilayda and coughed.

Hands still buried in his pockets, Philip stepped across the slickly polished floor. "What's going on?"

Erik crossed his arms. "It's a briefing."

Orlando snorted from where he stood leaning into the far corner. "If this is a briefing, then I'm a diplomat." He tilted his teacup toward his mouth. "At least, my sort of briefings never featured tea."

Arliss set her cup down on the long central table and stared hard at him. Orlando needed to shut up before he let slip something too important. He was hinting too closely at his background as a spy. For Thane. For Anmór.

Orlianna's eyelashes flicked dangerously, but she didn't respond to his hints. "This is not a war briefing. This is preparation. And I appreciate that you enjoy my cabin's snuggery."

Arliss nodded. On the entry side, opaque glass doors hid the room from the crew's view. On the opposite wall, a wide window gave full view of the dim ocean spreading out on either side. Above her head, five simple chandeliers flickered around the table like points of a star. Bookshelves lined the walls on either side.

Orlianna touched the map. "Here we are—just past the eastern lee of the Isle of Light. At this rate, we'll reach my city…" She traced her finger up the map to a mountain-lined bay further north. "…Cahair, within ten days, if the wind holds true. Which means you have ten days to become acquainted with Ikarra and its ways."

Arliss swallowed. She hadn't considered how simple and unsophisticated Reinholdian manners probably were to the Ikarrans. They'd stuck out like blunt arrowheads in Anmór. Ikarra was likely just as much—or more—refined.

Philip sat and scratched a hand through his hair. "What's expected of us?"

Orlianna looked at the floor. "Well, I'm not sure if *anything* is expected of you."

"I suppose that's good," Ilayda quipped.

Arliss screeched her chair up to the table. "Do you mean your people are forgiving of newcomers?"

Orlianna reached for her necklace. "I only mean you aren't what they are expecting at all."

Philip exhaled. "So we have to make a good impression in order for this friendship thing to work."

Orlianna wrapped her finger in the chain of her necklace. "At least."

Arliss stared at the necklace. It hung down the middle of Orlianna's chest like a flower made of metal. Petals of alternating silver and ivory swept around beneath a golden cap. It was beautiful, ancient—the most magnificent pendant Arliss had ever seen.

Arliss froze with her teacup halfway to her lips. *Pendant.* Could it be?

No, it wasn't possible. How could the Reinholdian pendant have found its way into the hands of an Ikarran princess, especially with their clan's isolation these past decades?

Arliss glanced up. Orlianna was staring at her. She looked away, but Orlianna had already seen, and her green eyes narrowed.

Philip framed his forehead with his fingers and stared at the map. "I suppose we start with geography."

Orlianna came closer to the table. She motioned left and right. "Start with whatever you like. I have plenty of books."

Erik finally sat beside Ilayda. "Excellent. I do enjoy reading."

"You'll have plenty of it if you want to know even a smattering about Ikarra," Orlianna said.

Orlando retreated from the corner and joined the throng around the table. "What is the perception about us in Ikarra?"

Orlianna tilted her head. "I'm not sure I understand your question."

"I mean, what do people think about our coming? Are they awaiting us with parades—or swords?"

Arliss nodded to show Orlianna she, too, wanted that question answered. Were the Reinholdians the long-lost clan, the prodigal sons? Or were they the outcasts, the barbarians, the warmongers? And what would they think of Orlando when they all—like Orlianna—realized he was Anmórian?

Orlianna hesitated. "Perhaps I have been too covert in my speech. When I told you that you aren't what my people are expecting at all, I meant it in the deepest possible way."

Arliss leaned over the table. The smooth wood felt cool beneath her splayed palms. "I thought you said you were doing this to prove yourself to your grandmother."

Orlianna groaned softly. "I shouldn't have kept this from you. But I feared it would keep you from coming."

Arliss's stomach muscles clenched.

"No one knows about my mission—except for Harrison and my crew. I left in secret." Orlianna stood. "Not even my grandmother Maeve knows about this."

Arliss collapsed back into her chair and stared out the gray window.

So they were going all this way to a country that didn't even know they were coming. What could have possessed Orlianna to think this was a good idea? If things didn't go off perfectly, they would be packed up and shipped back to Reinhold—at best.

At worst…

Arliss wanted to speak, but the words piled up at the bottom of her throat and choked her breath.

She grabbed at the table edge, trying to focus on something, anything, to anchor herself. Her eyes clapped onto the cabin window and for the briefest second, the world stopped spinning.

A long, contorted tentacle oozed its way up the wide cabin window. Slimy cups of gray flesh suctioned to the window as another tentacle crept up the other side.

Ilayda grabbed Arliss's hand beneath the table.

A hideous hiss, a gurgling growl, shook the cabin for several horrible moments.

Glass shattered. Enormous jaws snapped, teeth shredding through glass, crackling wood. Water squelched the chandeliers.

Orlando leapt across the table and tackled Orlianna to the floor. Arliss dropped to the ground and rolled toward the doors.

The jaws retreated from the crater they had made in the front of the ship.

Arliss pulled her bow from where she'd propped it by the door.

Orlando jerked Orlianna to her feet. They had to get out of this cabin and onto the deck. Another moment, and that creature would shove its jaws back into the stateroom.

Orlianna froze by the doors.

He squeezed her hand, but her eyes remained wide—fixed on the shattered wall.

"What was that?" Ilayda's voice trembled so much Orlando wondered how she could talk at all.

He shook his head. "I don't know. I've never seen anything like it."

"A monster of legend," Orlianna whispered. "A fiend of Anmór. And so the war begins, with even the free seas enslaved."

Shouts echoed from the other side of the doors. The lookout must have spotted the creature. The warbling growl bubbled up from the water and shook the darkened chandeliers. Orlianna stared, unblinking, not even breathing.

Orlando grabbed her forearm. "What do we do?"

Her lips tightened, and she blinked twice. She shook free of his hand. Then she turned and jerked open the doors to the deck.

"Orli!" Garrick shouted from the helm. "Something's upon us! I don't know what it is."

Her footsteps sped up as Orlando followed her across the deck. "Have you heard the legends of the *crogall?*"

Garrick's knuckles tightened around the helm. "Not much of a reader."

"Even you should remember the childhood stories—nightmares used to frighten children into obedience."

"I've tried to forget."

Orlando leaned around into Orlianna's field of vision. "These must be uniquely Ikarran legends. I can't say I've heard of them."

Orlianna scoffed. "Anmórians don't have time for legends of any sort, do they?"

He swallowed. There wasn't much to say to this kind of sharp truth.

She whirled and addressed the crew. "All hands on deck! Make ready your weapons! All hands on deck!"

The crew rushed into position with the fluidity of a train. Sailors ran belowdecks and reemerged with bows and barbed harpoons. Others unfolded sails for extra speed. Erik ran to the prow with an arrow nocked. Philip joined a sailor in roping a sail into submission.

Orlianna rushed to the helm. "Garrick, command the archers, and look for a way out of this. We need a heading."

Garrick hesitated with one hand on the wheel. "Who will take the helm?"

She grabbed the spokes. "I will."

The sea ahead was quiet and ripplingly still.

A spatter of rain made Orlando blink.

He opened his eyes. The creature exploded from the waters, tentacles waving, jaws clenching. Its long snout thrust high in the air, reaching nearly as high as the ship's deck. Its hide was thick, with sharp ridges serrating its back. Yet it had no fierce claws, no arms or legs. Instead, eight suctioning tentacles waved in every direction, latching onto the ship.

Orlianna was mistaken if she thought this beast was from Anmór. Orlando had seen nothing like it in his life. Nonetheless, he knew the blatant truth: it could kill them all.

Arliss clenched her bow. Everyone—even Ilayda—rushed around as if they knew what they were doing. She couldn't claim the same confidence. So many people trying to do the same thing—she would be just one more useless body. She stepped one stair up toward the elevated helm.

Orlianna's mouth was open, and her clenched teeth shone.

Arliss lifted her bow. "What can I do?"

Orlianna dipped her chin. "Kill it."

Still gripping her bow, Arliss drew her long knife and ran for the prow.

Everyone was already trying to kill it, so she wasn't alone. But no one could take down the beast. Garrick thrust a javelin which drowned in the murky water. Erik fired arrow after arrow at the scaly hide, but they bounced off.

Massive teeth chomped between equally massive jaws as the creature squeezed itself up the ship's side. Tentacles trickled over the edge of the deck.

The crogall widened its mouth around the ship's nose.

One snap, and the wooden unicorn at the prow disappeared with a crackle.

Philip hacked at one of the encroaching tentacles. The tip splattered on the deck, but the rest of the arm continued to snake its way along, unhindered. It shot toward Philip and looped around his left leg. The creature's black blood spewed down the leg of Philip's trousers and onto his boot.

Arliss dropped her knife, drew an arrow, and fired at a tentacle.

The creature shrieked and withdrew its tentacle, the arrow imbedded within.

Philip nodded his thanks in her direction.

She knelt and retrieved her knife, sliding it into her quiver with her arrows. They couldn't pierce its hide with anything, and the tentacles seemed resistant to pain. But if they could cut them off at their source...

The creature edged its jaws up on the prow and growled, spreading its fleshy mouth wide. That made another vulnerable area. Arliss's arms twitched. It was either cut off the tentacles, or get into its throat.

Before she could think or speak, before Philip could stop her, she rushed to the prow and nocked an arrow for the creature's mouth.

Orlianna ignored her aching knuckles as they strangled the helm. All blood had left them. They were whiter than snow, than death.

The crogall had pulled itself halfway onto the ship already, and still her crew couldn't stop it. Tentacles weren't just suctioning to the ship now. They were waving through the air in her direction.

The creature's strength pulled against her own movements at the wheel. So many weapons hung at her disposal—her claw knives, dagger, and stiletto all on her belt—but she couldn't manage the helm with just one hand. The beast was too powerful.

Contorted limbs surrounded her now, waving like faceless snakes on either side of the helm deck.

She glanced heavenward. The sky held nothing but clouded rain. She bit down hard. "God, do not let this be my end—strangled by some monster from hell."

Both tentacles shot toward her.

Orlando rushed up the stairs, knife in one hand, sword in the other. He sliced through the tip of one tentacle with his knife and batted the other away with his sword.

She exhaled and refocused on the helm. It was getting harder and harder to control as the ship listed more and more forward.

Orlando spun like a dancer, his soggy burgundy cape flapping as his two blades sparked back and forth. Who was this fellow—truly? He was no typical Anmórian citizen or soldier. This kind of skill was beyond anything she'd ever seen.

The tension in her body slowly turned to focus. She had no fear of the beast. With this cloaked spy whirling around her, she was impenetrable. It couldn't touch her.

The jaws snapped three paces from Arliss's face. Her first arrow pinged off its snout and clattered to the deck.

Kill it, kill it, kill it. Her brain rotated madly around the thought.

She dropped to retrieve the arrow, but her hand froze. Why did her body refuse to comply? Her heart stopped as she willed her quivering hand to grab the arrow.

The crogall roared and seized her moment of hesitation. One of its central tentacles wrapped around her legs and cinched them together.

She pulled the arrow onto the string.

The slimy limb jerked her off the deck. The ground melted into air beneath her feet. Rain pelted her face as the crogall suspended her high above the deck. It curled her up as if to strike—or to throw.

"Philip!" she shouted.

He was there—below her—shouting something indistinguishable. He sliced through the towering tentacle. Blood gushed onto the deck below. Just as the fleshy extension split from itself, it contracted outward.

Arliss hurtled through the rainy air and over the side of the deck.

She was falling. She was about to be drowned. Water would fill her lungs as the beast gnawed at her flesh bit by bit.

She drew the knife and stabbed it into the blackness.

The ship was closer than she'd thought. The blade slit into the wood all the way to the hilt and jerked her to a hanging halt. Pain shot down her arm and into her shoulder as she hung from the side of the ship by her knife.

The water beneath her erupted. Salt ocean filled her nostrils, and she snorted it out. Tentacles reached for her again. They would yank her down, down, down.

Philip shouted from above her. "Arliss!"

She strained. "I'm here!"

He gaped, then firmly gripped the edge of the deck. He was

going to jump over.

She shook her head. He would kill himself, and have nothing for his chivalry.

But her muscles were burning. Her strength wouldn't last forever.

A tentacle grabbed her foot and nearly jerked her wet palm from the knife handle. She reached up and placed her hand atop the one wrapping the hilt. The slippery creature noosed her legs and crept up toward her waist.

In a moment it would pry her off. She looked up at Philip. "Get ready!"

"What?"

The crogall tugged her from the wall, but she gripped the knife like death. It slid free of the ship.

Jaws slavered below her. The crogall lifted her high, dangling its meal high above. The circulation in her legs was nearly gone, but she couldn't act just yet. It lifted her higher...higher. Almost parallel with the deck.

The crogall hissed, spouting water into her face.

She slashed the knife down and severed the tentacle.

The limb split, and the dying muscles contracted. She flew through the air. The beast's screech blasted her hearing into silvery nothingness.

She collided with Philip. His strong arms circled her as he tumbled backward into the deck, breaking her fall. She fell atop him, gasping wet breaths into his chest. He refused to let her go for a long moment.

He finally relaxed, and she rolled onto the deck. One look at his eyes and all her thanks were made.

Orlando stood panting near Orlianna's upright form at the helm. "I don't think it'll follow us. I hope not."

Arliss pushed herself up. "What does this mean? Is Anmór after us?"

Orlianna stared into the north. "Someone is. Someone is trying to stop our voyage."

Orlando still looked shocked. "Who do you think is behind these creatures?"

"I don't know," Orlianna said. "But whoever it is, they've just started this war we're all trying to prevent."

CHAPTER TWELVE:
WELCOME TO IKARRA

ARLISS STARED OUT FROM THE SHATTERED PROW. THE SEA WAS crisp, but storms whispered on the horizon.

In the week since the crogall's attack, she'd glued herself here, desperate for the first glimpse of Ikarra. Philip sometimes joined her with a cup of tea and a snatch of information from his studying. They'd all been studying—Erik and Philip especially—but she hadn't felt up to it. The sight of the patched-up stateroom window still sparked chills up her spine.

And, of course, she didn't feel like speaking to Orlianna. The nerve of her—enticing them into a voyage, then telling them the whole thing was a bloody secret. What if this Maeve woman got wind of things before they returned? There could be an ambush waiting, or even an all-out assault.

Orlianna swished silently beside Arliss. "I know you're angry at me."

"*Confused* might be a better word." Since when was underhanded manipulation the way to preserve diplomacy?

"Perhaps I should have told you. But I don't think you truly understand the situation."

Arliss cocked her head. "Excuse me, but I think I do. You left Ikarra without your grandmother's blessing on a mission no one would support, then tricked us all into thinking we were coming to help you build a bridge that was already in position. And once we're well on our way" —Arliss smacked the back of her hand against her palm— "you reveal the truth. They know nothing about us. And they probably don't want to."

Orlianna's eyes rolled upward. "What else could I have done?"

"You could have told us the truth!"

"I did." Orlianna glared. "You met Harrison. You spoke with him."

"Yes." Arliss gripped the splintered deck railing.

"Then you know what you have said is not true. The Ikarrans do know about you. And they are ready to reignite our relationship."

"Then why the secrecy?"

"That is an excellent question, and not an easy one to answer. Suffice it to say that—though most would agree with me—there are some who would have prevented me from going."

"Your grandmother?" Arliss asked.

"Precisely."

"And why is your grandmother against us?"

"She isn't. She's against war." Orlianna trembled. "She sees things. She understands things, more than most. More than anything, she wants to see unity between the clans."

Arliss smiled. Maybe this Maeve wasn't so awful after all. If she wanted unity of the clans, the absence of war, then they both had the same goals.

"However," Orlianna said, "Until now, 'the clans' has only meant Ikarra and Anmór. Reinhold makes things triply complicated."

Arliss's heartbeat clogged. "So you think she would put your relationship with Anmór before one with Reinhold."

"Perhaps so. Especially considering how little friendship there is between your people and Anmór. If Maeve supports you, Anmór could take it as war. And she cannot risk that."

Arliss stared down into the indigo waters. "But why? If she really wants unity, she could try to reconcile all three clans. What special attention does she owe Anmór?"

Orlianna gasped a wry laugh. "Don't you understand? I thought you knew."

Knew *what?* Orlianna kept too many secrets and spoke in too many riddles. Arliss's stomach whisked itself together.

"Forgive me for being too guarded. Sometimes I forget what I've told which people…which secrets are common knowledge." Orlianna took a step back. "My grandmother Maeve is the sister of Queen Merna of Anmór."

Arliss gripped the rail. A barbed splinter stabbed her palm.

"I assumed you knew after your visit to Anmór."

Memories flushed Arliss's head as pain flooded her palm. "I guess…I don't really remember."

"Well, it is true. Our clans are united, despite the conflict which cuts like a knife, higher than the mountain range that divides our realms. Maeve would never go to war—for any reason. And most certainly not over Reinhold."

Arliss plucked the bloodied splinter out of her palm. The muscle beneath her thumb knotted in resistance against the pain. "So how do you plan to convince your grandmother?"

"We're going to make a very good first impression."

Arliss arched one eyebrow. "Somehow I don't think good first impressions are going to come easy since we're an unwanted surprise."

"It'll certainly take some panache. A shot of nerves, too, and maybe of something stronger."

Arliss pressed her thumb against the drop of beading blood.

Orlianna inhaled sharply. "Well, then. Here it is."

Arliss faced the ocean again. This time, more than water and clouds greeted her. To the left, the beginnings of a line of mountains jutted out of distant mist. The land couldn't be more than half a league away.

A breeze tossed Arliss's hair about her face. It also whispered into the sails, rushing the ship along toward the mountains. But as they neared, Arliss saw they were going beyond the mountains. The ocean eddied away into a bay—or perhaps a river.

Orlianna turned. "Ready to turn us about, Garrick."

Garrick nodded and spun the wheel.

They had come parallel to the mountains now. The ship swerved, its shattered nose pointing straight down the bay-river.

Arliss swallowed the excitement that burned her throat. This waterway was all that separated her from Ikarra.

Ilayda stumbled up the stairs from belowdecks, frantically dragging her fingers through her thick hair. Erik had popped his head into her chamber long enough for her to understand she needed to be on deck—but not why. Something about mountains and bays and a lighthouse. Whatever *that* was.

She rushed up onto the deck. The crew bustled around with an unmistakable urgency. They were almost home, and their feet were starting to itch.

Ilayda hid her hand in her hair and scratched the back of her head. She was starting to itch for home herself. But home was where Brallaghan was. And that could never be home.

Erik nearly knocked her over as he ran by her. Drat him and his long legs.

She huffed in his face. "Excuse me, but what's up?"

"Ikarra." He pointed in the direction of the nose (west, wasn't it?). "Right there. We'll be there within the hour."

The boat's surroundings were changing. On the left, mountains peaked all the way down the narrow bay. On the right, a peninsula of land shaved to a point just parallel to them. Some sort of ruins crowded its sandy terrain. At the beach's edge, a gray tower stood guard. Light flickered from its highest windows.

"What's that?"

"Ruins. I read about them in some of Orlianna's books."

"Yes, but what's the tower?"

"A lighthouse."

"What's it for?"

"I don't know half of much about Ikarra yet." He turned and kept moving down the deck.

She started to follow him.

"Ilayda!" Orlianna shouted from the prow.

Ilayda winced with one foot in midair. "Your…Grace?"

"May I speak with you?"

She walked over to Orlianna. "What is it?"

"We'll be disembarking soon. We are going to be quite the surprise to everyone in my city, so I'd rather like to get to the palace without being noticed. Particularly, I don't want any questions about who Orlando is, or about why I am suddenly showing up with five unwelcome visitors. Understood?"

Ilayda shrugged. "What are you wanting me to do?"

"Whatever happens, lie low, and do as you're told." Orlianna ran her finger down a curious three-slotted scabbard which hung from her belt. "And make sure Orlando stays hidden."

"Is that all?"

Orlianna's lips twisted. "Make sure Arliss doesn't do anything stupid."

The familiar odor of fish and lavender filled Orlianna's nose as the ship's starboard side pulled parallel to the high dock. The dock was quiet today. Only a few ships meandered in the narrowing bay downriver; only a few carriages waited for wares. That could be good or bad. Either Maeve hadn't found anything out, or she knew everything and was waiting for a moment to strike.

Either way, it felt good to be home. Cahair hadn't changed in the past four weeks. The same lofty buildings guarded the first cantar—the section of the city that bordered the bay and its dock. Beyond that, the squattier homes and stores of the second cantar stretched out along the river.

The ship floated to a halt. She yanked up her skirt and stepped onto the creaking platform.

Garrick exhaled beside her. "Good to be back. Let's hope my little cantar hasn't fallen to bits without me."

"If anything, Domnall's probably seized it and set it in some order."

"Are you being serious, Orrels?"

She regarded him. "As serious as you are."

Garrick suddenly cleared his throat and grasped his hands behind his back. "Speaking of Domnall."

Lord Domnall—tall, imposing, and frowning like a mad dog—stalked up the steps to the raised dock. The bunched muscles in his neck betrayed his tension.

Domnall's chest heaved beneath a snug tunic of black leather. "What is your business?"

Orlianna smirked. "A 'welcome home, Princess,' would do nicely."

"After what you've done, I think you do not deserve any such welcome."

She rolled her eyes. Such an idiot with words, and yet the entire city fell before his feet. The way of the world. "So, you think I *do* deserve *some* such welcome?"

"I think you deserve nothing."

Garrick chimed in, "Are you sure she doesn't not deserve any nothing?"

Domnall's fist clenched in unison with his teeth. "Quiet, Garrick."

Garrick puckered his lips. "Yes, your highness."

Orlianna inhaled. These two lords—both so different in age, stature, and temperament—never could reconcile themselves. But the last thing she needed now was a fight. They had to get to the castle before Maeve found out she was here.

She glanced back at the ship. None of her Reinholdian cargo was visible, but the arrow stuck in the side of the mast told her they were ready. That was Arliss's signal.

"Excuse me." She traipsed down the stairs past Domnall. "But we can't lollygag here all day."

Domnall jumped down after her. "What're you doing?"

"Going home. I have salt water in my hair—and my eyes—and

this dress isn't exactly tip-top shape." She motioned down at the green linen mess. "And a shot of brandy might do me good right about now."

Domnall tucked his thumbs into his belt, which held a silver moon-shaped buckle. "You aren't going anywhere."

"Excuse me?"

"You are not going anywhere, not till we've done the usual inspections."

Garrick stumbled down the stairs. "You mean, we aren't not going some of nowhere until—"

"Shut your bleeding mouth." The veins in Domnall's neck pulsed. "You disappeared for nearly a month with no leave or explanation. Your ship is in quite a state. This kind of behavior is unacceptable, and Maeve intends to show you just what she thinks."

Orlianna flicked her pendant. "I already know just what she'll say. 'Orlianna, do you think of nothing before you do it? This is why you are not ready to be queen. Imagine what your *mother* would think!' I've heard it all from her a million times over."

Domnall leaned close. "Maybe you should actually listen."

"Maybe you" —Orlianna locked his gaze— "should get out of my way."

He obviously didn't see her punch coming. It hit him full-on across the jaw, and before he could react, Garrick punched Domnall's stomach. Domnall buckled, coughing.

Orlianna didn't waste time. She grabbed Domnall's left wrist, locked her leg around his left ankle, and jerked. He toppled onto the dock's wooden beams. Then she started walking. The wood chopped off into stone road beneath her boots.

She sped her gait into a run. Dock workers stared as she passed.

Arliss pounded down the stairs from the platform with Philip, Erik, Ilayda, and Orlando behind her. "What do we do?"

Orlianna pointed straight ahead at a row of three carriages parked along the street that separated them from the first line of enormous homes. "Get in one of those carriages, stay low, and drive like the devil."

Philip jogged alongside them. "Who's driving?"

"Me." Orlianna reached the middle carriage and pulled herself into the curving, covered seat.

Garrick untied the horses' reins, tossed them to her, and jumped in on the other side. "Domnall's up, and he's angry."

"Good." She pulled tension into the reins. Domnall ran across the dock toward them, chest heaving. "He can have one of the other carriages. Everyone in?"

Orlando stuck his head into the covered cab. "Everyone."

She glared at him. "Stay down. Especially you."

He disappeared back into the cargo compartment.

A horse whinnied beside them—not their own. A blurred figure leapt into the carriage on the right and cut the reins. The person grabbed the frayed ends and goaded the horses into action. Hooves clattered on stone as the carriage careened around and exploded down the street toward the library. Domnall?

Orlianna wrenched her own reins. "But Domnall is still over there…"

Garrick grabbed her elbow. "Go—now!"

"What is it?"

"Go!" he shouted. "It's a spy. He sent them ahead to warn Maeve. We have to stop them!"

She snapped the reins, and the wheels started crunching down the stony street.

Domnall's shout erupted behind them as his third carriage joined the chase.

Arliss dug her fingers into the sides of the compartment as the carriage jostled its way along, the wheels beneath her feet vibrating into a blur.

Orlando had his ear against the opening up to the driver's cab.

The wheels jutted over a crevice in the stone.

Arliss nearly fell on top of Ilayda. "What's going on?"

Orlando pressed his palms against the side. "We're chasing, and we're being chased."

Philip folded his arms, not holding onto anything as he sat on the floor. "So much for subtlety."

Orlando eased his way across the tottering car to Arliss. He slid open a metal panel. "Window."

She peeked out. The vivid smell of flowers and something fishy nearly overwhelmed her other senses.

She squinted. Three-storied houses rose to the sky all along their road. All sported different shades, but they were all painted green—some deep and verdant, some pale, some emerald. She'd never imagined so many living quarters could exist in an entire country, much less one part of a city.

But what stuck out were the dozens, hundreds, of people who streamed in and out of her vision as they rattled along. She saw more people in one fleeting glance than lived in the entire city of Reinhold. They peered out of wide windows, streamed out of first-story taverns, and stopped along the flat stone road just to stare.

"The first cantar." Erik noted—probably from all that geography study she should have done on the ship. "It's one of the two city districts. Rich, and controls trade. The second cantar is behind it, and that's Garrick's domain."

Arliss peeped through the tiny window. Beyond the street of houses, a domed building of shimmering glass marked the beginning of a arching bridge. "And that glass thing?"

"The library."

Orlianna shouted into the compartment. "Arliss, get your head back in here!"

The carriage jerked left and threw Arliss across the car into Erik. He braced her up.

Something dark scraped over the open window and swallowed the light.

"What happened?" Ilayda asked. Arliss could barely see her in the darkness.

Orlando hissed. "That lord's beside us now."

The carriage careened further left. Arliss's back slammed into the metal wall. A horse shrieked.

Something pounded against Arliss from outside. They'd been hit.

Orlando slid open the other window. "That lord on the other side, the spy on this one."

Arliss licked her lips. They tasted like metal. "We're stuck in between."

She glanced at Orlando, then stumbled to the front of the car and pulled herself onto the driver's seat between Orlianna and Garrick.

"Get back in." Orlianna didn't even look at her.

Arliss pointed. "We're coming up on that library too fast."

"And what do you recommend?"

"Slow down."

"How?"

"Garrick gets on one of the horses and charges on."

Orlianna's bare forearms knotted as she wrapped the reins another thickness around her palms. "They'll catch us."

"Why don't we cut them back a bit?"

Orlianna took her eyes off the road for a second. "Do you know what you're doing?"

Arliss glanced back at Orlando. "I've done something like this before."

"Do it." Orlianna tapped Garrick's shoulder.

He looked bewildered, but jumped on the right horse's back. Arliss drew her knife and severed the reins. The carriage jerked backward, and Garrick shot on ahead toward the library and the bridge beyond.

Arliss motioned to Orlando. "Grab my legs."

He climbed up onto the seat between them. "What?"

"Do it!"

His grip fastened around her ankles as she crouched onto the floorboard. She pressed her face into the iron floor and pointed her knife outward. The sides were open, and a carriage wheel whirled a handbreadth from her face.

"A little faster," Arliss instructed.

Orlianna snapped the reins.

The carriage sidled up further. Arliss stared into the gap between the horses and the carriage itself now. "Push me out." She nodded up at Orlando.

He eased her head out into the sliver that separated the two carriages.

She raised the knife and slashed down across the reins of Domnall's horses.

Leather split. The creatures galloped madly ahead as the carriage clattered to a crash behind them. Domnall rolled out onto the street away from the wreckage.

"Other side." Arliss pushed herself up and lay down over the top of Orlianna's feet. Orlando repositioned his hands around her ankles.

Orlianna's voice quavered uncharacteristically. "Arliss…"

Arliss strained, rolling her shoulders to get a better position. "I'm trying."

"Arliss, there are people on the bridge. We'll run them over, or crash into the library, one."

Arliss stretched her arm out until she thought her shoulder would pop. She backhanded the knife and pulled it toward her. Leather snapped, frayed reins whipping into her face. The carriage tipped onto its side and skidded along behind them as the horses ran free.

Orlianna pulled the reins to her sides. "Hold on!"

The carriage swerved, tipping onto two wheels. Arliss held onto the edge of the floorboard like death. Orlando's hands choked the circulation in her ankles as he fought to keep her in the cab.

The horses clambered to a halt as the carriage righted itself.

Arliss pushed herself back up onto the seat. She hadn't breathed for a long time, so her deep exhalation stung her lungs.

Orlianna dropped the reins. Arliss looked at the bridge beyond the glass library. Several people had gathered on the bridge, all clearly royal or at least noble. In the front shone one particular woman—tall, slim, and clothed in a loose silver gown that matched her hair. She stared at the carriage with expectant eyes.

Orlianna cursed beneath her breath and dismounted the cab. "Come on. All of you may as well get out."

Arliss and Orlando followed her, and the rest exited the back of the car.

The silver woman strode toward them. The charms along her girdle—some resembling the moon, some the stars—jingled as she walked. She regarded Orlianna, then scanned the line of the company behind her. Her eyes fixed on Arliss last—and longest—of all. Still she said nothing.

"I'm back," Orlianna said.

Domnall stormed around the carriage. Blood ran in a thin line down his forehead. "Your Grace, detain her at once! A chase through the city, the destruction of my two best carriages, and a horrible scene suitable only for tavern gossips."

Arliss looked to Orlianna. There wasn't much excuse for it all, was there?

Orlianna cocked her head. "If you hadn't chased me and sent your spies ahead, there would have been no scene."

Domnall opened and closed his mouth. "My lady, silence her! All this secrecy and foolishness—and for what? A ragged band of Anmórian peasants?"

"They're not Anmórian," Orlianna said quickly.

Arliss nodded. It was true, mostly. Not counting Orlando.

Orlianna advanced toward the bridge. "Grandmother, these are Reinholdian guests. They come to reunite the old friendship."

Arliss gasped. So this silver woman was Orlianna's grandmother, the sister of Merna. This was Maeve. Her gray hair and wrinkled lips could have belonged to someone of seventy, but her body was straight and hard, her jaw firm.

"Please accept them. They wish to preserve the unity of the clans."

Maeve's gray eyes widened with flame. Then she caught her breath, and her eyelids dropped.

Here it was. Either she shunned them and drew swords, or accepted and offered tea. Orlianna's reputation hung upon it, without a doubt. But beyond that, the entire reputation and history of Reinhold swung upon her words.

Maeve smiled and spread her arms wide. "Welcome to Ikarra."

CHAPTER THIRTEEN:
THE FIRST BALL

ORLANDO LET HIS SHOULDERS DROP AS EVERYONE AROUND HIM BREATHED a collective sigh of relief. They were welcomed. They were guests. And they were home, for now. Orlianna walked past Maeve and onto the bridge. The others followed.

He lingered behind. Maeve's words didn't comfort him. She'd welcomed the *Reinholdians* to Ikarra—not him. And try as he might, he couldn't conceal his identity. Sure, he could mask his accent and slip a few fibs, but that might cause more trouble than it was worth.

Maeve glanced over her shoulder at the rest of Orlianna's company, then turned to Orlando. "You are one of them, too, I presume."

He nodded stiffly. "I am a member of the princess's council."

"And this is your first visit to Ikarra?"

"I have not had the pleasure of coming to Cahair before, no." If these questions got any deeper, they would be impossible to answer without flat-out lies.

"I do hope you find it welcoming." Maeve motioned toward the bridge. It arched over the river and onto an island of rock. Built into and upon the rock, mounding and spiking upwards, gleamed a castle of emerald stone.

Orlando nodded his thanks. The river surrounded the castle's island, thus cutting it off from the mainland—yet still within easy access and sight.

Maeve gave him a glance up and down, then turned and walked

away.

He curled his fingers into a fist. Ríon had warned him that the Ikarrans wanted his ring. Maybe there wasn't anything but air in that. But Maeve's look seemed searching, hungry.

He pulled his cloak tighter around his shoulders and tromped up the high arch to the middle of the bridge. Arliss stood beside Philip, glancing around with narrowed eyes. Erik was pointing out landmarks to Ilayda.

Orlianna stood embracing a broad, smoky-haired man.

The man kissed the top of Orlianna's head, then gripped her shoulders and pulled her away. "It's only been a month."

"Any time is a lifetime without you, Harrison."

So this was Harrison, the friend and counselor she'd spoken so much about. He still didn't quite understand their relationship, and this helped nothing. They seemed deeply, madly in love, yet fifteen long years stretched between them. Harrison had a warrior's body, but his silvering hair and dead eye gave away his age and experience. Orlianna, on the other hand, was the image of youth, power, strength.

Orlianna laughed and turned to the others. "Excuse me. This is—"

"Harrison!" Arliss stepped forward and grasped his hand.

Harrison chuckled. "Indeed. How I've longed to meet again, Princess Arliss. And who are your companions?"

"My husband-to-be, Philip. And this is Orlando, my…"

Orlando sucked in air. What was he to her? Bodyguard? Trainer? Accomplice?

"My friend," she said at last.

Harrison bowed. "It's a pleasure you have your lot here with us. There's so much to catch up on. I'm sure Orlianna has much to show you. Eh, little darling?"

Orlianna jabbed him with her elbow. "Yes, I do. We'll do plenty of exploring together. There are lots of ways of getting around here."

Harrison gave her a knowing glance. "Indeed. Ikarra has many secrets."

Orlando slid his hand in his jerkin and stroked his knives. "Such as?"

"You will see, Sir Orlando," Harrison laughed. "You will see."

Maeve strode in between them all, her expression cold. "Exploration can be saved for later. I have sent couriers ahead to prepare rooms for all our guests. We will have a grand party this evening in their honor, so I propose you escort them to their rooms straightaway, Orlianna."

Orlianna nodded. "May I choose their rooms?"

"If you must." Maeve stalked over the other side of the bridge.

Orlianna motioned to Orlando. "Come."

Ilayda leaned over the white, round stone railing and stared at the dancing waters below. Cool sunlight flickered through the river and shimmered up like a thousand underwater candles. How cool it was here, for it to be nearly May! Reinhold would already be warm by now.

She suddenly noticed Erik's lanky form beside her.

Erik pulled at her arm. "They're leaving for the castle."

"Good for them."

"Come on, silly. We've got to get ready."

She rubbed her eyes. "What did I miss?"

"There's a party planned for this evening."

"Oh, joy. I *do* love large groups of people staring at me."

He grinned and pulled her away from the edge of the bridge. "You'll do fine. Now let's go."

She glanced back at the city. The roofs of the first cantar scraped the sky in front of her, and the second cantar spanned the width of the quiet river to her left.

"Sometimes I wish moments like this could last forever."

He released her arm. "If they did, they wouldn't be moments."

"Moments define our lives. They change us. Sometimes they

break us."

"Only if you let them." He reached for her hand. "The moments that define you are the moments you won't let go of—good or bad."

She looked away. He was so sincere, but her pain—her heartbreak—was too real. "I wish that was true. There are things I would let go of if I could, trust me."

"I do trust you." He held her hand in the air dangerously close to his mouth. "But you're mistaken. And you will not be complete until you let pieces go."

Her breath wadded up her lungs.

He closed his eyes, his lips parting. They hovered over her hand a moment.

Then he dropped her hand and walked down the other side of the bridge.

Arliss had hardly been escorted to her room by a scrawny-armed servant before there came a knock on the door.

Couldn't they give her a moment's peace—even to look around the room? She dropped her trunk on the floor and ran to the mahogany door.

"Who is it?"

The lock clicked, and the door swung inward. Orlianna flipped a key between her fingers. "Someone who has a key to just about every room in the castle."

Arliss laughed. "Just about?"

Orlianna stepped in and shut the door. "Maeve has a secret study with all her relics. She changes the lock once every five months or so." She clicked the lock shut again.

Arliss knelt and unclasped her trunk. "What are you doing here?"

"I needed to talk with you alone, before everything explodes beyond my control." Orlianna knelt, grimacing. "Though I fear it already has."

"I think things have gotten off well."

Orlianna shook her head. "I made such a scene. I've turned Maeve against you from the outset."

"She *welcomed* us."

"She's being diplomatic, that's all. You have yet to see the many sides of my grandmother."

Arliss lifted her bow out of the trunk and set it on the floor. "I'm not afraid of her. You said she wants to stop this war. So do I. I think that alone will make us friends from the outset."

Orlianna stood and walked over to the lone window that spanned floor to ceiling and overlooked the river below. "I wish I had your confidence. But I've seen too much. I know too much."

Arliss set her bow aside and joined Orlianna by the window. "You're afraid, aren't you?"

Orlianna crossed her arms. "What would I be afraid of?"

Arliss shrugged.

Orlianna huffed and changed the subject. "I chose your room for a reason. See this?"

She opened a little brass door halfway up the wall and stuck her hand into the cubby inside. Arliss peered in. Layers of dusty air floated above the stone. It clearly hadn't been used for some time.

"This chute runs the length of the chambers on this side of the castle. Mine is at the top. Anyone on any floor can drop a message in the box, crank this wheel the proper number of times, and it shoots down or up. I put as many of you in these rooms as I could."

"Who's in which room?"

"Philip is right below you. Ilayda is two rooms up. Erik I could not get into this side, but he is on Ilayda's floor, not far away."

"And Orlando?"

Orlianna blinked. "Yes, him too, right above you." She turned for the door.

Questions erupted in Arliss's head. What did they expect her to do at the party? How long would they stay here, if all went well? And what if all *didn't* go well? How far was Cahair from Anmór?

If they were close, she might—horror of horrors—have to meet Merna again.

She sprang after Orlianna. "Wait. I have so many questions."

Orlianna held up her hand. "There will be time. For now, you must get ready. The ball will begin within an hour."

"Wait…ball?"

Orlianna smiled and opened the door. "What is dinner without dancing?"

Orlando's footsteps echoed down the winding staircase. He slowed down, setting his feet down like he was walking on glass, but that only seemed to make it louder.

There wasn't much sense in drawing this on. He *had* to go to the party, and he couldn't hide. Especially since Maeve had already spoken to him, his absence would be more conspicuous than his presence. He rushed down the last few stairs and onto the dark, silent landing of the fourth floor.

He glanced around. Sconces hung on either wall with unlit candles, but the hall stretched down and disappeared into a burst of light. So the party was just ahead—probably down another set of stairs.

He looked back down the other end of the hall. A richly carved mahogany door was the wall's only ornament—and the doorway to Arliss's room, if Orlianna's directions were correct.

They were. The door clicked open and Arliss slipped out, smoothing out the folds of her dress. It was a ravishing garment— bold green wrapping her body like a leaf and slipping down the far edges of her shoulders. A golden sash braceleted her waist, but her hair flowed free.

He exhaled slowly. He'd been drawn to her once, and it wasn't hard to see why. For every ounce of courage and wit Arliss had, she had beauty to match it.

She smiled, dipped in a half-curtsey, then came down the hall.

"Good evening."

He bowed. "I…I don't know what to say."

"About what?"

"You."

She suppressed a smile. "Be careful how you talk. Philip'll clobber you."

"I'm not too afraid of him. But really—he's lucky." He stared at her. "He almost wasn't, you know."

Arliss bit her lip. "You mean when he almost lost me."

"That wasn't an accident. That was my mission." Orlando closed his eyes. "Thane didn't want me to kill you if I didn't have to. He just wanted to break you apart."

She frowned. "Why?"

"I don't know." He gnawed on the inside of his mouth. "Really, though, you look beautiful."

"You do, too. I mean, you look…"

"Like I always do?" He motioned down his body. The trousers were new and rough, and the tunic was silk—rubbing slickly against his skin—but the burgundy cloak hid it all and made him feel more like himself.

"No, you look quite fine. Practically royal. One could actually believe you are a prince."

He swallowed. "Their beliefs wouldn't be too far from the truth."

"No." Arliss sighed. Then her face relaxed, her mouth lifting. "And what does the prince say about finding a princess?"

"If you can find a princess in the three realms who will put up with my tedious self, then maybe I'll believe in miracles. Because that's what that'd be."

Footsteps pattered behind them. Philip jumped down the last three steps onto the hallway landing, with Ilayda hurrying behind. "What's a miracle—the fact that Erik's late, or that Ilayda got here before him?"

Ilayda slapped his shoulder.

More footsteps: the clump of light boots and the click of high heels. Erik and Orlianna stepped down to join them.

Erik crossed his arms. "I'm not late. The princess of Ikarra herself has just arrived, so I think that makes me right on time."

Orlando grabbed his jaw to stop himself from gawking.

Orlianna was absolutely gleaming in a strapless yellow gown with a beaded bodice and chiffon train. Her flaming hair was gathered up in the back of her head, but loose strands still framed her face. She nodded at Arliss. "Are we ready?"

Arliss took a shaky breath. "I think so."

Orlianna smiled and glanced around the room. Her smile melted when she saw Orlando. She tromped up to him. "Take it off."

"What?"

"That hideous cloak."

He tucked his thumbs beneath the collar. "It's something of an old friend."

"Well, that friendship needs to end. It's dirty, and your eyes look nicer without it."

He sucked in his lips. What right did she have to tell him what to wear? All the same, if she didn't approve, would anyone else? He put on a jaunty smile. "You look stunning. I assume they let you pick your own clothes out?"

She licked her lips. "Flattery never got anyone anywhere—especially not with me."

"No, I'm serious." He lowered his voice. "You're the most beautiful woman I've met."

"And you've met a lot, I take it?" She turned and started walking, jerking her head for him to follow. Everyone else paced behind.

He jogged to catch up. "What do you mean by that?"

"I don't know." She peered at him. "Probably as much as you meant about 'practicing your skills' on me."

They'd almost reached the end of the hall. Endless lengths of steps stretched out into an enormous cavern of light. He spun and grabbed her arm. "I don't know what you think I want, or who you think I am, but you're wrong."

"Then take your blanket off. You can have it back before you go to bed."

He chomped down on a hundred things he wanted to spit at her. Then he unlaced the cloak and let it fall to the floor.

Her lips twisted into a smile as she descended the stairs.

Arliss squinted as the hallway ended, spitting the party out at the top landing of a staircase that stretched down into the ballroom.

She glanced up. Intricate candelabras hung at intervals all along the ceiling, not one candle missing a flame. Below, a long table had been spread at the far end of the room, boasting branching candlesticks—as well as what seemed to be the court of Ikarra.

Arliss caught her breath. If the room wasn't dazzling enough already, white marble floors spread out beneath them with swirling gold inlays. They flickered light onto the tall windows that spanned floor to ceiling, overlooking the river on either side.

This was so far from anything Reinhold had ever been—even what Reinhold could ever be. This room held more history and secrets than the entirety of her city did. But it wasn't Anmór, either. There was too much light—and space—and welcome.

Orlianna nudged Arliss's shoulder and whispered, "Harrison is going to introduce us."

Arliss blinked. Harrison stood just down the steps on the middle landing. She nodded, accepting Philip's hand, and descended the stairs to Harrison.

She leaned over and put her lips to Philip's ear. "Don't let me say anything stupid."

He cut his eyes at her. "That'll be hard."

She laughed silently, but her heartbeat was exploding.

Harrison winked his good eye at her and gave a little bow. Then he turned and addressed the court gathered at the banquet table. "Good evening, my friends. Tonight, we come with unexpected guests from the realm of Reinhold. I would like to introduce them to you."

He nodded back at Arliss and Philip. "I present Princess Arliss of Reinhold, escorted by Sir Philip of Reinhold."

Philip led Arliss up and bowed low. She quickly mimicked him. But was that wrong? Was a curtsey more proper?

And what next? She glanced to Harrison for instruction. But Philip was already leading her down the stairs.

Behind them, Harrison marched along with the introductions. "I present Lady Ilayda of Reinhold, escorted by Sir Erik of Reinhold."

Arliss fixed her eyes on Maeve. The woman stood from the far head of the table and inspected every visitor that drifted down her endless staircase.

"And last, I present to you Sir Orlando…" Harrison hesitated.

"Of Reinhold." Orlando's whisper was so quiet Arliss could barely hear it.

"…of Reinhold," Harrison boomed.

The Ikarrans around the table clapped. Arliss tilted her head. That was a new method of welcoming someone. She and Philip reached the end of the stairs. Ilayda, Erik, and Orlando stepped down as well, edging off to the side.

With Harrison escorting her, Orlianna slipped down the final stairs and came between the Reinholdians and the banquet table. She tucked a wisp of red hair behind her ear. "I thank you for your welcome. And I apologize for any confusion I may have caused today."

Maeve coughed quietly.

Orlianna tossed her head back. "These are my guests, distinguished royalty from Reinhold. They come on business that will be of interest to all of you."

Maeve's chin jutted out. "And what is that business?"

Orlianna glanced over her shoulder at Arliss.

Arliss widened her eyes. Did they now expect her to extemporize a speech? She hated speaking in front of people, especially when she had no forewarning. And especially when people she knew—people who were counting on her—were watching.

Orlianna motioned for Arliss to step up and speak.

Arliss took two steps and swallowed the knot in her throat. "Thank you…very much. Your castle…it's lovely."

Someone at the table cleared their throat.

"I think we will all be great friends." Arliss choked on her words the moment they came out. What was she saying? Such common diction—she didn't even sound half as educated as Orlianna.

Maeve sighed. "What is your purpose in coming? Orlianna says your business will be of interest to us."

"Yes. It certainly will." Arliss composed herself, her next words starting to line up in her mind. "I come to ensure peace and friendship. I come to renew old alliances. I come to preserve the unity of the clans."

Maeve smiled. "The unity of the clans?"

Orlianna joined in. "Yes, grandmother. Princess Arliss desires the same thing as you—as we all do. Please, accept them. Renew our old alliance."

"Come, sit." Maeve beckoned. "Alliances are dangerous things in this dangerous time. Even unity can be a harsh idea to some."

Arliss came forward to the empty right-hand side of the table. The others quickly followed suit. Philip sat at her left, Orlianna on her right.

She sat. The tart smells of fish and citrus mingled strangely with sharp wine and floral perfumes. The lords and ladies around the table all stared at her unflinchingly.

She shook her head and focused on Maeve. "My parents send their blessing. Until recently, Reinhold has been isolated from the other clans. We want to end that isolation and replace it with friendship."

Maeve's face tightened, as though with a dozen things to say, a hundred secrets, a thousand revelations.

Then she lifted her glass of wine. "I propose a toast, then. To unity."

Philip sat stiffly against the chair's twisting silver back. Part of the intricate metalwork bulged out and poked him in the shoulder.

He shifted forward slightly, just enough. There, that did it.

He reached for a snatch of bread and examined the contents of the plate before him. Broiled fish, shrimp served with citrus, and little cylinders of some white, fleshy meat. It looked to be a toothsome feast. Hopefully it might turn these Ikarran hearts even more in their favor.

More than twenty people surrounded the long table. At the right head sat Maeve—watchful, silent, eating nothing. At the left head, an old man, slouching down in his seat.

Philip leaned over to Arliss and whispered so that she and Orlianna could hear. "Who is the old man at the end?"

Orlianna stared. "That is my father, King Lachlan."

Philip sat back. "The king? But…"

"I know, he seems even older than Maeve. But he is her son. His health has always been ill. Ever since my mother's death and then my brother's, he has been sickly."

Philip looked down. "I know what that's like."

Orlianna nodded, but didn't ask him to elaborate. He didn't need to. Her green eyes already held every pound of loss and grief—like weights that hung in the back of the mind.

Arliss lifted her water glass. "Does he still rule the people?"

"In name only. Maeve and I do thrice what he does." She reached for her necklace. "That is why I fear war. Because if it comes, I don't think he would last long."

Philip forked one of the white cylinders. "How do we keep the peace?"

"That's what Harrison and I have been contemplating." Orlianna stared into her glass. "We have an…invention that might aid us. The clan that owns this thing could be the most powerful in the realms."

"One of the gifts?" Arliss asked.

"No. But it is perhaps as pivotal as the gifts."

Philip popped the bite in his mouth. It was surprisingly tasty for such bland color and texture. "So what is this invention?"

Orlianna looked askance at Maeve. "I'll share later. Tomorrow, in fact."

Philip grinned, an involuntary rush of adrenaline spiking his pulse. "Brilliant."

Orlianna leaned over her untouched plate and stared at her father. So he really did look that old—it wasn't just her fancy. She sighed. Perhaps she ought to be happy that her father was still alive. Yet somehow, in her mind, he had died long ago. It had been many years since he had been truly *alive*.

Harrison leaned to her ear. "Do you think your grandmother overheard you?"

"What, about the birds? No, I don't."

"Do you think she already knows?"

She swallowed and glanced at where Domnall sat to Maeve's right. "If she does, it's because the wonderful lord of the first cantar has been spying on us."

"You know you can't keep them a secret forever."

Her chest constricted. "I know. And once I show the Reinholdians, it won't stay quiet long. She will know soon enough." If she didn't already know. Maeve knew so many things—too many things. Her eyes and ears hid everywhere, surrounding everything, discovering all. Secrets were hard to keep in Cahair.

Harrison sat upright and called down the table to Maeve. "My lady, what do you say to some dancing right about now?"

Maeve wet her lips with a sip of wine. "I do not see anything particularly wrong with it, nor do I see any reason for it. But the final course has not yet been served."

Harrison waved his hand. "A trifle. The final course is nothing but wine and cakes. It can be enjoyed between dances."

Maeve clinked her glass onto the table. "As you wish."

Orlianna wiped her mouth to hide her smile. She hadn't had a chance to dance in at least six months.

Harrison stood and raised his hands. "A dance! Come on, everyone, up and to the dancing!"

Domnall glared beneath a thin bandage on his forehead. "Some of us do not feel up to dancing. Carriage wrecks are not ever the nicest thing to experience."

Orlianna pushed herself up. "Some of us recover just fine."

"Isn't that fine for you?" Domnall sneered.

"Oh, but isn't it just?"

Garrick stood, his eyes twinkling. "Orli, are you sure it isn't *not ever never sometimes—*"

She held up her hand. "Not now."

Domnall drained his glass sulkily.

Harrison strode into the middle of the ballroom. "What dance, princess?"

She followed him. The sun was sinking through the windows to her left, so the vast sparks of candlelight gleamed even brighter. "Fisherman's Waltz?"

"Fisherman's Waltz it is!" Harrison shouted up the stairs. "Musicians!"

The musicians had been waiting in the upstairs hall. Now they hurried down to the middle landing, dragging two fiddles, a fiddlard, and a lute.

"Will you dance?" Harrison asked.

Orlianna shook her head. "Not right away. I prefer to watch the first."

She turned. Arliss and the others were still seated. She waved them toward her, nodding.

Arliss stood slowly, glancing around. She still seemed worried about making a good impression.

Orlianna smiled encouragingly. They had made as good an impression as they could. Maeve was appeased, on their side. She knew nothing of Orlando's nationality. She knew nothing of the birds. What more could they do?

The musicians warmed up with discordant coils of notes as Arliss turned to Philip. "Are you going to ask me to dance?"

He shrugged. "I thought about it."

She smoothed out her skirt. "Let me know when you decide."

"I will. Will you say yes when I do?"

"Probably."

He lifted her hand and led her to the center of the floor. Other couples crowded around them, forming a long line of couples. Ilayda and Erik lined up right beside them.

Philip kissed her hand and gave a slight bow.

Oh, how she adored him. And how she missed this sort of thing—simple dancing, just the two of them, no ulterior motives, no external pressures.

Yet it wasn't that simple, really. They weren't alone. And despite Maeve's welcome—and Orlianna's promises—the pressure was still there.

If nothing else, Ríon's warnings still hung in her mind unanswered. What were he and Clare up to now? Still sucking up to Merna? She hoped not. Perhaps they'd meet. Not that she wanted to visit Anmór again, but maybe he would come here. No, that wouldn't happen. If he had murdered Orlianna's brother, he himself would be killed the moment he stepped over the mountains.

Then there was her mother's command: find out the truth about everything that had happened with Thane and Merna and Anmór. Weave together the story. Make sense of it.

And, deeper still, her father's expectations. He expected her to come back from Ikarra ready to grab the crown and have the coronation right then and there. But she wasn't—and she wouldn't be.

Philip gripped her hand. "Ready?"

"I don't know this dance. Is someone calling it?" She glanced at Orlianna. The princess wasn't dancing this one.

He nodded up at the stairs. "It seems so."

Maeve ascended the steps, the charms on her silver belt jingling as she walked. She reached the landing and turned, clasping her hands together. A nod to the musicians, a bow to the dancers, and she began calling the steps. The glassy walls echoed with wandering notes.

"Cross by right hands, all the way around."

They circled around. Philip's hand was warm against hers.

"Cross by left hands, all the way around."

They did. The thrill, the spark, started to work its way up Arliss's legs.

"Cast down and back up to place."

Arliss pressed away from Philip, rounded Ilayda to her left and let Philip lead her back up to the head of the line. She looked up to Maeve.

Maeve's eyes widened as if she had come to her favorite part of the dance. "Now—sashay right, sashay left, two-hand turn. Sashay right, sashay left, two-hand turn back to place."

Arliss smiled. Beautiful, but simple. Most of the best dances were. They cast down around Erik and Ilayda, and the dance began again. She caught a glimpse of Orlianna again—standing by Harrison with her arms folded and her brows low.

Maeve cleared her throat. "Now—sashay right, sashay left, two-hand turn. Sashay, sashay, two-hand turn."

Did Maeve intend to call the entire dance? They knew it after one round.

But Maeve didn't stop. She called it—a third time, then a fourth.

Arliss focused on Philip. "I forgot how good a dancer you were."

"We don't do it often enough. When you're queen, hold more balls than your parents do."

"That I can promise you."

Orlianna suddenly appeared beside her. "Do you mind if I slip in? Harrison wants a moment with you."

Arliss released Philip's hand. What could be important enough to break her away from the dance?

Orlianna joined with Philip as Maeve began another round of "sashay, sashay…"

Perhaps Orlianna wanted to share something with Philip without being suspected. Perhaps she just wanted to give her and Harrison a chance to catch up. Who really knew what went on in the Ikarran princess's head?

With a long look at Orlianna, Arliss turned away.

Philip flattened his palm against Orlianna's. They pushed away from each other and cast down around the next couple. There was a strength—a restrained power—in Orlianna's hands. This woman was no ordinary princess. She was a warrioress.

They faced each other and turned around by right hands. As they passed, Orlianna whispered to Philip.

"You have lovely footwork."

He snorted. "Must come from so much swordplay."

"Feet are half the battle, aren't they?" She looked thoughtful. "Unless you aren't touching the ground."

They cast down again. Philip rounded the next man, waiting for elaboration. Not touching the ground? What on earth could that mean?

They met again and he led her back up the center.

He started to turn by right hands, but she stopped him and leaned close. "For centuries man has tried to rise above the restraints of gravity, to leave the imprisonment of earth. He has never succeeded. Most gave up, thinking only God could create wings that did not melt in the sun."

Philip's brain spun. Wings? *Gravity?* "What are you talking about?"

"What I show you tomorrow is crucial. And it must remain a secret from everyone."

"You mean, from Maeve."

"Especially Maeve."

He forced her to turn by lefts. "Why don't you trust her?"

Orlianna glanced over where Arliss and Harrison stood by the staircase. "I hardly trust anyone."

"Wings? I don't understand." Arliss stared at the line of dancers. The glowing room around her seemed to warp around her, swallowing up the details in a wash of light.

"You will understand tomorrow, dear one," Harrison said. "God willing, at least."

She shook her head. "If this new invention is so important, then why must it be kept secret from Maeve? She's essentially the queen."

"Don't let Orlianna hear you saying any of that tripe. She'll quarter you on the spot." The lines on his forehead cut deep. "But you are perceptive indeed. And though Maeve is not queen in name, she acts like she governs the whole ruddy clan—and sometimes the other clans, too."

"So she's a meddler?"

"She likes to be in control."

Arliss glanced up at the maze of chandeliers hanging from the ceiling. One particular candle sputtered, its wick dying out. She fixed her eyes on it. "Harrison, I need you to tell me something."

"Anything."

"What does Maeve know about me and my story? If you could find out the truth, couldn't she?"

"Of course she could."

The candle high above her seemed to go out entirely. "I'm just afraid. Maeve is Merna's sister, and you know how much Merna did to aid Thane. What…what if Maeve had a hand in the pot as well?"

Harrison inhaled. "I wouldn't worry yourself. I have never in all my years seen Merna ask her older sister for help or advice. They spurn each other and their actions. Maeve is a nuisance—and sometimes a threatening one—but she is not a traitor."

The candle flicked back to life.

Arliss sighed. "I'm unsettled—in my heart. Orlianna said her grandmother is too closely allied with Anmór." She faced him. "If they come for us, do you really think she would protect us?"

"*I* would protect you, to the end." His cool blue eyes sent splashes of warmth through her heart. "But do not fret. There may be a day when we draw swords at a ball, but I pray I do not see it. This is not a time of war."

Arliss bit her lip. No, it was not yet a time of war.

Not yet.

CHAPTER FOURTEEN:
THE RUINS' REVELATION

IT WAS EASILY MIDNIGHT WHEN PHILIP escorted ARLISS BACK TO her room. He didn't have to. It meant another set of stairs to walk, since his room was a floor below hers.

But of course he did it anyway.

She slipped the key Orlianna had given her into the lock. It was an unnecessary precaution, really—locking the door. But her stay in the Anmórian palace still left her on edge.

Philip hesitated at the door, about to walk away.

She caught his eye, shrugged one shoulder, and walked into the room. He stayed in the doorway.

She yanked off the high-heeled shoes and tossed them aside. "What a night."

"Some party, though. The whole place is brilliant."

Arliss faced her bed and started to untie the ribbon that held her hair back. "Full of history. The very streets are covers to stories just waiting to be read."

She'd left the far window open earlier, and now a gust of wind made streamers of the sheer curtains. Moonlight glistened across the wood floor. She shivered.

All at once the warmth of Philip's hands pressed on her neck. His fingers found hers and slowly untied the ribbon, letting her hair cascade down her back. Their hands intertwined, her back still to him.

She could feel his breaths falling heavy against her head. "What's on your mind?"

"Have you thought about any names?"

She frowned. He really must've had a bit much wine at the party. "What *names?*"

"For our children."

She coughed. "I think you're getting a bit ahead of yourself."

"Maybe." He spun her to face him. "But have you?"

"Actually…" She looked away. Then back to his eyes swimming with color. Her voice cracked. "Nathanael. I want to name our first son Nathanael."

He nodded, leaning closer.

She shifted—just edging back towards her bed.

He released her hands. "I should go."

She nodded slowly.

The door shut behind him. Arliss shivered a moment before crossing to close the open window.

The sun had long disappeared, and half the candles flickered out, when Orlianna sat alone at the long banquet table. She fingered the stem of a full wineglass. The empty ballroom still echoed with the ghosts of the party.

She closed her eyes. She could still see the dancers in a row— Arliss and Philip gliding around together, as happy as any two people had a right to be. Why couldn't she have that? Not so much the romance—that would never do, really—but why could she not feel that same joy? She wanted it, more than anything, but the more she wanted it, the more the pit in her soul burned like fire.

Her brother was gone.

Her mother was gone.

Her father was as good as dead.

That left her with Harrison. He—only he, never any other—was her heart, her soul, her balance. Maeve could never be that. Garrick could not either, despite his attempts. Her mother had been a confidant, a strong tower. And so had William—with his quiet ways and listening ears. But they had been taken from her.

She raised the wineglass and sipped, letting the sharp, red liquid burn the back of her throat.

Boots echoed softly on the marble behind her chair. "You shouldn't drink away your sorrows."

She set the glass down. "I'm not. I just needed some refreshment."

Harrison strode around the table. "Promise me you won't become like your father. That you won't slide down and let grief overtake you."

She crossed her arms over her chest. "I would rather die."

"And promise me also that you won't become a ruddy meddler like your grandmother. She's already shown her true power to your friends. Arliss told me" —his eyebrows tightened— "she sensed that Maeve was essentially the queen, so—"

"Damn whatever Arliss told you." Orlianna slammed her fist onto the table. Did everyone still view Maeve as the queen? She leaned her head back. "I'm sorry. I only can't bear having that manipulating, overthrowing..."

Harrison twitched a warning eyebrow at her.

She exhaled sharply. "It's quite late. I should shut up before I make a fool of myself."

He nodded. "I'm off to bed. And so should you. Tomorrow seems a grand day, by the sound of your promises to your guests." He walked away, his steps echoing softly up the staircase before he disappeared beyond the dimming candlelight.

Orlianna stood, her glass in hand. She strode to the far window and stared out—across the river at her beautiful city of Cahair. It absolutely glistened in the moonlight, every street a row of stars.

She gulped the wine. This beautiful place had always been home. All her life, she'd never felt it threatened, never felt unsafe. Yet somehow, her return to Ikarra with the Reinholdians threatened to tip over her entire life. This very castle, once so settled and secure into the rocky island, now seemed a fragile decoration.

It wasn't Arliss. No, of course not. And it wasn't even Ríon—

cursed outlaw—nor his conniving mother. No, the thing that made her blood turn came from within her own realm.

She stared down into the cup of red wine. At once it seemed transformed. The bubbles and ripples swirled into a nightmarish vision. Armies gathered and fought, drawing swords. Blood spilled. The blood of all three clans, but especially the blood of her people. All she loved fell beneath the red rage. The very oceans turned themselves inside out for the immutable flow.

She gasped. The cup slipped from her hands.

The glass hit marble and shattered in a million directions. A pool of wine spattered across the floor at her feet.

No. *No.* This would not end in the fall of Ikarra. This would not end with Anmór's victory, nor with Maeve coming to power. She, Orlianna, would rise. She would be queen.

She turned away from the window.

Maeve stared back at her. Still in her blue-gray gown from the ball, standing like a stone pillar.

"Granddaughter? Are you all right?"

"I'm—I'm fine. I was just thinking."

Maeve glanced at the broken glass. "I'll send a servant to clean it up."

Silence piled up for several moments. Orlianna finally started for the stairs.

"Orlianna, wait." Maeve called after her.

She halted. "What?"

"Tonight went quite well, I think, despite the situation." Maeve cleared her throat. "You were very foolish to go to Reinhold without my blessing."

Orlianna whirled. "As if you would have helped me! You would have stopped me, and we both know it."

Maeve held up her hand. "It is past. I cannot say what I would have done. I only say you must be careful."

"I have never been one to be careful."

"I know. But I do worry for you. Especially now."

Orlianna tilted her head. "Why now?"

Maeve stared out the window. "Because the three clans are converging. And Ikarra will need a queen."

The next morning, Ilayda stood before her bedroom's stone balcony and gazed out at the river. The other side of the castle opened up on a view of the grand city of Cahair, but this side looked down the far side of the rock island. The river gushed over worn rock hundreds of feet beneath her.

Beyond the river spanned a wide field, with nothing but a ruined tower to disturb the endless grasses. An uneven wind rustled the grasses on its way to the castle.

The city wasn't where she wanted to be right now. Too many people, too many strange things. It was like an enormous party that never ended. But this—this view—it was peaceful. And after that hideously long ball last night, she thirsted for peace.

Quiet footsteps marked the floors in the open room behind her.

She glanced over her shoulder through the balcony doors with their fluttering curtains. Erik. "What are you doing in here, sir?"

He stepped out onto the balcony. "Your door was open."

"You shouldn't come into ladies' rooms uninvited. People might say nasty things."

He leaned onto the stone guardrail beside her. "People will always say nasty things. The trick is to live in such a way that everyone knows they can't be true."

She brushed a strand of hair out of her face. "I can't say that for myself."

"What's your meaning?"

"I mean I've done plenty of nasty things that everyone knows *are* true."

"Just because nasty things happened to you doesn't mean you caused them."

The wind gusted across the naked balcony. She shivered. "I guess I'm not naive enough to believe that anymore."

He stared out at the fields, his chin in his hands. "Orlianna's taking the others to see the ruins. Are you ready?"

She pursed her lips. The rest were all ready to jump along to the next adventure, never savoring the one they were in, never pausing to ask the questions that needed to be asked. She couldn't do that.

Let them go. She would sit in her room alone. Or—better yet—she'd explore the castle. The ball had sparked a hundred questions. She could find a hundred more and answer them all.

"My head's still spinning from everything. I don't feel up to visiting the ruins. Go enjoy it without me."

He pressed his palms into the stone—very close to hers. "Look, we don't have to go with them, if you don't feel well enough for it. We can go anywhere or do anything you want."

She caught her breath. So she wasn't alone in wanting to savor this moment. And all the time she'd known him, they'd been utter opposites—barely friends, but hardly even that. And now he was the one thing she most wanted. A friend.

He smiled. "Where do *you* want to go?"

She paused. Then she placed her hand on his.

Arliss sucked in the briny air as her hair wisped around her face. She shivered, hiding her hands in the sagging green sleeves of her gown. For it to be almost May, this chill was surprising. Reinhold always warmed well before summer. Then again, they weren't in Reinhold.

She looked over her shoulder. Cahair lay half a mile down the peninsula behind them.

Philip and Orlianna walked a few paces behind, chatting as if they were old friends. Arliss smiled. Philip could befriend anyone—man or woman, young or old. Yet he never strayed from his true friends—especially not from Arliss. Perhaps that was why his and Orlianna's friendship made her so happy, for, as close as their confidence might be, her own was always closer.

Orlando trudged through sandy grass ten paces behind, filching glances at Orlianna. Why did he linger behind? He'd been in such a sour mood this morning. He'd hardly even seemed excited about seeing the ruins.

The ruins. The words alone made her heart stutter.

There they were—looming ever closer at the end of the peninsula. The further they walked, the more the grass turned into sand beneath them, and the taller the five-storied sprawl of a tower grew.

Philip and Orlianna came up on either side of her.

Arliss took Philip's arm.

Orlianna regarded the tower with a sharp breath. "There it is. The ruinous tower of Ikarra, in all its glory. A century of history and mystery hide within."

Arliss squinted. "It doesn't look like a ruin to me. Everything still stands."

"Yes, but it's abandoned. If not repaired soon it may fall beyond fixing. But..." Orlianna narrowed her eyes, secrets brimming beneath her lashes. "It is not beyond use. Not yet."

Orlando caught up beside her. "Come on, out with it. What're you hiding?"

Orlianna pursed her lips. "You are presumptuous. And these things are better shown than told."

So it was *that* sort of secret—something so delicious they couldn't know until it was staring them in the face. Very well. She could wait. Even if they had to walk up to the very top floor.

She glanced up. The top of the aquamarine tower looked flat and bare, but it was too far away to tell. If one could stand at the top, surely they could see everything. But this wasn't just a watchtower. Why would it be so wide around? She could have fit three of the old tower of Reinhold in it. And as for height, it was easily twice her destroyed home.

She turned to Orlianna. "Why was it built?"

Orlianna's eyes glinted like a storyteller with a great tale. "At high tide, the ocean laps at the tower's marble foundation."

Orlando laughed. "That's the reason?"

"Quiet." Orlianna's gaze flashed. "There is a legend that the men of Ikarra built the tower long ago so they could hear the mermaids sing. They made it tall enough to be watchtower, storehouse, and home. The mermaids then wanted to reach the top of the tower and be with the men. But a great sea-monster—much like the crogall—blocked the way whenever the tide came up to the tower."

Arliss could practically feel the creature's tentacle strangling her again. She shuddered. "What happened?"

"The mermaid queen sacrificed herself to kill the monster. Her blood was the only way for them to forsake their tails and fins for a human life."

Philip looked thoughtful. "It sounds like another story I know."

"All good stories do." Orlianna reached for her pendant. "There must always be sacrifice before the end."

Arliss stared at the pendant. White petals, edged in purple, formed the rounded gem—or flask—that hung from the thin silver chain. The threaded cap was also in silver.

Orlianna lifted her eyebrows. "My pendant—you've been staring at it ever since we first met. Go ahead. Ask what it is."

Arliss gasped a false laugh. Orlianna's bluntly open manner was unexpected. She nodded to indicate she considered the question asked.

Orlianna ran her finger up the delicate chain. "It's one of the gifts of Reinhold."

Philip made a sound like he was choking.

Arliss swallowed. Somehow, she'd known the whole time that *this* was the pendant of Reinhold. An heirloom of her people. And if it was like the other secret gift she'd discovered—the vial—then it held great power.

"I didn't want to tell you at first because I thought you might take it from me," Orlianna said. "But I see now that you are not greedy like so many others in the realm. You give where you expect nothing in return."

Arliss wet her lips, but couldn't soften her dry throat. "I could command you to hand it to me."

"You aren't unequal to me in a fight."

Arliss nodded off the compliment. "I don't really want to find out. The pendant is yours."

Philip smoothed out the wrinkled leather of his snug sleeveless jerkin, then rolled up his shirt's linen sleeves. "Well, I know what *I* want to find out."

Orlianna took his hint. She picked up her skirts and ran to the tower.

Arliss steadied her breathing. If revealing the pendant was a small matter to Orlianna, what could she possibly be hiding within those marble pillars?

She ran after the others.

Orlando leapt up stone steps that seemed at least half as tall as he was. Now that they were on the tower's doorstep—the opposite side—he couldn't see Cahair anymore. He reached the top stair and turned around.

At the base of the steps, gravelly sand splayed out into a quiet ocean. Low tide. There wouldn't be any mermaids singing right now. A lone lighthouse stood lifeless on a clump of rocks farther out.

He made for the door as the others clambered up on either side. He jiggled one of the ringed handles, then let it slam back into the stone. "Locked?"

Orlianna gripped the other ring. "No one's even thought about this place for at least forty years."

How was that? As big and grand as the tower was, surely everyone hadn't ignored it. By the stars! This thing could probably be seen in some parts of Anmór. Surely so. How was it that no one had seized it for their base camp?

Philip grabbed the other handle. He and Orlianna tugged the double doors open.

Orlando tiptoed inside. Darkness. Dust. And the whole thing smelled like smoke and rusty iron.

The doors pounded shut behind him. He stood in nothingness for a moment.

Then Orlianna struck a flame. Her face gleamed red. "How about some light?"

Orlando's chest tightened. Here it came. The striking of one torch, and this big secret came to light.

He winced inwardly. Secrets coming to light—it didn't have a pleasant sound. Maybe if he had fewer secrets himself. But he couldn't erase them. No one could.

Not even Orlianna, open as she was to the visitors. She seemed to be growing more and more curious about him, which gave him no choice but to keep his distance. She knew he was Anmórian, and that he'd worked for Thane, yes. But if she knew he was Merwin's son…if she knew he had the ring of Reinhold…

The tiny flicker burst into a flame as Orlianna lit the torch. She walked into the room's center, shedding light on the room's contents.

Nothing.

It was enormous, and it was empty, except for a staircase on the far wall. The ceiling was more than twenty feet, but it held neither tapestry nor window. The blue-green marble reverberated with four pairs of footsteps.

"Some secret this is!" Orlando's voice came swirling back to him from the edges of the room.

"Further up, friends!" Orlianna called. The flare of torchlight rose in the darkness. She'd mounted the steps.

He made his way up mostly in darkness, since she'd already made it up to the second floor. Arliss and Philip panted behind him.

Slits in the wall at four even intervals made the second floor considerably brighter, but the shadows were still stronger. Still, the light revealed an unusual sight: three gilded thrones, silently glinting in the thin light. At the fringes of the floor, rows of stone seats were staggered into the wall itself. The window slits broke up what seemed to be a stadium around a stage, a stage set for three rulers.

Arliss paused as a hush murmured through the tower. "What is this place?"

"An ancient meeting-place," Orlianna said. "For monarchs of the three clans. It has been generations since it was used."

"It has been generations since the three clans were together," Arliss pointed out.

"Quite right." Orlianna strode between the three thrones and for the opposite staircase. "But come. There are better things above us."

The third floor was naked compared to the second—only brighter, and utterly clean. The four slits in the wall were wider than the ones below. They ran from floor to ceiling, overlooking the outside. Otherwise it was just a huge empty chamber.

Orlando flapped his cloak. "Are we running up stairs for nothing?"

Orlianna's teeth flashed. "You don't like exercise?"

Arliss gathered up her hair. "It's certainly invigorating."

"Just wait until we get to the fifth floor." Orlianna swept the torch high.

Orlando started for the next staircase.

He froze.

A groan rattled up through the marble beneath his feet. The grating vibration whispered through the whole structure.

It stopped. Orlianna widened her eyes, and her upraised arm froze.

Then she crept across the floor, handing the torch to Philip. She pressed herself against the wall right near one of the openings. Her gaze traveled down to what must have been the steps.

She gasped.

"What?" Arliss whispered.

Orlianna lifted a finger to her lips.

Orlando refused to breathe.

Stone cracked shut. The sound shot up the tower like an arrow. It was unmistakable. The doors had been opened, and now they had just been closed.

Orlando neared Orlianna.

She tucked her pendant into her dress. "We're under attack."

Philip reached for his sword. "Who is it?"

"A band of Anmórian outlaws, but clearly not with the colors of the crown." She smirked grimly. "Your friend Ríon."

Orlando reached for his twin knives. Ríon had been a friend to Arliss, but he'd never been that to him.

He was, however, his brother.

Arliss was choking. She stared at Orlianna. "It can't be him."

"It's him, all right. Same scraggly bunch. I even saw a woman among them—seems Ríon has some of the same untraditional ideas about warfare that I do."

"Exactly." Arliss clenched her teeth. "That's why you have to talk to him. Come to peace. Imagine what this would do for the unity of the clans."

"Do you think I can have peace with my brother's murderer? And upon that, he's a trespasser." Orlianna headed for the stairs. "Philip, Orlando—come with me. I need two strong men if this is going to work."

"If *what's* going to work?" Arliss demanded.

Orlianna stopped mid-staircase and squared her shoulders. "The grand secret I have is something with wings. I do not intend for it to fall into Ríon's hands. I intend to fly it out of here."

Philip looked back at Arliss. "I'm not leaving her."

Arliss tried to ignore the echoes from downstairs. "What will I do?"

"Stay here and keep Ríon at bay. Try to talk to him. We'll come back for you." Orlianna disappeared upstairs. Orlando followed.

Philip faltered at the bottom of the stairs. "Arliss—"

"Go." She backed up nearer the staircase and levied her bow. If Orlianna needed him, he had to help. Besides, she wouldn't need to fight Ríon.

He nodded and hurried up the stairs.

She inhaled. Ríon wouldn't be expecting to see her in Ikarra. But once he did, he'd stop whatever madness he was on, and they would talk sensibly.

Footsteps pounded from below.

She lowered her arrow. He wouldn't talk with her if she was threatening him.

The footsteps grew closer.

Her heart raced against her will. She wasn't afraid of Ríon, and she *wasn't* going to fight him. But it was all happening so suddenly—Orlianna's secrets, Ríon breaking in unlawfully. And she was alone.

The steps stopped.

Ríon leapt up into the natural light of the third floor.

Arliss swallowed hard, arms tightening. She kept her bow pointed at the floor.

Ríon's eyes were an almost unnaturally bright blue, and now they flicked over to her with conflicting emotion. Confusion. Curiosity. Anger.

"Hello, friend." She took a step across the floor that separated them.

He stood silhouetted in front of one of the openings. "If we're friends, why are you pointing a bow at me?"

"I'm not pointing it at you." She nodded at his knife. "And why are you holding a knife?"

He scowled. "What're you doing here, Arliss?"

"Preserving the unity of the clans."

He laughed. "That never existed. Surely you can see that. I thought I warned you about the Ikarrans?"

"Even the smartest can be proven wrong."

"I don't claim to be the smartest."

"Then all the more you have been proven wrong."

He stalked closer, his shoulder twitching. "Where are your friends? Philip. Ilayda. Orlando. And of course, Orlianna."

"Where are yours?"

"I know she's here. And I know she's hiding something in the locked fifth floor."

"And that's why you're here—to break in someone else's property? You really are your mother's son."

He grated his teeth, but said nothing.

Arliss took small steps back toward the stairs. "Is Clare here?"

"Stop avoiding my question." He breathed hate into his typically chipper Anmórian accent. "Tell me what's in here, and we won't have any trouble."

She tightened her fingers around the arrow nock. "I don't know what the secret is." That was true enough, for now.

"You're a liar."

"When have I ever been that? We fought together. We would have died together! Don't you remember?"

"Things were different then." He raised his fist and his knife. "You didn't stand in my way."

The tingle of a fight burned through her core and down to her fingers. She spoke the foolish words in her head before she could change her mind.

"If I'm in your way, then move me."

He roared and ran straight at her.

Her bow was instantly useless—short-range fight. She started to drop it, but he lunged at her with his knife, aiming for her string. She jerked back.

His other hand clamped around the top curve of her bow.

She clawed for the nock. If she could angle it right, she could get an arrow in his shoulder and debilitate him for the moment.

He let go of her bow and grabbed her grip arm, snatching at her draw arm with his other hand. The anger in his hideously blue eyes fizzled into confusion, even terror.

She tried to draw back the arrow, but he twisted her grip forearm, trying to break her hold. She gritted her teeth. Pain torqued through her elbow and shoulder. He twisted her arm further. The bow was nearly upside down now.

Orlando's training rushed into her memory. *Use your whole body.*

She brought her leg up and stomped down through the bottom corner of her bow. Ríon's twist snapped away as the bow smacked him across his face.

Jumping behind him, she grabbed both ends of the bow and pulled it over his head. The handgrip slammed against his throat. Gasping, he circled his hands behind himself, trying to pull her off.

She tugged at her bow-choke and kicked him in the calf.

He leaned back and struggled for a breath. She held fast, despite his height advantage.

He snapped his body forward—throwing himself to the floor.

The bow slipped over his head. Arliss flipped through the air. Her hair tangled across her eyes as her heart went weightless.

Marble crushed into her back as she slid along the floor. She smacked the stone to bring herself to a halt. Spikes of pain sheared through her ribs.

She squinted into a barrage of light.

She had slid to the very edge of the window-like slit. Nothing separated her from a fifty-foot fall onto the rocky seashore below. She clutched her bow and pressed herself onto her knees, coughing.

Ríon sauntered across the room. "You don't know what you're gettin' yourself into here. There is no unity to be found in Ikarra."

Arliss staggered up, drawing an arrow. "Lady Maeve says that is her aim. So does Orlianna. We all want to stop war from breaking out. Isn't that what you wanted, too?"

"The war has already begun." He pointed his knife at her. "You have started it."

Orlando hurried up the last set of stairs after Orlianna. She was moving quicker than ever—her mind clearly on only one thing.

Whatever was up there, they had to get it out before Ríon got his hands on it.

Unlike the other floors, this one was barred by a locked door. Orlianna pulled a key from her pocket. "Ready?"

Orlando nodded. The excitement, the bewilderment, were tearing him apart.

She clicked the key and shoved the door open.

He and Philip stepped inside.

Philip still held the torch, but he didn't need it. The windows in this room were the widest yet—two on either side. Together they erased more than half the marble walls. They shed enough light to fully illuminate the secret that lay in the floor's center.

Philip stole a step closer. "Is it—"

"Yes." Orlianna smiled proudly.

Orlando reached out to touch the wooden frame, the skeletal canvas wings. "A flying machine."

She stepped up onto the machine's central wooden platform. "This is one of the birds of Ikarra."

"*One* of?" Orlando echoed.

"The others are in other hiding spots. We've kept our best prototype here for safekeeping. Until now I have never feared for it. But now that that *beast* is here..."

Orlando choked on unspoken words. He didn't like Ríon either. But for her to call his own brother a beast? And to seem angry enough that she refused to consort with him?

Then again, she blamed her brother's death on Ríon. Hatred was a natural response to her brother's murderer. He exhaled the pressure in his lungs.

Orlianna flipped her hair behind her shoulder. "Climb on, both of you."

Philip mounted the thing like it was a horse. "We're flying it out?"

Orlando scanned the contraption. The flying machine was strapped down to a long track on the floor. Across the track spread a semicircular arch with a rope pulley system stretching across. The rope notched into place behind the aircraft's frame.

It was just like a bow—nock the plane, then shoot it, and it would fly. Incredible.

He put his hands on his hips. "How do we nock this arrow?"

Orlianna slid her feet into frontal pedals. "Pull it back until it locks. Jerk that lever back" —she pointed to the rear of the enormous bow— "then jump on and hold on like death."

"And then how does it work?"

Orlianna rolled her eyes. "That engine there has something to do with it. But I imagine it's far too complex for your mind to comprehend."

Orlando wanted to strangle her.

Philip jumped off the wooden platform. "What about Arliss?"

"She'll be fine."

He grabbed the wing. "I refuse to leave this place without her."

Orlianna shot him a glare. "Don't crush the wing. And we aren't leaving without her. We will get her."

"How?" Philip sounded so angry Orlando thought he might *really* break the wing.

"Help me," Orlianna demanded, "And we'll get her out safely."

Orlando strode to the back of the plane to meet Philip. Safe—hah. Safe from what?

Philip nodded. They started to drag the aircraft backward, drawing the bow.

Orlando poured his strength into the task. Getting Arliss out safely meant keeping her safe from Ríon. But if Orlianna was wise, she wouldn't be worried about Ríon—the outlaw who had fought *against* Thane, *against* Merna.

She would have been worried about *him*.

"I only wanted to speak to you." Arliss tried to keep her voice calm. "I didn't want to fight. Please listen to me."

Ríon opened his mouth, but a voice echoing up the stairs cut him off.

"Stop! Listen to her!" Clare rushed up onto the third floor. The highlights in her hair shone in the natural light from the slits in the wall. Her blue eyes flicked with fury.

Ríon turned to her. "What are you doing, my heart?"

Clare's jaw jutted out as she strode toward them. "Trying to speak sense into ya, before you mess everything up."

"Clare, please—"

"No." She held her hand up. "Arliss deserves to know."

Arliss lowered her bow. "To know what?"

"Ríon has officially joined Merna's forces. We're here—"

"Stop." Ríon seethed. "I forbid you."

"I can't keep this from her." Clare tossed her hair. "Merna sent us to scout this tower. To scout Ikarra. I didn't want to, but I was overruled by my beloved—not to mention *your* own cousins."

Arliss widened her eyes. "Fiach and Finín? Are they here?"

As if at her words, Eamon's sons rushed onto the landing. They both looked stronger and healthier, but even more rough and ragged than usual. She stared at them, the weight in her heart making her shoulders sag. These were her friends—and family—and now they had turned against her. They had joined with Merna.

She chewed on her lip. "Why?"

"Because we don't want war!" Ríon slammed his knife in its sheath. "Relations between Ikarra and Anmór have always been at a tipping point. Reinhold is going to be the thing that pushes us all over the edge."

"*You* all?" She gestured around her. "As if there were only two clans. Reinhold is a part of whatever happens." She looked to her cousins. "Finín, how could you do this?"

Finín's scowl looked just like Eamon's used to. "Because Merna has promised to bring peace—and to mend what Thane did."

"She's lying." Arliss backed up to the window. A whisper of a noise flashed through her imagination. She pointed her arrow at Ríon. "I thought I knew you. But I don't anymore, and not only because you've turned on me. You killed Orlianna's brother."

He grunted. "Is that what they told you?"

Her pulse stuttered. Would he deny even this? Her friend had become someone she didn't know anymore.

A rustling noise disturbed the air above. She took a risk and stuck her head out the tower and glanced up. A shadow—flapping, gliding—dove down straight toward her. She leaned back in at the last minute.

The flyer shot past her window, almost crashed into the ocean, then leveled out. It soared up to meet her.

She faced them. "I'm confused. I thought I knew you all. I certainly never thought it would come to this."

Ríon advanced. "You've chosen the wrong side of this fight, Arliss."

"Perhaps." She edged her heels up to the end of the stone. "But then again, perhaps not."

She threw herself from the window.

Air whistled around her ears, casting her hair and the slits of her dress all around. Her insides jumbled together, and her ribcage felt empty.

Canvas rustled. Something bumped her. Philip's hands hugged her close and pulled her into safety, but not out of the rushing wind.

"If you change your mind," Ríon shouted, "you know where to find me!"

Arliss forced her eyelids open despite the wind. Orlando sat just behind Orlianna, working two oar-like levers, his eyes wide. Orlianna controlled two steering sticks in front.

Then the reality of the moment hit Arliss.

They were flying.

Chapter Fifteen: Choices

"Order!" Orlianna pounded the gavel on the podium. "Come to order!"

For once, no one hearkened to her. The circular council hall continued to reverberate with the chatter of a hundred voices—merchants, courtiers, ladies, and lords, lords, lords all around. She couldn't even spot Garrick and Domnall in the mix.

She cast the gavel onto the podium. It wasn't doing her any good. Nothing could settle this upheaved council—nor her unsettled mind. Because above it all, the injustice—the *wrongness* of it all—could not be answered. The aircraft had been the secret of all secrets. For an Anmórian outlaw to conveniently show up at their exact location precisely when she was showing them to her Reinholdian guests…

It was too perfect to be coincidence.

She glanced down at the bottom rows of seats in the upward-sloping auditorium—the seats reserved for royalty and royal guests. Arliss looked deeply unsettled. Orlando looked petrified. Ilayda looked bewildered.

Maeve tilted her neck toward Orlianna, her gray eyes flaring. She tapped her fingers on her arms.

"Quiet!" Orlianna struck the podium with both hands.

A thread of silence worked through the crowd. Lords started sitting down. Ladies stopped sharing opinions on what was really going on. Merchants stopped selling gossip. The kerfuffle melted into a thick, black silence. It hung over the circular tiers of seats in the theatre until Orlianna felt like an actor about to perform a soliloquy.

She filled her lungs. Then she used every ounce of air to blast her voice through the hall. "How does this happen? Answer me!"

No one did.

"What traitor is there among you who would sell Ikarran intelligence to Anmór!"

Maeve stood. "Orlianna, I think these revelations have taken your country by surprise as much as they have Anmór. You have not made yourself very free."

Domnall stood, a few rows higher up. "She's right. You have kept these flying machines a secret from everyone. That is not a way to secure your people's trust."

A murmur of consent rippled through the crowd.

Orlianna snorted. "Don't pretend your spies didn't already know something was afoot."

"Spies?" Domnall lifted his arms. "I don't know a thing what you're talking about. Though I'm sure our young Lord Garrick does."

Garrick stood. "Orlianna only works with those she trusts. This project happened to be of utmost importance and secrecy." He cast her a jaunty grin. "I suppose I've earned her trust more than some."

"That is enough." Maeve took a step down the aisle—more of a staircase than a typical aisle. "There are greater matters at stake here than squabbles between the two cantars."

Garrick sat, cheeks flushing.

Orlianna tucked her finger beneath her necklace chain. "What do you think is at stake, Grandmother?"

Maeve reached the bottom of the navy-carpeted stairs. "The balance of the clans. The peace between them. What happened at the ruins is tantamount to the beginning of a war."

Arliss jumped up suddenly. "That's a hasty conclusion. War with whom?"

Maeve turned halfway to face Arliss, her face hard. "With Anmór. Specifically Ríon, it would seem."

"But who was behind Ríon?" Arliss pressed.

This was too forward. Orlianna flicked a warning brow in

Arliss's direction, but she was too far away. The Reinholdian princess didn't notice. She kept talking, looking around the auditorium as she spoke.

"Ríon has acted rashly, but I think he is a good man. He fought with the clan of Reinhold once in a desperate battle."

Domnall grabbed the railings which lined the front of each row. "A battle against *whom*?"

Arliss hesitated. "A greedy warlord…named Thane."

"Thane?" Maeve's fingers twitched. "And who was this man? You have not spoken of him before."

"I—I do not speak of him unless I must."

Maeve whirled to Orlianna. "How many secrets do you keep from me? From us all?"

Orlianna worked her fingers down to her pendant. Her chest squeezed tightly around her lungs, pinching her breaths. Maeve was right. She kept too many secrets, bottled them up within herself. But how else could she live? If they came out, it would be like a volcano's eruption.

She tucked the pendant in her breast and steadied herself on the podium. "I always intended to reveal the aircraft. But I was waiting for the necessary moment. At present, they are useful only as weapons of war. I didn't want to stir that up."

Maeve crossed the stage to the podium. "But you did."

Arliss sat and stared at the floor. She looked small, as if the incident had shaken her foundation. "I think Ríon has good intentions, despite what he did."

Orlianna bit her lower lip and spat it out again. Good intentions? How could trespassing—not to mention cold murder—come from anything but the darkest of hearts? "I don't care about Ríon's 'good intentions.' He's the son of Merwin and Merna, so his very blood is tainted."

Arliss looked up, the smallness in her appearance disappearing. "Shut up."

Orlianna coughed. "You are extremely presumptuous to speak to me in such a manner. In fact, you are presumptuous to speak in this council at all. I think perhaps we should hear from a wider span of sources."

"Indeed." Maeve elbowed around to the back of the podium. She hissed in Orlianna's ear. "Sit down and stop making a fool with your pride."

Orlianna gasped, but she could say nothing. Every word she spoke dug her deeper into this pit of confusion and mistrust. She may have even alienated Arliss—her newest and thus her purest friend—with hasty words.

But her *pride?* Maeve knew nothing. There was no arrogance in her heart—nothing even like it. She was broken! She had suffered the loss of a brother, a mother, and (in many ways) a father. The grief hung heavy always. Now, as she walked to her seat at the base of the stairs, it seemed it was going to drag her to the carpet.

Arliss crossed her arms across her chest and leaned back into the plush chair as Orlianna sidestepped down the row toward her. To Arliss's left, the seats were all full of the rest of the Reinholdian company. But to her right, the five seats sat empty, but for Harrison at the very end.

Orlianna hesitated, then sat right beside Arliss.

Maeve had begun a grand introduction of sorts. Arliss ignored it and focused on her own thoughts: Ríon's motivations, Orlianna's reasoning, and—above all—what Merna was really up to.

Orlianna leaned close. "I'm sorry."

"No, I shouldn't have spoken," Arliss whispered. "It was out of turn."

"But perhaps it wasn't. You know a side of this story that many here do not. The forces behind Thane could be the same ones behind these developments. Did you consider that?"

Arliss tried to breath normally. "Of course I considered it. It's what terrifies me most."

"It begs the question of who else was behind Thane, besides

Merna."

"I don't know if there was anyone else."

Orlianna shook her head. "If Merna was his only support, she would have surely attacked and seized Reinhold by now. But she hasn't."

Arliss's stomach curdled. "Not that we *know* of." Who knew what was going on in Reinhold right now.

Orlianna stopped talking and nodded at Maeve. Apparently the speech was getting interesting.

Maeve stepped away from the podium, nearer to the crowd. "The princess has spoken harsh words against the rulers of Anmór. I think she forgets that Queen Merna is my sister, and thus there is an inseverable bond between our clans. I would not cut that bond over some random skirmish."

"What would you do?" a lord at the top of the auditorium called out.

Maeve clasped her hands. "I would unify us."

Orlianna squeezed the guardrail. "You always say that! But what do you mean by it?"

"I mean what the word means. To unify is to make one. If the three clans—" she twirled her fingers around each other "—were to become one—" she interlocked them "—all our problems would be solved."

Orlianna's face grew pale. "You mean squeeze us all into one clan?"

"Yes." Maeve stepped back. "With divided districts and governors, of course, but with one ruler overseeing it all."

Arliss swallowed. Maeve clearly wanted to be that one ruler. But this wouldn't solve their problems. Even as one, the three clans would still exist. There would be civil war after civil war until this "unified" clan burned itself to the ground.

Domnall's broad chest expanded as his voice boomed through the auditorium. "How would this come about, practically?"dd

Maeve exhaled. "I have been contemplating that myself for a long time."

"So you have secrets, too." The words jumped out before Arliss could catch them.

Maeve glared over at her. "Everyone has secrets, Princess Arliss. Have you heard of a *rigdal mór*?"

It struck a chord of familiarity, as if she'd read it in a book before. She still shook her head.

Maeve looked upward. "In the Anmórian tongue, a rigdal mór is a great royal meeting. A meeting of royalty from all the clans. It used to happen every year on the last full moon of spring. Now, with the disappearance of Reinhold and the conflict between Ikarra and Anmór, the tradition has been lost. But we are only two weeks from the full moon. I have arranged with Merna for there to be a rigdal mór in her capital."

Orlianna leapt up. "So you're colluding with our enemy?"

"Anmór is not our enemy!"

"Their prince just attacked our lands."

Maeve exploded, raising a wrinkled hand. "I don't care about those dilapidated ruins! Nor do I care about your flying contraptions! All I know is that, if you want to start a war, you're doing a splendid job."

Orlianna collapsed into her seat.

Arliss reached for the guardrail and winced. Her arm still hurt from Ríon's twisting. Maybe she should say something—defend Orlianna.

Harrison stood. He hadn't spoken yet, so every eye and ear turned in his direction. "Wise as she is, I think my dear Orlianna has missed some of the point. But you Maeve, have missed the point entirely."

Maeve laughed uncomfortably. "Do explain."

He walked onto the central staircase. "There are too many wills at work here, and so few of them point in the same direction. You speak of uniting all the clans into one. But when I look around this room—around this world—I do not see that possibility. I see multiple hearts, all with different aims. They can be made to point in near the same direction. But they cannot be made the same."

Arliss nodded. Harrison was right. The clans could not be combined into one. The sheer diversity of opinion in this room alone was enough to spark a fight.

Maeve clenched her fists at her sides. "So you think I am wrong, Harrison. What if you are the only one who thinks the way you do?"

Arliss stood, wetting her lips. "What if *you* are the only one who thinks the way *you* do?"

Maeve stared at Arliss, openmouthed. Then she lifted the gavel and struck the podium. "This council is dismissed."

Orlianna and Philip stood on either side of her as the hall rustled back to life. Orlianna leaned close. "That was brave. It needed to be said. Thank you."

Arliss smiled and shrugged.

Orlianna sighed, her eyes wavering somewhere near tears. "I cannot ask you to stay in Ikarra. No matter what Maeve says, war is an imminent possibility. I do not want you to come to harm."

So it *was* that serious, especially if Orlianna had given up hope of holding off war. They'd only just arrived in Ikarra. Surely they couldn't leave so soon. But with so much danger…

Philip placed his hand on her shoulder. "We need to talk."

She glanced around. "Here?"

He shrugged, a wry grin teasing the corners of his mouth. "No. But I saw a hill down the peninsula that looked quite romantic."

The last few lords trickled out around Orlianna as she lingered in the dark hallway out of the auditorium. She glanced around the long, paneled walls. In winter, coats were hung here and overshoes were cast on the benches. Now, though, very few wore even the lightest of cloaks.

She took a step nearer the door, then turned around again. Maeve was still in the auditorium. As much as she didn't want another confrontation, they needed to talk. In front of a hundred people, their communication was too guarded. She needed bluntness.

Then again, nothing she could say would change Maeve's mind. She'd be better off following Arliss and Philip and counseling them.

She strode for the open door, passing the last cloak still hanging—silvery velvet, edged with crescent charms.

"Granddaughter?"

Orlianna froze. She closed her eyes, swallowing the resentment that stung her throat. "Yes, grandmother?"

"I am sorry for the clash back there."

"So am I." She stared through the crack of a doorway out onto the busy, sunlit street.

"I am even sorrier that we do not agree. I wish you could see my side. You have so much potential. It burns me to see you wasting it on warmongering."

Orlianna whirled, her fist striking the air. "I am not warmongering! Who is the one who encouraged Harrison's ambassadorial trips to Anmór? Me. Who led an expedition to stop Anmór's border encroachment before it grew out of hand? I did. And who made an effort to renew the friendship with Reinhold? Tell me—did you have a hand in *any* of that?"

"Well." Maeve inhaled shortly. "None of those things have worked. Anmór is still hostile. Your brother died on that mission— a mission *you* led. And now, these Reinholdian guests seem to be drawing war like a magnet."

Orlianna plucked the ties that crisscrossed her bodice. "At least I tried. What have you done?"

"More than you know." Maeve's lashes fluttered. "And to think that you are my successor—"

"I am not your successor. I am my father's, as he was yours."

Maeve shook her head. "Your father is impotent. Were we attacked, could he lead our armies? No. He could only guide from afar. But you—you are a leader, a speaker, a warrior. The people respect you, and I do not want that to change."

Orlianna wrapped her arms around her lower ribs. Maeve had never been so harsh before. Yet she had also never praised her this highly before. Perhaps she was warming to the idea of her being queen. If so, maybe she just needed a little proof.

"So you would groom me to be your successor?"

Maeve lifted her cloak from its hook. "The truth is, I will not be around forever. I would like to be immortal. I'd like to…"

"To watch and guide me forever?"

Maeve pressed her palm into the black paneling. "Yes. I would like that indeed."

"If you think I can lead the people, give me a chance." Orlianna edged to the other side of the hallway. "If I can find out what Ríon's up to—even find out the forces behind all this—I think we can prevent war. Then perhaps you could see me as queen."

Maeve slung her cloak about her shoulders and headed for the door. "I doubt even you can find out the truth in time. But I see no harm in you trying."

"So we have a bargain?"

"Indeed." Maeve stepped into the afternoon light. "Just don't bring your Reinholdian friends into this."

A swish of silver and she was gone.

Orlianna smirked. Bringing her Reinholdian friends into it was precisely what she was going to do.

The sun's last embers trickled down across the gentle hill, casting long shadows back toward the city. At the base of the hill, sand meshed with tangled grasses before stretching into the waves.

Philip sighed and stared in the opposite direction—west, toward the sunset. Toward Reinhold.

Not that he could see Reinhold, or even the sea that separated them. A hulking beast of a tower stood in his way, obviously trying to remind him of the day's earlier excitement. Turmoil. It really had been a whirlwind of intentions and revelations.

Beside him, Arliss flopped down in the grass. She stared straight up at the starlit sky, speechless.

He leaned back into his palms and looked at her. She was beautiful. He'd always known it, and it was always obvious, but somehow in this moment—lit by the sunset and stars—her beauty grew even greater. The way her hair tangled about her shoulders as she lay, the way her lips parted just slightly as she stared…

She slipped from her daydream and caught his eye. "What are you staring at?"

"I'm not sure." He lowered himself onto his side in the grass beside her. "Who are you? A princess, an adventuress, a legend, a warrioress, a friend. Maybe even a queen."

She shook her head. "I'm just Arliss."

He relaxed and lay flat. Seagrass wisped around his head and tickled his ear. He reached for her hand. "We've gotten ourselves into quite a thing. What do we do?"

Her fingers flexed tighter around his. "I don't know. Orlianna suggested we leave. With all the uncertainty—with my own friends turning on me—I can't help but feel she's right. Maybe we belong back in Reinhold."

He turned his head to her, but she still looked straight up. This didn't sound like the Arliss he knew. She never hid from a fight. She never shied from an adventure.

She muttered to herself, "Who knows if we could even get back, with those monsters."

He sat up, then pulled her up beside him.

Her eyebrows arched like longbows.

He plucked a blade of seagrass from her hair. "You promised your mother you'd find out the truth about our story and how these other clans are connected with it. And you promised your father you'd at least try to come to grips with being queen. So far you haven't done either."

She cocked her head. "And of course I can't go home without checking off every item on my parents' grand to-do list."

"Going home won't help anything. We know too much. We've

done too much. It would just be prolonging a fight that's coming to us anyway."

She exhaled. "So either we stay here and fight, or we go home and wait for the fight to come to us."

"There'll be fighting either way."

"So what's your choice?" She scooted around to face him straight-on.

Ah, so she wanted *him* to make the hard choices for her. That wasn't happening. She was the royalty here. And if they were ever going to do anything as a couple—as king and queen—it had to start now. Together.

"I will follow my princess."

She grabbed his hand. "I'm asking you because I don't know."

"My queen, then. You are my queen."

She dropped his hand and turned away, squeezing her eyes shut. "I am not that! Can't you see I will never be that? I can't even make up my mind about the smallest thing!"

"This isn't a small thing. The tiniest decision can alter the entire course of history." He reached for her cheek and turned her head to face him. The tears that glistened in her eyes surprised him. He wiped them away with his thumb. "Listen. You have a power no one else has. You know so much about Thane—enough to find out why he did what he did. You know the truth about Orlando's heritage. And you know almost as much about the gifts as Gally himself."

She stared westward for a moment. Then she stood, pulling him up with her.

He stood beside her. A wild ocean wind whispered through them.

She exhaled into the breeze. "I feel like all my life before knowing you, even the best moments, was only the beginning of a sunrise. And now I cannot bear to see that sun set."

He pulled her close. "So what is our decision?"

"We stay." Her fingers trembled against his chest. "We fight."

BO BURNETTE/166

Chapter Sixteen:
A Quest of Spies

Orlianna paced the royal balcony box, scrutinizing every person in the sanctuary below her. Ever since she'd been given free reign to investigate matters, every crowd seemed full of spies, every dark doorway was a place for slipped secrets, and every gathering was a cover for something darker.

She couldn't help it. If Ríon had struck somewhere further away—even the catacombs again—it wouldn't have worried her so. But he had infiltrated the greatest landmark of Cahair itself.

Maeve cleared her throat behind Orlianna. "Sit down, granddaughter. We are in church."

"They are only singing."

The layers of harmonies resounded off wooden walls and vibrated the staves that supported the balcony and—further up—the rounded roof. A long aisle bisected the sanctuary below with a carpet the color of wet grass. The carpet led all the way up and across the altar, but at the head of the rows it split off on either side. From here, the shape of a cross was all too clear.

Maeve sat like a stave herself. "*Only* singing. Indeed. And everyone in this church is probably *only* staring at you making a fool of yourself."

Orlianna scanned the audience. Arliss and company took up the entire first left-hand row, but even they were preoccupied with the apparent grandness of the building.

For her part, she didn't understand the Reinholdians' wide-eyed curiosity. Stave churches were as typical as mountains in Ikarra, and just as varied in size and location. Yes, this one was decent-sized, but the church at North Havens was almost double its breadth.

And this was not the only thing. The past two days, Arliss had positively *drooled* over everything in the city. The cisterns for drinking and plumbing. The funicular cars for travel up and down the castle hill. The flat city transport boats. The rock caves where food was kept cool. Reinhold was a wilder land than it seemed if all these things were novelties.

The music dissipated. A hush smothered the building.

Orlianna glanced around. The priest stood by the altar, blessing a goblet of wine and a wafer of bread. An acolyte had risen to carry around the elements. She gathered her skirts beneath her and sat quickly.

Maeve sat to her left, Harrison to her right. She scooted as far right as she could.

Harrison eyed her. "Maeve tells me you've taken up a grand quest."

"Is that what she said?"

"More or less."

"She always means more and says less, or else means less and says more," Orlianna whispered.

"So where are you starting?"

Orlianna pressed her back into the wooden seat. "I don't know. But I have some clues."

"You're going after Ríon?"

"I'm going to try."

"How?"

She stared ahead over the balcony. "Orlando knows something. He seems to be especially connected with Ríon. I don't understand it, but I think I can use him to my advantage."

"Is that all he is to you? Something to be used and then cast aside."

She glanced away. What was Harrison getting at? That she didn't care enough about her new friends? Or worse—that she'd singled out Orlando for special attention. She glared at him.

He squinted at her, shook his head in amusement, then looked away.

Orlando was clever, and reasonably kind. But he was also secretive, mysterious, and locked like a chest with no key. She couldn't waste her emotions on a heart like that.

Orlando elbowed through the crowd that flooded from the stave church. The midday sun made the roads sparkle beneath the emerging throng of people. The service had ended, and now a pealing bell announced the oncoming deluge to the entirety of the first cantar.

A stumpy man bumped him. "Watch it."

"Sorry." He sidestepped. "Pardon me."

The man peered from beneath wispy eyebrows. "One of those foreigners, eh?"

Orlando backed toward the street's edge. "Yes."

"Hmph." The man turned, and the crowd swallowed him.

Orlando stared. It was strange, how so much mistrust could dwell in so beautiful a city. It was as if a messenger had come before him, telling them everything he'd ever done.

No. If they knew, they'd do worse than shun him. They would fight him. They would kill him.

Someone bumped him from behind.

"Excuse me," he muttered.

"You're excused. Now let's get on with it."

Orlianna. He spun. "What are you doing?"

"Walking out of a church. Why—do I look as if I'm spying or somesuch?"

"Yes. And I should know. I'm a spy."

"Ah! So now a whiff of truth slips out of those guarded lips."

He sucked air through clenched teeth. "I'm not hiding anything."

"That's what they all say." She started walking down sidewalk that spanned either side of the road, and she motioned for him to follow. "I must ask, since you admit to being a spy, whom are you a spy for?"

"*Was* a spy for."

"Naturally. Back when you were an Anmórian."

"I've never really been an Anmórian."

"That's believable enough, considering your accent is practically Ikarran. Quite what we call 'posh.' But you are Anmórian, accent or not. And I want to know who you were working for."

He glanced around. The further they got from the church, the more the crowds thinned out. The upper stories of the buildings overhung the sidewalk, creating a cool shade for the walkway. Vines draped out of window-boxes, dangling just above their heads.

"Why do you need to know?"

"Because I need a spy. And I need one I can trust."

He cut her a look. "You know the very concept of spies implies treachery and double-dealing?"

She smirked. "No, I know nothing of warfare and espionage. Please inform me."

If she wanted to play this game, so be it. He was quite good at it. "You see, spies have secrets. Dark secrets. So what they tell you isn't always the truth. Their informants may be your assassinators."

"The same can be said of princesses. So if you get killed on my watch, I can't say I'll be sorry." She picked up her speed and clapped once. "Excellent. We have a deal."

He jogged after her. She was going way too fast on several levels. "Wha—what? I—"

She kept talking. "Garrick has a whole network of spies that patrol the riverway, running from here at the head of the first cantar, all the way at the end of the second cantar."

"Where's that?"

She pointed. "Garrick's home, at the very end of this street."

Orlando squinted. He could barely make out a tall, thin blue mansion. Between them lay hundreds of yards of road. To the right, sandy fields narrowed out to the ruins. And to the left, the river circled its course by the city and around the castle.

He exhaled. "So what's my mission?"

She dropped her voice. "I received word that an Anmórian ambassador is here in the city. However, he's not here on public business. He's under deep cover."

"That can't be good."

"No. And I think it's connected with Ríon."

Orlando's heart stuttered. That name still made his chest sore, made his brain cloud. The brother he'd always had and never would have. He stiffened his arms beneath his cloak. "So you want me to find this ambassador and stop him alone."

"Yes. And no." Orlianna slowed. "You'll have company."

Arliss strode up on the other side. "You told him?"

Orlianna nodded. "He knows."

Orlando lifted his hands. "Wait, wait. I know nothing."

"That's all you need to know." Orlianna stopped and pressed her hands into Orlando and Arliss's backs. "Stay alongside the river. Find the spy. Stop him. And wait for me."

Orlando flexed the fingers of his ring hand, covered as always by a fingerless glove. "But—"

Orlianna touched her lips to his ear. A tingle rippled through his skin. "You can do this. And after all, if you change your mind, you know where to find me." She gave them a shove. "Go."

He followed Arliss across the street toward the riverway, his face hot, his pulse thrumming. And it wasn't because Orlianna had practically smooched his ear when she whispered into it. Of course not.

It was because she'd quoted his brother's words verbatim.

Arliss took the lead as they crossed the road, heading for the side of the street next to the river. Orlando held back, so she set the pace—a moderate stride, just slow enough that they wouldn't be suspect.

She'd been dying to see the riverway. Apparently it was the jewel of Cahair—a stretch of taverns and shops so close to the river they practically swam its shores. One could have a cup of tea whilst dangling their foot an inch from the water. But—she had to admit to herself—she hadn't been dying to see it like *this*.

She was not a spy.

That was what she'd told Orlianna. But Orlianna wouldn't accept no for an answer. "Anyone can do anything if they put their heart to it," she'd said.

They reached the other side of the street, jumping onto the sidewalk out of the way of a clattering carriage. Arliss swayed.

Orlando reached out to steady her. "Now what?"

She looked up. Four floors of overhanging apartments stretched up in front of her face in two identical buildings on either side. A narrow alley cut between the two structures. But this side of the road was dead except for a stray dog that nosed through a flowerbed.

Arliss slipped into the alley. "Let's go."

Orlando grabbed her arm. "Arliss, I—"

"Are you afraid? We aren't alone."

"No, I'm not. And yes, we are."

She kept hurrying down the constricting passage. "Orlianna's brought all of us into this, I think, but she told us all separately so the secret wouldn't slip out. Our friends are on this street somewhere."

He glanced around the dark alley as if he thought their friends were hiding in the mossy bricks. "Why us?"

She bit her lip. It was a fair question, why Orlianna used her Reinholdian friends to do something so secretive and dangerous. "We know more about the situation than anyone else. And we aren't biased toward the Ikarran or the Anmórian point of view."

"Aren't we?" Orlando's tone bit with some of his old sarcasm.

She edged along the damp brick, stroking her palms against it.

Either he meant she was biased to the Ikarrans, or that *he* was biased to Anmór. She brushed a crusty lichen and shivered. Orlando seemed a changed person, but a volatile streak still emerged every now and then. Supposing he turned them over to Anmór—to Ríon?

No. She would not believe these lies.

The alley spat them out six feet from the rush of the river. This side of the apartments was every bit as alive as the other side was dead. Citizens streamed up and down the riverway—drinking every manner of beverage—reclining in outdoor seating areas—peering from pleasure boats. Even in such a grand place, then, the Sabbath was a day of rest and fellowship.

She swallowed a guilty prick in her throat. They couldn't rest. They had work to do.

She stepped out and blended into the flow of passersby, Orlando sliding behind her.

He held down the edges of his cape. "Where are we going first?"

She nodded at the first building after the apartments. "Mícheál's Tavern. There are two taverns in the second cantar, one on either end of the street." Her voice dropped. "They also happen to be on either side of the theatre on the other side of the road, and they compete for business."

"Fascinating. But trivial."

"No. Not trivial." Hadn't Orlianna told him all about the spy chain? Or was he just playing dumb?

She patted her side where her quiver should have hung. She hadn't worn it to church—obviously—but now she wanted it. She looked at him. "Do you have your knives?"

He patted his chest. "Always."

She smirked. "Except for when I steal them."

"Naturally." He reddened. "So how do we find this Anmórian spy?"

So he really *was* ignorant. She huffed. "Didn't Orlianna tell you about the spy chain?"

"Not really."

"Garrick has spies placed in a zigzag all along the riverway. One of them is the owner of a tearoom in between the two taverns. But Mícheál himself may have information for us."

They reached the tavern's back door—or front, considering how you looked at it. More guests entered from the riverside, and the outdoor dining area was noisy with revelers. This wasn't the place to hide. But it was a place to blend in. Arliss walked up to the tall mahogany door and squinted into the glass panes.

Orlando joined her. "What are you doing?"

She flashed him a grin. "*You* are buying me a drink."

Arliss tilted the tiny glass to her lips and tried another sip. It wasn't any better the second time—harsh and bitter like rotted bread. The place was absolutely crawling with patrons eating, drinking, bellowing laughter. The dusky tavern around them didn't seem to notice the two foreigners huddled in a corner booth.

She coughed. "I don't like this drink you bought me."

"You don't have to like it." Orlando took a swig of his own. "You just have to drink it and look around."

She gagged. "What is this—spy lessons?"

"If so, you're a tedious trainee."

"You're a tedious instructor."

He rolled his eyes, then nodded past her.

She turned. A friendly young man with sharp features and a slick leather apron confronted their table.

"Anything I can get for ya?" His accent wasn't refined like Orlianna's. It drifted closer to the Anmórian brogue.

She smiled. "Master Mícheál, I presume?"

He wiped his hands on his apron. "Depends on who is presuming."

"Friends of Orlianna and Garrick."

"Ah." His dark eyes twitched. "Well, I don't have anything for Orlianna and Garrick's friends here beyond a refreshing drink or two.”

“Are you *sure?*” Arliss pushed.

He arched an eyebrow in annoyance. “Uh, yes. I meant what I said.”

Arliss tried to catch Orlando’s eye. Did they have the wrong Mícheál? Orlianna had sworn the tavern owner was part of the spy chain. But he seemed to be rejecting them, misunderstanding them. Either that, or there was a hidden meaning in his words.

Orlando leaned over his shot glass. “Pardon me for taking up your time. Do you know who might have something for us?”

“I don’t know for sure, but I hear the teapot over at Rose’s is whistling. Might try there.” He walked off, whistling just like said teapot.

Arliss drained her glass, sputtered, and stood. “Let’s go.”

He tilted his glass. “After you.”

Orlando edged his way in front of Arliss as they exited Mícheál’s. Maybe Orlianna had told her more, but she didn’t know twopence about spying. Everything Mícheál had said had been a double-meaning—even the bit about the drinks being all he had to give them.

Arliss hadn’t even seen the note Mícheál had slipped beneath his glass.

Orlando unfolded the crumpled scrap of paper. *He passed an hour ago. Didn’t stop. Rose will know—order tea with honey and extra cream on the side.*

He panted. The crowd was absolutely strangling, and it ruined what would have been a lovely river view. That assassin lurked somewhere down this street, and every step brought them closer.

Arliss walked so close their shoulders brushed. “What do we do?”

He passed her the note.

She nodded, then started to slip it into her pocket.

He snatched it away from her. “Don’t do that.”

"Why?"

"We have to destroy any evidence." He ripped the paper in half and handed her one piece. Then he stuffed his half in his mouth and swallowed. The paper almost wedged in his throat.

Her eyes widened. "I'm not doing that."

"Yes you are."

She slipped it between her teeth, chewed, and swallowed. She gagged.

He sidestepped right and slipped off the main thoroughfare. "How about some tea to wash it down?"

The tearoom looked more like a tiny wooden box with rotting black boards, but the outdoor patio stretched all the way across the stone sidewalk to the river's edge—with a walkway in the middle to allow passersby. The main building seemed to be under renovations. A few stray cats roamed the premises.

Orlando pulled out a chair for Arliss.

She sat, and he also settled into a black iron seat.

"I suppose we wait for this Rose person to take our order?" Arliss scanned the area.

Orlando surveyed the tearoom's courtyard. Half the tables were full, but only one woman made the rounds serving them. Must be Rose. She set a pot of tea on an adjoining table and trotted over to theirs. Her lavender tunic swished around black breeches. Her hair—a dark brown—caught the midday light and glinted with hints of gold and auburn.

She tucked a strand behind her ear. "How can I serve you?"

Orlando stared. She was young—hardly older than himself. She seemed too young to be a spy, much less run her own tearoom.

Arliss cleared her throat and answered for him. "We'll have two cups of tea with honey, and extra cream on the side."

Her dark eyebrows dropped, curving. "Did Mícheál recommend me?"

"He did."

A small smile spread across Rose's mouth. She glanced around, then pressed her hands on their table. "I'm glad you've come. The one you're looking for passed this way not fifteen minutes ago. He ordered black tea with sugar but no cream."

"I don't think it's important what tea he ordered," Arliss pointed out.

"True." Rose shrugged. "But honestly, with everything that's gone on, it might be. You need to be careful."

Orlando tried to take a steady breath, but the anticipation of a confrontation—a fight—thumped through his veins like a drum. "Is he near?"

She stepped back. "I think so."

Arliss stood. "Orlando, come on."

Rose smacked her hands together. "What about your tea?"

Arliss turned. "We'll come back later, okay?"

Rose nodded. "I'll be counting on it."

The crowds thinned out the further down the riverway they walked. They were nearing the second tavern now. Arliss inhaled: fish, ale, citrus. The sweet scent of vanilla wafted up from the river as a lone pleasure boat drifted by.

It was peaceful—too peaceful. She glanced right, past Orlando, through the crack between two buildings. The street on the other side of the riverway was quiet. The theatre across the road stood dark and empty.

A shadow flashed on the theatre steps.

Arliss batted Orlando's hand. "Look. Across the road."

He kept moving past the crack in the buildings. "Keep walking."

"Orlando—"

"I said keep walking."

They reached another alleyway. She darted a glance through. The shadowy figure was in the middle of the street now and walking swiftly toward the riverway.

She grabbed his hand. They had to stop and make a plan, or else this whole thing would fail. The assassin would get away—or worse, he'd kill them.

Orlando thrust her hand away. "Stay calm."

She snorted softly. As if a simple command from him could still her beating heart.

Another chink in the buildings flitted past, casting a ray of light across the shadowy riverway. Arliss squinted for a sight of the assassin. Nothing.

They were behind the second tavern now. The long building stretched down nearly to the road's end—where Garrick's home stood. Arliss stifled her panting as they sidled against the back of the endless tavern. Another ray of light stabbed into the shadows fifteen paces before them.

She filled her lungs.

Ten paces.

Her middle three fingers itched for an arrow—for something.

Five paces.

Orlando's gloved left hand flexed beside her.

They reached the end of the tavern.

A shadow exploded between her and Orlando. A knee jabbed into Arliss's stomach. She buckled, and the assassin tackled her. Her cheekbone smacked the road as he wrenched her arms behind her back. She winced at the strain.

She angled her knees beneath her and stomped a foot up into his belly. His grip loosened just enough for her to wriggle under him— right as Orlando grabbed his legs and flipped him onto his back.

Orlando shot a punch toward his downed opponent, but the assassin rolled away. Orlando's fist crushed into the pavement. He gasped in pain as blood trickled from his knuckles.

Arliss scrambled to her feet.

The assassin stood and stamped down on Orlando's back where he knelt. Air whooshed from Orlando's lips.

Arliss huffed. No one harmed her friend without paying for it. She lunged, jabbing her elbow into the assassin's chest.

He leapt back, whipping out a knife.

She reached for his knife hand forearm and found it knotted

with tight muscle. He pushed his weight down her left arm, forcing the knife closer to her. She squeezed his wrist. He had to drop the knife if this fight was going to be even.

She darted her right hand up into Orlando's signature move—locking her arm around her opponent's knife arm. She snapped her locked arms back.

The assassin's fingers crumpled open. The knife clattered to the stone.

He hissed through his teeth, jerked his arm free, and thrust her away. She tottered back, tripping over Orlando. Her back thudded into the pavement.

She strained for breath that had been expelled from her lungs. The assassin loomed over her, wielding his retrieved knife. He was waiting, baiting her. There was something almost familiar about his broad-shouldered bearing, his haughty stride.

She made the realization the moment she spoke it. "You're holding back."

"So are you."

That voice! It burned with familiarity in her mind. Yet still she couldn't place it.

"I don't want to kill you. I want you to tell me where Prince Ríon is."

Orlando rolled over beside her, holding his knuckles. "Personally, I wouldn't mind killing you."

She stood. "We don't mean harm to you or to your people. I don't know what Ríon is up to—and I'd like to find out—but for my part, I want to keep peace."

The assassin pointed his knife as Orlando also stood. "I know where Ríon is. And I know what he's up to. But I'm not telling you one blasted thing."

He stepped back toward the alley. "I'm leaving. If you follow me, you die."

Someone sprung from the alley, barreling into the assassin and knocking him off his feet.

Arliss's heart jumped into her throat. Philip.

Philip swung one fist into the assassin's chest, the other into his stomach. Then he drew his sword and held it to the coughing fellow's neck. "If you touch her again, I'll drain your blood."

Arliss stepped forward. "That won't be necessary. He was just offering to take us to Ríon's hiding place."

"I offered nothing."

Arliss gasped, recognition washing over her.

Orlianna faced the assassin. "You know Ríon's exact locale."

"What makes you think that?"

Arliss stepped between them. Philip lowered his sword, and Arliss came so close she could feel the hooded fellow's hot breath.

"Because you're part of his band." She jerked his hood back from his face. "Finín, son of Eamon."

Philip started. "Fin?"

Finín nodded. "Congratulations."

Arliss froze, her face inches from his. "How could you do this! How could you turn on me—on all of us! Especially after your father's sacrifice?"

Finín's chest heaved. "You're ignorant. And you forget my father was always allied with Anmór."

"And *you* forget why that alliance ended."

Finín jerked his chin upward. "What are those two chattering about?"

Arliss turned. Orlianna and Orlando had been huddled together, whispering quietly, and now turned back to the others.

Orlianna's lips curved with realization. "Well, Finín, I have a task for you."

Finín glared. "I don't take tasks from Ikarrans."

She pulled a pointed dagger. "Take us to Ríon." Her chest shuddered. "To the catacombs."

CHAPTER SEVENTEEN: CATACOMBS

ORLANDO SPOONED HIS OAR THROUGH THE GENTLE RIVER THAT SEPARATED the sandy peninsula from the green mountains. Trees clustered in soaring peaks up and down the opposite shore. They were going to the catacombs—those black tunnels of night that snaked through the mountains, over the border to Anmór.

He squeezed the oar tighter. He didn't want to get another step closer to Anmór. That would be like going back to the bondage of Thane. But even more than that, he didn't want to revisit the catacombs.

Orlianna tugged at an oar beside him. She hadn't spoken yet beyond a few words of direction to Arliss and Philip. They rowed in the prow of the small boat with Finín bound just behind them. Orlianna stared at the mountains like enemies to be conquered— or maybe more like demons that couldn't be banished.

He swallowed. She must've been thinking of her brother. How hard it had to be to come back to the place where he'd died.

She tossed her head, shaking her hair behind her back. "You are acquainted with Ríon, just like Arliss?"

His neck prickled. "Oh…yes. I am."

"How did he know you would know about the catacombs?"

"You know I was once a spy for Anmór."

"Yes, I know that—as of about an hour ago." She sighed. "I just don't understand what connection he has to you. Until recently, Ríon has been an accursed outlaw. Merna blamed everything on him. I want to know why—and why she stopped."

"You think I know?"

"I think you know more than you're telling. If you were a royal spy, you must have been tight with Merna or Merwin."

Orlando winced at the name of the man who fathered him—then abandoned him to be the protege of a volatile warlord. "I was never close with Merwin." He choked.

"Merna, then?"

He stared straight ahead. Their prow pointed south, the sun sinking to their right. They were almost to the mountainous shores.

Orlianna waited. "Orlando, I need to be able to trust you."

"You can't trust me," he whispered.

"Why?"

"If I told you, you wouldn't ever trust me, not in a thousand lifetimes."

She lowered her oar, and the boat started to drift left, but she didn't seem to notice. "What have you done that cannot be forgiven?"

He squeezed his eyes shut. There was so much. Should he tell her? Spill the secrets of a lifetime of sin, of hatred?

No. Of course he couldn't. It would kill her. It would kill *him*.

He faced her. "Sometimes there's so much in your past that it overwhelms you."

She looked away. "I understand that."

The boat scraped up on rocks. Orlando peered up at the looming green peaks. Somewhere between the two nearest mountains lay the entrance to the catacombs.

Arliss drew her knife and cut Finín's bonds. "Lead us to Ríon."

Ilayda brushed her hair out of her face as she entered her room. She'd left the balcony doors open, and a sharp breeze now fluttered the curtains and rustled the heavy bedcover.

Something else rustled in the far corner—light and papery.

She strode over to the open cabinet. Orlianna had shown it to her on the first day—the elevator message system that ran up and down the length of this side of the castle. Surely enough, a folded scrap of paper sat in the dusty box.

She pulled it out. How long had this been here? She'd only just gotten back from church, so her friends couldn't have been back at the castle long.

She unfolded the paper and read the scrawled message: *We know where Orlando's brother is, and we are going to find him. Stay at the castle. —Arliss*

Ilayda folded the paper and sighed. So they had all run off without her? Did they think she was useless simply because she couldn't wield a weapon as well as they could?

Or was it perhaps deeper, darker. The last time they'd all adventured in a foreign realm, she'd caused all their problems by running off and following her heart. Not only had she gotten herself captured, she'd almost gotten Brallaghan and Brédan killed.

She glanced toward the open balcony doors and blinked back tears. She should have stayed in Reinhold—Brallaghan or no Brallaghan. At least there she could have been useful. She could have helped rebuild the city. Here, she was nothing but extra baggage.

Someone cleared their throat behind her.

She turned, crumpling the paper slightly. Maeve stood in the doorway, her hand on the frame. A navy dress wrapped her slender figure, and her silvery hair was gathered at the back of her head.

Flustered, Ilayda dipped in a half-bow. "Your grace."

"Lady Ilayda," Maeve nodded. She glanced at the paper. "What is that?"

Ilayda smoothed out the paper. "Nothing. Just…a note from a friend."

"What friend?"

Ilayda wrinkled her brow. If Orlando was here, he'd have said it was none of her business. And he would have been right.

Maeve lifted her chin. "May I see it?" It was a request, but her tone was commanding.

Ilayda slowly stretched out the hand with the paper. Maeve strode forward and took it, her gray eyes scanning the short lines. Her mouth tightened as she read. Then she handed it back to Ilayda.

"Orlando's *brother*? And who might that be?"

Ilayda slipped the note in her pocket. "I have a strange feeling that you already know."

Maeve's eyes widened at her bluntness. "And what makes you feel that?"

"Someone who wants to rule all three realms must obviously know a lot about them all."

"This is true." Maeve stared into Ilayda's eyes, waiting, testing.

Ilayda could hold it in no longer. "So you knew Orlando and Ríon were brothers the whole time?"

"Yes. My sister Merna despises me, but she cannot keep secrets. Orlando has long been the subject of her contempt—and her dependence, it seems."

What else did Maeve know, then? If she and Merna communicated, this former Ikarran queen might know the entire story of Thane—from Anmór's perspective, of course. But then again, Maeve had acknowledged ignorance of Thane.

Unless, of course, that was a lie. But Maeve seemed too high, too wise, to speak outright lies.

Ilayda turned to shut the doors and block out the breeze.

Maeve's voice trembled slightly. "Arliss—does she aspire to soon be queen of Reinhold?"

Ilayda clicked the doors shut. "No. Not at all."

"Do you think she could come to accept one, unified clan in place of the three?"

This was ridiculous. Of course Arliss wouldn't—ever, never, not in a lifetime. In fact, this rigdal mór thing sounded like a grand disaster. But she couldn't slap Maeve in the face with another brash answer.

Ilayda turned. "Perhaps you should ask Arliss herself sometime."

Philip felt like he was breathing water. The underground air lay dank and thick, and it smelled like ashes and time. That's what the entrance to these catacombs had looked like too—charred wood, aged carvings, and letters that once meant something but were now too blurred to read.

He nudged Finín. "How much further?"

Finín walked between Philip and Arliss, his unbound hands tensing. "Calm down. Whenever we arrive, we'll be there."

Philip restrained the urge to kick Finín's legs out from under him. "This is taking too long."

"These tunnels are long, Master Philip. They stretch all the way to Anmór."

"And you're taking us all the way to Anmór, it seems!"

"That is true. Ríon's base is in these catacombs, but in the portion owned by Anmór."

Orlianna laughed dryly. "The portion brutally and unlawfully seized by Anmór, you mean."

Orlando flashed his torch to the side. "He's right, though. This journey's been tediously long. I don't remember the tunnels ever stretching this far."

Philip glanced back at Orlando. Sometimes it was easy to forget the fellow had once been a villain, a cruel spy who cared for nothing but himself.

Finín halted, his ears twitching upward in the torchlight. The tunnel widened above their heads and on either side, fanning out into a much larger passage.

Finín stepped to the left side of the tunnel and pressed his palm against the earth. "Do you feel that?"

Philip touched the oozing wall of dirt. He felt nothing but the damp sliver of a worm. "Nope."

"I feel noises. Voices. The clink of steel. We are getting close."

Finín spun and picked up speed, first a jog, then a run. He was trying to bolt from them. If he got to the hideout before them, Ríon's band would be at alert. Not even Clare's presence of mind could save them.

Philip dashed into the yawning blackness. Lights started to materialize around him.

Then something cracked into the back of his head. The lights wavered a moment before flicking out completely.

Arliss pumped her arms in time with her legs, willing herself to gather more speed. Philip had disappeared in the vague light before her.

Behind her, Orlianna and Orlando ran, the torch casting wild shadows all around. She caught glimpses of things as they passed—crisscrossing side tunnels, curious carvings in ancient script. But all of it flicked by too quickly.

Something materialized in the distant darkness—or not so much a something, but less of nothing. The blackness softened with a pinch of gray, then a dash of uncertain orange.

Firelight. They were close.

She could hear the voices now, echoing as if from the walls of a cathedral.

Her heart was already exploding from running, and now it doubled its pace. Ríon, Clare, Fiach—the whole band—were right up ahead. And they would either listen to what Orlianna had to say, or they would kill them.

At least they were alone here in a dark, secret place. None of the rulers of the realms were there—not Orlianna's father, nor Maeve, nor Merna, nor Merwin. Not even Elowyn and Kenton. This was the next generation trying to make peace with each other.

The tunnel ended suddenly, spitting Arliss out into a vast underground chamber. It was so wide she couldn't have seen the other side but for the light that blazed in a round central firepit.

She blinked in the sudden wash of light. People gathered

everywhere, sharpening and practicing with weapons. It was vast, cavernous…noises echoing, echoing, echoing. She grabbed her head to steady its sway.

The noises cleared as she adjusted to the bowl-like cavern.

She gasped. Fiach and Finín held Philip down, ten paces in front of her. To her left and right, warriors aimed longbows and crossbows at Orlianna and Orlando. Ríon, his forearms plated with gold armor and folded across his chest, stood beside Philip's downed form. Clare stood a ways behind him, silhouetted by the firepit.

But none of them mattered for a moment in comparison with the person who faced her, not three paces away. None of them were so horrible, so unwanted, and so shocking as this one. The reek of wine and perfume stung Arliss's nostrils already. This woman had haunted her enough in one week to last a lifetime. The sister of Maeve. The wife of Merwin. The mother of Ríon. The queen of Anmór.

Merna threw her head back and laughed, and the sound echoed off the dirt ceiling.

"I *found* you!"

CHAPTER EIGHTEEN: DARKNESS

ARLISS REACHED FOR AN ARROW AS THE BAND OF WARRIORS circled her, Orlando, and Orlianna. This wasn't how she'd planned for this to go. She had planned to walk calmly into Ríon's hideout, hold a parley, and leave with a satisfying solution.

But none of those plans factored in the snake-tongued queen of Anmór.

Merna's nostrils flared. "Oh, Arliss, it has been too long. How I missed your company!"

Arliss fingered a nock. "I can't say the same."

Ríon stepped beside his mother. "Release that arrow."

Arliss jerked her bow from around her back. "From this, I presume?"

A dozen arrows instantly pointed at her from all around the cavern.

Ríon ground his teeth. "*Drop it.*"

She held her ground. "Or what?"

He pointed his sword in her direction. "You all die."

Well, this was darker than Ríon's usual merry smile. She tilted the arrow back and forth. "Odd how quickly you abandoned your goal of peace."

"Killing you would be a great step toward peace."

"So I am the cause of every conflict I step into, then?"

Merna held up her hands. "Everyone, hush-hush. We can talk about petty matters later. I myself want to know something. Why are you here, Arliss?"

Arliss motioned at Merna with the arrow. "I could ask you the same question."

Merna chortled. "You expected me to be reclining back at my castle?"

"Yes, essentially. Sitting and waiting for this grand rigdal mór when all the clans get squashed into one by your foreboding sister."

Orlianna whispered, "*Foreboding*—nicely done."

Merna's arms stiffened. "Who sent you? Does my sister know we are here?"

Arliss inhaled the smoky air. Merna was afraid of Maeve, or at least wary. And that meant things weren't quite so close to being unified as Maeve thought.

Merna stepped forward. "Did Maeve send you? Does she know?"

"If she knows about this, she hasn't said anything to me."

Merna dropped her shoulders. "Good, very good. She always tries to manage everyone's affairs! At least this is hidden from her." She cut a glare up at Arliss. "Until now."

"Indeed." Orlianna stepped near Arliss, disregarding the bevy of arrows pointed at her. "This region belongs to Ikarra. I command you to leave—all of you."

Ríon cocked his head. "Does it? A few years ago, Anmór secured these mountains in a fierce battle—in these very catacombs, in fact."

Orlianna strode past Arliss, her shoulders tightening as if to restrain her from ripping Ríon to shreds. "Do not presume to teach me the history of *your* murdering self."

Ríon narrowed one eye but said nothing.

Merna laughed. "You presume too much about the past, Orlianna. And you have neither authority nor ability to command us to leave."

Arliss looked around. It was true. At least two dozen band members surrounded them, not counting those gathered closer—Merna, Ríon, Clare, Fiach, and Finín. Philip had been downed when she arrived, but he didn't seem seriously wounded. The rest of them were free, but what were three against thirty?

Arliss glanced up. A huge stone hung from the ceiling by thick ropes, dangling over the central firepit. It must have been a forge of some sort. But if the ropes were severed, the fire would go out. All would be darkness.

Merna edged toward Arliss and Orlianna. "You have nothing."

Orlianna reached behind her neck and undid her necklace, dangling it in Merna's face. "I have this."

The heat of torchlight shone against the back of Orlianna's hand, but the pendant felt cool beneath her palm. Quiet. Sleeping. Waiting for its power to be made known.

Merna's lips contorted, trying to form words. She finally stammered, "Th—the pendant! You have found it."

"I have always carried it."

"Thief! It does not belong to you."

Orlianna pulled the chain closer. "It doesn't belong to you, either."

"And you've done your fair share of pinching other clans' gifts," Arliss added. "I barely recovered my own treasures from under your nose."

Merna waved her hand. "The gifts are powerful things. They shouldn't be in the hands of simpletons. And this—the pendant of Reinhold—this tops all."

Orlianna refastened it about her neck and let the pendant drop familiarly against her breast. "You want it, don't you?"

Merna licked her lips. "I want all of them."

"Do you know how powerful it is?"

"No. But I know one who does."

Orlianna arched a brow. "Whom?" There were none in Ikarra who were experts in gift-lore. She, Maeve, and Harrison likely knew more than anyone else—and even that wasn't much.

Arliss drew closer, her eyes fixed on where Philip lay upon the ground. "I think I know whom. But if I am right, it shocks me that someone so good as Galcobhar could turn to your side, Merna."

Merna laughed—long, full, letting her revelry reverberate through the head of every person in the cavern.

Orlianna reached for her ears. The hideous tintinnabulation recalled the battle which occurred in this very cave six years ago. William had lain just where Philip now pushed himself up; Ríon had stood over him the way he did now.

Merna swallowed her laughter. "You know nothing. None of you. By the time you know what is upon you, you will all be dead."

Orlianna worked her fingers to her belt. Her claw knives hung there, ready to be drawn. "You intend to kill us? So much for a grand council of the clans.'"

"You will kill yourselves!" Merna raged.

"I came to speak with Ríon!" Orlianna shouted. "I came for peace."

Ríon glanced between them and Philip's rising form. "Really? This looks an awful lot like a fight."

Clare grabbed his shoulder. "Listen to her."

He shook free. "I won't listen to any of these fools."

Arliss gasped. "What about your *friends*?" Her voice rose to a scream. "What about your brother?"

Ríon drew his sword. "That murderer? I'll never call him brother."

Orlianna flicked out her claw knives—three short blades that poked between her fingers, attached by a common hilt. "You're the murderer, prince of Anmór."

Ríon flashed white teeth. "What about those you have killed, Orlianna? Don't think Ikarra is the only one with losses from the border wars."

Orlianna restrained the anger that burned her neck. William's death alone outweighed any grief this villain might feel. She wanted him dead—gone.

Arliss nocked an arrow as the circle of people tightened. "Border disputes are nothing to what Merna has done. She tried to use Thane as a pawn to destroy Reinhold. Ríon, you're nothing but a traitor—a second Thane!"

Merna flipped the edges of her satin skirt. "You can stop talking about me as if I'm not right in front of you. And speaking of traitors, you harbor one in your midst."

Orlando readied his twin knives, his face tight. He was obviously still afraid of Merna. So he must have been her personal spy—just as she had suspected. How awful, how horrible, to come back to this woman who had tainted his former life.

Orlianna stepped in front of him. "He's changed. He is no longer a spy for you."

Merna motioned for Ríon's troops to advance. "He is mine."

"Then try to harm him." She pointed her claws at Ríon. "Try! I dare you to fight us."

"Wait!" Arliss's voice rang out.

Orlianna whirled. Arliss had slipped out of the ring of debaters and now stood a few paces off, her arrow aimed into the cavern, not at any person, but at the ropes which suspended the stone forge from the ceiling.

Orlianna smiled. The Reinholdian princess was rash, but also brilliant.

Arliss drew her shot all the way. "You can fight us, but there is one condition. We'll be in the dark."

She released the arrow. The rope split. Stone plummeted and cracked into the firepit, pounding the flames to ashes.

Darkness swallowed Orlianna until all she could see was the faint silver glow of her pendant.

Arliss blinked back the rush of darkness, the spray of ashes from the firepit, and rushed straight into the midst of the fray.

Philip had leapt up against Fiach, and their swords flew like lightning. Ríon and Orlianna rushed at each other, Orlianna drawing her three-bladed claw knife as she ran. Orlando faced off against Clare, but neither made a move. Finín was nowhere in the darkness, but the rest of the band rushed—shouting—from the other side of the cavern.

And Merna stepped off to the side beside a lone torch in the wall, watching it all, her silken arms folded tight.

Arliss drew an arrow. This couldn't end well if they waited. They had to leave. Orlando was closest to her, so she headed for him. Merna she kept at the edge of her vision.

Orlando turned to her, his cloak rendering him one shadow in the darkness. "We need to leave this place."

Arliss nodded, then remembered he couldn't see her. She blinked as her eyes adjusted to the dimness. "You have to break the fights up."

Clare rushed between them. "How? They're consumed by madness."

Arliss grabbed Clare's shoulder. "Call him out of it! Make Ríon see that he needs to speak with us."

"He isn't the only mad one." Clare shrugged Arliss's hand off. "And nothing you could say would change his mind now."

"Why?" Arliss clenched her bow. "What has Merna told him?"

Clare's worried blue eyes flickered. "Many things."

Arliss held her gaze. The sizzling blades around them did nothing to drown out the realization she found in Clare's eyes: Ríon had been lied to. He had been manipulated, bribed. And he had learned something that had changed his mind about everything.

She exhaled. Only one thing could have changed his mind about everything that had come before. That would be knowing who was really the true mastermind behind Thane, before he gained Merna's troops, before he built his fortress in Reinhold.

Someone who knew everything about the clans.

Everything about the gifts.

A person wiser than all.

Galcobhar.

Gally.

Arliss tightened her draw hand and addressed Clare. "Is it your grandfather?"

Clare caught her breath. Her mouth opened, but nothing came out.

"*Cease!*" Merna screeched. "No more!"

Philip and Fiach lowered their swords. Ríon shoved Orlianna off him. Everyone looked at Merna.

She had mounted the crushed firepit and lifted her hands. "These Reinholdians—and Ikarrans—have come to us for a parley, not a fight. And now I will give you a chance, Arliss, to ask your question."

Arliss shook her head. Orlianna was the one who should do the talking. But no one else spoke. She inhaled and took the lead. "I need to know more about my story. My parents want me to be the queen of Reinhold. But I can't settle down until I have answers about my world, about everything that has happened."

Merna's fingers twitched against her crossed arms.

Arliss still held her drawn bow. "If you weren't the only one behind Thane, who was?"

"I know the whole story about Thane. I always have."

"Of course you do. You've been involved since the very beginning."

She chortled. "Is that what you think? It isn't true."

Orlianna intruded. "Since when did you care about truth?"

"Never. Truth doesn't exist beyond one's own mind. But hard facts *do* exist—such as the fact that I was never Thane's greatest benefactor."

"Tell me." Arliss raised her bow in warning. It couldn't be Gally. She couldn't believe it. His kindness and wisdom contradicted it.

Merna spread her hands wide. "I tell you only one thing—you will leave this place before you cause anymore ruckus. Rigdál mór is coming. We cannot have a war already begun."

Philip spoke up. "You started this war long ago when you helped Thane."

"I did not start this war!" Merna leapt from the firepit-podium. "And now you will leave!"

Ríon swung his sword and shouted a command in the Anmórian tongue. A dozen fighters lined up, facing Orlianna's posse.

Arliss's hand went numb around her bow.

Orlando flashed his other knife out of his sheath and leaned close to Arliss. "Plan?"

"Get out of here." She drew her arrow. "Now."

Ríon's line of troops rushed closer. Orlando swallowed. The hate that burned in his brother's eyes looked like death. Was he fighting to kill?

They couldn't stay to find out. Arliss stepped backward, jerking her elbow at Philip and Orlianna. "Come on!"

"But Arliss—" Philip's sword froze in a standard guard.

"She's right." Orlando followed Arliss, starting to run. "We have to leave. Ríon won't be reasoned with."

Orlianna rushed alongside them. "And his mother won't hear a ruddy thing either. It's no use."

The cavern narrowed down to a passageway that disappeared into a snaking darkness. Without a torch to guide them, they would be running blind.

Whoops erupted behind them as the line of fighters neared.

They had no other choice but to let the dark devour them.

Orlando ran straight, always making sure he could hear Orlianna's quiet panting right beside him. He sheathed one knife and fished through a jerkin pocket. Crusty petals brushed his bare fingers. If only they had some flame...

"Arliss?"

"Yes?" Her voice was thin.

"You remember the Lasairbláth you gave me long ago, on the Isle of Light? I still have some."

"Good thing it doesn't go bad," Arliss muttered.

Orlianna cleared her throat. "Lasairbláth gains power with age. At least, so it is rumored."

Wet earth squished beneath Orlando's boots. They didn't need darkness, wetness. They needed light—fire.

Something flickered in the furthest edge of his vision. He swiveled his head. One of Ríon's band bore a torch. And they were moving steadily nearer.

Philip pivoted and planted his feet. "They're on us! Out weapons!"

Arliss's golden hair flicked into view as the torchlight neared. "We can't stay. We are outnumbered. Nothing good will come of this."

Orlianna dropped her gaze. "Maeve will be furious."

Arliss's chest heaved. "Maeve should have known about this."

Orlando dug in his pocket for the aged flowers. Yes, Maeve should have known something of this, if she was so wise—and since she was Merna's sister. Then again, what if she did know—and was hiding it?

Either way, she would know *now.*

He fisted the Lasairbláth and ran straight toward the light.

Light flashed toward Arliss, creating ripples of brightness down the tunnel. Then, almost before she knew what was happening, the flames were upon them.

Ríon's distinctive, bloodcurdling yell bellowed somewhere to her right. Orlianna's flaming hair swirled as she spun into the fight. Orlando was in there, too, his fist raised—still clenching the Lasairbláth. He was going to try to blow up the tunnel.

Someone slammed into Arliss, blasting the breath from her lungs.

She staggered back. Arms looped around her, jerking her bow arm back. She struggled, but her opponent was too strong, and he had surprised her.

She thrashed and kicked back at his shins.

He leaned close. His breath whistled into her ear. "Fight me."

Finín. She stopped struggling but stayed tense. "Why?"

He released her. "I have a secret to tell you."

She sheathed her arrow and held her bow horizontally in front of her. "There's no time. Fin, you have to get back down the tunnel."

"Why?"

"Because we have to leave. Things may get interesting in a moment."

He stood still. "All I know is this—Anmór is coming for Ikarra. They are coming for *you*. I do not think the rigdál mór will be a council of peace."

Arliss scanned the tunnel. The fighting was deadlocked—even though both Orlianna and Philip faced two opponents at once. Orlando had seized a torch. Now he was bending down, scattering Lasairbláth across the ground.

Orlando stood and called to her. "Arliss! We have to get out of here!"

She grabbed Finín's shoulder. "Please, cousin, get the band out of here. I don't want harm to come to them."

He stepped away. "You need to find out the truth, Arliss."

"I will."

He paused, uncertainty written in his eyes. "Anmór isn't the only clan with secrets." Then he fled.

Orlando had pulled Orlianna from her fight, and they were running like mad for Arliss. Finín jerked his comrades in the opposite direction.

"Philip!" Arliss shouted.

He shoved his opponent into the ground and ran.

Orlando threw the torch at the line of Lasairbláth on the ground.

Arliss kept running as the darkness grew.

Then the light exploded. Dirt shot down the tunnel toward them. The earth groaned, a shudder wreaking devastation through the catacombs. The ceiling caved in.

The tunnel swallowed itself behind them. Arliss kept running for the light.

CHAPTER NINETEEN: RELICS

ORLIANNA STUMBLED OUT OF THE FUNICULAR TRAIN CAR THE MOMENT it hit the top of the ascent to the castle. She gripped her skirts, not even nodding to the conductor as the rushed across the rocky hilltop to the castle. Bleak midnight fell thick around her. Their trip through the catacombs and back had taken the whole rest of the day.

She'd sent the others on back, slipping Arliss a spare key for one of the back entrances. She herself had needed to get the message to Garrick about the catacomb incident before word got to Maeve. Now, the sabbath was long over. Who knew what unholy hour of the morning of Dialuna it was.

She rushed up the main entrance to the ballroom. At this hour, there was no need to use secret entrances. No sane person would be awake.

A light twinkled through the huge glass windows. Only two people could be there at this hour. One, she never minded seeing. The other, she'd rather not have to face.

She twisted the key in the door and pulled it open.

At the end of the bare banquet table, Harrison held a candle's light to a book.

Orlianna exhaled. At least she wouldn't have to face Maeve's interrogation until after a good night's sleep.

"What're you reading?"

Focused, he didn't look up.

"A little something I borrowed from Arliss." Then realization knotted his brow. He jerked his head up. "Orlianna! Darling, where the devil have you been?"

"Nowhere." She strode past him toward the stairs.

He grabbed her arm and pulled himself up. His good eye glared as he examined her, his grip on her arm practically cutting off her circulation. "You've been gone for half a day. Maeve is furious. I expect an explanation."

"Maeve should sit down. She invited me to do what I did."

Harrison's eyebrows rose to their pinnacle.

She huffed. "I went to the catacombs to find Ríon to speak peace with him. We found him…and a few other things we weren't expecting."

"*We?*" His voice rose. "Don't tell me you dragged the Reinholdians into this."

"Where do you think they were this whole time—sipping tea on the riverway?"

"Why didn't you tell me?" Harrison seemed suddenly to grow to the size he'd been when she was only ten and he twenty-five, when he had first begun to train her. "I should have come with you."

Yes, he was the ambassador. But she hadn't the time. And she could not have risked his life. He was too valuable.

"I didn't need you," she said.

His lips parted hesitantly. He released her arm. "You're right. I've trained you in everything I know."

"No, it's not that." She bit down the burning of her heart. "It's that I *do* need you. And that is why I didn't tell you I was going, because I knew you would come with me, and I could not risk—"

He pressed his finger to her lips.

A tear slipped down her cheek before she knew she was crying. "If something happened to you—"

"Hush," he whispered. "Why do you fear the future?"

"I don't fear the future. There is hope for Ikarra." She glanced around the dimly glittering room to try to erase the fresh memories—and stale ones—of the catacombs. "You know it is not the future I fear."

"Then why do you fear the past? This is a troubled time. Why should you carry the weight of grief and guilt?"

"Because I must!" She grabbed his shoulders for support. "Do you think I still want to grieve? I loved my mother, and no matter how hard she tries, my grandmother will never be half what she was to me. And the catacombs, they only made me think of those souls…"

"That was not your fault. You should be blaming Anmór rather than yourself."

Orlianna steadied her breathing as the tears stopped. She walked away from the table, toward the far window that overlooked the river and the fields beyond. Harrison watched, but didn't follow her.

She reached out to touch the glass. "I'm sorry you have to see me like this. But there is no one else I can talk to this way."

"I'm much obliged to hear you. But what about Arliss? You can confide in her."

Orlianna shook her hair behind her shoulders. "Arliss has enough of her own problems. Her parents' pressures, her friends' struggles. She's still trying to figure out how Reinhold fits into this mess. I cannot weigh her down any more."

Harrison looked down, his voice quiet. "What about Orlando?"

Her heartbeat quickened. "Or—Orlando? I hardly know him."

"Ruddy nonsense! You spent two weeks on a boat with him. And he's been here a few days yet."

She cocked her head toward him. "I can't just go blubbing to anyone I like. I can't even do this to my father, and I hardly ever did it to my mother. I just have you."

"Orlando doesn't have anyone, though. And I can see in his eyes he has more troubles than any of us know."

It was true. The catacombs seemed to have haunted him as much as they had her. Had ashes of memory been cast in his eyes as well?

She headed for the stairs. "We need to get some sleep. I'm flying the aircraft out on a scouting mission early tomorrow."

He paced after her. "Why? What did you find out?"

"Anmór is closer than we think. And they may not be coming for rigdál mór." She grasped the stair railing. "They may be coming for battle."

Arliss stroked the gilded leaf at the edge of the book's page—an aged volume she'd borrowed from the castle library. Like everything here in Ikarra, it answered questions—then asked a dozen more.

The door to the room swung open and Ilayda rushed in, breathless.

Arliss glanced up from her book. She'd been so tired last night (or that morning, rather) that she must have forgotten to lock the door. She combed her fingers through her tangled hair. "What do you want?"

Ilayda jumped on the bed beside Arliss. "Where'd you go? I scoured the castle—the whole city—for you! Maeve was beside herself."

Arliss closed the book. "Maeve knows we were gone?"

Ilayda rolled her eyes. "Of course she does. And she's going to want the full story. But first, I want it."

"We went to the catacombs to find Ríon. We found him." She smacked the book onto the nightstand. "We fought him."

"Everything's going wrong. Our friends are our enemies. The lands of legend are dark and mysterious." Ilayda's gaze drifted around the room. "I was right."

"Right about what?"

She stared out toward Arliss's open balcony. "I told Erik yesterday that we would be better off back in Reinhold—safe, away from all this trouble. Yes, there are troubles back home, but they're nothing to what has happened here."

"Ilayda, I can't abandon Orlianna and her people. She needs me—needs our clan to bring balance." As if they had done anything so far to right the scales of the conflict. Arliss swallowed. "I promised my mother that I would find out why Thane did what he did. I promised my father I would accept my role as queen. I haven't done either of those, and I haven't really even come close."

Ilayda's brown eyes became focused and sharp. "You should talk to Maeve."

"Why?"

"She knows things. I feel she's a sort of…storyteller."

"She saw my note?"

"Yes. While you were gone, she asked me…questions." Ilayda's chest deflated. "Maeve knows more than anyone about what's going on. And she wants to turn all of our clans into one."

Arliss stood. "Why did she speak to you about this?"

Ilayda tilted her head, musing. "I think she was afraid."

Arliss made for the door, bare feet sliding against the hardwood floor. Orlianna's borrowed set of keys still jingled in her pocket. Maybe one of these would open Maeve's secret tower room.

Arliss reached for the door handle. Ilayda had a perception about other people's thoughts and emotions that often went deeper than she realized.

"What do you think Maeve is afraid of?"

Ilayda looked over her shoulder at Arliss. "You."

The keys rattled unfamiliarly in Arliss's hand as she jabbed each one into the lock of the ancient door, trying to find the right one. Orlianna had given her these keys the evening before to get back into the castle. Surely she wouldn't mind her using them just one more time.

A dull noise echoed close by.

She whirled, but the armory's aisles were still dark and empty. Entire suits of armor stood, silently guarding legions of bows, swords, and spears. The far stone wall was completely blotted out by intricately painted shields.

She turned back to the door. The blackened piece of wood hardly seemed worthy of the tower it attached to. Maeve's tower could be seen from anywhere in the city, and even Orlianna had praised the depth of her relic collection.

The lock finally swallowed one key. She gave it a twist. The door groaned inward.

She slipped in and shut it behind her. The room within was the size of her closet. There were no lights—not even a sconce or candelabra—but well-placed windows swirled upward, casting blades of light on the stone stairs.

She leapt the stairs, listening to the way her footsteps swirled up, then down to her again. Fifty-five steps which all seemed to grow longer the higher she got.

She reached the top and froze.

The uppermost chamber was unlike anything she'd ever seen. It widened beyond the span of the supporting tower beneath. Windows were cut into the stone walls with perfect precision. Light sliced down from above and bled together, illuminating the whole tower.

Wooden pedestals, built into the circular stone floor, stood at even intervals around the wall—until they reached another small staircase. It wound upward to another floor, half-open to the tower's light. And then again, up to a smaller upper platform. And above that, above the relics and the staircase, hung half a dozen of the richest tapestries.

Arliss slipped the keys in her pocket and took a deep breath. The bodice of her jade silk gown seemed to tighten. Where to begin? What might this room reveal about Maeve—and all Ikarra?

She walked the edge of the room. Some of the relics weren't so remarkable—a gold crown with a missing gem, a curl of rope, a silver goblet. She walked faster. If Ikarra still had their gifts—like those given to Reinhold long ago—they would be kept in this room.

She hurried up the stairs to the second level.

This was much like the first. Strange objects occupied their pedestals without so much as a placard to denote what they were, or had once been. She would need the most learned guide in the realms to explain this place.

Silver flashed the sun in her eyes. She halted. A long sword with an emerald scabbard spanned across two pedestals. This had to be the sword of Ikarra.

She exhaled in confirmation. Next to it sat a twisted circlet; within that, a jeweled ring.

Well, there they were: ordinary gifts. As far as she knew, Reinhold's gifts were the only ones with unique powers. And that was only because they unlocked the secret gifts.

The sword had unlocked the vial.

They had the ring, but it unlocked nothing.

They had the crown, but it unlocked nothing.

But Orlianna's pendant—she claimed it was the pendant of Reinhold.

That left one more gift: the sphere. The elusive one. Not even Gally knew what it was or where it had gone. Unless, of course, he *did* know and hid it from her.

The narrow sunlight shifted enticingly up the stairs. She pressed her hand into the stone and drifted up them.

At the top, more relics crowded the space. Her brow tightened. These were odder than the ones downstairs.

A chunk of stone. A pile of burnt, fluttery paper. More ropes—these smaller, and stained dark in places. A jar filled with rocky sand.

None of it made sense, and none of it went together.

Then she glanced at the last item, and her heart stumbled.

A fiddle wasn't a remarkable thing, but she'd seen this one before. It had the same mahogany luster, the interlocking designs on the edging. This *had* to be the violin from Thane's fortress—Orlando's violin. She reached for the neck.

"A spy, eh?"

Arliss whirled, flashing her knife out.

Maeve raised her open palms. "There's no need to point weapons at me, Arliss."

Arliss kept the knife level as shock trembled through her muscles. "You startled me."

"By sneaking up on you as *you* trespassed in my private collection? Indeed." Maeve laughed. "How did you get in?"

Arliss swallowed.

"Orlianna gave you keys, didn't she?" Maeve arched an eyebrow. "Don't pretend she didn't. I know you two have been colluding."

"As if you haven't colluded. You seem to get a steady stream of information from Merna."

"She is my sister."

Arliss realized she was still holding the knife. "She's a liar. Right now she's aiding Ríon through the catacombs. Her army may be marching on this city already."

"They come for rigdál mór."

"How can you be so sure?"

Maeve strode toward the first pedestal and stroked the chunk of rock. "Because she knows she cannot avoid the unity of the clans. It is meant to come to pass—written in the stars, as some foolish folk say. I like to think it was written *by* the stars—by those who possess the power and will to write the story of the world."

Arliss choked on her own saliva and coughed. "So you expect us all to become one? For the sun, moon, and stars to bow at your command?"

Maeve pursed her lips. "First unity—" She picked up the rope. Arliss saw now the stains were dried blood. "—then balance—" Maeve folded the rope. "—then all are one."

She pulled the knot tight.

"And the gifts can go safely on display in a museum?" Arliss clenched her fist as her blood heated. "Along with a few portraits and a little tablet explaining what Thane did. Explaining why my uncles died fighting him. And explaining how—*somehow*—Thane had nothing to do with any of this!"

"Are you accusing me?"

Arliss looked away. "You clearly know much about the three realms. I have reason to believe that someone else was behind everything. I thought you might have a guess."

Maeve walked to the slit of a window, her hands clasped behind her back. The sun glinted in her grey eyes. "Arliss, I have heard much about your story, both directly and indirectly. And everything—the kingdom in the wild lands, the rise of Thane, the fiery arrow, the journey to Anmór, the battle in your own land, and even your voyage here—they all revolve around just one person."

Arliss thought of all these things. Wasn't Thane involved in most of them? Or was there someone else behind everything?

Maeve glanced at her. "That person is you."

"Me? You would hold me responsible for my own uncles' deaths?"

"Conflict has trailed you like a train on its tracks."

Arliss stopped herself from drawing the knife again. "Your sister caused more conflict than I did."

Maeve faced her and nodded. "What Merna did was rash. And I am sorry for the death of your uncles."

Arliss leaned back. This kind of sympathy, from Maeve? It caught her off guard a bit. Just because Merna told Maeve things, didn't mean they were colluding. But if they were, if they had been…

Her eyes went to the fiddle. The only way Maeve could have gotten it was through Merna.

"If your sister had come to you—if she *had* asked your advice—what would you have told her?"

Maeve shook her head. "I can never know what I would have done. Only what I will do."

"And what is that?"

"I will bring peace to our clans, so that there need be no more death—not in my realm, or in yours."

Orlianna glanced up at the veranda of Garrick's narrow blue mansion as she, Orlando, and Harrison reached the street's end. The upturned flowerpot at the top of the stairs meant he wasn't at home—which meant he probably didn't know anything about her mission. All the better. He would have talked her out of it—or worse, tried to come with her.

She swept her hair behind her shoulders. Her emotions were in enough of a state without Garrick's badgering. Maybe it was just her imagination, but he seemed to be pressing even closer to her since the Reinholdians' arrival. Didn't he know she wasn't going to pour out her heart to *anyone?*

At least not in that way. That silly, frivolous way of people who were in love.

In love.

She choked on her own spit. Romance was ridiculous. And love—well, it was ridiculous, too, though not as useless. Love had once had a place in her heart. And it still did, but too much of it had fermented into bitter grief.

Wild seagrass reached up her short dress and scratched her knees as she waded through the field beside Garrick's house. The open-faced building behind his house was three stories of ugly, unadorned wood and iron. No one knew why it had been built. But now it found a use as a place to park and launch the aircraft. The ugliness actually helped hide the secret: no one wondered about the building, no one asked questions.

She reached the rusty door and was about to open it when Orlando reached in front of her.

"Allow me," he said.

She bit her lip and nodded, staring at the metal. As she entered, she let her fingers linger in the indentions in the doorframe—the place where she and her brother had carved their names as children.

He swept the door open and let her and Harrison enter first. The door hissed shut behind him.

Orlianna inhaled the old wood and new sunlight. Birds' nests clustered the corners of the room, and the screech of hatchlings echoed in the barn-like building.

Orlando glanced around, confused. "How do we—?"

She placed her hand on the bottom rung of an iron ladder that cut straight up through the ceiling. "This way."

On the third floor, Arliss stood with her head on Philip's shoulder.

Orlianna pulled herself through the floor and stepped onto the platform. Boots clicking, she paced to the three aircraft in the center of the room. "Arliss. Philip. Over here."

Arliss snapped to attention, her golden waves spinning. "I was afraid to touch them without you here."

"Good." Orlianna stroked the bird's canvas wing where it lay on the central crossbow mechanism—just like the one in the ruined tower. "But now I'm here, and that means our mission can begin."

"What is our mission?"

"Fly over Cahair, over the river, over the mountains. To the very border of Ikarra. From there we can see if Anmór is on the move above ground, now that the catacombs are closed off for the time."

Arliss ran her hand up the aircraft's silky wood props. "Rigdál mór is not for nearly four weeks. Why would they be coming now?"

"Your cousin said as much, didn't he? And who knows what Ríon might do. He doesn't give a damn about what or when anything is supposed to be."

Arliss stared at Orlianna. "You really do hate him, don't you?"

Orlianna exhaled, her stomach tightening. "What do you expect?"

From the other side of the room, Harrison waved at them. He and Orlando had been inspecting the other aircraft. "Ready for flight, my lady!"

Orlianna nodded once.

Arliss stared the empty space where the front wall should have been. Instead it was a wide window, a launching for the birds. The midday sun caught Arliss's eyes and turned them into sapphires. "I know something of how you feel, you know."

"What?"

"I lost a brother, too, long ago. He died just after birth. I never knew him. But the pain is still there."

Orlianna met Arliss's eyes and discovered a whole new depth of realization, of friendship, within them.

"It's hard, losing a brother." Arliss leaned against the wing. "It's like being tempted with a perfect life, but you lose it before you knew it was perfect. And then it's as if there is always something missing—something you need to look for. But you begin to realize you will never find it. There will always be a hole."

Orlianna's tears hid behind her eyes and stung her throat. "Then you understand."

Arliss placed her hand on Orlianna's shoulder.

"Engine's ready." Harrison booted up to them. "You want to fly with Arliss or Orlando?"

Orlianna shrugged, mainly to douse the sudden flutter of her heart. "It doesn't matter to me."

Harrison looked at the other two. "Any preference?"

Arliss shook her head.

But Orlando folded his arms, the burgundy cloak slipping to the side. "I'll go with Orlianna."

Orlianna pivoted and started preparing the bird: tightening the ropes, adjusting the rudder, ensuring the crossbow system was ready to shoot. She kneeled in the front, hand on the release lever, as Orlando clambered in and sat on the thin wooden platform behind her.

She looked over her shoulder. "Are you ready for this?"

"Yes."

"No, you aren't." She stared at the city just outside. "No one is."

She pushed the lever.

The bird rocketed down the platform.

CHAPTER TWENTY:
FEAR APPROACHES

FOR A FEW SECONDS, ORLANDO FELT LIKE THE MOMENTUM WAS going to throw him off the back of the aircraft and into the barn. The wheels swallowed up the runway as the giant crossbow shot them into the open air.

The plane jerked. Orlando's hands turned white around the nearest props.

Then wind rushed beneath them, lifting them upward. The canvas wings breathed a sigh of relief. Orlianna pulled the steering stick and tilted the wings upward. The wind's force sucked Orlando's lungs downward.

Then all at once, they were floating—flying—with the Jade City spreading out beneath them.

Orlando let go of one of the props and stuck his hand out into the wispy layers of air below them. Garrick's mansion was just a speck of blue at the end of rows of crisscrossing streets. The riverway was nothing more than a dark edging to the crystalline blue river that wove its way around the castle and back to the sea. And the castle—it stabbed up higher than everything else, its towers seeming almost close enough to touch.

The plane tilted, rounding the south side of the castle. Orlando grabbed the prop again. They flew along the river. Orlianna pushed the plane downward, and they hovered over the riverway rooftops that whistled by.

Something rustled in the air above them. He looked up.

Harrison flew the second bird, his face calm and focused. Arliss perched on the platform's edge, hanging on with one hand.

With the other she waved to him.

Arliss stuck her free hand straight out in the wind as her tension, her regret, melted away. She'd wanted Philip to be able to come, but Harrison insisted the aircraft could carry only two passengers. Not that Philip had cared. He had just shrugged and said he'd go later.

She smiled, partially because the rush of wind forced her lips apart. He never put himself first. It was always her, or his family, or his people. If only she herself could be half as selfless.

Then again, less was hanging on him. He was just a peasant carpenter who happened to catch the eye of the princess—happened to join her on her quests—happened to win her heart. No one expected anything of him. Anything he did was a victory and an achievement.

But for her, *everything* was expected. The whole fate of Reinhold seemed to be hung on her shoulders. It was a weight she didn't want. The crown of Reinhold had sat in its case on her dresser since the moment she'd arrived here. And now, with the wind flooding her lungs, she felt she never wanted its weight on her forehead.

Harrison tapped her. "Princess?"

She shook herself. "Sorry. I was daydreaming."

He was practically shouting in the wind. "Not a problem. I thought you might like a turn at the stick."

"I'm fine, actually. I'll trust it to better hands."

He glanced behind him, then pushed onward. "Looks like those two blighters are doing circles around the city. And *I* thought we had a mission to do."

She caught the hint in his eye. "Are you a matchmaker, Harrison?"

His eyebrows rose. "No. But I care very much about a certain princess. Her heart is my own."

Arliss peered down as they neared the edge of the peninsula, the wide river delta fanning out to their left. "Orlando is a good friend. He has earned much of my trust."

"Do you think he deserves Orlianna's?" Harrison turned his gaze back to the mountains on the other side of the river when Arliss did not answer. "I don't mean to be forward. But I do not want my girl's heart to be broken."

Arliss sighed. Harrison was right—Orlianna's heart was fragile, much more than even she probably realized. But so was Orlando's. And anyone could see from the shine in his eyes that he adored Orlianna. His heart could be shattered, too.

Something slipped into her sight on the furthest reach of the horizon—where the mountains that separated Ikarra from Anmór dipped down into a flat plain. She squinted. A black mass, like the crawl of raging ants, came into view.

Her heart thundered faster than she could breathe. She knew this sight all too well.

Harrison must have known it, too, for he jerked the plane up and forward. "You see it?"

She steadied her other hand against another prop. "Yes."

He pursed his lips. "I don't want to speculate on what it is."

"What else could it be?" In her mind, the prop became a bow grip. The black mass sparked with flashes of metal. "What else could it be but an army?"

Orlianna stared through her own wisping strands of hair as she tilted the wings forward, forcing the plane down. If this was to be a show for the people of Cahair, she needed to fly as close to the ground as possible. Her pulse sped up ever so slightly. She'd never flown anywhere but in the western fields or along the northern coastline.

But the birds were no longer a secret. And if the Ikarrans were going to find harmony with Anmór, they needed to be united. The incident at the ruins had shaken the people's trust in her—in her ideas.

But if they saw the beauty, the power, the fluidity, they might accept both her and her creations.

She lay down across the steering platform, one hand grasping the steering stick. With the other she brushed hair out of her face. Her linen jerkin scratched against the rough wood platform.

Orlando crouched beside her. "Low enough yet?"

"Not nearly." She eased the stick lower. "I want people's hats flying off when I sweep over them."

His eyes went wide. He pointed at the dock straight ahead. "Look."

She squinted. It was Domnall—no mistaking his broad bearing, nor his extravagant hat. A smirk spread through her lips. She dropped the plane even faster. She reached for the left-hand lever and twisted the crooked arm. The rudder in the back shifted, and the bird turned toward the dock.

Domnall glanced up, hand shielding his eyes from the sun's glare. He gaped at her.

She whizzed over him. The wind ripped his hat from his head and sent it spinning to the dock's edge.

Orlando laughed as they circled back around. She smiled in his direction. He had a fine laugh—like the vibrations of a resonant fiddle.

Domnall clutched the top of his head and shouted as she passed over him again. "Don't underestimate me!"

She circled again, putting one hand to her ear as if she hadn't heard. "What?"

"I'll shoot you down!" His cheeks ballooned with red.

She kept flying past the dock this time, then turned back toward the riverway.

Orlando glanced behind them. "If he's serious—"

"Don't listen to his malarkey. Never means a thing."

He grabbed the platform's edge. "But Orlianna…"

She stared at the approaching second cantar. "Just ignore him.

He's only frightening if you take him seriously."

"*Orlianna.*"

She looked at him. "What?"

He pointed to their left, back toward the dock. Domnall was just a tiny figurine.

Just as she looked, though, Domnall lifted his crossbow—aimed—fired—all within three seconds.

It was impossible not to aim a crossbow well, even from this distance. The arrow whistled over the tops of houses. The bird wouldn't move quite fast enough. The tip punctured the tail flap, ripping through the canvas.

The bird buckled beneath her. She reached for the rudder lever, but it was useless. The canvas flap had shredded completely off.

"Bloody idiot..." She breathed into the plywood.

Orlando's fingers angled the platform as the bird bungled its way over the first cantar. "What do we do?" he yelled.

She looked behind her at the flap. Tension spread through her arms. There was no steering the bird with that gone. At this rate, they'd crash into the castle—or worse, the riverway. She touched her chest as an idea rustled through her. If she could tie her jerkin to the frame...

She grabbed Orlando's arm. "Can you fly this thing?"

"I—I don't know—"

"Just hold onto this stick and keep the bird level. Then, when I tell you, twist this other lever."

He shook his head, but his eyebrows dropped in determination. He placed both hands on the stick and stretched out across the platform.

She inched toward the back of the bird. "God be with you."

He didn't look back. "And you."

As she reached for the flap, she stole a glance southward. Harrison and Arliss's bird was a speck on the horizon. She hoped their flight thus far had held less of the scent of war.

The mountains reached up like knobbly fingers of mossy stone grasping for the aircraft. Arliss peered over the side. The catacombs entrance lay far below, nestled in the foothills. That path surely wouldn't be much use now. She had no idea how extensive the Lasairbláth explosion had been, but a lengthy stretch of the roof must have caved in.

So now, it seemed, Ríon and Merna were carrying on their villainy above ground.

Harrison steered the aircraft lower, gliding straight between two spiraling pinnacles. The weather over Cahair had been clear, but in the mountains clouds clustered in thick blankets. The black mass they'd seen earlier was now invisible.

A cloud wisped right before them. They flew straight into it. The sun's light magnified tenfold, and all Arliss saw was light—pure, white light.

She lay on her stomach next to Harrison. "All is quiet. Peaceful."

"It's the enemy's greatest tactic—to appear what he is not."

"The enemy," Arliss mused. It was easy to throw Merna into that category. She'd helped Thane for a long time, if not from the beginning. But it was still hard to lump Ríon in with them. "From their perspective, aren't we the enemy, too?"

Harrison didn't bother turning his whole head so he could properly look at her. "Well, what are you fighting for, Arliss?"

She reached out to touch the swirling sky. "My friends. My parents. Philip. Reinhold."

"Deeper than that."

"I want to keep Philip alive. I want to discover the why and the how about Thane. I want to bring peace so we can finally write down the stories of our adventures."

He smiled at her, but his brows stayed taut. "Life. Truth. Stories. The enemy cares for none of those things. The enemy seeks death, lies. He cares nothing for stories."

The cloud melted away. At once the plain below became clear— a clumpy gray field of jagged rocks.

Arliss could only stare.

There, covering the plain like a layer of hot ash, marched the Anmórian army. She had never been good at estimating crowds, but their numbers must have been in the thousands. Horseman, bowmen, all flanked by a fleet of charioteers. She knew Ríon would be among their number.

At the head of the whole entourage rode King Merwin himself— his lengthy robes shrouding his body and making him look even paunchier than usual. The ceremonial shoulder and thigh armour did nothing to amend his outfit's stupidity.

But everything about him became nothing next to the rider at his right. Merna rode like the queen that she was, a deathly green silk chiffon shimmering beneath an elaborately engraved breastplate.

Harrison jerked the plane about, speeding back into the cloud.

Arliss stole one last glance over her shoulder as the army vanished into the vaporous air.

Orlando held onto the steering stick with both hands as the unruly bird pitched madly, trying to shake him off. The wind had picked up. A sour storm swirled toward Cahair from the mountains.

He stole a look behind him. Nothing—no sign of Arliss and Harrison.

Just Orlianna clutching the tail, fierce determination sparking in her eyes. She pulled her jerkin off, tugging it over her head. The rough fabric slid easily over the frame of the tail flap. But there was nothing to tie it with. She held it in place and called up to Orlando.

"If you had Lasairbláth sitting around in those pockets of yours, surely you have some rope?"

He took one hand off the stick and felt for his jerkin.

The aircraft dipped downward.

Grabbing the stick again, he pulled it level. "I—I can't do this!"

"Yes, you can! Just don't let go."

He slipped one hand from the stick and inched it toward his jerkin pocket. He pulled the short coil of rope out and held it in her direction. His arms spanned to their limit—but he couldn't reach her.

Her fingers stretched out, a few feet short of the rope. "I can't reach any further. The flap will whip off if I let go."

The wind whistled through the canvas wings as the bird continued to lurch unpredictably. A drop—two drops—of rain settled on Orlando's hand. They had to fix this now.

He narrowed his brows. There was only one way to get the rope to Orlianna.

"I'm going to let go."

Her eyes widened. "No. You'll kill yourself. Orlando—"

"You have to trust me."

Her chest heaved. She nodded.

He let go of the stick and slid backward down the platform to the tail. He drew a knife with his free hand. Their other hands met. She grabbed him more than she did the rope. He stuck a knife into the platform, pinning his chest and arms there. The rest of his body streamed out behind the bird.

Wind. The race of wind. Orlianna yelled something. The rain. The rain was getting harder. They had to land.

He opened his eyes. The unbalance of weight had swung the bird nose-upward.

Orlianna clutched at the smooth platform, clawing herself forward. Her pendant had come free of her dress, and it clanked against the wood. She strained to grasp the stick, then pushed the bird level.

The shift swung Orlando forward. He slid down the platform toward the nose.

Orlianna reached out to grab him—stop his fall. As she did, her hand caught in her pendant. The chain unclasped. The pendant slipped toward the wet lash of the open air.

Orlando grabbed for it, trusting Orlianna to hold onto his other hand. Cool metal burned the inside of his palm. Orlianna's chilled fingers clenched his other hand.

The wind quieted. The bird leveled out. He exhaled a breath he didn't know he'd taken.

Orlianna steered them toward Garrick's barn. She glanced at him, but like him, she couldn't say anything.

They were almost over Garrick's house when he summoned the strength to move, to offer her the pendant. As it passed his face, he caught the sharp, sweet scent of Lasairbláth.

"Here you go."

"Thank you."

A shadow flitted into Orlando's peripheral vision. Arliss and Harrison. They glided alongside, close enough that Orlando could read every expression on Arliss's face. The fear, the confusion. Then they came close enough that he could read her lips.

Anmór is coming.

CHAPTER TWENTY-ONE:
THE RIGDAL MOR

ILAYDA TILTED THE SPOON OF SUGAR OVER HER TEACUP AND watched as the granules spun ripples in the dark liquid. The conversation around her had grown stale, and she began to listen more to the wind that washed up from the river. Her gaze wandered out to the field beyond the river's far bank.

Their high tea with Maeve had been exquisitely set on a wide balcony on the castle's private side—facing the barren plains. From here, it was easy to forget the vastness of Cahair. The tea had taken so long to be set that Ilayda thought it might never come. But at last Maeve had ushered her and Erik through several winding passages and out onto this platform, where they were joined by Lord Garrick and King Lachlan.

Erik and Ilayda sat on either side of Maeve. Ilayda shifted in her seat. After Maeve's confrontation about the secret note, she hadn't been comfortable around her.

Erik sat opposite her, his long legs hooked around the legs of his chair to avoid stretching into Lachlan, who nestled in half a dozen pillows on a reclining chair.

Erik stirred his tea methodically.

Ilayda forced a tiny cough.

It caught his attention. He glanced at her, still stirring.

Since he faced the castle and the skies above it, he might be able to see any progress Arliss and the rest might have made. Ilayda glanced upward, then arched an eyebrow.

Erik scanned the sky, then shook his head.

So nothing. Either they were flying elsewhere, or something had called them home early. She'd spotted some distant rainclouds earlier, but they had all but melted away.

Maeve clinked her cup down at the table's head. "What do you think, Ilayda?"

Ilayda blinked. "I'm sorry, what were we talking about?"

Maeve stared, clearly irritated.

Garrick chuckled. "Maeve was discussing the cantars' different reactions to you and your friends. Apparently word's spreading that my cantar favors you. But there are other rumors trickling in from the first cantar." He eyed Maeve. "Speaking of which, where's Domnall? The old rascal should have joined us."

Maeve shrugged. "I invited him, but he had business at the docks."

"What a shame," Ilayda muttered.

"Pardon?" Maeve froze with her teacup in midair. "Did you perhaps want to comment on the topic at hand?"

Ilayda bit her tongue. So cold, so formal. This was nothing like even the stiffest meetings in Reinhold. She lifted her cup. "I think the Ikarrans have been very welcoming, for the most part. Don't you, Erik?"

He squinted at her, obviously not wanting to join the conversation. "Yes. Quite welcoming. Though it's all very different. And with war looming so close…"

It would be wiser for them all to return to Reinhold, Ilayda silently finished his sentence.

Lachlan glanced up, haggard eyes sagging. "War looms close? What news is there?"

"War is not looming close." Maeve set her cup down. "We are on the verge of peace. This great royal meeting will redefine the nature of our clans. As long as no one does anything rash—"

Maeve stopped short as footsteps pounded down the passage toward the balcony's glass doors. Ilayda twisted in her seat and felt her spine crackle.

Domnall swept the doors wide. They clanged shut behind him

as he crumpled into the chair beside Ilayda.

Ilayda shifted uncomfortably toward Maeve.

"What news, Lord Domnall?" Maeve asked.

Domnall gazed into the lacquered table. "Warmonger. Fool! She's going to bring the empire down around us."

Garrick leaned forward. "Who?"

Domnall fisted the table. "You shouldn't even have to ask. Your favorite—your darling pet. That infernal red-haired princess."

Ilayda exhaled. It was always amazing to hear how royalty spoke of other royalty when they weren't around.

Maeve lifted her tea. "What has she done to you now—plucked a feather from your favorite hat?"

"At least." Domnall glared. "She flew right over my head and practically knocked me off the dock. She's taken those flying machines for a turn all over the city."

"*What?*" Maeve's teacup clattered the few inches back down to the saucer. Tea sloshed over onto the table. "Where is Orlianna?"

"Here!" Red hair whooshing behind her, loose dress fluttering, Orlianna stormed out onto the balcony. She'd lost the jerkin she was wearing earlier, and her knee-length dress hung in tatters along the edges. Rain and sweat had tangled with her hair and turned it wild.

Maeve gaped. "Granddaughter! What are you doing?"

"Something rash, probably." Orlianna tossed her head. "But at least it's something. More than you're doing—sitting drinking tea with a crooked pinky while war marches on our doorstep."

Lachlan clenched his pillows. "Orlianna—"

The door slid open. Harrison held it for Arliss, Philip, and Orlando to tromp in behind Orlianna.

Domnall sneered. "What a fine party we have here. I won't say we haven't missed you."

Ilayda jumped up. "Arliss—what happened?"

Arliss glanced at Orlianna.

Orlianna leaned toward Maeve and pointed over the balcony. "Merwin and Merna have gathered the largest Anmórian army in history. They are rounding the mountains now, heading for these very plains. They'll be upon us in two days."

Ilayda swallowed her staggering pulse. All the questions, all the speculation—and now this. Battle was coming to Cahair.

They needed to leave.

Now.

Orlianna leaned over the table, waiting for Maeve to react. Her grandmother held her gaze, calculating a response—as if it the revelation didn't surprise her.

Nothing surprised Maeve. She might feign shock, but she reacted to everything as if it was normal, as if she herself was in control of the world. Now, with their enemies ready to attack, she seemed content to sit and drink tea overloaded with cream and sugar.

Orlianna stood tall. "Did you hear me?"

"Oh, I heard," Maeve said. "I heard the ravings of a warmonger."

"Merwin's army was already on the move. Our scouting flight did nothing to incite them."

"Perhaps not." Maeve stood, gritting her words like steel shards. "But your flight may lead the Ikarran people to think that there are matters of unrest—that the crown is nervous. When they hear that Anmór's forces are moving toward us, they will assume that they come for war. And they will blame you and your aircraft for starting the whole mess."

Lachlan cleared his throat. "With all due respect, mother, but what else would they be coming for?"

Maeve shrugged. "They come for rigdál mór."

Harrison shook his head. "It is a month until the full moon."

"I know the calendar, Harrison." Maeve inhaled. "I also know that my sister is impatient. Considering her past conflict with the Reinholdians, I understand she would be uneasy."

Orlianna clenched her fists. Uneasy—yes, enough to rally every one of her soldiers. They couldn't just sit around assuming this was to be a glorified parley. Cahair needed to be fortified for battle.

Maeve headed for the glass doors. The others parted to make way.

Orlianna didn't look over her shoulder at her grandmother, but she let the words slip her lips anyway. "Any fool can see that this is more than a simple meeting of royalty."

Maeve whirled in Orlianna's peripheral vision, her silver charms tinkling. "And I am the fool, am I? The one who has been the voice of reason and the guiding hand over Ikarra for years! You think you are wise? You think that you can win this battle by weapons and warfare? This is why you are not queen, Orlianna. And the people will never trust you until you show them peace."

She stalked off down the passage.

Orlianna panted. These words burned deeper than they should have, maybe because for the first time she felt they might actually be true. Maeve was the one fighting for peace. She herself had done nothing to bring unity.

Garrick touched her arm. "Orrels, your grandmother doesn't—"

She batted him away. "Don't touch me."

Harrison eyed her sternly. "You need to listen to her. She has wisdom."

Arliss nodded. "She may be right. Perhaps we jumped to conclusions."

Ilayda looked from Arliss to Orlianna. "I don't think we're safe here anymore. Should—should we leave?"

Orlianna reached for her ears. "I don't know. I *don't know*. Just leave me alone."

She ran. Her feet knew every path in the castle, in the whole city. She ran until she reached the library, until she collapsed on its floor which was painted like a map.

She lay convulsing in the middle of the glass-walled room, surrounded by volumes of history and legend. For once, the books weren't her friends.

They only reminded her that she was too broken to be queen.

Footsteps on the marble floor pounded up through Orlianna's skull. Her eyelashes fluttered open. Newborn sunlight streamed in through the far glass wall.

So she'd slept here the whole night. Good thing she'd awakened. Soon the city patrol would be coming to unlock the library for its public hours: sunrise to sunset.

The footsteps continued a few paces then stopped. Their echo still rattled through Orlianna's aching head. Heavy boots. Of course Harrison would have come to her, to check on her. But she didn't want more of his condescending advice right now.

She rolled onto her back, still staring at the gleaming windows. "It would probably be better if you left me alone right now."

Silence whispered through the library.

Orlianna eased pressure off her shoulder. "Harrison?"

"Granddaughter, I'm sorry."

Maeve? Orlianna pushed herself into a sitting position and turned. Her grandmother wore a dark gold silk and laced hiking boots. Her usually neat hair wisped around tired eyes. "I was wrong. You do have the makings of a queen."

Orlianna pressed into the marble. "Truly?"

"Yes. Imagine—one, great clan. Once I unify them, I can pass the rule over to you."

Orlianna sighed. Maeve's ideas sounded good in theory. But in actuality, they would crumble faster than a sugar cube in a cup of boiling tea.

She stood. "I don't want to rule the world. Just Ikarra."

Maeve stepped closer, her feet tracing the roads and rivers painted on the marble floor. "I want you as the successor. But neither I nor your father are comfortable with passing rule over to you while you continue to seek war."

Orlianna stared out into the burnished morning world, where

the green roofs of the first cantar turned into flame. "I'm not seeking war. I think it's seeking me."

Maeve touched her shoulder. "If you seek peace, you will find it."

Orlianna closed her eyes. She had sought peace for a long time. Somehow death and war crept after her like her own shadow. "Sometimes the only way to gain peace is by fighting for it."

Maeve dropped her hand, but she didn't contradict her.

The doors to the library burst open, and Garrick rushed in. "Lady Maeve! Scouts from King Merwin! He makes his camp in the Tuáma Fields and demands a meeting with you. They intend to have rigdál mór now."

So Maeve was right. They were coming for parley, not war. At least on the surface. Meeting them could still be a risky proposition.

Maeve caught Orlianna's eye, the question lingering unspoken.

Orlianna nodded deeply.

Maeve turned to Garrick. "Very well. Tell them to bring their royal court to the ruins at high noon tomorrow, and we will have the great royal meeting."

Arliss scratched her bare shoulder, shifting her weight on the stone seating. The Ikarran-style dress drifted off her shoulders, dragged on the floor, and laced up in the back (she'd needed Ilayda to help with that). But it was comfortable, and more than that, it made her look like an Ikarran.

The second floor of the ruinous tower spread out like a stage—the central three thrones the props, and the assembling councillors the players. The room had felt almost haunted when they had visited it four days earlier. Now, it had seemingly doubled in size. The harsh sunlight of midday burned through the four ceiling-high windows.

Philip leaned over to her. "The Ikarrans are all assembled. This is everyone."

Arliss glanced left, beyond Philip. Orlando, Erik, and Ilayda clustered together, their faces taut.

To her right, two rows of Ikarran nobility smothered the ascending rows of stone. Domnall, Garrick, Harrison, Maeve, Orlianna. King Lachlan sat in a special chair in front of Orlianna.

Arliss studied the king. Such a fragile man—his young eyes a dark contrast to his frail form. He looked like too much sunlight through the windows would melt him to nothing.

Suddenly a wrenching homesickness grabbed her stomach and tied it in a knot. She longed for her own father, her mother. The new city, rising upward each day. The old ruins, a reminder of Thane's villainy and of Reinhold's heroism.

Thane's villainy…one of many things she hoped would come to light during this council.

Philip elbowed her.

She glanced up. The Ikarran nobles were stirring, commenting. Something had drawn their attention.

People emerged from the stairs. The Anmórian envoys had arrived. Merna led the way to the other side of the room, flashing Arliss a smirk as she went. Merwin and Ríon walked behind her with grim faces.

And behind them, an old man in a brown cloak absorbed the whole scene with an unflinching stare.

Arliss gulped. Galcobhar—Gally. She hadn't seen him since she had stayed at his lodge, Glasberry, during her adventure in Anmór. He'd grown older since, and walked with the aid of a knobbly staff. It seemed that, despite his former criticisms of her, he was supporting Merna.

When the Anmórians were all seated, Maeve stood. Every person in the amphitheater hushed. Even crownless, throneless, Maeve looked every bit the queen she had once been. With her usual silver dress and bejeweled belt, she commanded everyone's attention by her simplicity.

Arliss held her breath. With everyone quiet, it was easy to think the three clans could really find peace. However, once the talking began, swords would be drawn as easily as words.

Maeve spread her hands wide. "Welcome, people of Ikarra—Anmór—Reinhold—to the first rigdál mór in many long decades. We come here as brother and sisters long separated, long sundered from each other. But we all seek the same goals. Peace. Unity."

Merna stood. "Pardon me, sister, but you have not been queen of Ikarra for many years."

Maeve stepped toward the thrones. "Lachlan has appointed me as his mouthpiece."

Lachlan raised his hand in approval.

Arliss noticed Orlianna's throat straining to swallow.

Maeve placed her hand on the high-backed Ikarran throne—the spikes that resembled horns of a unicorn. "Who will speak for Anmór?"

Merna came closer. "I shall."

Merwin sniffed. "What about the third throne, now?"

Arliss caught her breath. She'd been waiting for this moment, the moment when she would come forward. Orlianna had asked her the day before to be the representative of Reinhold. In the solace of the castle, it had seemed an honorable request.

Now, surrounded by all these friends and foes, sickness roiled in her stomach.

She stood, hoping no one could see her legs trembling. "I will speak for the clan of Reinhold."

Maeve frowned. "You will do nothing of the sort."

Orlianna leapt up. "I object!"

"You, also, will do nothing of the sort." Maeve crossed her arms. "Only ruling monarchs from the three clans, or those appointed by a monarch who is present, may speak from the three thrones. It is an ancient law."

"Then change it," Orlianna spat.

Maeve sat. "That is not in my power, but in the power of this assembly. So sit back down, *Princess* Arliss."

Arliss sat beside Philip, her cheeks burning. The title of princess meant nothing. She may as well have been a commoner by birth, a nobody.

Merna seated herself. The empty throne separated her from Maeve. "What say does Reinhold have in this matter, anyway? They cast themselves out years ago."

Arliss glared. "The stories actually say that your clan cast us out."

Merna squinted. "Be silent, girl, until you are called upon."

"She has a point." Maeve folded her hands in her lap. "This is a matter for all three clans. Unless we are *all* united, there cannot be peace."

"What do you propose?"

"I propose the three clans become one. One clan with one ruler."

A murmur rippled through the Anmórian side of the room. Even the Ikarran nobility, who had heard Maeve's intentions at the earlier council, commented among themselves.

Merna gasped. "And who would you propose to rule this clan?"

Maeve sat tall. "Myself."

Chaos erupted. The Anmórians leapt up, shouting threats. Merwin tried to heave himself up, but settled with inciting his lords into frenzy. Domnall tried to smother the dissent from the Ikarrans, but nothing could squelch Orlianna. She paced, shouting for attention.

No one but the Reinholdians heeded her.

Maeve bellowed through the hall, her voice like a dagger. "Enough! We will not behave like children." She inhaled as the crowd silenced. "Let Galcobhar come forth."

Gally hobbled to the center of the room, where he bowed to Merna and Maeve and the empty throne. Was he here, not to support Merna, but to assist Maeve in making peace? Maybe she had misjudged him.

Gally leaned into his staff. "Seasons come and go, but one thing remains the same—the three clans are as different as ever."

Maeve smiled stiffly. "Indeed. Perhaps you would like to elaborate on the proposed matters?"

Gally stared at her. "Of course. Meaning the stage is mine to play on, so to speak?"

Maeve nodded.

"Good." He grinned. "Arliss, come here."

Arliss glanced to Maeve for approval. Maeve bit her lip and grasped the arms of her throne, but she said nothing. Arliss stood, cast one glance back at Philip, and joined Gally in the center.

Gally patted her bare shoulder. His wrinkled hand sent chills down her spine. "If Arliss wishes to speak, I would do nothing to stop her. Speak, princess. Ask questions. Find answers."

Arliss's mouth dropped open as she forgot how to form words. What did she say—really? It seemed that every person from all her adventures was gathered in one place. Even the ghost of Thane seemed to hang over the whole place. How did she sum up her thoughts?

Maeve leaned forward, waiting. Merna tapped her fingernails on the arms of her throne.

Arliss closed her eyes and let her mind drift back to Reinhold. Her mother's parting words reverberated through her head.

"I want you to find out the truth about Thane—about our whole story. For my sake. And not just for mine, but for Eamon's. And not for his alone, but also for Nathanael's."

Her eyelids burned with unshed tears.

She opened them. "I want to know the truth about my story. For a long time, I've traveled a path of confusion. Everyone seems to know more about my world than I do. I have reasons to believe that people in this room are my enemies—that they have played a role in fighting my people, in killing my uncles."

Merna turned pale.

"So I want to know the whole story. I want to know the truth." Arliss curled her fingers. "About Thane."

Merna stammered an answer at once. "I—we—are not your enemy. I know things went rather ill in Anmór, but I tell you, it was never my intent to harm your people."

Arliss hitched up the skirt of her dress and stretched her leg out. Several nobles gasped. She pointed to the deep blemish on her calf.

"I still have a scar from where you stabbed me."

Merna's jaw trembled. "You have no evidence I did that."

"I have witnesses whom I will call up."

Maeve stood. "That is not necessary."

Arliss dropped her skirt. She was done with Maeve's niceties, her peacemaking. The truth needed to cut hard and deep into this crowd. "I think it *is* necessary. I think you all need to stop hiding the truth. Because it's there." She glanced toward Ríon. The set of his jaw proclaimed a confidence he hadn't had in the catacombs.

The catacombs. What was is that Fin had said to her there?

Anmór isn't the only clan with secrets.

Ikarra had secrets. Specifically, Maeve had secrets. Merna knew them. And Ríon did, too, according to Fin. They were all hiding it from her, hiding whatever dark secret they kept. Some hideous thread wound beneath all their stories.

She caught Maeve's gaze and held it. "You know the truth, don't you?"

Maeve's neck tensed. "I am not omniscient. I know many things, but not all."

Arliss felt her concealed indignation burning into a flame. "You have corresponded with Merna. I know you knew about me long before I came here. What else do you know?"

"I know that Thane wanted your land and your gifts."

Arliss jerked her head at Merna. "He wasn't the only one. She would kill to have the gifts of Reinhold. Ríon, tell them! Tell them what your mother said in the catacombs."

Ríon's chest swelled. "I don't take orders from you. But you're right, there are many here who want the gifts. That is why Gally is here."

Arliss glanced to Gally, confused.

Gally sighed. "We all know about the legendary gifts given to the clans—beautiful, but merely symbolic. But there were other gifts, three secret gifts given to the clan of Reinhold. These were scattered and almost lost. But now they have been found. The vial is in the hands of the Reinholdians."

Arliss caught Ilayda's eye. She probably had the vial in her pocket right now.

"The pendant is carried by the Ikarran princess."

Orlianna reached for her neck as if someone would snatch the necklace away.

Gally twisted his staff. "And the sphere—the most mysterious and unknown of all—is also in our midst."

Arliss inhaled. At last! All the searching, and now all the gifts of Reinhold were found. "Where is it?"

Gally reached into the bunched sleeves of his robe. "Here."

He could barely hold the sphere in one hand as he dangled it in front of Arliss' face. The silver ball shone so brightly that it was almost invisible. A dark hole pierced one side of the sphere. Intricate threading wrapped around the middle of the metal ball.

"Thief," Arliss whispered. This betrayal somehow hurt worse even than Ríon's. "That doesn't belong to you."

"It seems fitting, I say," Merna called out. "One secret gift for each clan."

Arliss backed away from Gally. "Are you all in league against us? This is no parley—no war council. I do not know who I'm fighting against!"

"Sit down!" Maeve loomed closer.

Arliss stood her ground. "I can't."

Maeve neared Arliss, her eyes flaring. "Yes, you can. Your time is up. Sit down, or you will regret it."

Philip jumped up. "If anyone lays a hand on Arliss, they will regret it—if they live long enough to, that is."

Merwin chuckled from across the room, his belly jiggling beneath an overstuffed doublet. "This is a parley. You have no weapons."

Philip raised a fist. "I need none."

Maeve shot Philip a glare, and for once something like fear lurked in her eyes. "That is quite enough."

Orlianna stood and joined Philip. "You are not the only voice here, grandmother. Everyone should have a say."

Lachlan leaned forward, wincing. "Orlianna, I appointed your grandmother to oversee this meeting. Please don't argue."

Merwin staggered to his feet. "Maeve, bring your people to sense now, or I will take this city and force you to it."

All hushed.

Arliss froze midstride. Was he serious? Would Anmór really attack on a whim?

Maeve snorted. "Merwin, you and I both know that fighting will get us nowhere. It will only turn this battle into one of blood and not of words."

"Don't you trifle with me." Merwin snarled. "We want the gifts, all of them. We want to own our rightful catacombs once and for all."

Merna added, "And we want the Reinholdians gone."

"*Bí cúramach, bean.*" Merwin snapped something at his wife in the secret Anmórian tongue.

She pushed herself up and thrust her head out at him. "*Tá mé sa cainteoir, ní agat.*"

Merwin blurted a string of words. "*Déanfaimid ionsaí anois. Ba mhaith liom an chathair a bheith linne.*"

Orlianna let out an audible gasp.

Arliss looked at her. Did she understand what they were saying? She'd never heard of anyone non-Anmórian knowing the secret language besides Thane and Eamon.

And…Orlando. He, too, seemed to comprehend the entire conversation.

Merna pointed at Maeve. "You will never rule over us all. I don't know why I have ever trusted you in the first place. You only use me the way you use everyone else. I am done with it."

"You know I am the only one capable of bringing peace," Maeve replied coolly.

Merna's face flamed red, her long eyelashes fluttering. "I don't need peace. I would be content to see this place run with blood as it crashes to the ground, if only the Reinholdian land and treasure could be *mine!* Arliss wants to know the truth. Why don't you tell her?"

Maeve arched her eyebrows. "*Féach ar do focal, deirfiúr. Níl sé am.*"

Orlianna seethed. "Why do you tell Merna to watch her words? What are you hiding?

Maeve gaped at Orlianna. She must not have known her granddaughter also knew the secret tongue.

Arliss flashed a smile. "I second Orlianna's question."

Maeve weighed her words before speaking. "I am hiding nothing. That is perhaps why I am the one qualified to rule these realms. No one detests me. No one contradicts me."

Detest and contradiction rose to the top of Arliss's throat and stuck there. Maeve was right. Somehow, no one in the auditorium denied it. All the nobles, both Ikarran and Anmórian, silently approved.

Arliss choked on the silence. If she was the queen of Reinhold already, they would give her full say about anything. She would be sitting in that empty throne. But she was nothing but a princess, and they were already tiring of hearing her dissension.

Maeve lifted her hands. "Arliss, Merna—please, put this to rest. Almost every soul in this tower is ready to put this all behind us. Are we not all in agreement?"

Arliss tried to speak but could not.

A new voice echoed up the stairs into the gathering. The voice spoke the word that summed up Arliss's mind.

"No!" Clare's sharp voice preceded her as she tromped into the middle of the assembly. "Not everyone. But how can people speak their mind when their tongues are cut off? Merna is holding knives to the throats of every one of her nobles to make them agree with her. And as for those who still disagreed, she simply didn't invite them." She tossed her golden-brown hair. "That means me."

Merna scoffed. "After all I have promised you, you ungrateful liar? And you are alone."

Clare's lips parted to reveal a threatening smile. "Not quite."

Four more people ascended behind her. Finín and Fiach, fully armed and wearing chainmail. And behind them, Rose—the owner of the riverway tearoom—with Mícheál the tavern-keeper at her side. Rose and Mícheál both carried longbows.

Lachlan stammered to Maeve, "Get these…outlaws…out of here."

Maeve clapped her hands. "Domnall!"

Domnall rose, drawing a concealed sword. "All of you, remove yourselves! Or else you will not find yourself here anymore."

Arliss joined Clare and her company. "You won't harm any of them!"

Orlianna rose. "How can you banish them for having weapons when your own right-hand man carries one?"

Lachlan's voice strained. "Orlianna, please! Sit…down."

Desperation edged Orlianna's voice. "I cannot! You are the king of Ikarra. Command them to stand down."

Clare reached for her blade. "We won't stand down."

Rose gripped Mícheál's shoulder. "Trust us, there are many in Ikarra who disagree."

Everyone had risen by now. All edged closer to the center of the room. Arliss found Philip at her back. Orlando stood next to Orlianna. Ilayda and Erik were caught behind the mass of Ikarran nobles.

Everyone had moved, except for King Lachlan in his chair. And as Maeve climbed onto the seat of her throne to elevate herself, he burst into a fit of coughing.

Maeve stopped mid-sentence, pointed finger raised.

Lachlan coughed violently. Blood trickled through his lips and stained the front of his cream overcoat.

A reverent hush smothered the conflict.

Orlianna and Harrison both rushed to his side. Lachlan's breathing had become erratic. His eyes lolled somewhere close to unconsciousness.

Orlianna knelt beside him. "This discord is aggravating his condition."

Harrison pressed the back of his hand to Lachlan's forehead.

"He's sick—very sick. We must take him back to the castle immediately."

The crowd parted as Garrick and another lord moved to help raise the king and carry him away.

Maeve still towered over the crowd. "Shall we adjourn the meeting, Merna, with nothing decided?"

Merna cocked her head. "I think we have made a decision."

"Aye." Merwin nodded, the folds of his neck squashing together. "Maeve, we demand it all—the secret gifts with the gifts that unlock them, the disputed territory in the mountains, and the Reinholdians. Especially that one." He pointed at Orlando.

"And he is very close to you, isn't he?" Maeve hissed.

Merwin wheezed. "Let my secrets be, or I will reveal yours."

Arliss wanted to disappear, to find one of the birds and fly away to Reinhold. But she had pledged to help Orlianna. She had promised Philip she would fight.

Maeve looked exhausted, defeated. She stepped down from the throne. "And if I do not concede to your demands?"

"We will attack your city and turn the river to blood." Merwin sniffed. "You have three days to make your decision."

The tower seemed to be collapsing around Arliss as the parley broke up. Orlianna rushed off with Harrison and the others to see to her father. Merna and Merwin retreated with their group. The echoes of footsteps slowly swirled away to silence.

When she looked up, only Philip, Rose, and Mícheál stood with her.

She glanced around at them. "Three days of agony. Waiting."

Mícheál frowned. "No. There's going to be a battle. There's no way around that."

Rose clamped her arms against her chest. "We need to get ready."

Arliss wanted to collapse onto the stone floor. "Maeve will not go to war."

"I think she will," Rose countered. "She's wanted Merna on her side for a long time. If she can defeat Anmór in battle, it might make her look like the queen of the world."

Arliss couldn't argue. Rose was a true Ikarran, and she was a spy. If anyone knew anything about this, she did.

So they had three days to prepare for the battle of their lifetimes. A battle between the three clans.

Another battle in a war that Thane had begun long ago.

CHAPTER TWENTY-TWO:
DEEPS OF THE HEART

ILAYDA FINALLY FOUND ARLISS SLUMPED AGAINST ONE OF THE FAR windows in the library, her face pressed against the glass. A dark purple sunset stretched its fingers across the sky toward Cahair. Arliss wasn't staring at the sunset, though. Her blue eyes reflected the eastern darkness as she stared—breathless—toward Reinhold.

Ilayda sat on the long marble windowsill beside her. "I should have thought to look here. You've always been the reader."

Arliss still stared beyond. "You've been a reader, too, for as long as I can remember."

"Yes. But it was only the books you shoved into my hands. Really, I think you practically locked me in the castle library sometimes just to make me read with you."

A smile tugged at Arliss's mouth. "Those were the days, weren't they? Days we can never have back."

Ilayda inhaled the scent of old leather and yellowed paper. That time was indeed gone. The old castle and its cozy library were long destroyed. The new city was going to have a much bigger library, much like this one in Cahair, with doors wide open to every citizen. But no matter how much bigger it was built, it would always be a memory—a shadow—of what had come before.

Ilayda flattened her palm against the cool glass. Her reflection peered back at her. "We can't stay here."

Arliss jerked her attention to Ilayda. "What?"

"You know that battle is coming. Neither Lachlan nor Maeve have decreed anything yet, but the rumors are spreading."

"That's why I'm going to be here. God has brought me to Ikarra for a reason. If battle is the way to peace, I will use what skill he has given me."

Ilayda clutched for Arliss's arm. "Arliss, this is why your father feared you coming here! He wanted you to come back alive."

"I swore to stay and fight. I can't back off just when the war is actually starting." Arliss glowered at her. "Are you afraid of death?"

"Yes." Ilayda choked for air. "I am afraid of death. Of blood. Afraid that everything we once called home will be gone forever."

Pressure rose through Ilayda's spine and spread through her ribs. She leaned back against the window, her eyes still on Arliss.

"Send me back," she whispered. "I can warn Kenton. Maybe he's finished his fleet by now. He can bring reinforcements."

Arliss's golden hair shook. "By the time he could return, the fate of the three clans would be decided." She reached for Ilayda's shoulder. "And I won't send you to your doom alone."

"She won't be alone," Erik intoned.

Ilayda turned. He and Orlianna had entered the library silently and now faced the pair by the window.

Arliss looked up at them. "The crogall are still out there. Crossing the ocean is more dangerous than staying here and fighting. And what do you expect to do—captain a ship by yourselves?"

"It's already decided." Erik crossed his arms, one reaching up to prop his chin. "Ilayda and I will take one of the aircraft to Reinhold and bring Kenton warning."

Orlianna nodded her affirmation. "We need every soul who can fight. There are only four birds, but I am willing to sacrifice one for Erik and Ilayda's venture. On the small chance Anmór delays their attack..."

"It is a very small chance." Arliss crossed her arms. "The world could have changed by the time they return."

"We shall see." Erik turned to leave.

Ilayda stood to follow him. Then she halted and reached in her pocket. "Here." She drew out the vial. "You may need this."

Arliss shook her head, her exhausted eyes finding their defiant glint. "Keep it. You need to make it to Reinhold alive."

Orlianna let the weight of the pendant drag her down the bridge toward the funicular that would jerk her up the hill to the castle—to her dying father.

She didn't want to go home. She didn't want to go anywhere. She wanted to climb on one of the birds and soar through the clouds, far beyond the hate which consumed Cahair. She could glide freely as far as she wished. Who could stop her from flying past the North Havens? Who could stop her from flying back to Éire itself?

Yet who knew if that world still existed. The three clans had escaped it long ago to find peace and solitude.

The funicular station stood empty. It seemed she always reached it at dusk, just when the conductor had slipped away. No matter. She unlatched the rusty door and climbed inside.

She popped open the secret compartment in the floor of the car. The smooth wood panel slid out easily, revealing a screw-like crank beneath. Her hands worked quickly, twisting the mechanism swiftly in a rightward arc.

The car staggered up the hill.

The castle was quiet, but lights wavered tenuously in Maeve's tower. No doubt she was counseling the darkness, meeting with her closest advisers, making a decision.

Somehow Orlianna failed to factor into that.

She stumbled across the hilltop to the doors, barely noticing when guards swept them open for her. They should have addressed her as queen. *She* should have been the speaker at the council, not Maeve. The people should answer to her.

Her hair stuck to her cheeks because of tears she didn't remember crying. Did they all want to break her? If only they could realize that she had been broken long ago. Her heart had hardened back into shape—unable to be moved or melded by anyone.

She staggered down a dark hallway. Her eyes were drunk with tears. It didn't matter where she was going anymore.

If battle came, she would fight until her last drop of blood.

Then she would die.

And they would mourn her then, the shadow of the queen that never was. Maeve would regret everything.

Shadows swirled around her.

Suddenly Orlando was right there in front of her, blocking her path down the dark hallway. Gasping for air, she stumbled into his arms. He held her, hesitantly stroking her hair.

She choked sobs into his pocketed jerkin.

"What's wrong?" he ventured.

"I can't do it anymore." She pressed her forehead into his chest. "Everyone casts their burdens upon me. For years I have led Ikarra while my father has gotten the title and Maeve the glory. I cannot anymore."

He examined her. "Are you leaving?"

She stood upright. They were the same height, the green of his eyes mirroring her own. She stepped backward. What was she doing? She couldn't throw her vulnerability upon him. He was too weak to handle it.

"I'm not leaving. I'm going to fight. I will sacrifice all I am."

Orlando set his jaw. "Your people need you. They need you as their leader."

She froze, her hand still on his shoulder. She tried to remove it, but her muscles refused to relax. "I am not a leader. No one follows me. Look at Arliss—all of you follow her. Even Ríon has the loyalty of his band. I have no one."

"That's not true." He touched her arm. His lips quivered as he tried to form his words. "I—I will follow you."

A light flickered in the hungry, desperate pit of her heart. "Even to war? To death?"

He held her gaze.

She leaned closer. "You would even follow me against your own brother?"

He dropped his hand from her shoulder, his dark eyebrows clenching.

She sighed. "He has done much evil. He deserves death."

But did he, truly? Orlando himself had been a spy for Maeve. Had not every soul in the realms done things deserving of death? Could Ríon be redeemed? She wasn't sure.

Orlando's face writhed in unspoken pain. "It's easy to run a sword through a stranger—someone you've never met and will never meet again. But through your own brother? You can't understand what you're asking me to do."

She reached to lift his chin. "Perhaps you can save him. It isn't too late."

He searched her eyes.

She let him bring her close, dangerously close, closer than she had let anyone come since William's death.

"You don't understand," he said. "You don't know the things I've done."

"Nothing is beyond forgiveness." His sandy hair, his emerald eyes, his ruddy lips, took up every bit of her vision. The murky hall vanished.

"How deeply do you mean that?"

"Deeply." She inhaled. For once, the pendant felt light on her chest. "I have not slept these past few days. I have had no rest, because I have been fighting myself."

He silently prodded her for an explanation.

She touched his cheek. It was almost smooth, the beard trimmed close. Much like her brother's had been. "I have searched the deeps of my heart, and I have found you there."

He blinked. "Then why are you fighting yourself?"

"Perhaps...because I do not know what to say."

He swept the last trickle of a tear from her cheek, tucked her hair behind her ear. "Sometimes you don't need to say anything."

And he kissed her.

She closed her eyes as the warmth of his lips melted her icy ones.

At first she wanted to fight it. But everything in her refused to move.

For once, she was loved.

She was followed.

For the first time in years, someone needed her as much as she needed him.

She lost herself in the taste of that. Her hands slipped around the back of his head. Pulling him close. Not wanting the moment to end.

He leaned away slowly, his breath hot against her face. Then he dipped in an awkward bow and slipped away.

As he left, he revealed the gray figure standing in the darkness at the end of the hall.

Maeve.

Orlianna silenced her beating heart. It didn't matter who knew about her feelings. Who knew who would remember it—even survive to remember it—with the impending battle.

Maeve swished down the hall and into the swath of torchlight.

Orlianna inclined her chin in greeting. "Where have you been?"

"Locked in my tower." Maeve waved behind herself. "Scouring every ancient book and map about great battles of old."

"And have you learned any good tactics?"

"I have learned only one thing." Maeve bit the corner of her upper lip. "War leads only to death and destruction."

"But wars end." Orlianna stroked the twisting silver stems on her pendant. "All wars end. If the battles were never fought, the wars would never end."

"If the battles were never begun, there wouldn't be any wars to end!" Maeve spread her arms wide, the drooping sleeves of her dress flapping.

"You can't control the actions of a whole country. Merwin and Merna are set on fighting us. Merna's greedy. She wants the land of Reinhold for her own. Don't you realize that's why she used Thane?"

"Do not speak to me of Thane, as if I know nothing."

Orlianna slid back one step. What *did* Maeve know of Thane? Her grandmother had revealed so many things this past week—knowledge of Reinhold, a desire to rule the realms, and her fluent Anmórian speech. It would be no surprise to find she hid something else.

Maeve hesitated. "If you think Merna greedy, surely you find me far more so, since I wish to rule not just one or two realms—but all three."

Orlianna sighed. This was the woman who raised her, bent her into a leader, fashioned her into a princess of iron. "You are not like Merna."

"Am I not?" Maeve mused, looking out one of the far windows into the nothingness of night. She cut her eyes back at Orlianna. "You seem to have become very free with your heart."

Orlianna winced. How much of the conversation had Maeve seen?

It did not matter. She had seen the kiss, at least, and that mattered more than anything else.

Maeve folded her arms. "I see the way you look at him, and I will not have it."

Orlianna thrust her chin out. "Who are you to command my heart?"

"Granddaughter, he was a villain—an assassin for Merna and for Thane. You cannot trust yourself to him."

"I can't stop myself! I have lost so much of my heart that what is left…it is no longer mine. I cannot control it."

Maeve stared at her, lips parted in disgust. "You are so proud," she hissed. "You think you are the only one in the world who has suffered—and you pride yourself on it! Do you think that the death of my husband did nothing to me? Do you think it has not pained me to watch my son grow more aged and feeble than I?"

Orlianna wanted to hide her face, to run back down the hall and up to her chambers.

Maeve dropped her voice to a rasp. "Or to see my granddaughter rally for war when we should seek peace?"

Orlianna opened her mouth to speak, but what could she say? She could see no other route but fighting. War wasn't the only thing that brought death. Her mother had died in peace. Her brother had been killed during a time of alleged peace.

And the war had started long ago. Arliss was right—this war began in Reinhold with Thane. Merna may have had only a vague connection with him, perhaps. Maeve had clearly never met him. But they were his successors in a fight that would never be over until it was fought.

Maeve reached out to touch Orlianna's shoulder, but recoiled her hand. "Be careful with your heart." She glanced up suddenly, her eyebrows arching as she looked beyond Orlianna.

Orlianna turned. Garrick stood there, his hands clasped together. He looked strangely grim and quiet in the shadows.

Fear caught Orlianna's lungs and squeezed them shut. He didn't have to speak. She knew what he was going to say.

Maeve must have known too, because she could not hide the crack in her voice. "What news, Garrick?"

"My ladies." He paused for a long time, far too long. "The king." His voice broke.

The stone beneath Orlianna's feet melted away.

"He's gone."

CHAPTER TWENTY-THREE: RALLY

ARLISS TROMPED THROUGH YELLOW GRASSES THAT DANCED UP TO HER knees. The area around Garrick's house was absolutely blooming with the stuff—spiny seagrass and sweet vanilla grass mingled together. Using her unstrung bow, she shoved them out of her way as she waded through toward the encampment.

The encampment. It had sprung up overnight in the acre of flat land near the river, in between Garrick's mansion and the Tuáma Fields. Green tents, spread out like crouching frogs, ballooned beneath the sinking sun. High wooden racks held rows of longbows and spears and swords, glinting with anticipation. And everywhere more people kept coming—fighters of all types.

How strange that, ten minutes' walk from the most civilized city in the world, one could find such a primitive settlement. War seemed to bring humankind back to the lowest, basest elements of living. Yet it also brought out the best—the heroic, the noble, the sacrificial.

There had been no grand funeral or mourning for King Lachlan. There was no time. There would be battle on the next morning. All grief would have to wait.

Arliss spotted someone jogging toward her—an attractive young soldier with a snug navy tunic and leather body armor. As he came closer, she saw he wore matching leather vambraces, and that the leather armor was reinforced with chainmail.

She tilted her head at him and waited for him to slow down. He didn't. She called to him. "In a hurry?"

"Yes!" Philip was almost to her. "Harrison needs me back at the castle."

She blocked his way and forced him to stop. "I think they need you here."

His boots tore through grasses as he halted. "That's not false. But Maeve and Orlianna are asking for me, too." He kept walking.

"Then who's in charge here?"

"Ironically, the spies, our new friends who weren't invited to the council."

"And they aren't too miffed?"

Philip shrugged and kept running. "See for yourself. They need your help."

She sped into a jog, heading for the large central tent. Its green flaps were streaked with gold, and the unicorn flag spread from its top. Must have been the royal headquarters. A few horses stamped nearby, tied to a freshly-dug post. But there weren't any Ikarran royalty around.

She swept open the silken flap and slipped inside.

"That *woman!*" Rose was saying. "I'm just about done with her. I could do a better job handling this battle."

Mícheál eased the sword she was holding out of her hands. "Calm down. It's an awkward situation. No one could handle it well."

Arliss slipped in between them and saw the parchment they had rolled onto the round table. "I'm tempted to side with Rose. Maeve is keeping far too many secrets from all of us."

Mícheál set the sword on the table, leaned over the paper, and scratched a marking on it. "Don't encourage her."

Rose shot him a smirk that had at least a drop of amusement.

Arliss ran her finger across the map's lines and arrows. "Battle plans?"

"Something like that." Mícheál smoothed out his navy overcoat. "Not that anyone's taking my advice."

"Why wouldn't they?"

"My parents were Anmórian traders who settled in Cahair. So

despite the fact that I'm a respected businessman and spy, I've always been a bit of an outcast. I guess some people think I might betray Ikarra."

Arliss looked at the plan. It showed wings of the Ikarran army rushing across the Tuama Plains like spikes, stabbing into the Anmórian ranks. Behind that, he had drawn an image of a bow over a shaded oval. Archers. Her place.

She swallowed. It was really happening, the battle between the clans.

"Who's leading the archers?"

Rose exhaled. "That's what we've been trying to decide. Ikarrans are not known for their shooting skills. This is all based on the latest word from Harrison and the rest. But we don't really have anyone to lead the archers." She arched an eyebrow at Arliss, the question lingering.

"I'll do it."

Rose almost smiled. "Good. Mícheál and I will be in your numbers. He's the deadliest archer in the three realms."

"Really?" Arliss stuck the bottom end of her bow in the soft dirt. "That's quite a claim."

"You want to challenge it?" Mícheál asked.

Arliss cocked her head. "If we were at peace, I would challenge you to a round of archery this moment. But now…"

A hush settled over the tent. Hoofs stamped outside, metal clanked as people rushed to and fro. The Anmórian camp on the other side of the fields would be just like this one: planning and waiting.

Rose grew grim, her lips drawn. "Sometimes I wish the world could be quiet. I wish we could all discuss things over a good cup of tea. But no."

"*Tuáma*," Mícheál muttered.

"What?" Arliss rested her bow against the table.

"*Tuáma*. It's the Anmórian word for 'tomb.' The Tuáma Fields—that's where this battle is to be fought."

Arliss gripped each of their shoulders. "I promise, if there is any power in my bow, those fields will not be our tomb."

Rose squeezed Arliss's shoulder. "We'll be with you—no matter what happens."

The castle ballroom had been transformed into an office of war. Councillors and fighters hunched over a maze of tables, buried beneath sheaves of yellowed paper, musty books, and empty pots of tea.

Philip squeezed between two chairs as he navigated the hall. No one noticed him or made any attempt to move their chairs further apart to let him pass.

Where was their fire, their adrenaline? There was to be a battle in the morning. Yet solemnity muffled the anticipation that should have been tangible.

Philip dropped his shoulders. It was understandable. Their king had just died. And for some of them, this wasn't a battle they wanted to fight.

Maeve sat with Harrison, Garrick, and Domnall at a long table at the back of the room, at the base of the grand staircase. A pair of spectacles pinched the end of her nose. Her usually kempt hair drooped in silver strands around her face.

She glanced up, examining him for a moment before returning her attention to her plans. "He's here, Harrison."

Harrison turned in his seat. "Come, lad. There's a little problem you might be able to solve for us."

"Anything." Philip brushed his hair away from his forehead and hooked his hands over the table's edge.

Garrick slid a paper down the table. "With your cousin taking one of the birds back to Reinhold, that leaves us with three. But the math isn't coming out with three pilots."

Dread blocked up Philip's throat and refused to let him swallow. He disliked where this was going.

Garrick rest his goateed chin on his fist. "Orlianna will fly one, of course. I will fly one. But there isn't anyone else qualified to fly. They're all too experienced or too valuable." Garrick cut his gaze up to Philip. "Except you."

"Me?" Philip's hands remained glued to the table. "I can't fly one of those things."

Harrison sat up and regarded Philip. "Orlando flew one briefly just days ago."

Was this some sort of challenge? Philip shot a protest right back. "That wasn't in battle. And if you're so sure of Orlando, why not ask him?"

Maeve caught Harrison's eye.

Harrison exhaled. "We…think it better to have Orlando on the ground, considering his past."

Philip ran his tongue around his teeth. "Does Orlianna agree with this?"

Maeve's fingers crinkled the edges of her map. "This is my command. I expect it to be unquestioned."

Philip scowled at her, then turned back to Harrison. "What about you?"

Harrison cleared his throat. "I'm leading the bulk of the ground forces. Maeve insists she can't spare me. Ikarra's army is very young, with little experience. They need someone with military experience."

Philip pushed up from the table and crossed his arms. They all knew he had experience. Even Maeve was conscious—probably more than conscious—of the fact that he had fought against Thane and Merna and everyone in between. "Then you take the third bird into the air. I will lead the ground troops."

Maeve pressed her map into the table and gaped up at him.

Domnall splayed his fingers out on the table. "Absurd."

"Absurd," Garrick stroked his chin, "But possible."

Harrison's mouth arched as he weighed it. "If Maeve has nothing against it, you have my consent and blessing."

Maeve's eyes searched invisible things—purposes and outcomes that were beyond the sight of those at the table. Philip watched her, waiting. Suddenly she nodded. "Very well. You will lead the infantry into the heart of the battle."

Philip's ears swallowed her words slowly as he realized what they meant. It meant he was walking into death's mouth.

Domnall leaned back. "Then our plan is complete. I call we send it out to the leaders and units. Let them prepare."

Philip started for the stairs. He needed to be alone to prepare for the morrow. He'd been faced with death before. But now, he was going to seek death out and bait it.

Orlando stood on the castle balcony with his hands clasped behind his back, trying to strike a royal posture. He was surrounded by royalty—Maeve and Harrison standing on the opposite side of the balcony, Arliss and Philip on this side. The crowd below them, across the river, gathered in bated expectation on the fringes of the Tuáma Fields.

He tightened his hands around each other. This was it. All the councils, all the plans, and now the fate of the three clans would be decided by a grand battle.

None of them had wanted this, had they? They'd all fought against it like it was hell itself.

Arliss had said so herself back in Reinhold. She'd said they were coming here to stop a war. Philip and Erik had agreed with her. As for Ilayda, she'd come just as much to get away from Reinhold as anything. But she was seeking peace, too, just like all the rest.

And the Ikarrans, weren't they all the same? Orlianna—haunted, driven by grief—wanted nothing more than to keep Anmór and Ikarra separate and peaceful. Harrison was an ambassador, so of course he followed suit. And Maeve's ceaseless cry was unity, unity, *unity*.

He inhaled, his chest straining against the restrictive itch of his layered armor. Loose threads of a linen tunic underlaid a shirt of mail and his usual leather jerkin—with polished shoulder guards of new steel. The burgundy cloak hung behind it all, for once looking dingy and out of place.

He glanced at Arliss beside him. She'd gathered her usually free hair to the side in a loose braid. Her face was tight, staring at the lavender horizon where the sun hesitated to make its ascent.

He sighed. "It's always come to a fight."

"Yes." She rubbed the leather vambrace on her bow arm. "I realize that now. Maybe I should have told myself the truth long ago."

Three stories below, the river churned against the rocks. "You told yourself the only truth you knew."

She shook her head. "It wasn't the truth. It was a hope—a possibility. But the truth is always more than possibility."

A lone horn blared a solemn tune: two ascending notes, then a descending scale that returned to the melody's beginning. Orlando freed his hands from behind his back and let blood flow to his fingers. The tune was almost sad, but the falling notes—even more than the rising ones—held a sense of finality, of resolution.

The hush among the army on the field started to melt. Murmurs snaked through the crowd.

Maeve held up her hand, and quiet settled again. She turned to Harrison. "It is time. She can wait no longer. I will rally them myself if I must."

Harrison made for the double doors. "I will fetch her."

Orlando swallowed as the doors slammed shut. If even Orlianna couldn't face the battle before him, could any of them?

The pounding on the door jarred Orlianna from a dreamless slumber. She jerked her head up from where she'd collapsed against the bed. Her hair had tangled with the sheets just inches from her father's face. She had not been able to let them take him. Not just yet.

The knock echoed through the hollow room again. "Orlianna,

it is time."

"The door isn't locked." She sat up as Harrison eased the door open.

He was arrayed for battle, his uniform cut down to the bare basics he would need for flying. The gray of his tidy beard and cropped hair did nothing to diminish his handsome appearance.

He crossed to the bed and lifted the leatherbound Bible from where it lay on the bed, open from last night. He scanned the pages. "The prophet Isaiah?"

"He faced dark times as well. He speaks as if it were a battle." She stood and stroked the silken pages. "Then shall your light break forth like the dawn, and your healing shall spring up speedily; your righteousness shall go before you; the glory of the Lord shall be your rear guard."

He faced her, the book open on his palms. "The people are waiting for you. They look to you to rally them—as their leader."

She folded her arms. "I am not their leader. Maeve is. Why does she not rally them? Father left her in charge."

She turned on her heel and paced to the intricate flight dress that hung, waiting, from her dressing screen. She grabbed up the folds of linen and leather and buried her face in them.

Harrison did not cross the room to comfort her as he so often had. He stood still, raising his voice. "You are their leader. A leader fights, no matter the state of her own heart, because her people matter more."

Orlianna clenched fistfuls of the dress as she pressed her forehead to the screen. "They do not call me queen. If we win this battle, if Maeve succeeds, they will look to her."

"If Maeve doesn't stand in your way, rule rightfully passes to you. And I don't care if you have the title. You are the queen in my eyes." His boots clicked as he stepped toward her. "You must rally the people."

She released the dress and faced him. She shuddered out a deep breath and let her lungs find their confidence.

He smiled and gripped the book with renewed animation as he

read, "Your ancient ruins shall be rebuilt. You shall raise up the foundations of many generations. You shall be called the repairer of the breach, and the restorer of streets to dwell in." He closed the book. "Such shall you be, Orlianna. Such shall you be."

The double doors to the balcony parted for Orlianna as she strode forward into the cloudy morning air. The western sky was thick with confusion, and the rising sun behind her was hidden in vapor.

Below, the army crowded the plains. Her army. They gathered below already in distinct units, already prepared for battle.

Beyond the Ikarran forces, half a mile of virgin field separated them from the Anmórian camp. Merwin's army had also assembled. They were a glint of silver death on the horizon—waiting.

She turned to her right. Arliss, Philip, and Orlando stood there, silently supporting her. How true they were! How little time she had known them, and yet they stuck like family. She would be proud to fight alongside them.

To her left, Maeve—the only real family she had left. And beside her, Harrison—her strength, her confidant, her right arm. He would fly beside her always.

She stepped forward and grasped the white marble railing. "People of Ikarra! We are gathered on ancient fields to continue an ancient battle—the clash between the three clans."

The people held their breath.

She filled her lungs with the bitterness of the April morning. "This is a fight that goes back further than the fight between Ikarra and Anmór. This is a fight between lordship and tyranny. It is a fight between freedom and slavery. It is between light and dark, truth and deception. This is the battle you will fight today!"

The crowd roared, raising weapons. Orlianna's fingers tingled. Her body knew better than her mind what was coming.

A sudden heat rushed up the back of her neck, and her shadow spread out below, onto the rocks and the river. She looked up behind her. The sun had broken free of the clouds and the castle.

She raised her hands. "Do you see the sunrise? It rises over a free Cahair, a free Ikarra. It rises over your families, your children. They are free to run in the fields, to swim in the rivers, to drink in the glory of God's world. And that is why you will fight. You will fight so that the sun may yet rise." She drew her long knife and stabbed it up into the glint of the sunrise. "For Ikarra."

A battle cry rumbled through the companies, starting at the front and rolling to the back like a wave. It shook the river's water and rattled the foundation of the castle itself. A shiver prickled the skin up and down Orlianna's spine. The people were responding to her words.

"For Ikarra!" The cry continued. "For Ikarra!"

Her world spun, and for once it was a world in which she was the queen.

She turned to her friends. Philip had raised his sword, Arliss her bow.

Beside her, Orlando raised nothing, but he nodded at her. "For Ikarra."

And if he was with her, little else mattered.

CHAPTER TWENTY-FOUR: THE FIRST CHARGE

PHILIP RUBBED SHOULDERS WITH THE TENSE FRONT LINE OF SOLDIERS. They were silent and stiff, no longer the rowdy lads who had roared in agreement with Orlianna's speech. Now—faced with such an enemy as lined the plains across from them—battle was real.

Philip's blood pulsated through his fingers as he curled them. The battle plans had been whittled down to simplicity. The three Ikarran companies would stab into the Anmórian ranks like three swords, leaving them vulnerable for attacks from the other, more unexpected, entities.

His company—which should have been Harrison's—stood exposed in the center of the battlefield. To his left, a lord named Rowan rode with a few other horsemen at the head of his contingent. Orlando was among their numbers. To the right, Domnall towered on his mount, a step ahead of his men.

Philip flared his nose. He wanted to be right here on the ground among the rest when the battle began.

And it was beginning. The silver flash of the Anmórian lines crept forward across the plains. They were all on foot, armed in glittering plate armor, wielding long spears and swords.

He glanced around. The Ikarran ranks did not shine. They blended in with the fields, the earth. Jerkins of muddy green and brown layered mail shirts. A few, such as himself, had plated shoulders. Domnall wore a full breastplate. But most dressed light.

He looked over his shoulder. The archers stayed behind the rest of the company, on the elevated span of rocks that lined the river. Arliss was back there. And back there—he hoped—she would stay.

Anmór broke into a full-on charge. Their yells thundered across the field. Philip's ears tingled. The hairs on the back of his neck turned into needles.

Somewhere in Domnall's company, someone started to beat a drum. It pulsed through the ground and got into the flow of Philip's blood.

The men of his company tensed, ready to charge.

He drew his sword and held it at arm's length. "Hold fast!"

Anmórian soldiers trampled the yellow grasses and speckled red flowers that carpeted the fields. They had closed half the distance now.

That meant they were within bowshot.

He lifted his sword high in the air so that it could be seen by all.

Arliss knew her fingers were shaking, so she gripped her bow harder. Merwin's army charged across the field, yet still none of their own companies advanced. Were they going to let themselves be run over?

A bright light flashed at the head of the center company. *Philip.* That was his signal.

She drew an arrow from the quiver at her side. It felt almost unfamiliar. It had been nigh five months since she had drawn her bow in true battle.

"Arrows on string!" she shouted.

Rose at her left, Mícheál at her right, nocked arrows as the other fifty or so archers did the same.

"Now?" Rose asked.

Arliss raised her bow and fixed her eyes on the head of the Anmórian lines. They were barely within bowshot. And Philip's company had not yet charged. "Not yet."

She closed her eyes.

The drumbeat raged in Philip's bones now, pulsing as blood rushed through his head.

Fight.

He closed his eyes. He saw Reinhold—as it was, as it had been. The city he had grown up in. The city he had seen fall.

Kill.

The images flicked beneath his eyelids too fast. The snakes in the forests of Reinhold. The crogall bursting from the sea. Thane on his throne, fingering a goblet. Maeve lifting her glass, toasting unity.

Conquer.

Thane's fortress crumbling as he disappeared. Merna's dress in flames. Eamon's body lying in the snow. The last glance of Reinhold's shores before they had come to Ikarra.

He inhaled, and the visions fled. He opened his eyes.

"Charge!" He leapt forward, sword up, arms pumping, picking up speed, feeling like he was running through water. The field swept along beneath him.

"Now, Arliss," he whispered to himself. The lines were thirty paces away. "Now."

A gust of wind forced Arliss to open her eyes. A west wind—in their favor. She stared heavenward. The clouds swirled, threatening mist or even rain.

But this wind was the breath of God himself, flowing across the fields in the direction of her shots.

She drew back her arrow. The other archers did the same.

"Fire!"

She relaxed her fingers and let the first arrow of the battle fly.

Orlando sprinted through his company, outpacing every Ikarran soldier. He wasn't going to hide comfortably in the middle of the contingent. He would be the first to join blades with Anmór.

He squeezed through the mob. Was this right? He was an Anmórian by birth. These were his countrymen, even his family.

But they had abandoned him. They had enslaved him. Now, they had demanded his life as a ransom price.

He drew his sword and one of his knives. He—the prized pupil of Thane, pet of Merna—would chop straight through their ranks. They would learn the true value of his life.

Orlando broke free of his unit, boots pounding over free grass.

A volley of arrows swept over his head and into the enemy's front lines.

The two armies met.

A sound like a train hitting a stone wall erupted all around him. Battle cries turned to strangled yells. The first casualties were trampled into the dead grasses below.

He leveled an enemy warrior and kept running. After the initial clash, the battle would thin out—spread out—and it would be hard to keep up with what was going on. Arliss's arrows had already cast the initial Anmórian charge into confusion.

A thickly armored soldier sprang at him, screeching, "*Maidir le fuil!*"

The enemy cut straight down toward Orlando's head.

He dropped to his knees and raised both his weapons. He cut straight through the soldier's sword arm just as his knife disappeared in his chest.

The soldier and his arm dropped separately onto the field.

Orlando kept running, but his stomach tried to drag him down. Nausea burned deep in his belly. He wanted to slap himself across the face. What was this—weakness? He'd never shied from a fight before. Under Merna, the blood of his enemies had been his fuel.

Merna. She was going to pay for this. She was going to answer for her crimes.

He scanned the chaos. Philip's company was shearing through the Anmórians. Further away, Domnall's company met with stronger resistance, and they were scattered—just like his own company.

On the opposing side, Merwin's troops continued their forward march. Where was their command coming from? Orlando didn't see Merwin anywhere on the battlefield.

He looked to the square tower of rotting stone that obstructed the center of the fields.

Merna stood at its pinnacle, in flashing armor overlaying a dress that shimmered green even in the cloudiness. With one hand she made signals to her troops.

With the other, she held a ball of light.

The sphere of Reinhold. Orlando clenched his sword.

He ran for the watchtower, legs pumping, heart flipping over itself. Merna's evil was going to come to an end.

Arliss lost sight of Philip the moment the armies collided, but that didn't stop her from scouring the field for him as she drew back a fourth arrow. He simply wasn't there.

She blinked, her chest throbbing. She forced herself to take even breaths. There was no need to worry about Philip. His skill with the sword outmatched every enemy he'd faced.

Unless, of course, this enemy was different.

She released her arrow and watched a distant soldier collapse near the base of the watchtower. The structure was barely within bowshot. In fact, most of the other archers weren't even aiming that far. She was surprised to have made the shot.

Merna stood atop the tower, surrounded by a circle of armored guards. It would take both fire and sword to reach her.

Arliss stepped to the very edge of the ridge the archers stood on. It was three heights of a man to the bottom—four in some places.

Her boots scraped gravel off the edge of the cliff, and it rained to the ground below.

She nocked an arrow and raised it, letting the tip block out Merna from her vision. If the wind was just right, if the height was perfect…

She huffed, lowered her aim, and loosed the arrow at another soldier in front of the tower. There was no hitting Merna from up here. But she *had* to be stopped. From there, she could control her entire army and give them a unity that the Ikarran forces simply didn't have.

Mícheál nudged her with his bow. "Anmór is moving east—toward us."

"But why?" Rose lowered her bow. "If they get much closer, we'll send them a volley."

Mícheál was on to something. Arliss peered at Merna. The Anmórian queen was raising her hands dramatically. Her raised hand seemed to be glinting in the erratic shafts of sunlight that stabbed through the clouds. She was giving a signal—a change of direction.

Then she saw it. A cloud of dust smoked the fields far to the right of the main Anmórian army. The wave of dirt rolled across the fields—fast—eastward.

Arliss gulped. Chariots. And those chariots could only be led by one person.

"Arliss—" Rose nocked an arrow.

Arliss felt like she'd been punched in the stomach. The chariots were not heading for the battle. They were speeding toward Cahair itself.

She gripped her bow and sprinted along the ridge's edge.

Rose and Mícheál's footsteps pounded behind her. The chariots emerged from the cloud of dusty grasses they churned up. She could see Ríon now—clad in gold and riding at the head.

Rose rushed alongside her. "Plan?"

"Ríon's chariots—they're trying to cut us off." Arliss panted. "They're riding straight for the city."

It was all so obvious now. Merna had personal feuds with the Reinholdians. She wanted them all dead, their heads served to her on platters. But Merwin was the one in charge of this battle's plans. And his tactics turned out to be simpler: storm Ikarra, enter the city, and take it.

Why had they not expected this? They had anticipated Merna's snaking mind. But Merwin's heavy hand was making the first move.

And what was more—if Ríon made it to Cahair, he would reach Garrick's barn first. If Orlianna had not yet taken off, he would destroy the birds before they made it to the battle.

She kept running. Her calves were flaming. The ridge curved—the dropoff to her left, the river rushing along to her right, with the castle just beyond.

The chariots were closing in.

Arliss slid to a halt at the cliff's edge. "We have to stop him. Before he gets to the city."

Rose lowered her chin. "I'm with you."

Arliss turned to Mícheál and motioned at the archers clustered all along the ridge. "Stay and lead the archers in my stead. We will return."

Mícheál only stared, his head cocked slightly. "Just because you're in charge doesn't mean you get to command me."

Arliss's brows shot up. She hadn't expected that out of him. "Mícheál, the archers need a leader."

"Then stay with them." He adjusted his bow grip. "Because I'm going where Rose goes."

Rose smirked.

Arliss found herself nodding. They had to stay together. She swiveled to face the incoming chariots. Their wheels rumbled toward them. Ríon had the horses' reins wrapped around one hand.

She slipped her bow around her torso. If she timed it just right, and Ríon didn't change course, she could catch an easy ride.

Rose had read Arliss's movements. "You aren't really doing this."

Arliss fixed on the chariot, her legs tense and slightly crouched. "Why not?"

Mícheál crouched beside her, his sharp jaw thrust out. "Jumping onto a moving chariot is a little dangerous, you know."

The chariots would pass below the ridge in a few seconds. Arliss's heartbeat swirled beyond count. "I've done it before."

Rose tensed. "Ríon's insane. He'll kill you."

"Actually, last time I jumped onto a moving chariot, it was Ríon's."

Arliss revisited the moment in her mind. The backs of her arms prickled. She could almost feel the snow that covered the ground in *that* battle.

She opened her eyes, focused.

She jumped.

The air felt like water, like the breath of ghosts trying to force her upwards. Each second retreated into itself. She turned weightless. The end of the fall would never come.

She hit the chariot's metal platform so hard she was sure she'd broken a few fingers. The force rattled up through her bones. Then, just as suddenly, the chariot's momentum sent her sliding off the back.

She grappled for anything she could hold. Her palm slapped against leather. Ríon's boot. She grabbed and held.

Ríon tried to kick free, but she held fiercely on. He fell forward against the front of the chariot, his mouth hitting the edge. She used his leverage to pull herself up as he turned on her.

"Fool!" He spat out blood. "You should be dead after that stunt."

"Well, I'm not." Arliss steadied herself with one hand and drew her long knife.

"No matter." Ríon flashed a grin. Still holding the reins, he drew a short sword. "I can kill you just fine myself."

Arliss took a shaky step back. He was restrained by the reins, so he couldn't quite reach her if she leaned back. It was just far enough.

So she took the risk. She sheathed her knife and inhaled. Dusty river air bogged in her lungs.

"Please. See sense. Don't keep fighting this on the wrong side."

Ríon's hand turned white were the straps wrapped around it. He casually faced the ground before them. "The wrong side? How does that figure?"

Arliss wanted to kick his turned back. "The side who helped Thane? The side who killed both my uncles! The side that rejected you for years. How could that possibly be the right side?"

Ríon turned his head halfway. "The side who helped Thane, indeed. You know so little."

"I'm sick of people pretending like I don't know my own story. I have *lived* it. I am Thane's own cousin. I know the truth."

"But you don't." Ríon pulled the horses right as the river kept curving. The chariot slowed around the curve. "You never have."

Arliss looked up. The ridge was drooping down into an actual riverbank, and Rose was running along its brink. Mícheál wasn't with her. Rose looked down at the chariot.

They only caught eyes for just a moment, but Arliss knew Rose understood her mind as well as she did hers.

Rose threw herself from the side.

Her jump seemed so quick compared to the eternity Arliss had leapt through. She hit the chariot standing up, and Arliss reached out to steady her and break her fall.

Ríon whirled. "Who the devil are you?"

"Nobody." Rose clenched her fists at her side. "Just someone who likes the truth and will fight for it."

Arliss nudged Rose's foot and mouthed Mícheál's name.

Rose glanced beyond Arliss.

Arliss turned just as another chariot swerved so close it almost collided with theirs.

Ríon swore and jerked right, nearly driving them into the river.

Mícheál gripped the reins, guiding his commandeered chariot so close that the whirling wheels nearly sparked flames with Ríon's. "You won't set foot in Cahair!"

Ríon thrust his sword at Arliss. "I *will* kill you both."

Rose drew an arrow, tottering to keep her balance. "I don't think so."

"Stopping me won't do anything." Ríon's attention lurched back and forth between his driving and the two ladies. "The real battle is behind us."

"You're stalling." Arliss drew an arrow. Her other hand vibrated where she gripped the wooden edging. "Turn this chariot around."

"*No.*"

Arliss let go of the side and nocked her arrow. Before Ríon could react, she made her shot—right through the reins that attached the right horse.

The chariot swerved left, almost flinging Rose off. Rose slammed into the far side. The horse kept running along the river, but the chariot weaved wildly away.

Ríon lost his grip on the other rein. He stumbled into Rose.

Arliss grabbed for the rein that whipped in the wind.

Suddenly the chariot was hers. Every turn of the wheels crunched up through the leather and rattled her bones. She pulled tension into the reins, but this was nothing like riding Kirras. The remaining horse had been bred for battle, so it kept going—but she had no idea how to control it.

Mícheál still sped along them. Rose pushed Ríon off, pulled herself up the side of the chariot, and leapt over onto Mícheál's platform.

"Arliss, come on!" Rose motioned.

Arliss took a panicked glance around. They were heading back into the thick of battle. Misaimed arrows or spears could fly right through them, and they'd all be dead.

Then she remembered the tower. Merna. That's where they would go.

Ríon staggered to his feet. "Drop the reins, idiot."

"Don't you dare." Rose drew her arrow in the other chariot, her eyes huge.

Ríon placed the tip of the blade against Arliss's back. Her shoulders went taut. "Drop them."

Rose's voice tottered. "I will kill you!"

"No!" Arliss stared at the battlefield as they wormed through empty spaces between combatants. "Don't kill him."

"He's dangerous!" Mícheál affirmed. "Finish him."

"He is dangerous," Arliss agreed. "But he is my friend."

The poking tip slipped from between her shoulder blades. Ríon exhaled sharply.

She relaxed.

Then Ríon grabbed her by the shoulders and ripped her away from the reins, throwing her over the side.

She grabbed the indented edge as her toes scraped through the grass.

Blood fled her fingers as she fought to stay on, to not be dragged through the field and trampled into mush. She knew Rose was shouting something at her, but she couldn't hear over the rasp of the wheels.

She looked up. They were almost to the watchtower. And they weren't slowing down.

Watchtower. Merna. Sword. Fire.

Fire.

She struggled to get air into her lungs. "Rose! Fire! A fiery arrow!"

Her arms burned, the muscles almost spent. She screamed in pain as she pulled herself halfway back onto the chariot.

Beside them, Mícheál had transferred the reins to one hand. With the other he drew a sword and rested it against his chariot's turbulent wheels.

Sparks jumped from the metal. One hit Arliss's cheek and burned for a second.

Rose had cut a strip from the reins and wrapped it around her arrowhead. She stuck it next to the river of sparks that rushed from the friction. And she shot—her arrow sticking in the wooden rim that edged the whole chariot.

The flames spread around the chariot's edge and down the wooden harness. They licked at the horse's side, chewed through the last of the reins.

The horse bolted free of Ríon's chariot. The chariot crashed into Mícheál's with a sickening, metallic crunch.

All four riders were thrown into the grass.

Arliss's head slammed into the ground. For a few moments she felt only basic sensations. Grass tickling the inside of her ear, blood filling her mouth.

Then she heard Merna's laugh.

CHAPTER TWENTY-FIVE:
TRUTH

PHILIP KEPT THE RUINED WATCHTOWER DEAD AHEAD AS HE CHARGED through the Anmórian ranks, scything the enemy wherever they dared oppose him. His blood had turned into a river that filled his muscles with new life, new strength. This was a fight in a foreign land, on a strange field with unfamiliar flowers and grasses.

But he was fighting for Reinhold.

He was fighting for Arliss.

He spun, arcing his sword through an opponent, and glanced toward the archers' ridge. Arliss's dark green hunter's garb and golden hair weren't up there anymore.

He swallowed the saliva that filled the papery insides of his mouth. He'd told her to stay put on the ridge. He didn't have time to head the main wing of the army *and* protect her.

And now she'd run off like a bloody fool, probably straight into the midst of the battle.

A yell stung his ears from behind. He turned, blocked the enemy's thrust, bashed him across the face, and let his sword find its mark.

He glanced back again, beyond the ridge. Across the river on the castle balcony, a tall shape glinted like moonlight at midday. Maeve was nothing but a pillar of gray light from this distance. But he knew she took in everything that went on.

"Philip!"

He whirled in the direction of his name. It was Orlando—his

burgundy cape streaming behind him as he fought his way through two opponents at once.

Philip grabbed an axe from his recently felled opponent and sent it whirling into one of Orlando's assailants. The enemy crumpled, and Orlando bounded the last few paces.

Philip grasped his shoulder. "I'm glad you made it."

"Any clue as to Merwin's plans?"

"None. He's nowhere to be found, but his soldiers are swarming like flies."

Orlando pointed with his knife. "Perhaps *she* has something to do with it."

Philip faced the tower again. Merna and her guards stood like grim statues atop it, almost inviting an attack. And if he knew Arliss, she was probably headed straight for the Anmórian queen.

He levied his sword. "What're we waiting for?"

Orlando stiffened. He stared west—just beyond the further fringe of Anmórian troops. A rusty cloud billowed across the fields toward the river—toward the city. It sparked like lightning.

"What is—" Philip stepped forward.

"Chariots." Orlando caught his eye. "Ríon."

Then Philip saw three figures running along the ridge, right in the path of the chariots. The bow in the lead figure's hand only made her silhouette all the clearer.

He headed toward the ridge. "Arliss is over there."

Orlando grabbed his left shoulder plate. "She can handle herself. Merna must be stopped."

"Stop her yourself." Philip whirled, blood burning the inside of his cheeks. "Arliss is more important than your personal agenda."

Orlando leaned back, head cocked, but his eyes looked hurt. "She's *your* personal agenda, Philip. We all have a score to settle with Merna. And I want to hear the truth from her lips. She's obviously kept secrets about Thane. I want to know who I used to work for—really." He glanced skyward. "And Arliss won't be alone."

Philip clenched his teeth to stifle a groan. He followed Orlando back toward the watchtower.

But he couldn't help glancing back. When he did, Arliss, Rose, and Mícheál had disappeared from the ridge, and he could no longer see the chariots due to the shadowy fray of battle between them. Yet something new dotted the plain—a new shape, clad in silvery gray, leaping from the ridge, darting across the plain.

Philip grabbed Orlando's arm and forced him to stop.

The gray figure stopped and pivoted, lifting an arm as if in a signal.

Up on the balcony, Maeve raised both hands, then thrust them down again.

The figure turned and kept running, straight toward Merna's tower.

Philip reached for his second sword, which he hadn't yet drawn. Something was wrong—very, terribly wrong. Maeve…this strange newcomer…secret signals. His entire torso tensed. His breath balled up in his lungs. This messenger was sent by Maeve, the extemporaneous leader of Ikarra. But everything in him, as sure as if it was the voice of God himself, screamed that this was a move of the enemy.

He spun, taking a quick view of the battlefield as he prayed. *Lord, where am I to go? Which enemy am I to fight?*

Orlando's eyebrows went up. Waiting.

Philip exhaled. *Who is the enemy?*

He started moving again, picking up speed. "That messenger— something's not right about him. He's heading straight for the tower. I'm going to intercept him and find out what's going on."

"But Merna?"

"We'll deal with Merna, too."

Darkness suddenly shrouded the ground before Philip's feet. A shadow flicked between him and the clouded sun. He glanced up, legs straining to speed across the field.

Orlando whooped and raised his blade.

A cheer rippled through the Ikarran troops.

Three of the birds were flying—swooping above the battle. A

flash of red fieriness streaked in the foremost plane. Orlianna had arrived.

But she wasn't the only one.

The vehicles flitted by in two seconds, but Philip saw them clearly: two chariots, one driven by Mícheál with Rose on board, the other driven by Ríon with Arliss hanging desperately on.

He ran faster than he'd ever run in his life, forcing his body to do more than it thought it could. Burning pain screamed up his legs. He licked his dry lips and let the pain fuel him.

The silhouette of Orlianna's aircraft was still right above them. She swooped lower now, using a crossbow to fire at the enemy while she steered with one hand. She cleared the fields before him and Orlando, creating a clear path for them.

Everything had become a blur, even Orlando beside him.

All he knew was he had to get to Arliss.

Orlianna knew that, to Philip and Orlando on the ground, the battle was a confusing mess. But to her, high above, she could see the greater picture—the companies converging and blending, the two armies clashing in a systematic cacophony of metal.

But, for the life of her, she couldn't determine why Ikarra's two best foot soldiers were running *away* from the battle.

Philip and Orlando were no cowards. Yet there they were, dashing madly from the thick of the fray and toward the ruined watchtower. She couldn't just turn about and let them be cut down. She had no choice but to fly right above them and shoot down whoever and whatever jumped in their path.

Her right forearm was starting to ache where she gripped the steering stick. She jerked her weight to the other side and swapped hands, dropping the crossbow from her left hand and grabbing it from the air with her right.

She smiled. Ah, that was better. She eased the plane a touch lower and surveyed the skies behind her.

Harrison and Garrick spread out to either side, causing confusion of their own among the main Anmórian forces. Bloody good. She could follow this trail for a moment.

Wind breathed straight through her leather getup and linen dress, and it burned her skin. She opened her mouth and laughed into the wind. The very nature of Ikarra was fighting these Anmórian infidels.

Soldiers fell left and right, her crossbow bolts in their backs. The rest scattered, screaming in confusion.

These were the birds of Ikarra.

She was the wind, the sky.

None could bring her down.

Philip had seen her now, and he was waving at her. "Orlianna!"

She dropped low, nearly brushing through the grasses as she circled him. "What?"

He cupped his hands to his mouth. "The messenger!" He pointed back toward the castle.

She flew in that direction now, so she scoured the fields for said messenger. There he was—one of Maeve's grey-clad errand boys. What was one of them doing in the middle of a battle?

She circled Philip again and caught the three words he shouted. "Merna—Maeve—treachery!"

She swallowed, and her throat sank down into her stomach. This couldn't be. But Philip had an intuitiveness about him, a perception that rivaled even her own practiced senses. She could trust him with anything.

She pulled the bird up higher again. The air turned colder. She shivered. The cold was a friend to her. She had never feared it, never despised it. She flew a few spans higher and took a fuller view of the battlefield.

Philip's and Rowan's companies had merged into one. They had pierced through the main Anmórian army and now spread out. With Philip gone, though, they lacked a sense of direction.

She pivoted the bird again, heading back toward the watchtower. To the left, Domnall was making valiant headway, but he couldn't break the enemy lines.

And the archers on the ridge…they had scattered all along, even where the river curved around the castle. What had drawn them?

She held her breath. Chariots. A dozen of them. Some were driving straight through the battle, but others headed toward the city.

Her hand trembled on the steering stick. She could fly over them and cut them off. The battle would be fine without her.

But Philip needed her aid as well. He was onto something. Merna's command post was the ruinous watchtower. If they could destroy it, her plans would be foiled.

But if even *one* chariot rampaged the city…if even some innocent Cahairian civilians fell when she could have done something…

She had to go to the city. She *would* go to the city.

She glanced down once more. Philip, she could not spot. He blended in too much. But she could make out one warrior in a burgundy cloak, almost to the watchtower.

Orlando turned and searched the skies for her.

She dropped a few feet through the wispy clouds.

He waved frantically at her, pointing toward the tower's base.

And then she saw the chariot wreck.

Orlando's muscles iced over as he reached the tangled heap of metal—the remains of two of Ríon's chariots.

Philip stumbled to a halt beside him, panting hard. "Arliss?"

Orlando scanned the wreckage. Charred wood lay amidst the twisted metal, and patches of dry grass coughed up remnants of a flame. The wreckage stretched nearly to the old watchtower.

He looked to the tower and felt like the air had been punched from his lungs. There at the base, golden hair tangling with the grass, lay Arliss. She wasn't moving. He couldn't even tell from here if she was breathing.

He pointed. "Over there."

Philip's staggered forward. "Arliss!"

A hand appeared from the middle of the wreckage. Ríon heaved himself over the side of the overturned chariot and landed in the grass with a thud. His hair had swept into his eyes and now stuck to his bloodied forehead.

Orlando swallowed and raised his knives. They had to get to Arliss.

Ríon spat. "Look who it is—my bastard brother and his barbarian companion! Dandy. I can do away with you both at once."

"Move," Philip pointed both his swords, "or I'll rip every one of your limbs from your body."

Ríon knelt in the grass and lifted a piece from the wreckage—a long metal pole, taller than he was. He held it at arm's length. "Go ahead."

Philip charged Ríon with a yell.

Orlando ran toward Arliss, but another new figure rose up and blocked his path. Her jade silk swished beneath the clank of a gaudy breastplate. She held no weapon, unless the silver ball in her left hand counted. But she still made his mouth turn dry.

Merna licked her lips. "Just who I wanted to see."

Orlando edged toward Philip's fight. "I can't say the same."

"You always were afraid. Always leaning toward weakness." She lifted the ball. "I never should have trusted in you."

"Why did you, then?" He seethed.

"Because you were the most talented warrior in Anmór, even greater than the son who was truly mine." Her eyes flickered. "And when Thane needed a spy, it was an easy way to get rid of you without having to kill you."

Of course she had always despised him. Back when he served her, he'd wondered why. When he found out his true identity, it all made sense. Naturally she would spurn the offspring of her husband's infidelity.

But to have her spell out that she had always wanted him dead...

He pointed the twin knives at her. The mother-of-pearl rubbed familiarly against his palms. "Then why not kill me now?"

"Good idea." She inclined her chin, looking beyond him. "Do not worry. Your death is on its way."

He stole a glance behind him. The gray messenger still sped toward them.

Philip was oblivious. He wielded both swords against Ríon's staff as they both spun around the wreckage in a whirlwind of metal.

Behind Merna, Arliss had shoved herself up. Blood trickled down her forehead and cheek, and her slit skirt and leather armor were dirty and singed. But she still had her bow and a half-quiver of arrows.

Orlando snapped his gaze to Merna again, but she had already followed his eyeline. She turned and saw Arliss placing an arrow on her bow.

Arliss stood tall. "Call off your company."

Merna's chest rose and fell quickly. "Arliss, Arliss, dear girl. You are confused. This battle cannot be stopped now. It will rage on until victory is decided."

Arliss shook her head. "I *will* kill you."

The blood left Merna's face. "You couldn't kill me. I know too much—too many things you wish you could know. No one else will tell you. If you kill me, my secrets die with me."

Orlando glanced between Merna and the approaching messenger, then tried to catch Arliss's eye. "What secrets?"

"If I told you, they'd no longer be secrets." Merna backed away.

Arliss looked at Orlando. She looked ready to release her arrow.

He shook his head and glanced at the castle. *Treachery.* He mouthed. *Kill the messenger.*

She turned back to Merna, but the corner of her mouth twitched with a restrained smirk. The messenger was almost within bowshot. But they had to keep Merna's attention from their unspoken plan.

Orlando filled his chest with air. "I am free of you. I'm no longer afraid."

Merna snorted. "Everyone is afraid. And I know your fears. I know what haunts you and refuses to let you sleep in the bitter shadows of the night. I know what makes your breaths shallow and your laughter thin."

He wheezed for air. If she cast his past sins in his face—as only *she* could—she could break him in an instant.

He kept his voice steady. "You don't control me anymore."

"I can break you in an instant. Do they know your secrets?" Merna glanced skyward. "Does Orlianna know all your secrets?"

Above, Orlianna circled the watchtower, flying lower. She was watching everything intensely. Was she going to try to land? Surely she wouldn't risk the bird falling into Anmórian hands.

Behind him, Ríon shouted angrily. He still whirled his metal pole, but it was hooked at one end—probably twisted by a blow from Philip. But they weren't fighting anymore. A different soldier had engaged Philip.

Ríon fled up the staircase that was built into the side of the square tower. He was trying to get higher. High enough to bring Orlianna down.

Orlando bolted for the tower

Merna screeched, "Stop!"

He froze. What could she do to stop him?

Arliss raised her bow in warning. "No, you stop. We know what you're up to, and we can bring you down in an instant."

Merna motioned up to where Ríon readied his hooked spear atop the tower. "So can we."

Orlando's abdomen clenched. He was being pulled apart—to pursue Ríon, to face Merna, to meet the approaching messenger. And from above, Orlianna. If she fell, and he could have stopped it...

He darted for the staircase.

It was too late. Ríon threw his projectile at the swooping bird. The spear tore through the left wing, and its hooked end stuck in the frame. The bird jerked left and down. Orlianna fought madly for control.

Merna screamed.

Orlando whirled. The gray messenger had collapsed, Arliss's arrow in his chest. The parcel he had been carrying dropped into a patch of burning grass.

He ran. But Merna had been ready. Before he could reach her, she had nudged the parcel out of the flame and lifted its contents. The paper casing had burned away, revealing the crown of Reinhold.

Arliss's crown.

Orlando froze. This was Maeve's messenger. Maeve...*she* had sent this gift to Merna?

Merna smirked, fingering the sphere in one hand and the crown in the other. "One secret gift for each gift of Reinhold. Like a lock—" She lined the crown up with the sphere. It wrapped like a vine around the silver ball. "—with a key."

A crackle of wood and a rush of grassy wind interrupted her. Orlianna's bird crashed, tearing through the field as it skidded to a halt.

Orlando's heart sagged. He needed to go to her. He needed to know she was all right.

Merna faced him with a triumphant smile. "I want you to see how blind you have been. I want you to see this new life that you *think* you've found crumble around you. I want you to know that you will never be free."

She twisted the crown around the sphere.

He rushed at her with his knives.

A blast of fire shot from the hole in the front of the sphere. He ducked, but it still blasted his left hand and side.

Pain seared his hand. He dropped his dagger and fell in the grass, rolling to smother the flames that gnawed at his jerkin and cloak. His burned fingers curled up in a fist, and he gritted his teeth.

His whole left side felt like it was on fire.

Fire.

Red.

Hair.

Orlianna.

Orlianna.

Merna turned on her heel and stalked toward where Arliss and Philip were running to Orlianna's downed bird. Ríon rushed down the tower staircase. Around a dozen of Maeve's guards had withdrawn from the battle and surrounded the wreck.

Orlando staggered to his feet.

Orlianna clawed away the canvas that flapped in her eyes. She spat out grass—and a little blood—and stood up in the middle of the wreckage.

The bird was ruined. Its left wing had been bent, nearly snapped off by Ríon's weapon. The hooked spear still stuck in the wooden frame. And the ropes, the steering stick—both destroyed.

She glanced up from the destruction of the thing she'd worked so long for.

Ten warriors surrounded her bird's wreckage, trudging closer. A circle of white nacre graced their helmets. These were from Merna's private guard—the best of her fighters.

And she was alone.

She climbed over the warped wing and brushed her skirts off. This was flight and not battle attire, so it afforded her hardly any protection. Her crossbow she had lost in the crash. Now her only weapons were her dagger and her claw knives.

She took one more look at the bird, her lips parting. The cut in the corner of her mouth split back open. The coppery taste of blood seeped into her mouth.

She turned and glared at the advancing warriors. She drew her claw knives with each hand. And she licked the trickle of blood away from the corner of her mouth.

All ten guards charged at once.

She whirled at them, clawing through the chest of the first man. She punched her other set of claws deep into his upper back. He dropped.

She sheathed one set of claws and picked up the dead man's sword. She swung it up to meet the next attacker. She blocked his sword, batting it away. He stepped back, surprised.

She kept swinging around. The blade sliced through the third warrior's neck, then back around to the second. He raised a small shield and blocked her blow. The vibration rattled up her arm to her shoulder.

She glanced around as she parried his next cut. Far to her right, one warrior aimed his crossbow at her.

She parried her opponent's sword, stole another look at the man with the crossbow.

She ducked.

The crossbow bolt—intended for her—pierced the heart of her opponent. He fell with a choking scream.

The man with the crossbow charged her, weapon jerking beyond aim. She clawed at his free arm, then grabbed the forearm that held the crossbow.

He tried to fire anyway.

She forced his arm back. The bolt whistled through his esophagus.

The other six warriors tensed with tangible fear. She pressed her lips together and waited. They had underestimated the princess of Ikarra before. But not now. They would fear her. They would pay for their atrocities.

A flash of burgundy streaked toward her. Orlando half-ran, half-limped alongside Arliss and Philip. Rose and Mícheál hurried right behind.

She looked out over the battlefield. Arliss was supposed to be leading the archers—among whom were supposed to be Rose and Mícheál. Philip had a wing of the army to lead. And Orlando wasn't supposed to be confronting Merna.

But it mattered not. God had seen fit to bring them all together in this one spot. She dropped the stolen sword and raised both claws.

They would fight together.

Arliss spun to face a charging opponent, releasing her arrow into his chest. Merna's guards were all around them. But they were together—all of them—and together they were even stronger. Even the elite of Anmór could not kill them.

She tossed her head back to shake the hair out of her eyes. Her braid had come undone in the chariot wreck. Blood was rushing to her brain and narrowing her vision.

She blinked. What was really happening here? Merna had received a parcel—from Maeve, it seemed like. And she'd only glimpsed it for an instant, but she was *sure* the item was the crown of Reinhold. Her crown. And now Merna had married it to the sphere, to deadly effect.

She drew an arrow and aimed at another enemy. Something was wrong, horribly wrong. There were invisible forces beneath this whole battle. Beneath her whole story, in fact. And they all seemed to be coming to a head.

She fired her arrow and glanced where she'd last seen Philip. He and Orlando were still together, but they were no longer on the battlefield. They pounded up the stairs of the watchtower in pursuit of someone.

A flash of gaudy green whipped around the corner of the top of the tower. Merna.

She jogged toward the tower. Orlianna hewed through a warrior on her way to join Arliss.

Arliss skidded to a stop, her palm slapping the tower's stone base. She looked up the moss-covered stairs.

Orlianna rushed beside her. "She's up there, isn't she?"

Arliss nodded. "We can end this."

"She has gained a power beyond her own. Otherwise she would never corner herself in like this."

"I know." Arliss ascended the first steps. "She clearly wants an audience."

"We'll give it to her." Orlianna hurried behind.

At the top of the tower, Merna stood on the other side of the square battlement, near the opposite stair. Ríon stood beside her, facing Orlando and Philip—all tensed with upraised swords. But they didn't charge. Arliss scanned the parapet for an explanation.

Between them lay a line of Lasairbláth petals.

And Ríon held a glowing torch.

Arliss lowered her nocked arrow.

Merna chortled. "I thought you might see my point of view rather quickly."

"Nothing of the sort," Orlianna snapped. "But anyone can see you want an audience. And we're terribly good listeners."

Arliss's chest heaved against her will, her breaths becoming shallow and quick. Merna was about to say something that could only be said to this private audience. And she was willing to kill them if they didn't listen to her.

Merna knew many rumors and gossips. She was the queen of secrets. But there was only one secret Arliss had ever wanted to ask of her.

She stepped closer to the line of Lasairbláth. "Can you tell me now?"

"Tell you what?" Merna's lips flicked, toying with her.

"Tell me the truth about Thane!" Arliss screamed into the sudden gust of wind. "Tell me why my country was invaded. Why *you* deny involvement. Why even here in Ikarra, I feel like I'm being hunted. Why my uncles died!"

Merna shook her head. "It's almost amusing. You are this close to knowing, yet you are all so clueless."

Arliss gritted her teeth and faced Ríon. "You, then. You know. You were on the verge of telling me in the catacombs."

"Of course I know. That's why I'm doing what I'm doing. Because I found the truth." Ríon tilted the torch in her direction. "I found out who Thane was with from the beginning."

Merna slitted her eyes at him.

Ríon half-smiled. "I was surprised. But then it all made sense. And I realized how foolish I was to fight it."

"Foolish to fight tyranny—injustice?" Philip demanded. "That is never foolish."

Ríon turned. "No, foolish to fight the power that no one could defeat."

Orlando spoke quietly. "Lies never defeat the truth."

Merna glared at him, and he shifted backward. "Oh, I have the truth—the real truth. Are you ready to discover the truth, Arliss?"

Arliss's fingers ached around her bow grip. "Why should I believe anything you say?"

"You will believe." Merna raised her hands. The clash of battle still raged on far below them beneath darkening clouds. "I only say it to prove to you how blind you all have been. It does not matter that you know. No one will listen to your ravings. You are not the queen of Reinhold. And you will *never* be the queen."

Arliss clenched her teeth. "I might one day be. And then you'll see that you have chosen wrongly."

"You think you are on the right side? You could never be more wrong."

Vomit churned in Arliss's stomach, but she couldn't be sick. She could do nothing but stand there as the threads of her story laced her heart tighter and tighter together.

"Do you want to know who Thane first came to after he fled from the Isle of Light? You want to know who advised Thane on his venture in Reinhold. You want to know who sent him to *me*, asked me to aid him. You want to know who suggested your fate—" Merna pointed at Orlando "—by hiding you away as Thane's spy. Who told me to tear you two apart—" she flipped her hand at Arliss and Philip "—and who has been lying to *you* since the very beginning." She jutted her chin at Orlianna.

Orlianna gasped.

Arliss drew her arrow. "Tell me now, or your secret dies with you."

Ríon readied the torch.

"Very well," Merna said. "You'd best lower that arrow, though."

Arliss lowered her bow and caught Philip's eye. Everything they had been through together—was it all about to be changed forever?

She swallowed the rawness in her throat.

The stone pulsated through her feet with the drums and blows of the battle.

"Maeve," Merna finally said. "Maeve was behind Thane from the beginning."

Chapter Twenty~Six: Victorious

"You're a liar!" Orlianna shouted. "My grandmother is not who you say she is."

Maeve—the force behind Thane? There wasn't a shred of truth in this. Maeve had not even heard the name of Thane until a week ago. She was just as surprised as the rest of them to find the clan of Reinhold alive and well—thriving beyond expectation.

Yet Maeve knew so much. She was so learned, so wise. Could she truly have been ignorant this whole time?

No. Her stomach tensed. It wasn't possible. She would not believe it.

Merna lifted the sphere in her grasping fingers. "Maeve is not who you think she is."

"Why should I believe a word you say?" Orlianna growled.

"Why shouldn't you?" Merna demanded shrilly. "She has disregarded you and suppressed you. By taking charge in Lachlan's stead instead of passing rule immediately over to you, she is refuting ancient customs."

Orlianna stamped her foot. "She's doing what's best for the people."

"The people of Ikarra are all as blind as you, trust me." Merna snorted. "She's duped them all into following her grand scheme to rule the world. But it will not happen. Not if I have any say in it."

Orlianna reached for her pendant. "You *don't* have any say in it." She backed away toward the staircase they had come up by.

Ríon edged closer both to her and the line of Lasairbláth. "You can't leave. Not now."

"Why not?" Arliss drew closer to Orlianna, arrow still on her string.

"Because you know the truth now," Ríon said. "And there are still people down there that will believe you."

Arliss's voice trembled. "So it is true, then."

Orlianna grabbed her arm and pulled her toward the stairs. "It's not true. And we are leaving. Orlando, Philip—come."

She stepped onto the upper landing.

Merna pointed the sphere at them. "You don't want to do that, trust me. This tower is surrounded by my guards."

Orlianna sucked in air, her muscles tightening with frustration. How could she have been so foolish to come rushing up here after Merna? Now the tower was surrounded. They had no way out.

But, perhaps a way…up. Over.

The sky was the color of ashes, and the sun had disappeared within it. Garrick's plane was doing corkscrews over the plains near the river. Harrison flew much closer, gliding close enough that she could make out his shining silver jerkin.

She whirled to face Merna. "Make me believe you, then. Show me the truth."

"Is this not proof enough?" Merna held the sphere above her head, the crown of Reinhold wrapped around it. "She has stolen from your guests to bargain with me."

It was the very crown Arliss had worn in Reinhold, the one she had brought on the journey. There was no denying it.

Philip spoke up. "What was the bargain?"

"She gave me the crown of Reinhold, as well as a promise that I would not be blamed for any of this battle's negative outcomes. She also ensured that all the Reinholdian guests would be placed in the most dangerous positions."

Orlianna diaphragm constricted around her empty stomach.

Merna smirked. "And in return, I promised her the death of those who stood in her way."

"Liar," Orlianna spat.

"Can you deny the facts even as they slap you in the face? Why else would she place a relative unknown like Philip as the head of the central charge of Ikarra's forces? Why would Arliss be allowed to lead the archers? Because Maeve wants them *dead.*"

Orlianna squinted at Merna, but in her peripheral vision she saw Harrison's bird swooping lower. "Whose deaths did Maeve bargain for?"

Merna smiled. "Ah, so you *do* believe me, at least a little. And you care, because you are afraid that your own grandmother bargained for your death, eh?"

"She would never do that."

Arliss nudged her. "If Maeve was behind Thane the whole time, who knows what she would do."

"No!" Orlianna glared. "My grandmother is—"

"The moon." Arliss froze, looking dazed. She looked out at the battlefield below.

Orlianna peered at her, wondering if she'd heard her correctly. The moon? What on earth was she speaking of? The clouds made it impossible to reckon the time, but it couldn't have been past midday. There was no moon to be seen.

Philip edged along the wall, sneaking toward Arliss and Orlianna. "What about the moon?"

"The *moon,*" Arliss repeated, clarity filling her blue eyes.

Orlando looked at her, the same realization flooding his face. "*She* was the moon—the whole time."

Arliss nodded slowly.

Orlianna bit down exasperation, knowing that Harrison would be closing in soon. "What on earth are you two talking about?"

Arliss reached into one of her jerkin pockets and pulled out a thick silver necklace chain. She fisted the whole length of chain and let the large pendant dangle at arm's length. "This came from Thane's fortress."

The interlocking chain was thicker than most, rather like much of Maeve's jewelry. But that was not the only similarity. Orlianna stared at the glinting curve of the dangling pendant.

It was a knife.

It was also a moon.

And it had once belonged to her grandmother.

She backed up against the crenelated wall, feeling behind her. The rugged stone had been worn smooth by time, but divots in the rock still scratched her palm. She cut her eyes down between the two crenelations. If she missed, it would be a long fall.

She stepped back, pulling herself up to stand between the crenels.

Ríon moved toward her, flashing his torch. "What're you doing?"

She ignored him and addressed Merna. "I want to know: was I on Maeve's kill list?"

"No," Merna said. "But you are on mine."

Orlianna jumped just as Harrison swooped over and caught her up into the air.

Arliss's arm shook, rattling the necklace chain. She'd stolen this from Thane's fortress, long ago. Back then, she had not thought to question why he had a necklace with a curved moon-knife hanging from it. But now she saw that it was merely a symbol—a gift.

A gift from Maeve to Thane.

Philip had been edging to her, and now he reached for her shaking hand. The warmth of his fingers sent chills up her arm. His hand was steady, but his multicolored eyes swirled with confusion.

Orlianna—clutching the bottom of Harrison's bird—swept over them, red hair streaming.

Ríon moved for the stairs on his side of the tower, teeth bared. "I'm going after them."

"Don't." Merna waved her hand. "We have the three we need right here."

Arliss met Philip's eyes, then Orlando's beside him. They all readied their weapons.

Merna held the sphere in both hands. "Fighting will only hasten your death."

"Then let's hasten it." Philip pointed his sword at Ríon.

Merna nodded at Ríon. "Kill them."

"I don't think so." A new voice—high, clear—sliced through the tower's tension.

Rose pulled herself up the stairs behind Arliss.

Arliss's heart pounded. How on earth had she gotten past Merna's guards? And where was Mícheál?

Merna wrinkled her nose. "Drop the bow, gypsy."

"Drop the ball, queen," Rose retorted.

Merna gripped the sphere. "You can kill *her*, too."

"I don't think so." Mícheál emerged from the staircase behind Merna and Ríon.

Ríon jumped—eyes bulging—and swung his sword at Mícheál.

Mícheál dove beneath the sword and somersaulted over the line of Lasairbláth.

Merna seized her chance. She fled down the open staircase.

"Stop her!" Rose fired an arrow, but it pinged off stone.

Ríon laughed, long and deep. Arliss hated it. He was becoming so much like his parents, it scared her. If only he could see what he'd become.

"If you'll excuse me." Ríon tossed the torch up in the air and dashed down the stairs after his mother.

Time slowed. Arliss watched the torch spin, flames licking the air, ready to explode into flashes of white when they hit the petals below.

Mícheál tried to grab the torch out of midair.

Rose fired an arrow into the sky in an attempt to stop it.

Philip and Orlando lunged for it.

Arliss threw herself at the torch, grasped it, hurled herself to the ground—anything to keep the fire from meeting the petals. She hit the stone near the opposite staircase.

The torch tumbled down the steps.

And in that same moment, clattering steel and shouts echoed up the other staircase—coming toward Philip, Orlando, Rose, and Mícheál.

Philip readied his sword. "Arliss, go."

She rose. "I'm not—"

"Go!" He shouted. "The people need to know the truth about Maeve."

She stared a moment at her friends. She couldn't leave them. But there were others still out there, unaccounted for—Orlianna, Clare, Garrick, Harrison.

"Arliss, go." Rose lifted her eyebrows. "We've got this."

Wind whistled through Orlianna's ears as she clawed her way onto the wooden platform beside Harrison. He didn't even glance at her, just kept seamlessly working the steering stick and the tail lever. He hovered above the battle, making a turnabout toward the river.

"Thanks," she panted.

"Hm." He nodded sharply.

Below, the ruinous tower shrunk away, seeming small in the midst of the dark, cluttered fields. It was hard to make out much in the fracas. But one thing shone clearly: Ikarra was winning.

Their troops had lost no ground back toward the castle. In fact, they had battered Merwin's forces back toward the old tower. Garrick and Harrison had scattered the outlying enemy contingents. And as for the chariots...

Without Ríon at their head, they were a jumbled mess. It almost looked as if they were fighting *against* Anmór rather than for it.

An icy chill seized Orlianna's heart and squeezed her pulse to a halt. She gripped Harrison's arm.

Now he looked at her. "What is it, love?"

"Merna. She told me something. I don't want to believe it. I will not believe it. But..."

"But you do believe it, deep down."

"Yes."

His forehead creased with deep ridges. "Tell me what she told you." He jerked the bird left to dodge a projectile from below. "Quickly."

She froze, her fingers turning to stone around his arm. Her saying it would be an admission that it was true. The words blocked up in the bottom of her throat.

"*Orlianna.* Tell me."

"Maeve," her voice cracked, "is the enemy. She was behind Thane. She is colluding with Merna. She has been behind everything."

Even...

No. She released Harrison's arm and grabbed the wood platform so firmly she thought splinters would stab her palms. More than anything, she could not think Maeve responsible for William's death.

Harrison didn't seem shocked by the truth. He merely nodded. "And you left Arliss, Philip, and Orlando to fend with her alone?"

"She was on the verge of killing me."

"You should not have left them."

"I—I was so shocked. I just wasn't thinking."

They were almost to the river—to the castle—but he jerked the plane around and headed straight back the way they'd come. He huffed through his teeth. "Ruddy idiot. They could be dead by now."

She stiffened, but couldn't contradict him. She had been an idiot. And now she had left the three people on this battlefield she trusted most at the mercy of a malicious witch.

Harrison lowered their altitude as they neared the tower. "See below us? Merwin's retreating."

"Retreating? Why?"

Harrison shook his head. "I can't say. But either he thinks he can't win this fight, or he's trying to draw us away."

"Or both."

"Very well." Harrison shoved the steering stick forward. "We'll play his game."

The bird pitched downward. The grassy field rushed up toward them at an alarming rate.

Orlianna grabbed at one of the posts to keep from sliding off the front. "What madness are you doing?"

"I'm landing."

Arliss's shins ached as she pounded down the stone steps of the watchtower. Sounds of battle had grown thicker around her. The fight had shifted from the river, and now the tower stood in the center of the conflict. Anmórian chariots circled the dusty cloud of combatants, causing mayhem.

But somehow...Ikarra was prevailing.

Arliss descended the last step. Grasses brushed against her legs.

The lead charioteer jerked around and headed straight for the tower. It was a woman, as quick and poised a driver as Ríon himself. She rattled toward Arliss, taking out an Anmórian cavalryman on her way.

Arliss froze. This woman was fighting *with* them.

The driver turned her head, and the wind flung back the hood of her cloak. Waves of golden-brown hair streamed out.

Clare. She pulled back on the reins, the wheels whining to a halt beside the tower. "Get on, quick."

Arliss jumped on without hesitation. Ríon may not have been on their side, but Clare seemed to be.

Clare snapped the reins. The horses whinnied and charged forward.

Arliss steadied herself on the side of the chariot. "Where've you been?"

"Biding my time." Clare scanned the battlefield. "Waiting for my moment."

"Your moment to do what?"

"This." Clare motioned at the Anmórian retreat. "Cause chaos. Destroy Merna's plans. Help you."

"So you're fighting against Ríon?"

Clare steered away from the thicker combat. "Ríon doesn't know what he's doing."

"He'll be furious."

"He's already furious, and I don't care. It's for his own good. Merna may have him drunk on her empty promises, but she hasn't persuaded me."

"Even with the promise of the throne of Anmór?"

Clare did not respond. She pointed at the sky ahead. They were free of the battle now, driving through fields scattered with dead and wounded.

Arliss looked up just as Harrison and Orlianna's bird dropped low and—with a violent whisper—skidded through the grass and landed.

Clare stopped just short of the aircraft as Harrison jumped off the platform.

Orlianna tumbled off, drawing her claw knives. "What is this?"

"It's all right!" Arliss dismounted the chariot, rushing around the stamping horses. "She's on our side."

Clare lifted her chin. "Hello, Orlianna. How nice to finally meet."

"Indeed." Orlianna arched an eyebrow.

Harrison strode past Orlianna and stroked one of the horses' manes, his good eye scanning the fields. "If we don't finish this now, it may never end."

Arliss climbed back on the chariot. Philip was still on that tower. Hopefully they could hold off Merna's guards. Perhaps even get away. But no matter what he said, she *had* to go back to him—with help. "How many can ride on this thing?"

"All of us." Clare tightened the reins. "Come on."

Harrison jumped on beside Arliss.

Orlianna stepped barely on, the heels of her boots backing up against the edge of the chariot. She held on with one hand as the horses pulled the vehicle forward. "Plan?"

Arliss pointed to the tower. "Merwin may be retreating, but Merna has plans of her own. We have to stop her."

"We have to focus our efforts on Merwin right now. If he retreats, the battle is lost for Anmór anyway," Harrison said.

"But Philip and Orlando and—" Arliss began.

The ruined watchtower exploded in a flash of white fire.

Orlianna grasped the edge of the chariot like it was life itself—because right now, it was. Her heart thumped against her rib cage as if trying to dislodge the pendant that hung heavy over her chest.

Last she had seen him, Orlando was atop that tower. Now, it had crumbled down to half its former height, and even that was collapsing. Chunks of blackened stone scattered the fields around. Dry patches of grass had caught fire.

But who had set the Lasairbláth aflame? And how had they escaped? They would have been blown to bits. Whoever had lit it had only done so knowing they could get away in time.

Arliss stood tense on the platform in front of her, hardly shaking even when Clare jerked the chariot to avoid a pile of rubble. They raced through the destruction now, but the battle had pushed even further away, and the field around the tower was quiet.

Anmór was retreating.

Ikarra was victorious.

Orlianna closed her eyes as the bitter irony of her own thoughts turned her stomach sour. Victorious? The smell of death settled thick around her. Lives had been lost—too many lives.

But even just one life, just one Ikarran casualty, was one too many. And that one life had been lost long ago.

The chariot slowed its rattle. She opened her eyes. Arliss had an arrow on her bow. Clare pulled gently to halt the exhausted horses.

All around, death littered the ground. Anmórians. Ikarrans. They had all died—some supporting a treacherous witch, the others supporting…

She exhaled tightly. If Maeve was who Merna had revealed her to be, there were no words for *her* treachery, her witchcraft.

Arliss's blue eyes burned with unspoken fears. She scanned their murky surroundings.

Harrison bounded off the chariot while it rolled to a stop. "Look!"

Orlianna peered into the smoking haze. A lone soldier, his steps steadfast, his bearing strong, strode towards them through the smoke.

"Philip!" Arliss leapt to the ground with a joyous gasp. She ran to him, almost stumbling over stony debris. They embraced each other.

Orlianna stepped off the chariot slowly, but Clare stayed on. Philip couldn't be alone. She knew him too well for that. If Orlando was alive—even wounded, even half-dead—Philip would never have left him.

She swallowed her scream.

A flash of burgundy materialized in the fog behind Philip, limping toward them.

She ran.

Their hands met, grasping as if to make sure each other were real. Orlando brushed his hands frantically through her hair as she felt for his cheek, grabbed at the folds of his dirty cloak. Blood trickled down his left cheek. She wiped it away, but it spurted fresh from the cut.

She kissed his cheek, long, hard, anything to stop the flow, anything to assure herself that he was alive.

He gasped a hot breath into her ear. "You're all right. When you jumped—"

"When the tower exploded…" She leaned back, shaking her head. "I could only pray."

Harrison edged toward them. "We can speak of this battle once it is won for good. Right now Merwin is retreating with no one in pursuit."

Orlianna strained to fully exhale. "Our troops are spent."

"No," Philip mused. "There are enough. They just need to be rallied—led."

Harrison knelt and lifted a sword from a fallen soldier, strapping it around his waist. He jerked his chin southwest, where the Anmórian army fled into the wilderness. "They're going back to their capital. But God knows they'll raid every Ikarran village between here and there until they are nothing but a ruddy pile of ash."

Orlianna stared at the tower's crumbling ruins. She knew what was in his mind. "You *can't* go after them."

Harrison grabbed her shoulder and pulled her away from Orlando, closer to him. "You can't tell me what to do."

"I am your princess."

"You are my *queen*." Harrison squeezed her hands. "But you cannot stop me from doing what must be done."

She shuddered. He was right. He was always right. But now, more than ever, she wanted him to be wrong. She wanted him to stay with her and sing her to sleep the way he had done when she was a child, protecting her from the nightmares that had always haunted her. He wanted her to whisper in her ear and tell her that the hell she had been through this day had only been a dream.

"Let me go with you," she managed.

He shook his head. "You will be needed here. Ikarra is about to be thrown into chaos. Only you can save them."

She bit her lip. Could she save anyone—from anything?

Philip rested his hand on his sword pommel. "I will go with you."

Harrison nodded in approval, but Arliss reached for Philip. "No…"

Orlando limped toward Harrison. "I as well."

"Not in your condition." Harrison pressed a hand on his shoulder. "And someone has to look after Orlianna."

Orlianna choked as she tried to restrain her sob. She inhaled deeply, squared her shoulders, and faced Harrison.

His good eye regarded her sadly for a moment.

He turned and ran to join his troops.

She turned toward the castle.

Arliss held onto Philip's back as Harrison turned to leave, as if holding onto him would keep him from going. They *could not* be separated. That had happened before—each time with almost deathly consequences.

He stood tall, broad shoulders squared as he faced her. "You have to let me go."

She clenched her teeth. "Give me one reason why I can't come with you."

His hand went around the back of her head. "I promised your father I'd keep you safe."

She jerked her hand at the bloody fields behind them. "And you think letting me fight in this mess was safe? Philip, we're beyond safety. This is beyond anything my parents supposed. This is war. This is the fate of the three clans."

He cocked his head at her, curious eyes searching hers. "You sound like your mother. Like you're seeing things."

Was she seeing things—the future? Her mother had always had the gift of knowledge, of foresight. Yet she herself had never felt imbued with such a gift. What would it feel like, to glimpse the things that were to come?

The ground beneath her felt like it was shaking. She staggered into Philip. "I—I must go with you. It is my duty."

"No." He wrapped his arms around her. "You do have a duty, but this isn't it."

"What, then?"

He combed his fingers through her tangled hair. "Until Ilayda and Erik return—God willing, with your father's fleet—you are the voice of Reinhold here in Ikarra. If you come with me there will be no one left to speak out."

Of course. It had almost slipped her mind in the intensity of the past week of battles and meetings and revelations. But she was supposed to be becoming the queen of Reinhold, wasn't she? Or at least acting like it.

She pressed her forehead against his chest. "I can't do this."

"Your father thought you could." He leaned back and lifted her chin. "And so do I."

"But not without you."

"I will come back. Once I make this right."

She shuddered as she inhaled. He let go of her, and the sting of the overcast wind turned her bones cold. He half-bowed, then turned to go.

"What about that kiss you promised me?"

He froze with his back to her. "I told you, I will give you that honor once you are crowned queen."

She licked her lips. "I just…wanted to make sure I got it. Better early than never."

He turned back to her. A smile tugged at his mouth. "I'll see you soon, Arliss. Farewell."

Tears blurred her eyes so she could not see him walk away.

CHAPTER TWENTY-SEVEN: LETTERS OF THE MOON

ILAYDA YAWNED AND ROLLED ONTO HER SIDE, HER SPINE CRACKLING all the way down as she shifted on the wooden platform. The air that rushed beneath the bird was smooth, peaceful. Wisps of clouds reached through and stroked her face as she blinked slowly in the brightness.

Erik glanced at her, then looked back down at his hands on the steering stick.

She sighed. They'd been on this floating contraption for nearly three days, and he'd hardly said a word to her. His eyes were full of unspoken thoughts. His arms were knotted with tension from steering the bird for so long, and his lips were parted tensely—as if he was permanently on the verge of saying something.

She rolled all the way onto her back and felt for the satchel. She'd knotted the strap around one of the support beams. Sticking her hand inside, she found nothing but air and old leather. They had drained the last of the meager provisions Orlianna had sent.

She huffed air through her teeth. "Reinhold had better be close."

Erik's voice sounded dry and underused. "I think it may be just below us soon. We shall see."

"Can we see a bit sooner?" She flipped onto her stomach.

The aircraft jostled, and he put both hands on the steering stick. He shot her a sharp glare. "Watch it."

She peeked over the edge and stared into the clouds. They magnified the sun's light and surrounding the bird in an explosion of brilliance. If Erik would drop a little lower, they could pass below the clouds and see what lay below them. But he had an uncanny sense for calculating directions. If he thought they weren't there yet, he was probably right.

She tried a more subtle attempt. "I miss my parents. And Arden. My father's probably been making himself sick this whole time."

"I miss mine, too." He nodded. "And Keelin. And our new house. We'd only just finished the frame when I left."

"They were still thatching my roof," she mused. Reinhold had seemed like an imaginary realm while she was in Ikarra. Now, with the wild eastern air burning in her nostrils, it felt real once again. The images from home drifted through her mind. "Father was telling them they'd made the doorway too narrow. Mother was making sure the kitchen windows were positioned so that sunlight would come through all times of the day. She'll miss living in the castle."

"Will *you* miss it?"

She shrugged. "I have the feeling I will split my time between homes. Arliss is just as much my family as my own."

Who knew what Arliss was doing right now? If things had gone badly, she might be fighting for her life. Alone. All because Ilayda had not been able to stay, not been able to face the enemy.

She chewed on her lip, hard. It wasn't like there weren't difficult things to face here. The thought of facing Brallaghan again still terrified her. But at least now she *could* face him. Her time in Ikarra had shown her that much.

Erik pushed down on the stick. The bird fell through the clouds. The light dimmed around them.

And suddenly she could see shapes, colors. The dark undulations of the ocean. The white line of sand. And cliffs—the glorious Cliffs of Áill—rising up to meet them.

She exhaled. They were *home*.

The clifftops rushed up toward them at an alarming rate. She braced herself for the landing, the wind stinging her wide eyes. But Erik held the bird steady. It whooshed smoothly to a halt atop the grassy cliffs.

The back gates to the city swept open as Ilayda rushed across the clifftops toward them, jerking up her skirts. The gates scraped up a cloud of sandy dust that stung her cheeks. A few particles stuck in her nose.

Arden stepped through the gates just as she reached them.

She wrapped her arms around her brother, squeezing his shoulders tight. He'd grown taller—if it was possible—in the few weeks she'd been gone. In fact, he *might* have *almost* been taller than her.

She patted his head as if to reinforce that he was not. "I've missed you, I suppose."

His eyes were wide. "What're you doing here?"

She sneezed out the sand in her nose. "I could ask the same question. Why are you in Cladach, anyway? I thought Mummy and Dadda were staying at the capital until the homes were finished."

He ignored her, pointing at the bird and at Erik approaching. "What is *that*?"

"That is Erik. I believe you've met."

He rolled his eyes. "Yes, I've met your boyfriend many times."

She clenched her teeth and shot him a fierce glare as Erik approached. Hopefully he hadn't heard. And hopefully *he* would keep his mouth shut.

Arden stuck out his hand. "Sir Erik."

Erik shook it once—hard. "If I'm Sir Erik, you're Lord Arden, so watch it."

"And, Lord Arden, you still haven't answered my question." Ilayda put her hands on her hips. There was no reason for Arden to be in Cladach, just *waiting* for them. He wasn't expecting them.

Arden nodded. "If you're thinking I've been staying in Cladach just waiting for a lovely couple like you to show back up, you're dead wrong. I'm here on a mission."

Ilayda reached out her hands as if to choke him. "So are we, so make it snappy."

Erik walked past Arden. "I don't have time for chitchat. We need to get to the king now. Every moment we waste is a moment our friends could be fighting for their lives."

"I—I'll send for a carriage." Arden's face turned serious. "Arliss—Philip—where are they?"

"Back in Ikarra." Ilayda jerked her head behind her, as if Ikarra lay just a stone's throw across the water.

Erik kept walking. "Come on, Ilayda."

Arden ran after them. "You won't find the king or queen at the city. That's why I'm here. They sent me to fetch Lord Brédan to join them."

"Where?" Erik asked.

"The ruins of Thane's fortress." Arden inhaled slowly. "They've found something very interesting. Something about Thane."

Ilayda sucked in salty air. Arliss had been talking about this the whole time—the *reason* behind Thane, the *force* behind Thane. Maybe she really had been onto something.

Erik clenched his fists. "Then it's even more urgent we get to the king."

Arden rushed ahead of them, waving his arm. "I'll have a carriage ready in ten minutes!"

"We don't have ten minutes!" Ilayda shouted after him.

"Of course we don't." Erik kept a level stride. "We'll go on horseback."

Ilayda kept her head down as branches smacked it, tangling with her hair as she rode. The setting sun sank through the trees behind her and cast long shadows that reached along the forest floor before her mount's hooves.

In front of her, Erik jerked his horse left, toward the river. He sat tall in the saddle, turning his head every direction with eyes and ears on edge. He slowed to a canter, searching the trees.

Then he shot off again with refreshed energy.

She leaned forward onto her horse's smoky mane. They had to be close. Erik knew these woods better than anyone.

The path ahead widened as it paralleled the river. The jolting force of her horse's hooves became smoother as the road evened out. And then the boundary stones started flicking by like catapult projectiles.

She gripped the reins. These stones had come from the ruins of Thane's fortress. They were close. Already the mountains rose high above her—mountains that surrounded the dark dell.

Erik snapped his reins and maneuvered his horse closer to the river.

Ilayda squinted at his movements, wrapped the reins once around her hand, and mimicked them.

Her horse slowed to a lazy trot.

Stupid thing. It never listened to her. She tapped her heels on its sides and yanked the reins upward. "Get on!"

The horse glanced at her out of the corner of its eye. Then it jerked left and plunged between the boundary stones and into the river.

She gasped as the frigid water turned her legs to pillars of ice. The current tugged them forward, and her mount followed it. She fumbled with the reins, trying to get the horse to go anywhere but further down the river. It refused.

She shivered and glanced ahead, but Erik was almost out of sight. She could see the dell now, and a crowd of several dozen people gathered there. Most clustered around the left side, where Thane's chambers had once stood.

She smacked the horse's muscled shoulder. "Get out of the river. Now!"

It snorted a huge, watery sneeze and kept going, legs casting up spouts of water on every side. She closed her eyes and pressed her face into its mane. At this rate, it would ram them both into the stone mound at the back of the clearing.

"*Ilayda!*" Someone was screaming her name. Her mother?

She raised her head just as the horse bounded out of the river, stamping around in a circular halt. The sudden stop jerked her from the saddle. She felt her spine crackle all the way down. She tumbled through the air.

Someone caught her, steadying her as her feet stumbled somewhere between standing and falling.

"It's okay," he was saying. "Stand up."

Water glued her eyelashes together. She leaned her wet head back into her rescuer's shoulder. Erik, of course. He always was there for her, wasn't he?

Her chest strained against her drenched bodice. She blinked open her eyes as her mind cleared. This wasn't Erik. He wasn't tall or slender enough.

She turned and nearly screamed.

Brallaghan leaned toward her, his face tight with confusion. "Are you hurt?"

She pushed herself away, shivering from cold and the shock. "I'm fine."

The crowd behind them drifted toward them just as Erik's horse leapt the river and cantered to a stop on the other side. He swung himself out of the saddle and guided the beast toward the others.

Brallaghan swept his hand down his red tabard. His shirtsleeves were rolled up to his elbows as if he'd been working. "What—what are you doing here? I mean, I thought you were in Ikarra."

"I'm not." She crossed her arms.

A voice—most certainly her mother's voice this time—drifted toward her. "Ilayda, my dear!"

Ilayda twisted her hair to wring the water out. She wasn't ready for a bunch more fuss.

Brallaghan motioned at the crowd. "You should get over there. There…there are secrets in these mountains we never dreamed."

She stepped awkwardly to the side. Should she say anything more? High above the clouds, it had seemed so easy to say she had gotten beyond the ways he had hurt her. Now—with him staring her in the face—she didn't have the same strength.

He reached to touch her shoulder as she walked away. His touch sent a tingle down her arm. "Ilayda, I—"

She turned, and his hand slipped away. "Please, don't. You can't change the past. We both need to move on."

"That's what I wanted to say." He paused. "That I am sorry. I never wanted to hurt you. I know you went to Ikarra to try to get away from me. And I thought I could forget what had happened, with you gone. But I could not. And now…"

"You can't keep driving yourself mad?" She stared into the mountainous walls, knowing all too well what he was feeling.

He nodded.

She breathed—deep, straining, shuddering. She reached a hand toward him cautiously. Then she hugged him for one moment. "I forgive you."

She stepped back, inhaling the thickness of the air between them. They would never be the same—the way they had once been. But they were *friends* again. And the peaceful tingle in the bottom of her heart told her that was all that mattered.

Her mother reached her and grabbed her by the shoulders, spinning her to face her. Ilayda shook as her mother's long fingers stroked her dripping cheeks.

"You're here," Elisabeth gasped. "You're alive."

Ilayda hesitated, unable to speak. It didn't seem such a miracle for her to be here, alive, when Arliss wasn't here, and might not be…

Iciness snaked up her body and pricked her skin like needles.

"Oh, you're chilled through." Elisabeth pulled her to the larger group. "Come. There is much to see."

Her father jogged toward them, his long face lighting up.

"Ilayda! My dear!" Adam threw his arms around her. A wave of warmth passed through her body.

Then someone swung a thick woolen blanket over her. It settled over her like a wave, wrapping her in snug shadows. She closed her eyes and tugged it tight about herself.

Hands settled on her shoulders, smoothing out the wrinkles. "You all right?"

She opened her eyes. Erik stood in front of her, head leaned forward so that his eyes faced hers. She nodded quickly. "I'll be fine."

He pressed his lips together, gave a quick nod, and patted her arm once. Then he turned to join the rest.

The crowd—twenty or so people—was comprised mostly of nobles and knights. Both lords' families were all there. A contingent of guards stood by in raiment like Brallaghan's. And—in the middle of the whole thing—Kenton and Elowyn waited.

It dawned on Ilayda that they were waiting for *her.* She lifted the fringes of the blanket and stumbled along, following Erik through the crowd.

Elowyn's face was tight, but she spread her arms toward her. "My child. You have returned."

Ilayda embraced the queen. "It is good to be home."

"This is not home." Elowyn looked upward, dark eyes searching. "Not this place. Darkness lurks here."

Ilayda glanced around, noticing the cave that stretched deep into the mountain. Arliss had once been kept in a room down that very hall. Surely nothing still lived here. What then could the queen be speaking of?

Kenton grasped Erik's hand. "I am glad you are here. Though I must ask why."

Erik exhaled. "Arliss sent us. It's a long story."

Kenton gestured with the torch he gripped. "Orlianna said 'tis two weeks' trip to Ikarra. You cannot have been there and back in little more than three."

"But we have."

"How?" Kenton's brow wrinkled.

"Wind travels faster than water."

Ilayda looked up, recalling the flight through the skies. The sky was now dark—dark as nothing, except where hopeful stars pierced through the expanse. The moon she could not see. Perhaps it was hiding behind clouds.

"You can tell us all later." Elowyn moved toward the cave. "Now there are more pressing matters."

Erik rushed after her. "I beg your pardon, my queen, but I have matters just as pressing."

Elowyn froze at the sharpness in his tone. "It's Arliss, isn't it?"

He nodded.

"Is she safe?" Kenton demanded.

Ilayda tilted her head. "Philip is with her."

"Is she *safe?*" Kenton repeated.

Ilayda quieted. She couldn't answer this. If the battle *had* broken out, not a soul in Cahair would find safety. And even if she had delayed the fighting, there could be trouble elsewhere.

Erik motioned around. "No one is safe right now. Anmór is ready for war. They may even now be marching upon Cahair."

Kenton gritted his teeth. "Then why did you return alone?"

"Arliss and Orlianna made the decision. And I agreed with it." Erik hesitated. "Orlianna calls for your aid, my king. She needs the ships of Reinhold."

Ilayda held her breath. Kenton said nothing.

Elowyn lifted her chin. "Orlianna spoke much of her grandmother while she was here. Did...Maeve agree to send you?"

Erik paused, glancing upward as he tried to remember.

Ilayda shook her head. "They didn't consult her."

Elowyn gasped. "Then they are all in graver danger than we could imagine."

Ilayda arched an eyebrow. What did Maeve have to do with danger, or with Reinhold coming to aid Ikarra? "What are you talking about?"

"You will have to see for yourself." Kenton handed Erik his torch and motioned toward the dark cave.

Ilayda stepped forward, Erik beside her. Kenton, Elowyn, Adam, and Elisabeth followed at a distance. The darkness seemed ready to swallow her up. But at every step, Erik's light frightened away the shadows and sent them scurrying into oblivion.

She loosened the blanket around her shoulders as she neared the room at the end of the stony hallway. She had spent little time in Thane's fortress before its destruction—less than half an hour. But Arliss had told her stories about the rooms she was kept in and the places she was shown.

She had even shown her a stolen trinket: a necklace with an intricate pendant, a dagger in the shape of a crescent moon.

And it had come from this very room.

Thane's room.

She stepped through the stone doorway as Erik's light peeled away the darkness.

It was a mess. Water from the breaking of the dam must have made its way even in here. Rotting bedsheets and muddy clothes were strewn in shreds on the floor. The whole place stank of rust and mold.

But everywhere there were papers. Maps. Charts. Plans. But most of all, letters. Letters smothered the desk along the right wall so that the top of the desk was hidden.

Ilayda picked up one of the letters and admired the wiry script. "Lovely penmanship."

Elowyn's voice echoed through the doorway. "Read it."

Erik motioned for her to go ahead.

Ilayda lifted the letter into the torchlight and read:

My dearest Thane,

Your reports alarm me greatly, but I do not yet think our plans at risk. We shall continue as planned, but with all vigilance.

First, the matter of Merna and her spy. She is foolish and selfish. All she wants is to add Reinhold's territory to that of Anmór. But Orlando is useful—useful, but not necessary. Let her do as she wishes with him for the time. If you are both successful, all will be well. And if Orlando fails in this mission, I will ensure that you have command over him. For my part, I think it is wise to send him to the city during your attack. It will confuse and distract them. As for the other notion, I realize you care for him, but all soldiers are expendable.

The second issue is far more concerning. I realize that by the time you read this much may have changed. Since you have captured Arliss, you may bring the wrath of her city upon you. This was rash, but I know you could do little else. Since you have her, use her as bait. Do not attack straightaway as you planned. Keep her locked away until you can discover more uses for her.

You have found a use already. This peasant Philip you speak of makes things doubly dangerous for us. If they are both educated in the ancient ways, if they both believe in the power of the old legends, if they both know of Lasairbláth, we are truly doomed. Your goal must be to separate them by whatever means. They may be but sixteen years old. This matters not. A future union between them could ruin all.

I will say it simply: they are the most dangerous couple in the three realms, and they must be eliminated.

Ilayda choked, trembling. The blanket slipped off her shoulders and pooled on the floor around her feet. This was *the* person—the one Arliss and Elowyn had been searching for. The one behind Thane from the beginning.

Her stomach twisted. She knew who this was. She did not need to read on. But she did anyway.

If circumstances force you to it, proceed with your attack. My spells will be in your favor. One day, the three thrones will be made into one and you will be my right hand.

Until then, I shall ever be,

Your lady—the moon

Maeve

Ilayda wanted to scream. Erik was talking, but the shadows plugged up her ears. The letter drifted back to the desk as she reached to cover her face.

"No," she moaned. "We left Arliss to her death."

"What?" Kenton tensed. "What is Maeve doing now?"

Ilayda looked up, tears streaking her cheeks. "She is arguing for peace and unity. But she says those can only come if *she* rules all the realms. When we left, she was trying to ward off a battle with Anmór. But I can guess well enough her true intentions."

Elowyn trembled. She staggered, collapsing into Ilayda.

Ilayda reached for the queen, struggling to keep her upright. Something had seized her limbs, and she could not stand. She seemed to have drifted from her own body.

Elowyn swayed a moment.

Kenton reached for her.

Then she stood straight, blinking. "It has happened."

"What did you see?" Ilayda ventured.

"Battle. Bloodshed." Elowyn let silent tears flood her eyes. "The breaking of the unity of the three clans."

Ilayda stood there a moment, staring at the letters spread out across the desk. The torchlight made them look like fallen autumn leaves.

Maeve had been the enemy the whole time. She'd had a bad feeling about her. Maybe she should have said more. Maybe she shouldn't have left Cahair. Did Arliss know by now, too? Or was she fighting the wrong enemy?

Erik strummed his fingernail in the nock of one of his arrows. "She's going to try to kill them."

Ilayda looked at him. "Who?"

"Maeve," he said. "*They are the most dangerous couple in the three realms, and they must be eliminated.*"

"We have to get back to Cahair," Ilayda said.

Erik strode out of the room, between the others gathered, and back toward the main clearing.

Kenton rushed after them. "You just arrived. You aren't going anywhere."

"Indeed," Adam affirmed.

Ilayda marched beside Erik. No one could stop them. Not now. "Can we get the bird back in the air?"

Erik nodded, stepping out of the cavelike hall. "We'll hook it up to a carriage and have them drive like mad to the edge of the cliffs. Then, cut the cords—"

And they would go straight over the side.

She bit her lip. "Worth a try."

Kenton grabbed them both by the shoulders and jerked them to a halt. "One moment, you two."

Erik's eyes brimmed with irritation, but his subtle squint betrayed a tinge of amusement. Kenton was wise, wiser than they. They needed to listen to his advice.

"Don't rush off without a plan," Kenton urged. "Breathe. Prepare yourselves. Tell us everything that has happened, so that we can piece together the full story. *Then* we can make our battle plans."

Ilayda nodded, but discomfort still gnawed in her gut. Her friend was across an ocean fighting—maybe dying. And she could do nothing about it by sitting and waiting.

Brallaghan walked up and gestured over his shoulder. "Your horses are waiting, if you are ready."

"We need to hurry." Ilayda strode for her horse. "Arliss is in grave danger."

CHAPTER TWENTY-EIGHT: RISE AGAIN

Everywhere Arliss looked, she saw death.

The Tuáma Fields were bestrewn with bodies. Some already stank from a day of decay. Others wavered between life and death, holding on till one of the Cahairian medics reached them. But there were only so few to help so many.

Arliss walked silently, choking on the smell of ash as she neared the crumbled watchtower. The chariot wreckage still lay there in a mangled heap. But Orlianna's bird was gone—stolen away by Ríon, no doubt.

What Anmór had not taken were their fallen soldiers. They slept now alongside Ikarrans, somber reminders of the unity which had been shattered beyond reparation.

It was as Mícheál had said: Tuáma meant tomb, and these fields now entombed soldiers from both clans.

But those who had died were gone. She could not bring them back.

She could, however, bring back the missing—the unknown.

Arliss sighed. The bedraggled, bloody remnants of Harrison's pursuit had returned to Cahair in the wee hours. Merwin had been driven away from Ikarra's key cities, they said. But there was no sign of either Philip or Harrison. No one knew their fate.

She turned to Rose who walked beside her. "He could be anywhere."

Rose didn't pull Arliss close to comfort her, but her deep eyes yearned with understanding and regret. "We'll find him."

Arliss let her arms hang at her sides. There was no telling how far Philip or Harrison had made it.

Behind them, Orlianna drifted past every body as Mícheál searched for survivors. The medics would not be far behind.

Mícheál suddenly knelt beside one young soldier. "He's alive." He glanced warily up at Orlianna. "And he's Anmórian."

Arliss froze, waiting for Orlianna's response.

Orlianna looked up into the rising sun, her red hair flaming. "Save whoever you can. It matters not what clan they are from. Right now, a life is a life."

Because they were all fighting one enemy now: Maeve. She had manipulated them all.

Arliss ascended a grassy knoll and shuddered. What would it be like to face Maeve, now that she knew what she knew? She couldn't pretend otherwise. But Merna was right: no one would believe her when she revealed the truth.

Rose suddenly pointed west. "Look."

Arliss glanced that direction. She whirled, choking on her own attempt to swallow. "Orlianna!"

Orlianna picked up her skirts and ran to join them atop the knoll. "What do you see?"

Arliss bit her lip. "It's Harrison."

Orlianna ran down the hill and toward his fallen body.

Orlianna dropped to her knees in the grass beside Harrison, her skirts whooshing around her.

His eyes were closed, but his lips quavered as air whistled through them. His chest stretched slowly beneath a tabard stained dark with blood. She reached out shaking hands to touch him. He'd been wounded more than once.

But he had kept fighting, fighting until his task was complete.

Her lungs were filled with stone. She gasped, glancing around. *Who* had done this—this treachery? She would kill them a hundred times over.

Harrison suddenly gripped her hand. His fingers were chilled in the morning air, but they were still strong.

She leaned toward his pale, bearded face. "Harrison, speak to me."

Air wheezed from his lips. "You're here. You found me."

"Yes. I'm here."

"I'm glad you came." He squeezed her hand. "I did not want to part without one last word."

"Don't speak that way. The medics are here. They will help you. You can make it back to Cahair, I know you can. In a few weeks' time—"

"Orlianna." He said her name firmly. "My wounds are too deep. It is time for you to let go."

She trembled, sobbing. "But I *cannot*. You are the truest friend I have ever had. You are my very heart!"

"You will have to learn to give yourself to others."

Orlando.

Orlianna took his hand again. "If you leave, you will take what is left of me with you."

"No." He reached up and tucked her hair behind her ear. "There is much more of you left to give. You will become the queen of Ikarra, the greatest one to ever sit on the emerald throne. 'Your ancient ruins shall be rebuilt. You shall raise up the foundations of many generations. You shall be called the repairer of the breach, the restorer of streets to dwell in.' So shall you be."

"How?" she managed.

"You keep fighting until the fight is done." His words were short and halting now. His chin shook as his hand dropped from her hair. "But promise me this, Orlianna, that you will not let them break you. You must always rise again. You must never stop fighting."

She held his hand with both of hers. "For you, I will."

He smiled, his eyes almost closed. "Farewell, darling."

Then his face relaxed, his head falling back into the pillow of grasses. His fingers loosened around hers. His last warm breath drifted up to her cheek.

She lay over him, sobbing as his blood stained her dress. "No, Harrison. Please…" Her voice died away, but she still wept his name. Over and over she said it. Harrison. Harrison. Harrison.

But he did not answer her.

He was gone.

Arliss stood tall as she followed the procession down Cahair's main road which cut straight through the first cantar. Her cloak dragged her shoulders down, but she kept her head up—meeting the sorrowful faces of those who lined the road.

Old women clustered beneath overhanging apartments, faces haggard with understanding. Shopkeepers stood outside their darkened businesses. Even the children's play was halted with reverence.

By rights, the procession was one of heroes and victors. But there were no cheers, no trumpets. Those on biers and stretchers were almost as many as those marching.

Arliss sucked in the dense air. Beside her, Orlianna stared at the ground, her breaths so shallow her chest barely moved with each one. Beside Orlianna, four castle guards supported a bier. Harrison lay atop it. His face peaceful, pointed heavenward.

Arliss blinked back tears. At least they knew what had happened to Harrison. It was almost worse for Philip—not knowing whether he was alive or not.

A drum pounded in time with the procession. She glanced up. They were near to the end of the road. The stave church rose on her left. A little further, the glass library guarded the bridge to the castle.

Her heart thumped in time with the beat. It rattled through her sore bones. Across that bridge, within that castle, she would have to face the true enemy. For the first time, she *knew*. Knew who she was fighting and what she had to do.

What would Maeve do, though? Would she strike against Anmór? Would she assassinate the Reinholdians one by one? Would she crown herself queen of the world?

Arliss looked down at the smooth pavement and exhaled shudderingly. If that happened, many good things in the world would be ruined—lost—forever.

And she could have prevented it, couldn't she? At the rigdál mór, Maeve and Merna—both queens—had given their say. But she, the princess on a gilded throne, had no such sway.

A tightness wrapped around her stomach. If she had heeded her father's prodding and taken up the mantle of queen, she might have been able to stop this whole mess. At least she would have respect among the people of Ikarra. She would have a voice.

She raised her head again. She had to be strong, for Orlianna's sake.

They passed the library. The glass walls glimmered and flashed vague glimpses of the sun in her eyes. She squinted away and faced the castle again. The stony island with its sprawling palace lay quiet. One would have thought it empty.

Except for the lone figure who stood on the balcony, watching the procession. She had cloaked herself in a black robe to signify her mourning, but her silvery dress still shimmered beneath, along with her usual belt, hung with charms resembling the moon and stars.

They reached the arched bridge. Spires and stone loomed above.

Maeve looked down—straight at Arliss. Their eyes met. A chill pierced Arliss's blood, but she refused to look away.

Maeve's lips parted. She tilted her chin up as if to say, *see how high I am. See how low you are.*

Arliss lowered her chin and narrowed her eyes. She was beaten down, exhausted, and without the man who had been her rock for the past two years. But she still had a mission.

Whatever it took to bring down Maeve, she would do it.

CHAPTER TWENTY-NINE: MAEVE'S GAME

ORLANDO JOGGED DOWN THE STAIRS INTO THE BALLROOM. THE SAME setup remained from before the battle, the long tables arranged with maps and charts splayed out. But everything was quieter. Grimmer. No expectant buzz rustled through the lords and scribes and accountants.

Instead, there was a silence. At first it seemed a respectful silence—a mourning for the fallen.

But as Orlando descended the last step and walked between the first two tables, he realized what kind of silence it really was. The whiff of wine and stale bread only masked it. This was a silence of secrets.

The pain from the wound in his side flamed up again. Shards of fire shot through his bloodstream. He limped through the ballroom.

"Young man." The voice demanded he stop.

He turned. Lord Domnall sat hunched over stacks of paper, his graying hair tangled, his jaw slack. No doubt he was tallying the dead. Deciding where to bury them. The sort of decisions no one ever wants to make.

"Yes, sir?" Orlando said.

Domnall rested his fisted writing hand on the table. "Maeve has ordered for no one to leave the castle."

Orlando tensed. This was bad on several accounts. First, Maeve was either onto them or was at least preparing for some grand development. And second, because Arliss had already left the castle early that morning—in great secrecy, just in case.

And because he had helped her, they could both be accused of treason.

He swallowed hard. As if the things he'd done under Merna and Thane weren't treason enough.

Domnall cleared his throat, waiting for a response. "Is that clear?"

"Utterly so." Orlando shook himself from his drifting thoughts. "I'm only going to the armory. My knives are there, being sharpened—"

"Go." Domnall waved him away. "But make sure your companions know that they are not to go any other place besides here until otherwise notified. Am I clear?"

"*Utterly so.*" Orlando grated the words through his teeth. Though the old arse wasn't anything like *clear*. He filtered his thoughts through so many negatives and technicalities that his meaning wandered off.

He turned on his heel—trying to hide his limp—and strode through the wide opening out of the ballroom.

Turning left down the gilded passage, he breathed slow and deep in spite of the pain that seared his side. This hall was the place that, not four days ago, he had kissed Orlianna. *Her,* the princess of Ikarra!

And she had kissed him back. Or so it seemed. He thought it would have been more clear. But of course it wasn't.

Intricate mirrors with mahogany frames lined the right side of the hallway, all the way down to the armory. He glanced in one and frowned. The battle had stained and darkened the burgundy cloak more than ever before. His dark eyebrows drooped low over eyes deep with shame.

He looked away. What was he, that the Ikarran princess would ever love him? He shoved through the door and into the armory.

More silence. A smoldering fire and the sharp smell of iron meant there had been smithing going on not long ago. But the craftsmen and weaponers had cleared.

He stepped around an anvil, a crooked sword laid atop it. He walked down one of the aisles of spears and longbows, but it was no more lively. Everyone had been sent away.

A whisper of footsteps pattered from the far corner.

He jerked, cape swishing. A rotting old door swung half-open in the back corner of the room, behind all the aisles and hanging shields.

His heart pattered. This was the entrance to Maeve's secret tower. He treaded closer as the door slowly started to slide shut.

She was up there.

They were alone. He could threaten her, reveal how much he knew.

He could save his friends.

And—perhaps—he could fully redeem himself. A deed such as this might in Orlianna's eyes counterbalance the other things he'd done. He could love her without reservation.

He stuck his foot in the jamb just in time to stop the door from closing. And he eased it open and ascended the dim, spiraling staircase.

A salty wind blew down the empty main road of the second cantar, blowing Arliss's cloak flat against her back. She shivered and pulled it tighter about herself. She needed to find Rose and Mícheál as soon as possible.

It shouldn't have been this cold on the first day of May. In Reinhold, it would have been warm by now—even hot, some years. But the flicker of warmth in Ikarra's weather had melted and died amidst the groans of battle. The skies were stale and looming. The winds swirled erratically.

Arliss started down the street. Not a soul in sight. The city was quiet. Stores had closed. No one wanted to venture out. No one wanted to acknowledge what had happened.

Everyone had been hurt by the battle. *Everyone.* And no one knew how to react.

Arliss checked behind her, back beyond the library and over the bridge to the castle. The silence from the crown hadn't helped matters. The people probably worried that the royalty didn't know what to do—or worse, that they didn't care.

Orlianna had skulked around the castle, not sleeping or eating. She'd stood on the balcony, facing the Tuáma Fields since early that morning.

Arliss stepped up onto the sidewalk and ran her hand along the brick of the houses. They squashed into each other with hardly enough room for a body to fit between. She glanced up, hoping to see signs of life. But dark curtains veiled all the round windows.

She sighed. Almost as well that no one saw her. If it got back to Maeve that she was spying about under *her* nose…

It could mean bad things. Things like execution.

She reached the end of the line of homes. The next alley was wider, warmer. The next building was no home. It was shorter in height, longer lengthwise, and smelled perpetually of fresh bread and cold ale. Mícheál's tavern. She smiled and slipped into the alley.

The voices on the other side sounded out of place after the quiet main road. She pressed herself into the brick and listened. Three men. Two of them with the clink of mail, which meant they were guards. She didn't recognize their voices. But the third voice she knew.

"I haven't seen her," Garrick was saying. "But why does it matter? You can tell Domnall to mind his own business."

One of the guards snorted. "This isn't just his business. It comes from a higher power."

Garrick scoffed. "I don't think my dear Orli cares where the Reinholdians go in their leisure time."

Arliss held her breath. For one thing, Garrick needed to let off the whole attraction to Orlianna. She and he would never be. Especially now, he needed to leave well alone.

But what were the guards asking about? Were they after *her*?

The guard's voice was stale. "This order does not come from the princess."

"Who has a higher authority than the princess? Hm?" Garrick demanded. "Lachlan's gone. Rule passes to his daughter. That's the law."

"That's what you think," the guard snapped. "Just watch yourself, Lord Garrick. Be sure you are on the side of peace."

The guards clicked their heels together in salute, then marched away toward the castle.

Arliss stepped away from the side of the alley. The mossy brick had turned her hands damp. She took shallow breaths. Should she show herself? The guard's words were all too clear: she was not supposed to be out of the castle. Would Garrick turn her in?

She had to risk it. She had to find someone who would help and believe her.

Swinging her arms and taking confident strides, she stepped out of the alley and onto the riverway.

Garrick had his back to her. He walked after the guards with a slower pace, staring meditatively at the river. He clasped his hands behind his back and mouthed something she couldn't hear.

She smirked and mounted the three steps to the mahogany door of Mícheál's tavern. The two glass panes in the door cast her reflection back in her face. The tavern within was dark—closed. Just like everything else in the city.

She tried the handle.

It jangled noisily and gave a sharp squeak, but it was locked.

It captured Garrick's attention, though. He came running back down the street as she turned to face him, still standing at the top step.

"Arliss!" He eyed her up and down.

"Garrick." She put her hands on her hips. "What's the news?"

He lowered an eyebrow. "What are you doing out here?"

"What are *you* doing out here?" She dismounted the steps. "I thought no one is supposed to be out of the castle. If they're looking for me, couldn't they come looking for you?"

He swallowed. "You heard."

"What's going on here?"

"No one's supposed to be out and about. Maeve's orders."

Arliss glanced at the tavern just as a flicker of shadow passed behind the glass panes. She turned and looked Garrick in the eyes. "I don't take orders from Maeve. Neither should you. Neither should anyone."

He snorted. "You're mad."

"Probably. But sanity is a cheap price to pay for goodness. Maeve is not who you think. She's after all of us. We have to stop her."

His eyes flared. Then he stalked away, boots pounding stone.

"Garrick, you have to listen to me!" she shouted after him. "If you care even the slightest bit about Orlianna, you have to listen!"

He spun to face her. "Oh, I'll listen to you. They will all listen to you. Because after what you've said, you will be brought before Maeve herself." He waved at the distant figures. "Guards! Over here!"

Arliss looked wildly around for an escape. She could dive into the river, but she could only swim unnoticed for so long. And who knew what lurked in any waters. More crogall?

The street was empty. All the stores were closed, darkened.

The guards were running toward Garrick now. They would be near her soon.

She stepped up and jiggled the handle of the tavern again. Locked tight. Here, the line of homes blocked her from their view. But they would round the corner and see her in a few seconds, and it would be three men's testimony against her, not just one.

She dug her fingers into the brick building. She could climb, dodge them by jumping roofs.

"Stay where you are!" Garrick's voice loomed from around the corner.

She drew her knife.

They must have heard the sizzle of metal. "Arliss, stand down!"

Strong fingers curled around her arm and jerked her backward into the darkness of the tavern.

The door clicked shut. She blinked, letting her eyes adjust to the lightless room. The person who had pulled her in was still holding to her arm.

Three pairs of footsteps pattered just outside, then halted.

"Where's she gone?"

The hand tensed around Arliss's arm. She held her breath.

Boots stomped up the stone stairs.

"Maybe in here." Garrick rattled the tavern door.

Arliss bit her lip to silence her breathing. If it wasn't locked back…the door would swing inward and smack her across the face. She'd be charged for disobeying Maeve *and* running from her minions.

The mahogany wood jittered in its frame, but it did not budge.

Outside, Garrick gave an irritated sigh as he stomped away. "You two, split up and look for her! I've got to find Lady Maeve."

Their footsteps retreated. Arliss exhaled.

The hand slipped from her arm. She turned and saw Mícheál's gray outline. He jerked his head backward, indicating her to follow him.

"What's going on, Mícheál?" she whispered. She had told them the revelation about Maeve, but he may have discovered something more in the meantime.

He shrugged, striding to the left side of the tavern. "No one really knows."

"We have guesses." Rose's voice echoed toward them. She struck a match and lit a lone candle, revealing where she sat on one of many stools against a counter. A mirror spanned the wall behind the bar, casting the candlelight in a million directions over tables and chairs all over the room.

Arliss eased herself onto one of the leather stools. "Everything has gone so wrong."

Rose's brows scrunched together. "What do you mean?"

"Everything I came here for—to bring peace, to reunite the three clans. I came here thinking this would be the end of the fighting. And I thought once my questions were answered, I could go home."

Rose stared into the mirrored wall, the sleeves of her navy gown draping around her elbows. "Home. What a strange word." She looked back at Arliss. "I don't think home will ever be the same for any of us."

Arliss crossed her arms and propped them on the counter. "It's already different for me. Thane destroyed my village. We're just barely starting to rebuild our lives."

Mícheál eased himself onto a stool on the other side of Rose. "At least you have somewhere to call home."

"Don't you two?"

Mícheál shrugged. "I've lived here all my life, but that can't change my Anmórian heritage. Now that Anmór has attacked us…some people think I should be imprisoned. Even banished."

So the quiet city was not so silent as it seemed. Rumors floated beneath the surface. Already ill things were spreading. Maeve was constructing a plan—and had both lords on her side.

Arliss groaned and pressed her face into her palms. "I wish we could leave. I just want to see my parents. My home."

Rose restrained a sigh that sounded almost like a sob.

Arliss looked at her. "What?"

"Cahair isn't really home for me." Rose crossed her arms tight across her chest. "I was born in the outlands. My family moved to the North Havens, by the sea. There my aunt trained me how to be a spy. The spy chain once ran all over Ikarra, but when my aunt died, it died with her. Now it's just in Cahair."

"And that is under attack, too," Arliss put in.

Rose nodded solemnly. "My family owned a restaurant in the North Havens. After my aunt's death, they sent me to Cahair to meet with a new supplier—a trading partner by the name of Conor."

Mícheál stared into the glass wall. "My father."

Rose tucked her hair behind her ear. "I arrived here at the tavern late—at sundown. It was the day of the accident that killed Mícheál's parents. In his grief, he had left the door unlocked, so I came upon him right here—" she traced the polished wood "—by himself. Weeping."

She reached for Mícheál's hand and let their fingers intertwine.

"All alone in that tavern, there was no one else. So I held him. And I wept with him. I've never left Cahair since."

Arliss nodded. "But you're still looking for home."

Rose cut her eyes at Arliss, offering a slight smile. "There's a wanderlust in me that I can't quite control."

Arliss stood and pressed a hand on each of their shoulders. "You would both be welcome to come to Reinhold to visit. Maybe even to stay. We're in need of a good tearoom."

For a long time, she stood in silence, savoring the peace—the friendship.

Her mind started to drift away.

Then the pain in her forehead jerked her back. Philip was gone. Harrison was dead. Maeve was onto them in a dangerous way. They had to *do* something.

She stepped away from the counter, her heels clicking on floor that gleamed dully. "We have to go the castle and stop this madness."

Rose looked up, her eyes clearing. "We'll come with you."

Mícheál strode across the tavern, his long coat flapping. He opened a narrow closet. He pulled two quivers and two bows out of it. "We'd best be armed. Who knows what we will meet."

"No one knows," Arliss agreed. The loyal Ikarrans had no idea the evil that was creeping upon them. Not even Orlianna, perhaps.

Not even Orlando.

Orlando crept up the staircase so carefully even he couldn't hear his own footsteps. The winding staircase circled up the tower in murky shadows, the only light drifting through slits in the walls. And even that wasn't much. The day outside was somber, hidden beneath a chainmail sheet of turbulent clouds.

Strong steps pattered above. He counted the last three steps: fifty-three, fifty-four, fifty-five. He stood on the landing and leaned his head back to look around.

Pedestals with relics on them bracketed the round room at perfectly spaced intervals. Opposite this stair, another one wound up to another platform; and above that, an even higher one. And all around the ceiling and high, round walls hung yards of draping tapestries.

The footsteps above him halted. Maeve was on the upper platform.

He felt in his jerkin for his knives. Who knew what she might do if she felt cornered and threatened? He had to be ready.

Heels clicked again, echoing down from above. The stairs groaned one by one. His throat swelled, tightening as he tried to swallow. This was it. He could mend *everything* right now—his past sins, his career of treachery, his undeserved love from Orlianna.

Maeve turned the corner and descended the last few steps. Her black cloak dragged behind her, pulling open to reveal the blatant shimmer of her gown. Her hand hovered just above the handrail. Her eyes speared straight into his.

Breaths swelled out against his chest. It was all her fault. She'd advised Thane—manipulated him, even. She may have even controlled Orlando's former destiny.

"Sir Orlando." Maeve inclined her chin. "This tower is private."

The *gall* of this woman. He forced himself not to draw his knives and rush right at her.

"You snake," he spat.

She stood a moment, lips parting, trying to speak. Her eyes grew terribly wide. Then she narrowed them. Her expression grew sharp as steel. "Get out."

"I will not."

"Get out! I am of a mind to kill you forthwith. If you value your life—"

"I don't!" He jerked his knives from their sheaths and advanced.

"And neither do you. Using Thane—using *me*—to accomplish your purposes. I thought I was working willingly for Merna. But I see now I was just a pawn in your grand game."

Maeve seemed unconcerned by his outburst. She plucked a ring from the nearest pedestal, holding it up in the vague light. "The game has just begun. Pawns are expendable. They come and go."

"Like Arliss's uncles? Like Harrison?"

"Yes." She flashed him a glare. "They had no power to stop me. The queen is the most powerful piece in the game."

"The queen can be destroyed without the game ending."

She gaped slightly, but her eyebrows twisted in something like amusement. "You mean to destroy me with your newfound knowledge, dear little prince?"

He exhaled through his teeth. "No one will follow you once they know the truth. Already all Orlianna's circle knows. You will never rule the realms."

Maeve cupped the ring in her palm. "This ring—I believe you have one like it."

He clenched his fists with their fingerless gloves. No one had brought up the ring of Reinhold in some time. But he had been thinking about it throughout the whole battle. If the sword unlocked the vial, and the crown unlocked the sphere, the ring could do only one thing.

Maeve held out her hand. "That ring unlocks a powerful weapon. Give it to me, and secure that weapon for me, and I will not reveal your secrets. I will bury them where no one will discover them."

"My secrets?" His stomach soured. Maeve *knew*. She knew everything he'd done.

She even knew about *that* day. She may have even arranged it.

With this, she could break him in a hundred ways with just a few words to certain people. She could crush him like the pawn that he'd always been.

His voice rasped like sand in his throat. "I will not give it to you. And I will never betray Orlianna either. The pendant will never be yours."

She set the ring on the pedestal. "Orlando, be sensible! Give them both to me, and I will let you both live. You can escape to the east and make a home in Reinhold, where no one will ever think to harm you."

He screamed, his voice echoing up the tower. "I would rather die than bargain with you!" He rushed at her, knives flicking.

She drew herself upright. She held both her hands out. And she bellowed something horrible and dark in the Anmórian tongue.

An earthquake shook the tower. Orlando stumbled. A rumbling like a growl rattled up through the foundations of the castle. He fell on his face at Maeve's feet.

"Your wish is granted. You will die."

He craned his neck up at her, pushing himself up with hands still gripping the knives. He didn't know what had caused the rumblings, but he couldn't threaten her again. The air of the tower had grown thick with dark power.

"You can break me if you like," he managed. "But know that we can break you. Arliss can break you."

"Arliss knows." Maeve's eyes went shot with fear. She glanced around, looking through Orlando almost as if she didn't see him. *"Arliss knows."*

He eased himself to his feet, flicking his burgundy cloak behind his heels.

She reached up and undid the tie of her cloak. She cast the black cloth on the floor and strode for the stairs down, not even casting him another glance. Whatever had seized her mind, it had made her forget him completely.

Orlando waited until her footsteps disappeared and the door cracked shut below. Then he rushed down the stairs.

He had to find Arliss.

Orlianna stared down at the castle below her, the river beneath the rocks, the fields beyond that. Her arms fastened like steel bars across her chest, restricting her breaths. She blinked and found her eyes clogged with tears.

She was dying.

Inside.

Harrison's death shredded through the deepest part of her soul. She had sometimes wondered what was left of her heart. Now she knew. There was still something there. But it was being crushed to death.

The balcony doors clicked open behind her and banged shut. She didn't turn around. She could not move.

"Where is Arliss?" Maeve snapped.

Orlianna clenched her teeth and closed her crusted eyelids. "As you know everything, I can hardly be expected to answer your questions."

Maeve inhaled sharply.

Orlianna waited, eyes closed. She had not spoken to her grandmother since before the battle. Then, she had seen her as a noble but misguided ruler, trying to mend an unmendable situation.

Now, she was a traitor. A villain. A murderer.

"I *don't* know everything," Maeve said.

"But I do, now. I know all, thanks to your loving sister." She swallowed, testing her grandmother's limits. "I know the truth."

Heels clicked toward Orlianna.

"Do you?" Maeve's voice was high with false perplexity. "And what is that?"

Orlianna seethed. *Enough.* Enough of the lies, the pretending. Enough of acting like Reinhold was a new idea, or that the name of Thane was unfamiliar. Enough of treating Merna like an enemy rather than the accomplice that she was. Enough of shunning responsibility for Harrison's death.

She whirled, fists clenched, her voice rising to a scream. "It was you—you fiend! Everything I have followed, everything I have tried to live up to? It is all a lie!" She stabbed her finger into the air inches from Maeve's face. "You are a lie. And I know the truth. We *all* know the truth. And you will never be our queen."

Maeve stared at her with cold, gray eyes. "Is that all?"

Orlianna gasped for air. She didn't know this woman. This was not her grandmother. "Who are you?"

"I am Maeve." She lifted her arms. The charms on her belt jingled. "I am the moon. I am the queen of the three realms."

Orlianna dropped her voice to a whisper. "How could you lie to your own granddaughter all these years?"

"It was for your own good. I always meant to reveal everything in time. But this story is beyond even my control, and things have spun in ways I could not predict."

Orlianna shook her head in disbelief.

Maeve hesitated, stretched her hand out. "Please, Orlianna. Reconsider. If you stand down and comply, I will not harm you or any of the Reinholdians. You can escape and begin again across the sea."

Orlianna's blood burned again. "I will never bargain with you."

"Orlando said the same." Maeve nodded. "Well, that's that, then."

"That's what?"

She strode for the doors. "It is time. Give the order—I want everyone in this city in the throne room within two hours."

"Why?" The throne room—which lay behind the ballroom, beneath these chambers—had not been used in years. Nestled in the rocky island, it was easily twice the size of the ballroom.

"You will see." Maeve swept open the doors. "You *will* see."

CHAPTER THIRTY:
CORONATION

ARLISS SWUNG THE DOOR OF THE TAVERN OPEN AND STEPPED out into a street wildly different from that of a few moments before. Citizens now packed the riverway road, shouldering their way along—all in the same direction. All toward the end of the road where the glass library stood.

All toward the castle.

Arliss jumped off the steps, Rose and Mícheál behind her. Something was up. This was a dense crowd already, and getting denser. Soon the street would be packed from the storefronts to the river's edge.

Rose hid her quiver under her skirts, slid her bow down her back, and drew up her hood. "What in the world?"

"Something's afoot." Mícheál pulled his hood over his head. "Let's be careful."

Arliss hooded herself and stepped into the crowd. People jostled her on every side. She sucked in her breath and tried to shrink the width of her shoulders. No one heeded her.

This morning, these people had been crushed with silent grief. Now their mood was uncomfortably festive. They should have been weeping, making monuments to the dead. Instead, they pressed on in rapt anticipation. Fathers carried children on their shoulders. Young women had strung their hair with flowers. Everyone wore their finest jewelry, and it glinted in the sinking sun.

All this—in such a short time! It had to be an order from the castle.

Arliss whispered to Rose, "A service commemorating the fallen?"

Rose shook her head. "These people are going to a party."

A sharp voice rose above the hubbub. "There she is! That Reinholdian princess!"

Arliss tugged her cloak about her head, looking for the speaker. Some of the crowd stopped, also glancing about.

Mícheál prodded her and Rose on, keeping them near the storefronts. "Keep moving."

"Stop them!" The accusing voice came again. "It's her!"

The crowd pressed about them, hemming them close to the backs of homes.

Arliss picked up her pace. This was bad. There was a watch for her. And she knew just who might have placed such a watch.

Another voice—a nearby woman—pointed right at Arliss. "You're right! It's Arliss."

"And that tavern lad! He's Anmórian, ain't he?" A cocky fisherman elbowed through the crowd and faced the three. He aimed his finger at Arliss. "There's a price on yer head, miss."

She kept her voice steady. "Where are all these people going?"

"Have you not heard?" The woman swept her hand skyward. "Everyone's been summoned to the castle. Maeve is making a great announcement."

Arliss's heart stumbled as she choked on her breath. Maeve was moving faster than she could prevent it. At this point it would be hard to stop her.

But they had to try.

She plowed into the crowd, forcing her way past the fisherman. "Let us through!"

The masses ahead were already rounding the library, crossing the bridge to the castle. But two dozen people had halted, watching the kerfuffle with Arliss, Rose, and Mícheál.

A burly man—a sailor, by the look of his uniform dress and calloused palms—stepped in their way. "It *is* them. I say we send 'em all back where they belong!"

Several around murmured in agreement.

"The Reinholdians—ship 'em back across the ocean. And that Anmórian tavern owner, he can take his blooming self back over the border. I've seen more live Anmórians than I ever want to see again!"

The crowd roared in approval. Someone shoved Arliss into Mícheál. He stumbled closer to the rowdy sailor.

"I am a citizen of Ikarra, Keefe." Mícheál's fists were tight. His cloak hid his bow.

"Not by my reckoning, lad."

Mícheál jabbed his fist up into the sailor's jaw.

Keefe spat in surprise, then swung his fist around and clobbered Mícheál across the face. Mícheál staggered backward into Rose and Arliss.

Rose tossed her hair behind her head, eyes flaming. "No you don't." She pushed both hands into Keefe's chest.

He grabbed her arms and twisted them to the side, contorting them in opposite directions. She gasped in pain, kicking him in the shins.

"Let her go." Arliss drew her knife and pointed it over Rose's shoulder at him. "Let us all go."

Keefe hesitated.

In that moment of hesitation, Mícheál rose—stringing his bow—and hooked it around Keefe's neck. He stepped behind Keefe, jerking the noose tight around his throat. Keefe released Rose's arms and grabbed at his throat.

Mícheál slipped the bow free and made a dash for the river. "Come on!"

Arliss and Rose pounded behind him, Keefe and a few others right behind. Arliss kept her knife ready. "We have to get to the castle. Any ideas?"

Mícheál sniffed. "When *don't* I have ideas?"

"Well—" Rose began.

Mícheál cut her off and pointed. Three narrow longboats floated on the peaceful waters. "Those."

They were almost to the edge of the riverway.

Arliss ran faster. Her hood swept off her head, and her hair tangled with the air behind her.

The crowd shouted close behind. Too close.

She looked behind. Keefe was ten strides away.

She looked ahead. At this rate it was either jump for a boat or fall headlong into the water.

She jumped.

Orlianna rushed down the ballroom steps, silk swishing about her heels. The formal dress with its ballooning skirt was a decoy. Underneath she wore a tightly fitted dress and a belt packed with weapons—the claw knives, a grappling hook, even a short sword. And, of course, the ancient dagger Kenton had given her. The dagger that belonged to Merwin.

The tension in her breast knotted tighter. Merwin had laid treachery on top of treachery. Not only had his son killed her brother, but now he himself had dealt the death blow to her closest friend.

She rubbed her skirts, tracing the outline of the leather scabbard. She recalled Kenton's words to her before they left Reinhold. He had called upon her to bring peace between the clans.

More than that, he had asked her to urge Arliss to rise to the role of queen.

Thus far, she had done neither.

The ballroom's high ceilings reverberated with the din of a crowd. Ikarrans from both cantars streamed through the double doors and across the ballroom in her direction. But they did not head up the stairs. All shoved forward on either side of the staircase—to the room that lay behind, beyond, below.

Orlianna swallowed. She had not entered the throne room since her mother's death nine years ago. *No one* had entered, to her knowledge. Maeve ruled from a distance, not face-to-face as her mother had. Lachlan was bedridden. And there had been no coronation to dust off the varnished floors and gilded thrones.

Until now.

She descended the last step as the crowd parted around her. They didn't seem to see her. She was invisible.

She scanned the ballroom. Orlando was shoving through the crowd toward her. He reached the base of the stairs and grabbed her hands.

"What's going on?" She released the breath in her lungs.

"Something awful." Orlando squeezed her hands. "Maeve is making the next move in her game."

"How do you know?"

"I confronted her. In her tower. She offered me safety. You as well, if only we would stand down and not resist her."

Orlianna stepped forward, pulling him with her, and her weapons jostled around her legs. "Not in a thousand ages."

"That's what I told her. So she threatened to kill me." He glanced around. "The tower shook. It felt like the foundations of the castle were trembling."

So that hadn't been a figment of her imagination. Good to know she wasn't drifting into insanity because of her grief.

"Orlianna!" Arliss's voice rose over the hubbub from the direction of the doors. She, Rose, and Mícheál dug their way through the drift of the crowd until they reached Orlianna and Orlando.

"Maeve is making a great announcement to all the people—in the throne room," Arliss said. "I think we can guess what that might be."

"We have to stop her." Orlianna turned on her heel and rounded the left side of the staircase, running her palm against the marble wall.

Mícheál edged alongside her. "Make way for the princess!"

A man cast them a dirty look. "Why? What's the princess to us?"

Mícheál's lips pulled back, his teeth bared. "The way I see it, she is your leader."

"Not as far's I can see. Maeve's the one who's carried us through this mess so far." The man continued plodding down the wide hall.

Orlianna reached for her pendant and clenched it. The people were already looking to Maeve as their leader—their savior. If she didn't tell them the truth, they would be under her spell before they knew what had happened.

"What's your plan?" Orlando asked. "Waltz down the aisle and snatch the crown out of Maeve's hand?"

"Just about." Orlianna danced her way through the crowd to the other side of the hall. "Follow me."

They all reached the other side, where an indentation in the marble walls held an iron door. Cobwebs wisped inside the large keyhole. The other four crowded in the alcove around Orlianna as she jerked her outer skirts up and pulled out her keychain. She hadn't use this one in a while. But the knotted key still clicked in the rusting metal. The door swung open.

Arliss inhaled. "A secret passage."

Orlianna stepped into the darkness. "It leads straight to the back of the throne room. I used to spy on royal councils in it as a girl."

The passage was dark as a tomb. They were half-underground now. The throne room was partially carved into the rocky island which the whole castle sat on.

Orlianna hesitated with the doorhandle at the other end of the passage. No matter what was about to happen in this room, it was not good. The way she acted—and reacted—would forever change her fate as a monarch of Ikarra.

She depressed the handle and pulled the door open.

Afternoon light flooded the vast room from windows that spanned the upper half of the far wall, behind the throne platform. The bottom half of the room was underground, but the light from above rendered everything clearly.

She'd never imagined the throne room could hold so many people. This was Ikarra at its finest. They had gathered so quickly. These were people hungry for leadership, thirsty for change. They had faced death and now desired life in excess.

And she could not give it to them. What life she had was cold and pallid.

The others filed out around her, and she shut the door. Right now—in the corner of the room—no one had noticed their entrance. But once they ascended the steps to the platform, everyone would see.

A hush crept over the crowd. They parted down the middle, some pressing themselves against the greenish stone walls to form an aisle.

Orlianna craned her neck to see over the heads.

Maeve marched down the aisle and mounted the platform, where she turned and raised her hands to hush the people. She wore the same silver gown, and had added a cape of purple crushed velvet. Her gray hair was gathered in a tight bun at the back of her head.

Domnall and Garrick stepped up on either side of Maeve. Orlianna reached for the back of her neck. Had everyone gone over to her side? Was no one loyal anymore?

Maeve's voice rang out like a trumpet in the room's precise acoustics. "People of Cahair, welcome! I know that these are hard times, times when we should gather to mourn. I do not ignore that. For it is because of these hard times that I have called this city together."

Arliss caught Orlianna's eye and glanced up toward the platform.

Orlianna shook her head. Not yet.

Maeve continued. "After the death of King Lachlan, and the recent conflict, Ikarra lies in an unstable place. If we are to move forward, you need a ruler."

The crowd murmured, mostly in what sounded like approval.

Domnall clasped his hands behind his back. "On his deathbed, Lachlan approved that—should he happen to not survive—Lady Maeve and the lords could appoint a temporary leader. And that leader stands before you. She is Maeve."

Maeve glanced around, assessing the people's response.

Silence echoed.

"Does anyone gainsay this nomination?" Domnall demanded.

Orlianna stamped up the stairs to the platform. "*I* gainsay it."

Maeve ended her scan of the room with her eyes piercing Orlianna. She held her chin high and smiled. "You think *you* could be queen?"

Orlianna strode across the dais, skirts rustling. "It is my right. I am the heir."

Maeve dropped her voice. "These people will never follow you." She turned to the assembly. "Orlianna has long urged us to fight and to seek conflict. By building her aircraft and flying them, she tempted Anmór's wrath. But we have no need for war with Anmór. If you will have me as your queen, I will bring you peace."

Several in the crowd applauded.

Orlianna gripped her skirts in exasperation. "Listen to me! You do not know what you are doing. Maeve is a fraud—a sorceress! She is in league with our enemies!"

"Silence, princess." Domnall edged toward her. "Get off."

She cocked her head at him. "Never."

Arliss mounted the platform behind her, pointing at Maeve. "It's true. She was behind Thane, if that name means anything to any of you."

"This discord is what caused this battle in the first place!" Maeve spread her arms wide. "Is there not agreement among us that we should seek unity?"

"Aye!" the crowd roared.

Maeve turned to the single throne that had been set. Beside it, a delicate crown shimmered atop a pedestal.

Orlianna shook her head. "You are lying to everyone, even yourself."

Maeve's eyes flashed like daggers. "Do you *want* more to die? Do you want the courtyards of this very palace to be stained with blood?"

Orlianna's hands curled. "No."

"Do you want all to become like Harrison?"

"*No!*" Orlianna thrashed her clenched fists. She shuddered, trying to regain composure. "But know that you are wrong. You will be brought to justice in the end."

"Wrongness depends on your perspective."

Orlianna gulped down the acid in her throat. "Then whose perspective is right?"

"Well, who wins?"

Maeve reached out and lifted the crown.

Orlianna stretched out her hand. "That was my mother's crown."

"Your mother is gone."

"*Put it down.*" Orlianna reached for her pendant.

Maeve faced the people. "Let a decree go forth through all the land: we are not at war with Anmór. We will seek peace. Anyone who fights against that peace will be eliminated."

"By whose authority?" Orlianna demanded.

Maeve raised the crown high. Then she placed it on her own head. "The queen's."

BO BURNETTE/342

Chapter Thirty-One: Deep Sorcery

ARLISS'S LIMBS HAD TURNED TO STONE. DESPITE THE WARMTH OF the mass gathered in the throne room, she felt icy. Frozen. Unable to move, to speak.

A scream gurgled somewhere in the bottom of her throat. She staggered across the platform toward where Maeve faced the crowd, arms upraised, the crown settling on her head.

The crowd roared, their applause thundering the foundations of the rocky island beneath them.

Arliss glanced over the crowd. These people had fought bravely against Anmór assault. If only they knew they were now supporting some of that same evil. If only they knew what she knew—that Maeve was a villainess.

But they knew not. And now they would not listen. Maeve had prematurely trounced any rebellion or riposte. The people wanted a leader who would bring peace and unity.

They were getting what they wanted.

Arliss stepped in front of Maeve, blocking the crowd's view of their new queen.

Maeve glared at her, lips twitching. "Move, girl."

"I am no *girl.*" Arliss clenched her fists, longing to reveal the bow she had hidden beneath her cloak. "I am the princess of Reinhold."

Maeve bellowed laughter toward the ceiling. "What challenge is that to me? Go home to your parents, child, and tell them how you have failed. Even your mother cannot have foreseen this."

Arliss's pulse raced. Maeve's reach may have grown so long she had touched even Reinhold. What if her parents—

"What do *you* know of my mother?"

"I know much of all people and all things." Maeve drew herself to her full height. She had always been a strikingly tall woman, but now she seemed to tower over Arliss. "You could never challenge me. You, a simple barbarian princess. What do you have to come against me?"

"I have the truth."

Maeve leaned so close her heavy breaths blasted hot into Arliss's eyes. "What do these people care for the truth? It doesn't matter anymore. Thane's name means nothing in Ikarra. The shock you felt when Merna revealed the truth belongs to you alone."

Arliss looked to Orlianna for support, but she was motionless.

Maeve adjusted the crown on her head. "Well, you heard my decree. Those who fight against peace must be eliminated. You will all leave—now."

"Who do you think you are?" Arliss snarled. "Do you mean to rule the universe with your twisted mind? Do you think you are *God?*" She realized she was screaming so loud everyone in the hall heard her.

"I am the goddess of these realms."

"You are no deity." Arliss drew her bow from behind her back. "You kill when and where you wish. You trample on the voices of all but yourself. You don't even care for your own family!"

The crowd gasped, murmuring.

Maeve's eyes bloomed at the sight of the bow. "Guards, seize her!"

Domnall drew his sword at once and advanced from the edge of the platform, but Garrick stayed, looking uncertain.

Guards shoved through the increasingly frenzied crowd on their way to the throne.

Arliss backed toward the secret passage, grabbing Orlianna's arm. Orlianna refused to budge. She stared at Maeve, her lips quivering.

Blood surging through her skull, Arliss jerked at Orlianna's arm.

"Come on!"

Orlando leapt onto the platform and helped her drag Orlianna to the door. Mícheál held the door open. Rose stood beside him, her jaw tight.

Arliss looked back. Two dozen guards were closing in fast.

"Stop them!" Maeve raised her hand. But she was hardly heard above the shouts of the people. Confusion gushed through the room's fading light.

Orlando pulled Orlianna into the murky doorway. Mícheál shoved Rose in and slipped in after her. Arliss squeezed through the closing door. It clanged shut behind her.

Metal crushed against metal from outside. Some of the guards must have run into the door, unable to halt in time.

"Arliss, run!" Rose grabbed her hand and yanked her down the narrow passage just as the door jerked open and orange light reached in.

Arliss ran.

The guards' footsteps echoed close behind.

They reached the other end of the passage and burst out into the wide hall leading to the ballroom. The creamy marble walls were cast with a reddish glow that flowed in from the ballroom. But no light came from the direction of the throne room.

The doors at the far end of the hallway had been thrown open, and the crowd rushed toward them like a horde of ants. Maeve and her guards tried to get through, but they could do little to stop the mob.

Arliss gripped her bow to her chest. They had to get out of here. Maeve may have crowned herself queen, but she didn't have full control. If they could escape her clutches and regroup—even find Philip—they could still have a chance at this thing.

She nudged Orlianna's back. "You have to lead us out of here."

Orlianna shuddered. She seemed unable to process what was going on. "I cannot."

Arliss exhaled, the buzz of the crowd behind her sending chills up her spine. She bit her lip. Fine. *She* would do it.

She strode into the ballroom. Everyone else followed her. She didn't have to command them. They just followed. Was she really just a girl—a simple princess? This felt like the authority of a queen.

But she did not want that authority. It threw itself upon her without asking. Every time she had assumed this role before, she had failed. Her uncles had died. Her city had been destroyed. She had lost Philip—maybe forever.

Orlando jogged beside her. "I may be wrong, but with a mob and a sorcerous queen at our heels, we might ought to run."

"True," Rose agreed, running up on the other side of Arliss.

Arliss's boots pummeled the ballroom floor, sending spikes of pain up her legs, which still ached from the battle. She swallowed the pain. She had a mission. The pain in her heart burned louder than her that of body. If they could make it to the Tuáma Fields, they could track down Philip.

If they could make it.

She threw the castle's double doors open to the sunset as the mob reached the end of the hallway, filling the ballroom behind them.

The company filed out of the castle—Orlianna, Orlando, Rose, Mícheál—running from the madness.

But the mob no longer led the way. Maeve ran at their head, flanked by Domnall and Garrick. The two lords calmed the crowd, but Maeve was fixed on Arliss's company.

Arliss scrambled onto the island's treacherous terrain. Clumps of rock jagged up in bouldering mounds all around. They all stopped atop one flattish rock, catching breaths.

Orlianna finally found her tongue. "Where are we going?"

Arliss pointed to the conductor's box at the edge of the island. "We have two boats moored at the base of the funicular track."

"And you intend to paddle our way to safety?"

"Do you have a better idea?" Arliss demanded.

The doors swung open, reflecting the sunset light into her eyes. Maeve stepped out onto the rocks—only twenty paces away.

"She doesn't," Rose quipped.

Maeve advanced.

"Run," Orlianna commanded.

Arliss waited for Maeve to speak, to do something. She seemed deep in thought. Her fingers moved in time with her muttering lips. She stared at the ground.

Then Maeve smiled. She looked around at the river that flowed about the castle island. Murky water gushed dark in the dying light. She raised her hands, fingers twitching. The words on her lips rose to audible volume. "*Crogaill den domhain, éist liom! Dúisigh! An comhrac in!*" She smirked straight at Arliss. "*Scriosann mo naimhde.*"

Arliss stood stunned by the evil in the words. What had Maeve said? It was Anmórian. After hearing it spoken she recognized the language's out-of-reach cadence. But why did Maeve use it now?

"No." Orlianna must have understood. Her eyelids revealed even more of her fearful, green eyes. "Run!"

Arliss stumbled to the rocky edge of the island.

The river gurgled violently forty feet below her. The two flat boats drifted into midstream, the water's turbulence nearly breaking their restraints.

Behind them, Maeve's guards exited the castle. They leapt boulders on their way across the crag.

"We have to get down there." Arliss pointed to the boats.

"Think again," Mícheál said wryly.

The raging waters parted in the middle. A knobbly, ridged shape rose up in the middle of the river. Almost like a mound of rock, but greenish and wet and shining like armor.

And with eight muscled tentacles swirling all around.

Arliss's stomach clenched with nausea. She'd never wanted to see another crogall in her life.

But there it was.

Orlianna grabbed her aching head. She *would not* let Maeve's treachery keep her from fighting. Like she had promised Harrison, she would fight to her last breath.

Arliss nocked an arrow on her bow and aimed it at the oncoming guards.

Orlando jerked his twin knives from their sheaths, his jaw thrust out.

Rose and Mícheál raised bows in like stance, rushing to meet Maeve's forces.

No—this did not need to become Ikarrans against Ikarrans. Maeve *was* the enemy. And the beasts in the river below needed to be destroyed. But some of these guards she had known for a long time.

"Wait!" Orlianna called. But it was too late. They released the first of their arrows and two of the guards crumpled into indentions in the rock.

And it was too late for Rose and Mícheál as well. Guards surrounded them, slashing their bowstrings and snatching their bows away.

Mícheál fumbled for his dagger. One of the guards slammed him in the temple with the butt of a spear. He dropped, limp.

"Mícheál, no!" Rose fell beside him, grasping his shoulders. "Mícheál!"

Arliss started forward, arrow ready.

Orlianna stretched her arm in front of Arliss, pushing her back. "Stop! You'll be killed."

"We have to help them."

Rose glanced up, strands of hair blowing away from her face. She gritted her teeth as guards surrounded her. "Keep going! Get out of here!"

Arliss wavered. "My friends—"

"*Go.*" Rose mouthed it again as the guards bound her hands.

Orlianna turned, hoping Arliss had the sense to follow. To her surprise, the Reinholdian princess turned and took the lead in their band of three.

Orlando jumped off the edge of the crag onto a flat just below.

"Are we just going to meet them head-on?"

"Them?" Orlianna demanded. She looked down at the thrashing creature in the water below. True enough, two crogall now stuck their toothy snouts up toward her. The catlike eyes narrowed, dripping nostrils snarling.

If Maeve controlled these, she could have been behind the others—

Orlianna jumped down beside Orlando. She was done making lists of the things Maeve had been behind. It sufficed to say that every evil in the three realms traced itself back to her grandmother.

Arliss jumped between them. "Are we going to kill these things, or not?"

"How?" Orlando asked.

Orlianna pressed a hand into the craggy stone, stroking her pendant with the other. Maeve wanted this gift. That meant it was very powerful indeed, if she thought she needed it to be fully queen of the realms.

Did Maeve know what she knew—that ancient Lasairbláth filled the pendant to bursting?

Or that, if her suspicions were true, the ring of Reinhold unlocked it?

Of course Maeve knew.

Orlianna heard her own voice echoing in her head: "Lasairbláth gains power with age. At least, so it is rumored." Perhaps it was the time to use it. Perhaps it had hung against her chest long enough. She could destroy these creatures in a moment. But what else would be destroyed along with it?

It was too risky. She climbed down after Arliss.

Arliss walked with a dancer's precision. A misstep could dislodge an avalanche of stones and hurtle her straight into the mouths of the crogall below. Not like she wasn't walking straight into their mouths, anyway.

A natural staircase cut down this side of the mountain, offering a passable—if treacherous—alternative to the funicular. Judging by the metallic cranking that crackled behind her, Maeve's guards were using the funicular already.

Orlianna's shout confirmed her suspicions. "Hurry! They're trying to cut us off."

"From what?" Arliss muttered. "The crogall?"

The funicular's clank distracted the attention of the two creatures, who drifted away underwater with uncanny silence.

Arliss kept going. This was their chance. Scramble down, jump in the boats while their backs were turned. They could be across the river and in the second cantar before the crogall turned around.

She waved Orlianna and Orlando forward. They were only a stone's throw from the water now. The uneven ripples cast troubled waves against the base of the island. The boats settled down, wood scraping the rocks.

"Quickly," she whispered. "Before they see us."

"They aren't the only ones we have to worry about." Orlianna still held onto her necklace with white fingers.

Arliss craned her neck. The castle, with its looming towers and vast windows, stretched away toward the sky. Closer, at the edge of the uppermost rocks, Maeve stared down at them. The diamonds in her crown glinted orange in the sunset.

Orlando gulped. "We're losing the light."

"We'll lose more than that if we don't hurry." Arliss shoved Orlianna toward the boats. "Go."

One crogall eased out of the water, tentacles swishing toward the funicular. It still hadn't seen them. The vehicle staggering down to the opposite shore was far more interesting.

Arliss glanced left. The empty fields were aflame with sunset.

Orlianna followed her eyeline and went rigid. "You're trying to leave Cahair, aren't you?"

"Of course I am," Arliss hissed. "What else is there? Maeve has turned us into outlaws. We have to find help and guidance, and it bloody well won't come from her."

"You want me to leave my people when they need me most?"

Arliss had heard enough. Another moment and they would all be chomped to bloody bits. "They don't need you. Not now."

Orlianna spun to face her, her lips contorting with a thousand words. She huffed and followed Orlando down to the boats.

Orlando jumped down into the longboat, and the wooden tub rocked back and forth a little.

Ripples pulsed outward through the waters.

One of the crogall turned and shot down the river toward them.

Orlando's ears reverberated with the sound of Orlianna screaming his name. The boat jiggled beneath his boots. He clenched his abdomen to hold his balance.

His stomach flipped over on itself when he looked down the river.

The two crogall shot toward him, parting the waters. Their flailing tentacles spanned the whole length of the river.

He scrambled to get out of the boat, but the vessel had drifted from shore, and the connecting rope was taut. Orlianna grabbed the rope and tried to tow him in, but time moved too quickly.

The first crogall nearly hit his boat head-on. It ducked underwater at the last moment, its jagged back scraping the boat's underside.

The force jerked the boat from the shore. The rope split. The boat whirled toward the other side of the river. Orlando grabbed the side to keep himself from falling overboard.

Orlianna stood almost in the water, her face desperate with the inability to do anything.

Arliss had an arrow drawn, but surely she knew by now that *that* would do nothing against these creatures.

Behind him, the crogall pivoted, dragging itself back around by its suctioning tentacles. They squelched their way along the rock, and the gigantic body faced Orlando again. The feline eyes slanted at him—just watching. Waiting.

He drew his knives slowly. They sizzled almost silently as they left their sheaths.

But the creature did not move.

Maeve's voice rang out from above. "Mo ghile, ionsaí! Scriosann!"

My darling, attack! Destroy!

Orlando's blood chilled.

Maeve was a black silhouette against the orange light. "Mharú dó!"

Kill him.

Orlando glanced around for an oar. It lay in the bottom of the boat. Still holding both knives, he drew out the oar and plunged it into the water. He dragged himself toward where Orlianna stood on the shore.

Maeve's next words could not have been meant for the beast. They were for her own enjoyment. And, since she knew he understood Anmórian, they were probably for him, too.

"Lig an abhainn sreabhadh le fuil!"

Let the river flow with blood.

Orlando glared up at her, then back at the crogall which now swam slowly toward him. "Blood, yes. But not ours."

Orlianna's heart pounded like a war drum, but her breathing slowed. Time slowed. The crogall floated lazily downriver. Orlando's boat slogged through the water toward her. Arliss's arrow spiraled from her bow, every second an eternity.

She inhaled. They were trapped on all sides. Harrison wasn't here to swoop in and save her anymore. She was *going* to die, one way or another. Maeve had made that certain.

And if she was going to die, she'd die protecting Orlando.

Arliss's arrow struck the crogall's hide and pinged off.

Orlianna leapt into the boat. It rocked, nearly keeling over into the water. She kneeled in the prow, reaching out to steady it.

Orlando gasped. "What on earth are you doing?"

"Shut up!" was all she could manage as she drew her claws against the crogall's approach. "And paddle!"

Stunned, he stabbed the paddle into the water and spun them toward the opposite shore. Orlianna let the metal claws become one with her hands. The hide was impenetrable, but there were at least the eyes. If she could get that close.

The crogall reached them, rising above the water—

It dove low, arcing deep beneath their boat. A wave spat into Orlianna's eyes. She blinked behind her.

Arliss had cut the other boat free and shoved it into midstream. She had finally put away her bow—useless thing—and wielded the formidable combination of knife and paddle. Not like she could do a thing with either. The way she stood, so invitingly insolent, the crogall would shatter her balance and swallow her whole.

Both crogall sped back down the river, darting over and under each other in a mischievous dance. The water churned, casting wild waves in their direction.

"Be ready!" Orlianna shouted over her shoulder.

The force of a train exploded into the boat. Water drenched her. Something crackled, either wood or her spine or both. She went flying.

Then swimming, water tangling her dress and hair and surging up her nose and drowning the shallow breaths in her lungs.

The rock-crowded river was dark. She blinked away the saline sting. Two dark ovals shifted above her, blocking out light that dripped through the water like blood.

Two other dark shapes rushed past her, blocking out the light entirely. A sticky tentacle wrapped round her legs. Both dresses stuck to her like plaster.

She clawed into the tentacle, stabbing so deep the point of the blade pressed dangerously against her thigh.

The tension snapped, jerking the claw from her hand. The crogall's wounded arm unrolled, hurling her deeper underwater.

She clawed her way up through the water, desperate for air.

Blood stained the water around her. Just that of the crogall—or of her companions?

She surfaced and found herself far downstream—nearly to the riverway. Rose's tearoom was within sight. Rose. Mícheál. Probably both dead by now. They might *all* be dead.

She took a watery breath. She flailed, remembering how to swim. Her muscles tightened. She took a deft stroke back toward the crogall.

The back of her hand smacked stone. She'd reached the opposite riverbank. Cahair spread out long and tall from her vantage point below the rocks that barricaded the river's edge.

She climbed out of the water and started running along the shoreline. Sandy rocks grated beneath her boots as she pounded toward the funicular's landing spot. She squinted.

Just as she'd guessed—the crogall were splitting up. One whirlpooled around Arliss's boat. The other dragged Orlando and his craft back near the funicular.

Up by the castle, Maeve's hands jerked apart, mimicking the crogall's movement. *Causing* it.

Orlianna ran faster. How could she have been so *blind?* All this time, her grandmother wasn't just trying to assume rule of the three clans. She was doing so by manipulation and sorcery.

Orlando's damp burgundy cape was a whirlwind as he spun his knives through the eight tentacles that dragged him further and further. He wouldn't hold out much longer, especially if the crogall decided to use more than just its tentacles.

And Arliss, too, was failing fast. The crogall lunged at her with its toothed snout open. And, for whatever inane reason, she'd gotten her bow back out.

Orlianna flew across the rocky river shoreline, the glass library to her left casting flaming flecks of light into her eyes. She could only help one of them. And the burgundy spy needed her more right now than the Reinholdian princess.

Arliss didn't know how she was still standing. Her legs were like water below her, her fingers like ice.

And the crogall snapped its toothy grin at her again and again.

It wasn't trying to devour her—yet. It toyed with her, baiting her. She'd already wasted three arrows confirming what she already knew: trying to pierce its hide was like trying to pierce a wall of thick steel.

On the left-hand ridge, Orlianna rushed to aid Orlando. She shouldn't have let the boats get separated. But the waters were too unruly to paddle. She'd long since cast the paddle in the bottom of the boat.

The crogall rose, jaws spreading wide. The teeth glinted like knives. The rough tongue flapped. But this time, the beast didn't duck at the last moment. It chomped down on the boat. The prow cracked.

Arliss tripped back into the stern, nearly dropping her bow.

She tightened her fist until she couldn't feel her hand. No matter what, no matter *anything*, she couldn't lose her bow. Philip had made this for her so long ago. It was like a friend to her now. And it was the one thing she could count on to keep her alive.

The crogall lifted the boat out of the water as if it was a toy. Then, scaly snout jerking, it hurled Arliss and the boat downriver toward the funicular.

Arliss grabbed one of the seat planks with her free hand. Her stomach swirled together the meager lunch she'd downed at Rose and Mícheál's earlier. This was flying, but not anything like the birds. This was terror and nausea and fear.

The boat smacked the water, spinning into Orlando's boat.

"Arliss!" He jerked his head up, gasping for air. He pointed behind her. "Look out!"

The crogall swam toward her again. On the other side, beneath the funicular track, the other crogall sped toward Orlando. The boats were trapped—cornered.

Orlianna screamed something vicious in Anmórian. She had burst through the gates, scaled the funicular car with its emerging Ikarran guards, and now leapt up the track. Distracted, the second crogall turned one eye to watch her.

Arliss nocked an arrow just as *her* crogall slammed into her boat. She collided with Orlando's again. Water flooded both their vessels now.

She drew her arrow. There were only two weak spots on these beasts. One was their tentacles. She'd found that out back on the ship on the way to Ikarra.

But cutting off tentacles wouldn't kill them. Maimed, the crogall still had two rows of a dozen knife-like teeth. And they were still the size of a train car.

The crogall emerged from the water, propping its massive head on the edge of her boat. The prow listed into the water. The boat started to sink.

Teeth snapped an arm's length from Arliss's face. A deep, throaty growl vibrated the boat.

She shuddered, barely breathing. The demonic creature stared her down.

She raised her bow as its mouth somehow spread even wider. The purpling rays of the sunset touched the pink flesh at the back of its throat.

The growl rattled louder.

She drew her arrow.

It lunged.

She gasped for air, loosening her grip on the worn wood. "I'm sorry, Philip."

And she released the arrow into the crogall's throat.

The growl exploded into a warbling cry. The crogall's final bite crushed the bow between its jaws. Wood splintered, stuck, crackled like firewood. A tooth nicked Arliss's arm as she threw herself backward into Orlando's boat.

The crogall drifted downward in a cloud of its own blood.

Orlianna planted her feet wide halfway up the ascending funicular track. The counterbalancing cars sat frozen at either end, one at the base of the hill near the bridge to the city, one atop the hill near the castle.

There Maeve stood, her tower behind her stabbing up into the darkening sky. Watching her minions do her bidding.

Orlianna looked down at the river below her. The body of the crogall Arliss had dispatched now sank to the bottom. But there was still one to deal with. And Arliss and Orlando—both struggling for balance in a sinking boat—couldn't do much against it.

A rattle shook the track, rocking her balance. She tensed, boots edging the wooden borders of the track. The cables vibrated with tension.

The cars moved toward her from either direction.

She glared up at Maeve. So she was trying to squish her flat? It was either get run over by a funicular car, or jump straight into the mouth of a crogall.

Orlianna tossed her hair and drew the knife Kenton had given her. Surely after twenty-five years, Maeve would know that it took more than simple tricks to stop her. Surely she knew that any question could have more than two answers. And even paths that forked only into two roads could simply be flown over.

She cut down the constricting bodice of her outer dress. The ancient steel split the already-shredded silk. She tore the dripping gown off, smoothing out the leather battle tog below it.

She waved the emerald silk above her head. "Up here!"

She got Arliss and Orlando's attention along with the crogall's.

"Get out of the river!" she yelled down at them. "Get clear of the funicular!"

"What're you doing?" Orlando bellowed.

"Just listen to me!" The cars rattled toward her on either side. "Trust me!"

Orlando nodded, but Arliss hesitated.

The crogall raised its serpentine head from the water, captivated by her shouting and waving the dress. It opened its mouth, tongue flicking.

"Get out!"

Orlando paddled for the shore. Arliss crouched in the stern, knife in hand.

The crogall's eyes followed them, and its tentacles tensed, ready to speed after them.

Orlianna drew a breath, her chest swelling against the snug leather bodice. She echoed the commands of her grandmother. "*Mo ghile, ionsaí! Scriosann!*"

Atop the hill, Maeve raised her hands. The sky was the color of violets. She was just a dark silhouette now, with only her gray eyes glinting in the moonlight. "*Mharú!*"

Orlianna nodded giddily, locking eyes with the crogall. "*Mharú!*"

The cars cranked toward her. Her muscles stretched the bare skin of her arms as she tensed everything to hold her balance on the rattling track. A rough night wind drifted over the castle from the west, prickling her skin.

"*Mharú!*" Maeve's tone turned desperate. "*Mharú!*"

"Yes!" Orlianna agreed, this time in Ikarran. "Go ahead, demon! Kill me!"

The crogall's eyes burned red. Its tentacles spun, readying for the lunge.

Maeve sputtered an endless stream of Anmórian incantations.

"*Mo ghile, ionsaí! Scriosann!* My darling, attack! Destroy!" Orlianna sheathed the dagger. "*Scriosann! Scriosann!*" She hurled the tattered dress at the crogall.

It jumped from the water, tentacles reaching for her, jaws hungry and wide.

The funicular cars were two arms' lengths on either side.

She jumped across to the other edge of the track.

The crogall's tentacles suctioned to the other side.

Maeve shrieked, seeing what was about to happen. But she could not stop it.

Orlianna dove from the track, recalling the diving lessons with Harrison so long ago. She'd never thought she'd put them to use in such a perilous situation. The water rushed up to meet her.

Above, the crogall's head landed on the track just as the cars met. They plowed into the creature, metal screeching as they tried to continue their course. Tentacles flailed. The track rocked.

The downward car caught on the edge of the toothy mouth and ripped the jaws apart, jerking half the beast's head off its body. Sinewy flesh tore as the dying growl gurgled to nothing.

The crogall's dismembered body crashed down into the river with both funicular cars.

It was a wave straight from a legend that threw Orlianna to shore.

CHAPTER THIRTY-TWO: PRINCE OF ANMOR

THE WAVE SPAT ORLIANNA ONTO A SANDY PATCH OF SHORE between clumps of rock. She pushed herself up, praising God for the placement of her landing. A few feet right or left, and she'd have bashed her brains against the rocks.

She staggered up, blinking saltwater from her burning eyes.

A hand closed around hers.

Orlando pulled her up the strand and toward the bridge that arched over from the castle. "Are you all right?"

She trembled, the chill of the water finally hitting her as her adrenaline settled. "I don't know."

"We have to keep moving." Arliss's dress flapped as she stalked up the grassy incline. She glanced at the bridge that arched over their heads. "The guards are crossing right now."

Orlianna dropped Orlando's clammy hand. "These are my people. I will not run from them."

Arliss whirled, eyes flaming. "You *will* if they're trying to kill you."

"Don't presume to lecture me."

Armor clanked on the bridge above.

Arliss stepped close enough to touch Orlianna, but still a step higher up the hill than she was, so their eyes were level. "You aren't thinking clearly. Maeve has made you an outlaw. She won't stop until she hunts you down. Stop letting your emotions run away with you."

"Let *my* emotions run away with me?" Orlianna felt her voice becoming shriller as it vibrated up her throat. "Everything you're doing is for yourself—for your love. I am no fool. Pull the plank from your eye before you draw the splinter from mine."

Maeve's voice sheared the air. "Orlianna!"

Her muscles turned to ice. This voice no longer meant wisdom and counsel. This voice meant death.

Maeve descended the bridge and stood at the top of the slope, the glass library in the near distance behind her. "Drop your weapons."

Arliss readied her knife. "You must not know me very well."

"Unfortunately, I do. But your weapon is not the one I am concerned about." Maeve stared at Orlianna. "Unfasten *it* and hand it over, and I will pardon you all. Otherwise you will never set foot in this city again."

Orlianna seethed. "What power do you have to do that?"

"The power of the people." Maeve motioned to the bridge. The guards all looked rather shaken from the crogall incident. But some of the rabble from the coronation (only the roughest and most daring sort) had also made their way down the broken funicular track, and they were livid with questions and accusations.

"She's attacking her own city!"

"I heard her speaking in demon's tongues!"

"Is it true that she is in league with Ríon?"

Orlianna choked on the mob's words as they trickled off the bridge, blocking her from the library—her refuge—and from the city—her home. How could these people have changed so? She had spent her life among them, helping them, serving them, never counting the title of princess as anything.

But, just like Arliss said, they didn't need her. They did not want her. They did not love her.

No one did.

She was too broken to be needed, wanted, loved.

She rushed up the hill into the crowd, raising her voice. "Don't you see? Maeve called these creatures out against me! She is meddling in dark magic. If she does this to her own granddaughter, what will she do to you when you disobey?"

The rabble hushed.

"*I* did not summon these creatures." Maeve pointed at Arliss. "She did."

Arliss snorted. "That is rich coming from you, you queen of liars."

"You brought them with you from your wild land across the sea. Do I not speak the truth?" Maeve looked to the crowd for support. "We have never seen these creatures in Cahair before. 'Twas Orlianna's voyage that disturbed them. She brought them back here with the Reinholdian barbarians."

Orlando flipped his knives. "If anyone's a barbarian, it's you."

"Silence, Anmórian scum," Maeve hissed. "I know who you are. You have no place to utter a word in the presence of royalty."

He clammed up, knives lowered.

Orlianna stomped up the hill to Maeve. She gripped her skirts and cringed at the touch. Her skirt was sticky, stained black with the crogall's blood.

Maeve inclined her chin. "Do you recant your rebellious acts?"

"No." Orlianna didn't have the breath for anything else.

"Will you hand over that weapon around your neck?"

She raised her blackened hands as if to shove Maeve away. "Never."

Maeve swallowed. "Then you give me no other choice but to banish you."

The sandy grass beneath Orlianna's feet sank. The streaming grasses wrapped around her dress like tentacles dragging her down. Her heart slowed, dragging her pulse with each painful thud.

Cahair was hers. Her home. Her life.

"Did you hear me?"

She reached to cover the ringing in her ears. Night was falling fast about her. Her vision tunneled, the world closing in about her. A warm wind hitting her, reminding that it was now May. Arliss's hand on her back.

"Orlianna…"

Maeve turned to the crowd. "Let it be known that Orlianna and her band of Reinholdian miscreants are hereby banished from the realm of Ikarra. Let no one aid them or harbor them, unless they hand over themselves and their gifts, by order of the queen."

Ikarra was hers. She couldn't be driven out of her own country. She was the princess.

"I will hide where you will never find me. And when I am strong—"

"You will never be strong!" Maeve jerked around to face her, and her belt jingled. "Do you not see that? You think you can stand on your feet for one moment, but all it takes is a single battle and the death of a friend, and you are shattered."

Orlianna sucked in the violent truth of Maeve's words. She was shattered. She was not just breakable. She was broken.

"And there is nowhere you can hide." Maeve turned to Domnall, who stood beside her with a leering grin. "Send word to the major cities—to Túrgarda, to Gormard, to North Havens—and let them know that Orlianna is not to be welcomed. She is banished."

The crowd had hushed, shocked by Maeve's declaration. But no one contested it.

Orlianna stood still.

Maeve thrust her hands toward Orlianna, then motioned for the guards. "Did you hear me? You are *banished*. Get out of this city."

Arliss gripped her arm. "Orlianna, we—"

"No!" She jerked free. "I will not!"

"*Orlianna.*" Orlando grasped her shoulders from behind and whispered into her ear. "Don't get yourself killed."

"I would rather die than face this hateful world!" She knew she was raving. It mattered not what anyone thought of her. She was nothing anymore.

The knot in her forehead blurred her vision as Arliss and Orlando dragged her away, past the library, toward the docks.

And as the last light fell from the sky, Maeve stood, the crown on her head disappearing into the night.

Arliss led the way to the docks, taking silent steps down the flat stone road. A line of carriages was parked alongside the dark wharf, and two vast Ikarran trade ships anchored out in the bay. The air reeked of fish from a catch that must have been sitting neglected in the wake of the battle.

Behind her, Orlando led Orlianna along. None of them had spoken a word in the trek from the castle. And strangely enough, no one had followed them.

Arliss glanced over her shoulder, back down the street at the library, and at the castle behind that. She still felt like she was being watched. Maeve had eyes everywhere. She would know where they were going.

Why hadn't Maeve just killed them? She'd just tried to with the crogall. And the crowd had been on her side…

But if they'd been slaughtered by the crogall, Maeve could have played it as an accident. Outright murdering her granddaughter in cold blood, on the other hand, would have turned the mob against her.

She gripped her cloak. It didn't matter. They were leaving.

She passed the steps to the elevated dock platform and turned right into the shadows. The darkness beneath the platform was so dense she could barely make out the row of longboats roped to the shore.

Orlianna seemed to awaken as Orlando led her down the sandy bank. "A boat?"

"Yes." Arliss crouched by the nearest boat and fiddled with the knot. The wound on her forearm from the crogall's tooth still throbbed.

"But you said we were going to the Tuáma Fields. To find—"

"I realize what I said." Arliss squeezed the rope. It scratched into her palms. "But we've been banished, so we cannot begin our search in Ikarra."

Orlando undid his sword belt and tucked it in the bottom of the boat. "Where are we going?"

Arliss could see in his eyes that he already knew the answer. "We can't get back across the sea to Reinhold. And we'll be fugitives anywhere in Ikarra. So our best bet is to go where we might still have allies."

Orlianna jerked her head up. "Anmór."

Arliss gazed out across the bay. The mountains loomed black in the night, as dark as the catacombs they hid. "Philip is out there somewhere."

Orlando stepped down into the boat and drew up an oar. "We'll need more than just Philip if you're going to try to face Maeve again." He hesitated. "You are going to face her, aren't you?"

Arliss sighed. "I don't know. That's why we're going Anmór—" she eyed Orlianna "—to find Ríon."

Orlianna glared. "Consorting with enemies to defeat enemies? How senseless are we?"

"He's not an enemy. He's been a bloody fool, but deep down, Ríon wants unity just like we do. He wants peace."

Orlianna wavered. "But Maeve has won."

"She hasn't won." Arliss slipped her bow beneath the planks into the bottom of the boat. "I'm still alive."

Orlianna's shoulders sagged. "I just don't see how we can win this fight."

Arliss took Orlianna's freezing hands. "Neither do I. But I promised I would stay and fight for Ikarra. And I never break my promises."

Orlianna grasped Arliss's hands with renewed strength. She took a shivering breath and let Orlando guide her into the boat.

A scream erupted from the shadows by the docks. Two guards burst forward, brandishing spears. Of course Maeve had sent someone after them. It couldn't have been this easy.

Pushing off from the side, Arliss jumped in and took up an oar.

One guard threw his spear like a javelin. Orlando shifted in front of Orlianna, but the spear overshot the boat and pierced the waves.

The other guard dropped his spear and drew his crossbow.

Arliss fumbled under the floorboards for her unstrung bow. No way to string it—

Orlando caught her eye and read her mind. He raised his palm.

She stuck the end of the bow in his palm and arched the bow, slipping the string over the other end. She spun to face the guard. Her arrow pierced the arm that held the crossbow.

He stumbled back into the shadows.

Orlando plunged the oars in and rowed. He stirred ripples in the black water as they glided toward the opposite shore.

She glanced down toward the wide opening of the bay, in the direction of her beloved Reinhold. Maybe it was just her imagination, but she thought she saw a scaly mound disturb the surface of the bay before disappearing underwater.

They reached the other side of the bay at midnight.

Arliss's boots dislodged stones as she trudged up the hill. Darkness had long consumed the mountains that spanned the land on either side, but she could see well enough to climb through the gray shadows before her feet. The gleam of an almost-full moon reigned in the skies above.

The steep hill leveled out. She climbed the last step and turned around, waiting for Orlando and Orlianna. Her companions had none of her urgency. Every step could bring them closer to Philip, or at least Ríon.

She brushed hair out of her face and stared out at the path they'd taken. The steep hill banked down into the bay. Across it, Cahair shimmered like a jeweled crown in the blackness. The river mirrored the lights of feasting and celebration.

She'd come here in hopes of uniting all their clans. But all she'd done was drag them all into a deeper war. Wasn't it this way every time she tried to solve things? She always left destruction and death in her wake.

"Why am I here?" She whispered the question to the night.

The wind laughed in her ears.

Orlando clambered up the incline beside her. "Why do you think?"

She crossed her arms and looked away. "I don't know anymore."

"Yes, you do." He leaned around to look her in the eye. "Perhaps you've just forgotten."

The wild chill of the ocean burned in her nostrils. She cast him a look, then turned further around, her back to him. She didn't need to be preached to. She just needed to keep going.

He touched her arm. "You know who you have to become."

"I am Arliss, princess of Reinhold. I don't need to be anything more."

"That isn't enough."

She shook his hand off. "You're being ridiculous."

Orlianna reached the top. She raised an eyebrow at both of them. "Are we moving on?"

"Yes." Arliss spoke through her teeth. "The catacombs entrance is just ahead."

Pain lurked in Orlianna's eyes, but she strode forward into the lead.

Arliss and Orlando followed silently behind. The narrow pass cut between two mountains which rose on either side like jaws ready to swallow them. The city and the river vanished behind as they passed deeper between the mountains.

Darkness loomed over them. Arliss blinked. Orlando's tired breaths beside her were the only thing that signaled he was there.

"I shouldn't have snapped at you," she said presently. "I should hear you out. But I already know what you're going to say. I heard it endlessly from my father, then from Philip, and even from our enemies."

"The question is, when are you going to start listening?" Orlando asked. "You're the only one who can stop this mess. And the only way to do that is to accept who you are."

"I am who I am. Accepting the title of queen won't change that. Those who didn't listen to me before won't listen to me any more seriously afterward."

"It's not about how others view you." Orlando reached for her hand, and his ring burned like ice against her palm. "It's about how you view yourself."

Orange light suddenly flooded the ravine. Five paces ahead, Orlianna wielded a torch that spun its flames up into the night.

Just ahead of her stood the gaping mouth that began the catacombs.

She let the other two catch up. They stood together, staring into the tunnel. The flicker of the torch revealed letters and borders etched into the surrounding stone.

"I suppose this place haunts all of us," Orlianna said. "Who knows what we will discover inside?"

"An empty path to Anmór." Arliss tightened her quiver belt. Unless Merna continued to use these tunnels for her leisure time. Or unless Ríon's band still encamped here… But after the events of the battle, that seemed unlikely.

"This path seems never to be empty."

Arliss stepped forward into the torchlight. "There's only one way to find out."

Orlando's empty stomach growled a counterpoint to his pounding heart. The unending darkness was beginning to become stale and almost frightening. Orlianna was too mentally distraught at the moment to realize it, and Arliss hadn't been through the training he had, but he knew what both of them didn't—that their mission was doomed.

They had no provisions. Banished from the castle as they had been, they hadn't the time to return for their things. They had only what had already been strapped to their bodies.

So no food. Or water. Or maps.

Just clothes, a few weapons, and two of the gifts of Reinhold.

Orlianna's pendant.

His own ring.

Like lock and key.

He spun the ring around his finger and let the torchlight play with the silver band. Etched threads circled the inside of the band against his finger. He'd always wondered why. Now, he knew.

He glanced up at Orlianna, who still carried the torch as she and Arliss walked in front. His fist curled. His ring unlocked her pendant—which, based on Maeve's desperate attempts to get ahold of it, was a powerful thing indeed.

Should he give it to her? In her state, she wouldn't know what to make of it. She was beautiful, powerful; but she was also volatile, dangerous.

He hid his hand beneath his cloak and picked up his pace. This wasn't the time. Not in this place. These tunnels knew too many things about his past transgressions.

And if his blind estimations were anything like correct, they were nearing that wide-open chamber where so many things lay buried.

Arliss broke the silence, her voice blunt and hollow in the dark. "Are we near the opening?"

"Yes." Orlando's voice was even quieter. "So you have a choice to make."

"Choice?"

"On the other side of the big chamber, the tunnel branches. One goes east to the capital, and the other goes further south to near Glasberry."

Arliss brushed her hand against the tunnel's hard dirt sides, freshly cleared out since the incident with the Lasairbláth the week before. "Why is there a royal tunnel going to Glasberry?"

Orlando shrugged. "Ríon has always used these tunnels."

"These tunnels weren't dug by Ríon." Orlianna lofted the torch high, scattering the ceiling shadows. "They were made by your people."

"*My* people?" Arliss scrunched her brows. This was an older and deeper history than she knew.

Orlianna nodded. "Long ago, before your clan fled, Reinhold dwelt in Anmór. They used these tunnels to do underground business with Ikarra—quite literally."

Arliss dropped her hand from the damp side of the tunnel. She took a breath that smelled like mud and felt just as squishy in her lungs. There was so much history in these realms, and much of it concerned Reinhold. If only she had the time to stop, to trace the threads, to sew them into a tapestry.

If only this war was over.

Maybe Orlando was right. If she could see herself as queen, she could summon her alliances, march up in brazen display, and throw down Maeve's regime—ignoring the odds. If she didn't end this, the evil and darkness that had started in Thane's fortress would spread until it consumed everything she had ever held dear. There would be no new city of Reinhold. There would be no royal wedding. There would be no one to tell this tapestry of stories.

She inhaled and let a song roll off her tongue, a song that had spun its melody along her path for so long now. Her voice reverberated richly down the tunnel.

"A princess on a gilded throne..."

Her voice returned to her, vibrating as if out of the sides of the bowl.

Orlianna jogged forward. "The opening! We're close."

Arliss kept singing. "...clothed in simple raiment."

They stepped out of the tunnel into the vast chamber with its central firepit.

And another voice joined hers. Not Orlianna's. Not Orlando's. Deeper, stronger. Full of life and hope and joy, even in this dim place, like a candle that no darkness could quench.

"A queenly look is in her eye."

"And grace is on her forehead." She ran across the cavern to Philip and threw her arms around him.

For a long time, she pressed her face into his chest. She breathed.

Huge, gasping breaths. He was alive. Right—here. She clutched the back of his jerkin, rubbed her cheek hard against him. Yes, he was real. She wasn't dreaming.

His chin brushed her forehead. She opened her eyes and snapped from her reverie.

"A beard?"

He shrugged. "Comes from being on the trail with no royal commodities."

"On whose trail?"

Philip motioned behind him.

And, as if on cue, Ríon stepped from the shadows.

Arliss tried to make her heart beat steadily. She shouldn't be afraid of him. He was the whole reason she'd come this way.

"Hello, Arliss." His tone was still the cocky swagger he'd used of late, but his eyes were lowered, hesitant.

Arliss started to answer, but Orlianna strode up beside her, flashing the torch. She drew her knife.

"*You.*"

Orlianna clutched the knife by her side, her taut muscles fighting the urge to run it right through Ríon's throat. The very sight of him made her sick. Arliss wanted to make an alliance with him, and perhaps that was the best course, but she couldn't help the sensations that rushed through her body like lava.

Fiach and Finín stepped out into the cavern behind Ríon. Finín's torch mingled with Orlianna's and illuminated the whole space. Orlianna levied her knife.

"Orlianna." Arliss's tone was condescending. "Put your knife away. There's no need."

"The quiver in your voice makes me question your surety." Orlianna pointed the knife at the ground, which she saw was scattered with dry Lasairbláth petals. "Why should I trust him now, after all he's done?"

Philip held up his hands. "Hear us out."

Orlianna gritted her teeth. Harrison's lessons on diplomacy and parley nagged the back of her brain. She sheathed the knife.

"I'm listening."

Philip nodded. "Brilliant. Well, it turns out we all may be on the same side after all."

"And how do you figure that?"

"We all have a score to settle with Maeve," Philip said. "Even Ríon."

Orlianna glared at Ríon for an explanation.

He fisted leather-gloved hands. "Until recently, Merna and Maeve managed to get along fine. Thane was the common denominator between them, and I became the scapegoat. Any problems or mistakes were simply blamed on me."

"Well deserved," Orlianna muttered.

"Now, there's no buffer." Ríon paced closer. "And I realize that what Maeve is doing—what she's always been doing—is wrong. My mother's lied to me. She heaps up empty promises of a throne, but in reality we're all just running down a path that leads to one thing: Maeve ruling over us all."

Orlianna swallowed. For once, she found herself agreeing with the prince of Anmór.

Arliss stepped out of Philip's embrace and regarded Ríon. "So you'll ally with us?"

"Yes." Ríon gnawed his lip. His gaze passed over Orlianna, then to Orlando. "If hesitantly."

Orlianna huffed. "If you have to hesitate, may as well not do it."

"She's right," Philip affirmed. "We do this together or not at all."

Together? There was no *together* with her brother's killer.

She took a large step back. "There's no question of my allying with him. I think all of you know that very well."

"Fine by me." Ríon set his jaw. "You're too dangerous, anyhow."

"Ríon, wait." Orlando reached toward his brother. "You have to trust her."

"Trust?" The sarcasm in Ríon's tone grated like steel. "As if you know anything about trust? You liar—deceiver. She still doesn't know, does she?"

Something in his words made Orlianna's heart throb inside her chest. Her pulse exploded, every heartbeat slamming against where the pendant hung over her heart. "What do I not know?"

Ríon threw his head back, mouth agape. "Oh, you've eaten every lie Maeve has fed you, haven't ya? Your whole life."

"What are you talking about?"

"They told you I killed your brother?"

"You *did!*" Orlianna shouted, her voice booming off the sides of the cavern. "In this very spot!"

Ríon shook his head. "They told you wrong."

"I heard it from William's own lips—'the prince of Anmór did this.' You cannot refute me."

Orlianna looked to the others for support. Beside her, Arliss stood by Philip and Ríon. Facing them stood Fiach and Finín, and a few paces off, Orlando.

Orlianna swallowed. Her throat felt like a serpent was strangling it.

"I thought you'd have put it together by now," Ríon said. "Surely you know that there is more than one prince of Anmór?"

No, no, no, went the drum of her heart.

She met Orlando's gaze. "Is this true?"

His face twisted. "It is."

The earth under her boots melted. She had given her heart away to a liar and deceiver. She had bared the depths of her soul to one who was not worthy even to be spoken to. How could she have been so blind?

She drew her knife. "How could you do this to me?"

He strained for air. "I tried to tell you…so many times."

"Excuses!" She stamped toward him. "You are the son of your father."

Arliss reached out a nervous hand. "Orlianna, please."

Orlianna batted it away. "Don't try to calm me! He murdered my brother."

Ríon drew his sword. "If you fight, you end whatever alliance you wanted to make here."

"Let it be so." She pointed her knife at him. "I will kill you both."

She dropped the torch and rushed at Ríon and Orlando.

The first explosion flashed up in Arliss's eyes, the heat of flame rushing up against her for half a second.

She leapt back, watching the fire from Orlianna's dropped torch snake through the winding paths of Lasairbláth. They had been woven through the cavern like a patchwork tapestry, a chain of explosions just waiting to be set off.

In her anger and haste, Orlianna had started it.

She and Orlando fought, spinning against each other with every bit of their skill and training showing.

Orlianna jammed her forearm into Orlando's throat, locking her knife arm around his. He jabbed his knee into her stomach, and she doubled back.

Arliss pressed Philip's shoulder. "We have to stop them."

"There's no stopping her. Not now."

Ríon eyed the ceiling. "No, he's right. If we don't get out of here, the ceiling'll crush us."

"You've led me into a trap?"

"Not my trap. Maeve's. She's been using this place to grow and store dried Lasairbláth for a long time."

White flame stung Arliss's eyes from the other side of the cavern. Crumbling rocks and dust rained from the ceiling and sprinkled in her hair. Clever woman. She'd probably corresponded with Thane and transplanted some of the Reinholdian flowers over here to Ikarra.

Once again, Thane's influence reached her even after his death.

She moved toward the brawl. It made her feel absolutely sick, watching these two friends bashing at each other with death in their eyes. And even worse, she didn't know which one was right.

Philip caught her hand. "I'll break it up. I don't want you getting hurt."

She looked him in the eyes. "They'll listen best to me."

Which probably wasn't true. But she could not stand by and watch.

Another flash. Another explosion. The ceiling rattled. Arliss squinted, coughing in the dust that steadily fogged the cavern. Time was crumbling away. One tunnel led away back toward Cahair; two opposite tunnels forked toward Anmór.

No matter what way, they had to get out.

Orlando dodged Orlianna's vicious kick and nearly stepped back into the nearest Lasairbláth explosion. He tripped, his foot catching in the dirty crater.

She stared, panting, evaluating her next move.

He stepped out of the crater and rotated his ankle. It was twisted, but not seriously wounded. But the physical pain was nothing compared to this. To having *her* fight him.

A flash lit up the cave. The fire danced through the trail of petals.

Orlianna lunged, stabbing her dagger backhanded through the air.

He grabbed her forearm and twisted the dagger away.

Her knuckles crunched into his cheekbone from the other side. The vertebrae in his neck crackled.

He stomached the pain. He couldn't hurt her. But he had to stop her.

He grabbed her free hand and pulled her close. He still had her knife hand torqued sideways, and the blade rested cold between their chests.

The muscles in her knife forearm rippled. The blade tilted out, slicing against his jerkin.

He stepped back, still clenching both her forearms. "Please don't do this."

"I have no choice." Refusing to look at him, she tried to twist her arm free.

"Everyone has a choice." His muscles burned, already exhausted by her tenacious strength. "I used to let my past define me. But I'm done doing that. You should be, too."

She finally looked at him, her green eyes livid. "You can never escape the fact that you are a *murderer.*"

She snapped his grip on her and shook free.

He panted hard, absorbing the hatred that filled the way she looked at him. His heart slowed from the rush of battle. She had once looked at him with trust, adoration. Now, there was nothing in those eyes but hatred.

She charged him, slashing.

He drew his twin knives.

Arliss rushed between them just before they reached each other.

Orlianna pulled back. "Move. This isn't your fight."

"Yes, it is. You're my friends. I won't let you do this to each other."

Orlando pointed his knives at the ground. "Arliss is right. We shouldn't fight."

"I will fight you!" Orlianna shouted above the volley of explosions. "Blow for blow, blood for blood, of what you did to William!"

Arliss raised her bow. "We have to get out of here before the tunnels cave in. Otherwise it's all for naught."

"Then get out! I shall finish this." Orlianna stepped around Arliss, edging toward Orlando.

His pulse picked back up.

Arliss swiveled, but didn't stop Orlianna. Her eyes jerked toward the right tunnel. She lowered her bow and caught Orlando's eye, mouthing something.

Get her out.

Orlando nodded. He flashed his knives at Orlianna, assuming an offensive combination that would push her back. And back.

And back.

After all, it was for her own good.

The ceiling shook so hard Philip could hardly hear anything else. Orlando and Orlianna's fight had become a blur through the falling dirt. All his senses seemed dulled in the smothering underground.

He tightened his sword belt and turned to Ríon. "You have our provisions?"

Ríon tightened his rucksack around his chest, then patted it. "Right 'ere."

Philip nodded to Fiach and Finín. "Ready, gentlemen?"

Eamon's sons nodded.

"Let's go."

The weapons and fragments of their camp strapped about them, they crossed the cavern, dodging the last of the explosions as they went. The fire had burned its way to the end.

Philip glanced up. The collapse was only just beginning. Lines fractured the hard dirt ceiling far above his head. Rocks and clods of dirt fell like hailstones.

Arliss waited at the mouth of the right-hand tunnel. Orlando had forced Orlianna back almost to her.

Philip jogged toward them. "Get in the tunnel!"

Arliss turned.

Chunks of ceiling fell all around them now. One hit Ríon in the head, and he swore, but kept running.

Philip scrambled over the former firepit, holding his shield over his head. The patter of stones rattled through it and vibrated it against his skull.

The right tunnel started to cave in.

He clenched his every muscle. They wouldn't reach it in time. He would be separated from Arliss—again. And she would have to find her way without him—again.

Arliss's voice rang clear through the avalanche of dirt. "Philip! What should we do?"

"Keep going!" He ran, legs pumping. "Go to Glasberry!"

Orlando rammed his full weight into Orlianna just to force her down the tunnel. She staggered back and disappeared into the dark. Orlando entered the tunnel.

And the entrance collapsed.

Philip pulled up to avoid toppling over the mound of dirt. He pressed his hands into it, squeezing up fistfuls of earth.

He cast dirt onto the floor. "We were so close."

Ríon sighed. "This whole cavern's about to be flat. There's two tunnels left. Which'll it be—Anmór or Ikarra?"

Philip stared down the darkness that led to the Anmórian capital, then back through the dust at the path to Cahair. He'd been to both. Both had wicked rulers. Both had imminent danger.

But for him, there was only one choice.

BO BURNETTE/380

Chapter Thirty-Three: Perspective

ARLISS STEPPED, BLINKING, OUT OF THE DARKNESS AS THE TUNNEL dropped away on either side, spreading out into a wide plateau. It had been dark—hardly sunrise—when they'd entered the catacombs from the Ikarran side, so it was strange to emerge here in Anmór with the sun glaring down at her.

She took in the surrounding landscape. The mountains behind her, beneath which the catacombs ran, vanished into flat lands that rolled out across the southern horizon. To her right, the land swelled with little green hills that rose up to become mountains in the west. To the left, a lake—and beyond that, spires of a city. Not the capital, but certainly a significant-looking place.

She examined the more imminent fixtures of her surroundings: her two companions. Orlando and Orlianna emerged from the tunnel, ragged and angry. The night without sleep—and with the harrowing tunnel collapse—had done them both ill.

Orlianna's dress, still stained dark with crogall blood, hung tight around her tense movements. "Well, we made it." She had stopped trying to kill Orlando after the tunnel collapsed behind them, but she still kept glancing at him.

Orlando's arms hung at his sides. "What now, Arliss?" Tiredness and defeat undercut his tone.

Arliss turned. "To Glasberry."

"And once we're there?" Orlianna spoke quickly.

"Clare wasn't with Ríon, so she must be there. Gally will be there, too. They will both have answers to our questions."

"And what *are* our questions?" Orlianna approached her.

Arliss jerked her head toward Orlianna. She'd grown tired of Orlianna's tone, her attitude, her...everything. Yes, her grandmother had turned against her. Yes, she'd lost her best friend. Yes, her newfound boyfriend had turned out to be her brother's murderer. But she needed to calm down and take a few breaths. Stomping around and antagonizing everyone would get them all no closer to stopping Maeve.

She sent a quick prayer for patience heavenward. "We all have questions. Like what Maeve will do next. Why does she want your pendant? Is she going to attack Anmór—or ally with them? Nothing is certain right now. Hopefully Gally can make it more so."

"Hopefully," Orlando agreed. "And hopefully he's got some victuals. I'm pretty near starved."

Orlianna shrugged, giving him a look that said she didn't care whether or not he starved.

Arliss turned and marched through the green brush of grasses toward the crystalline lake. The city beyond likely held a train station. A train would take them straight to Glasberry. It couldn't be far now.

And she and Orlando both had plenty of experience hopping trains.

The sunset lit up the rough landscape's blooming flowers. Wild shoots of orange and purple burst up through tangled seagrass. A path had been cut through the mangle of wildflowers, leading straight to the lodge, but it was dingy with overgrowth.

Arliss ran her hand through the flowers as she passed. The train they'd hopped on the way here rattled around Glasberry, shooting back down toward the capital. It swept past them, throwing her hair in every direction.

The flowers leaned back, grasses whispering. Arliss smoothed out her tangled mane. Here they were—Glasberry. The sunset falling across the lodge made the dark wood an even richer red. It was a squatty, level building with a flat roof. Long windows were shuttered tight—with no light glinting.

Orlianna walked beside her. "Is this it?"

Arliss nodded. "I've been here before—once."

"You came as a friend then." It was almost a question, almost a challenge.

"I come as a friend now." Arliss arched an eyebrow at Orlianna.

Orlianna's eyes flamed up, and she opened her mouth. Then she closed it and nodded tightly.

Orlando suddenly sped up, jogging through the wildflowers toward the wooden watchtower that connected to the lodge by a long staircase. He pointed. "Over there!"

Arliss followed, taking long strides as her slit skirt parted about her. The grasses cleared away, revealing the barren seaside. The watchtower loomed over them like a skeleton.

And at the base of the tower, Clare knelt in the sandy dirt, hands pressed into the ground.

Arliss ran to her and leaned down, but Clare hardly noticed. Her eyes flicked upward, but she didn't move.

"Clare?" Arliss prodded. "We've come to speak to you and Gally."

Clare stared at the ground. "Gally is dead."

Arliss froze. "Dead?"

Clare looked up, tears shimmering in her eyes. "He became unwell after the Rigdál Mór. Deep pains in his heart. I brought him back here directly after the battle. Haven't left his side once. Until this morning…" She stared out at the darkening sea.

Arliss knelt beside her and took one of her cold hands. "You should come inside."

"I can't. I've been shut up for three days." Clare looked up, finally noticing Orlando and Orlianna. Her jaw tensed. "Oh."

Orlando bowed.

Orlianna didn't.

Clare stood, wiping her eyes with a shuddering breath. "Come on. There's tea boilin' inside."

At the word *tea*, they all followed her into the lodge.

"How did you know already?" Orlianna tilted a splash of cream into her tea.

Clare leaned back against the divan, blowing to cool her cup. "News spreads fast among spies. You know Rose?"

"Of course." Orlianna stirred the cream in. "She's spied for me for years."

"She got a message sent by the hand of another spy who was at the coronation. He took it by horseback to Lochair, where a cousin of mine brought it down the tracks here."

Orlianna tapped the spoon on the side of her cup and set it down. She was lucky to have faithful, skilled friends such as Rose. Even in the midst of the horrifying event that was Maeve's coronation, she was still doing her job.

And especially *now*, with the sting of betrayal sucking the life from her blood, she valued the real friends like gold.

"Have you heard any other news?"

Clare paused, mouth open. "Yes, in fact. Maeve has left Cahair. She boarded a heavily guarded train headed for our capital."

So the old witch was making her first diplomatic move as queen of Ikarra. And it *was* diplomatic—not a motion of war, like so many would expect.

But if Maeve was heading for the capital…

They were so close…

This could all end. And Maeve would never expect it. She would assume Orlianna knew nothing of her voyage; or that if she did, she would return to Cahair in her absence.

Orlianna sipped her tea. "We have to go to the capital."

Arliss glanced up. "But, Philip—"

"Arliss, they're all there. We kill Merwin, we kill Merna. We end this madness."

"And we kill Maeve?"

The tea's bitter strength soured Orlianna's throat. "If it comes to it."

"Can you live with that—killing your grandmother?" Arliss asked. "I agree that it must be done. But it will be harder than you think."

Orlianna pursed her lips. "I am not the only killer among us."

Orlando stayed silent.

She leaned back. The shutters creaked as the divan pressed against them. "But I don't think we will have to. She has more sense than Merwin and Merna. She will speak to us."

"That won't work." Arliss set her cup down so hard some sloshed over the side. "We already tried that. We have to kill all of them, or none. If we don't stop them all, the death of one will only fuel their fire."

"We can at least make a start." Orlianna stood, pulling the knife Kenton had given her from her belt. It was single-edged, the blunt side shimmering with swirling engravings.

She pressed her finger to the blade. It was sharp—very sharp— even after disuse. This was an ancient blade—not Anmórian work. If she was not mistaken, it was one brought over from across the sea by their original ancestors.

And she would begin by thrusting it through the man who killed Harrison.

"Thane gave this knife to Merwin. I think I should return it to him."

Orlando sucked in air. "You realize Merwin is my father?"

Of course she realized it—especially now! She spun at him, knife drawn. "What kind of father was Merwin ever to you?"

He sank back on the divan.

"Thane was more of a father than he ever was!" She sheathed the dagger. "Orlando, you know that this has to be done. If not by me, then someone else. But it must be done."

He rose from the divan. "I know."

Arliss held the satchel Clare had lent her with one hand, shoveling food into it with the other. It was tempting to cram it all down her own throat. Clare had fed them well, but her stomach still gurgled in confusion after the day without eating.

The kitchen was void of windows. The light of a lone candle was just enough for her to peek at the bag's contents: six citrus the color of the sunrise, a thick side of bacon, several flat cakes of bread.

She reached up to a high shelf and pulled down a wheel of white cheese. It was hard and heavy and smelled delicious. She pinched off a chunk and stuffed it between her lips.

"I saw that."

Arliss dropped the cheese into her bag. "Saw what?"

Clare chuckled, walking into the kitchen. "Are ya ready to be off?"

Arliss cinched the satchel shut. "Are you?"

"I suppose." Clare looked around. "These halls aren't alive without him here anymore. And with Ríon elsewhere…I see no reason to remain at Glasberry."

Arliss held the candle between them. She'd related to Clare everything that had happened—up until the catacombs. She hadn't wanted to speak of the wounds that still raged in both Orlando and Orlianna's hearts.

And she hadn't wanted to broach the other subject, either. But it was her duty to Clare, as a friend.

She sighed, and the candle wavered. "I saw Ríon in the catacombs."

"Did you?" Clare's eyelids lifted. "Then why's he not here?"

"We were going to join. But Orlianna didn't want to, and before I could speak reason into her, the ceiling caved in. It cut us off from each other." The heat of the melting wax drifted up. "He's with Philip now, but who knows what direction they headed."

Clare walked out of the kitchen. "So he has changed sides once again."

Arliss followed with the light. "Do you think he's in the right now?"

Clare stopped. "Ríon hasn't known why he's fighting for a long time now. I thought I knew. But now I feel maybe I've chosen the wrong side."

"How could you say that?"

She shrugged. "Gally supported Merna, even to the end. He said he would die with his country rather than under Maeve."

It was a fair point. Patriotism. It was what had fueled her thus far, wasn't it? Love for Reinhold. The longing to be back home, to rebuild her city.

Clare tossed her golden-brown hair behind her shoulders. "I know Merna has done evil things in your realm. But the things she's doing could help Anmór—even help me. Maybe it's just a matter of perspective."

Arliss paused. Everyone was right in their own eyes, everyone else wrong. Each individual person and country had decided what they felt was right and true—and then fought against those who opposed them.

Was there weight to Clare's words? Maeve wanted good things, after all. She wanted peace and prosperity for all. Merna wanted a rich realm with a secure line of heirs. She, Arliss, wanted a rebuilt land and peace with the other clans.

The image of Nathanael's body lying limp on the steps of Thane's fortress flashed in her mind like the candle in front of her face.

Then Eamon—his blood seeping onto the snow, Thane's shadow looming behind her.

And she closed her eyes, taking a deep breath.

"No. One side is life, the other death. There is no perspective there."

Clare lifted the book she'd been holding at her side. "Gally believed that. And he would want you to have this. I think he knew that you'd choose the right side, that you'd rally the light to fight the darkness."

Arliss took the old book, handing the candle to Clare. It was heavy, the mottled old leather rubbing like sand against her hands. She turned the yellow pages as Clare held the light close.

She landed on a passage that screamed out from the paper like the voice of God himself.

There must be monarchs from all three clans present to hold a rigdál mór.

She gripped the book with both hands, holding it closer to her face.

A king or a queen from Ikarra, Anmór, and Reinhold must all be present for this meeting to occur. Any decision such a meeting makes without all three present is not binding for all. Any law so made, is not binding. Any war so declared, is not true. Any peace so made, is not true. The clans' gifts have been forged of old, cast in metals and gems and ancient spells. They will work ill in the hands of those who act in disunity.

Arliss gaped up at Clare, just as Orlianna and Orlando emerged from their rooms behind her, new clothes and weaponry strapped about them.

"What's the open mouth for?" Orlianna asked.

"I know how to stop Maeve." Arliss closed the book. "We must hold a rigdál mór."

Chapter Thirty-Four: Orlianna's Vengeance

Philip shivered, the water rushing around his bare skin like ice barely melted. The evening was a warm May breeze, but the water hadn't caught up yet and remained chilled by winter's touch. He took swift strokes, pulling himself through the turbulent channel.

The bay was empty. Few ships anchored at Cahair's docks, and none entered from the far side. He glimpsed a few carriages rattling from the docks toward the cantars, but they were just distant shapes. He swam for a different destination.

Ríon's shoulder-length hair was a tangled mess as he swam wildly beside Philip, making rough waves. He heaved his head above water. "Still for the ruins?"

Philip spat out saltwater. "I don't change my mind."

"I'm not trying to." Ríon ducked his head under and kept swimming.

Fiach and Finín had far outpaced both of them. The two young mariners had been born and bred on the seas, and the water seemed to flow in their veins. The brothers were already heaving themselves onto the beach near the tower. They stood and started walking.

Philip saw the light just quickly enough to shout a warning. "Get down!"

The ruined lighthouse—which hadn't once illuminated during their time in Ikarra—swung round, its light flashing in their direction.

Fiach and Finín dropped on the beach.

Philip gasped for air and dove underwater.

The light filtered down through the water a moment before disappearing.

He burst to the surface and paddled for shore, dragging himself onto the temporarily dark beach. He crouched beside Fin, keeping his breath tight in his chest as water streamed down his bare back.

"Are we spotted?" Ríon crawled onto the sand beside them.

"Not yet," Finín whispered. "But if we don't keep moving, we will be. Let's go."

Philip stood, crossing his arms across his chest. "I'm in charge, so I'm giving the orders."

Fin faced him, his head finding the same cocky tilt Eamon's had. He was taller than Philip, and nearly as muscled. "I'm just stating the obvious here."

"No need to state the obvious. Save yourself the breath."

Fin held his hands up. "You can relax."

"Can I?" Philip brushed a hand through his drenched hair. "I need to know you're all going to follow me. I won't have us all pursuing different goals."

Ríon shoved Philip's back. "Right now, I think we all want to get away from that spyin' lighthouse."

The light's reflection on the ocean swung toward them.

Philip ran with the other three, dashing for the ruined watchtower. It reached up toward the sky, casting down wide shadows with ample hiding space. The light passed over the tower just as Philip threw himself against the shadowy side.

He pressed his cold back into the even colder stone as the blade of light reached out beyond the edge of the tower. He exhaled. They were safe for the moment.

But why was the light in operation?

This had to be Maeve's doing. Ríon had gotten word of her grand move—crowning herself queen of Ikarra, and running off on an ambassadorial mission to Anmór. Which meant her home city was without its leader.

But not, apparently, unguarded.

Ríon tramped about in the darkness beside him, tugging his mostly-dry shirt from his satchel. "Invigorating little swim, I think. But d'you have a real plan?"

Philip leaned against the tower, letting the gentle breeze dry off his dripping body. "It's simple: stay undercover and find out who is still loyal to Orlianna. Then we assemble an army."

"Maeve is a bewitching leader. And she was once queen of Ikarra. Many people *want* her to be queen."

"Then we have to show them the truth. We have to show how evil she really is."

Ríon pulled his gray shirt over his head, then smoothed out his wild hair. "And what about Clare? Arliss?"

"Arliss will go to Glasberry. She'll find them, and then they'll come find us." Philip unfastened his satchel from around his waist and pulled out his boots. His wet bare feet were picking up sand everywhere he walked. "I know it."

"Do you know you're on the right side?" Ríon asked.

Philip tugged on the boots. "Yes. I always have. And I've never been surer than now."

"How?"

Philip stared out at the raging black sea. The lighthouse's revolving beam shone at intervals, casting light across the wrinkled water. Somewhere out there, Reinhold was still there. His aunt and uncle built a new home, a bigger shop, and waited for him to return. Erik and Ilayda would be with Kenton and Elowyn by now, calling for their aid. And Arliss would be summoning Clare to action, drawing her friends together in the way only she could.

But Ríon was right. How—how was he so sure? What was it that burned down in his soul and made him keep going?

The wind whistled past him and prickled gooseflesh all over his bare torso. He crossed his arms again.

It was Arliss, of course. The fact that she could be queen, and he king beside her, lay above and around everything.

But it was bigger than Arliss. It was bigger than *him*.

He faced Ríon. "It's because our side is the one that seeks life, even if some of us have to die. We seek peace, even if it takes war to get there. We follow God, even when others make themselves into gods. We laugh when the world around us demands we cry. When they tell us to bow to lies, we stand in truth. We love life, because in the end, that is the gift we have been given. And I'm going to give it every bloody bit of strength I have."

Ríon exhaled, and he got the joyous glint in his eyes that hadn't been there since the battle in Reinhold against Thane. He stepped closer to Philip and reached out his arm.

Philip clasped it.

Ríon nodded. "I will follow you to whatever end."

Orlianna leaned low over her mount's neck, trying to avoid the spray of sand as hooves gouged holes in the beach. Clare and Arliss galloped down the sand ahead of her, speeding toward the capital.

She sniffed the heavy salt air. She'd never been in this part of Anmór before, but she knew her maps. They could follow the shoreline to the fringes of the capital, but that would be like knocking on the front door. A safer route would be to veer west and enter the city from the back.

And when they got there…

Arliss clearly hadn't thought that far. But *she* had. They'd need disguises. And a door in. Apparently Arliss was on a first-name basis with an Anmórian waterman who could get them in.

But all Orlianna really needed was an opportune moment. She needed to be able to get to Merwin, just long enough to return his dagger to him. She needed to hear his dying breath.

"Hold up, would you?" Orlando struggled to get his mount to gallop. It fought him, jerking back into a lazy canter.

"Can't handle a horse?"

He glowered at her. "I've been handling horses my whole life. This one is just a special breed of stupid."

"You must get along well, then."

He finally tromped up alongside her. "I don't like *this* Orlianna. Can I have the other one back?"

She started to toss her hair before she remembered it was braided over her shoulder. She looked away from him, rolling her eyes. "You can't handle my sauciness?"

"There's a lot more going on with you than mere sauciness."

She cut him a look. "Quite frankly, I don't like this Orlando. Can I have the other one back?"

"There's only one."

"That's funny." She jerked her horse to a halt in front of his, cutting him off. "Because I fail to see how the man I sold my heart to and the man who ripped it out are the same."

He barely pulled up in time. Sand rained up toward her as his horse pawed the beach in irritation. "I did withhold a truth about myself from you, and that was wrong."

She stared. *Wrong* didn't even begin to describe it.

"But I did not deceive you about who I really am. The Orlando you fell in love with is the same Orlando who's standing in front of you right now."

It was true. What he had done, he had done. The fact that she knew did not change anything. But what hurt was that *he* had always known. He'd known the whole time he was seducing her that he'd killed William. But he chose to be the fool anyway.

"Maybe you are the same person I fell in love with." She tightened the reins. "But I feel I am no longer in love."

She urged the horse after Arliss and Clare, clamping her thighs to hold on as she galloped even faster than before.

She felt nothing for Orlando anymore. Nothing.

Nothing?

The doors to the throne room seemed ready to explode from the noise within. The hall outside, by contrast, was still eerily quiet. Arliss gulped. They were late, so their appearance would be even more conspicuous.

Arliss craned her neck around the corner of the hallway. The two blank-faced guards hadn't yet heard their approach.

"Ready?" Orlianna pushed herself into the wall beside Arliss. With her red hair stuffed beneath a white wimple, she hardly looked herself. Harsh makeup highlighted her already-prominent cheekbones.

Arliss pressed her ear to the wall, listening to the rumble of the assembly within. Her skin prickled with familiarity. The last party she'd attended in this vast hall hadn't exactly been a giddy time. But at least she hadn't been on a mission to overthrow a regime. The stakes were a lot higher this time.

Or maybe it was just because she *knew* the stakes this time.

Clare rubbed her lips together in anticipation. "Are we ready?"

Arliss looked back at Orlando. He nodded. She readied an arrow on her bow. "Go."

Orlianna trudged ahead of Clare, keeping her head down. Clare walked with regal posture, her black cloak streaming out behind her. She prodded Orlianna along like a mule.

The guards jumped to attention, hands on their flag-draped spears. "Who comes?"

Clare swept her arm wide. "Lady Eirann of Lochair, with the gift of a servant for their majesties."

Arliss held her breath from behind the corner of the wall. Would the guards take the bait?

Orlando's breath blasted down on her shoulder from behind.

She started. "Are you sure this is customary in Anmór?"

He nodded. "You'd be surprised what people use to bribe the crown."

The guards gave each other a suspicious glance. One of them pulled out a long parchment. "You are not on the guest list."

"I am a special friend of Prince Ríon," Clare insisted. "Trust me, you'll see his wrath if you do not admit me."

The guard lowered his pike at her. "See if I care."

The noises within the throne room had dropped to a lull. Arliss nocked an arrow on her bow, pulling tension into the string. They needed to get inside—now.

Clare stepped closer, holding the edges of her cloak. "*Let me in.*"

He pointed his pike at her chest. "Stand down, lady."

Arliss jumped around the corner with her bow raised.

The guard gaped. Orlianna seized his surprise and ripped his pike from his hand and clouted him across his temple. He dropped, unconscious.

The other guard thrust his pike at Clare. Arliss's arrow pierced his shoulder. He cried out and dropped the spear. It hit the marble floor with a sound like a thousand silver shards.

Orlianna dealt him a blow that blacked him out, too.

Arliss froze, expecting more guards to come running. But silence ruled.

"Come." Clare reached for the enormous double doors. "Orlianna, stay beside me. We need to find that sphere. Arliss and Orlando, keep to the back of the room. Try not to be noticed."

Arliss tucked her bow beneath her cloak as Orlando did the same with his crossbow. "We'll be watching you both."

"Good." Orlianna's darkened lips twisted into a smile as she pulled open one of the doors and followed Clare into the throne room.

Orlianna cringed at the boom of Merwin's ceremonious voice that hit her the moment she stepped through the doors. She could barely glimpse him through the maze of pillars and people as he stood before the thrones at the far back of the room. But he was there in the open—just as she'd hoped.

And better yet, no one seemed to notice them. Both Anmórian and Ikarran guests packed the room, all crowding to see and hear Merwin's speech. They didn't even bother to leave the carpeted aisle free. Bodies spread from wall to wall, around pillars, blocking every free space.

She eased her way between two silk-gowned Ikarran duchesses for whom she'd never cared.

Clare tugged at her wimple from behind. "Remember, I'm in charge," she whispered.

Orlianna huffed, adjusting the wimple. Clare needed to be more careful, not to mention less bossy. If her fiery locks slipped loose, she'd be recognized in an instant.

Clare placed a hand on her back and guided her along through the crowd.

Orlianna kept her head down, trying to avoid eye contact with the Ikarran duchesses. As much as they aggravated her with their pouting lips and overtrimmed dresses, she knew they'd recognize her in a jiffy. And somewhere deep down, it stung her to know that her grandmother had invited *these* wenches to her party and not her.

As they made their way through the maze, Merwin's speech became clearer. "So I thank you all for attending. My countrymen, my friends: you mean more than any amount of gold in the world."

Orlianna rolled her eyes at the marble floor. As if they hadn't all paid their worth in taxes or income from trade.

"We have come together in this dangerous time to seek peace." Merwin shifted his bulk to the center of the throne platform. "Because peace is something that cannot be achieved without each one of you."

Several clapped their agreement.

Orlianna took harsh, heavy steps, grinding her feet into the shimmering mother-of-pearl designs. They were approaching the thrones from the left. Clare guided her close beside the pillars that lined the wall down the room.

She stole a glance behind her. Arliss and Orlando stood cloaked in the far corner, watching.

Arliss gave her a sharp but encouraging nod.

Orlando only stared. His expression screamed terror.

Her heart sped up. He knew what she was about to do. And he seemed to have made peace with it. But now, she felt unsure, unsteady. The burgundy-cloaked spy was the most volatile force in the room.

And she was about to kill his father.

Arliss craned her neck above the mass, straining to catch every syllable of Merwin's thickly accented voice.

Merwin stepped back toward his throne. "So, without any further ado or whatnot, I introduce to you all the hostess of this gathering, Queen Maeve of Ikarra!" He threw his arms wide.

Maeve strode around the edge of the thrones, ascending the steps to stand beside Merwin and Merna. She lifted her chin with her usual smile.

The crowd applauded, the cheering rose to a roar.

Arliss's stomach knotted. They were probably all bribed to celebrate. How could they *really* all be so blind?

Maeve raised a hand and lowered it through the air. "Thank you all! Please, be silent."

Everyone went silent—slowly and not all at once.

Arliss had been standing still, but she gave a few final, resounding claps just for good measure. They resounded awkwardly through the ballroom.

Maeve squinted around the hall in irritation. "Well. Thank you for your welcome. It warms my heart to see so many people gathered in unity."

Arliss clenched her three middle fingers. It would warm *her* heart to stick an arrow in Maeve's right about now.

"As you know, I have recently reassumed rulership of Ikarra. This is a sudden change that will have vast effect on both our clans. For one thing, Ikarra will be ceding the catacombs and the surrounding lands to Anmór once and for all."

The crowd murmured, the diverse audience all reacting differently to the news. Arliss craned her neck to spot Orlianna. Near one of the right-hand pillars, Domnall leaned back, nodding in approval.

Maeve waved the crowd silent again. "I also, along with Merwin and Merna, move to establish peace between our two clans. In spite of the recent conflict, unity is closer than you may realize. I retake the throne I held for many years in the golden days of Ikarra. And I intend to spread those golden days to Anmór as well."

Arliss swallowed, breathing tightly. Apparently Reinhold didn't figure into Maeve's clannish unity politics. Either that meant she intended to ignore their existence…

Or that she planned to eliminate them.

Maeve kissed her fist, then spread her hand out to the crowd in an old Anmórian gesture. "So tonight is for you all. Meet each other. Speak to each other. And look forward to brighter days ahead."

She and Merna sat on either side, but Merwin remained standing in between.

"Shall any questions be made?" Merwin addressed the party. "Does anything withhold us from food and drink and song?"

The crowd held its breath in anticipation.

Arliss held her breath, too. Now was the moment for Orlianna to make her move.

Behind the thrones, a musician struck a reverberating drum, prematurely beginning the music. The drum struck again, rumbling through the silent hall.

Then Clare's voice rang out in response. "Wait!"

Orlianna kept her eyes fixed on the ground below the pedestal. Her face twitched with the effort it took not to look at her grandmother. That was all it would take. One meeting of the eyes, and Maeve would find her out.

Merwin's nostrils flared as he examined Clare. "Who are you, and what have you to say?"

"I am Lady Eirann of Lochair." Clare repeated the lie with a flourish and an even thicker accent than her usual. She truly sounded the part of a citizen of Lochair—the lake city they'd seen from afar the day before. "And I come bringing this servant as a gift to your majesties."

Orlianna folded her hands over her waistline, rubbing her wrist against the dagger that hung beneath her cloak. It would only take a moment. A breath. One move—

Merwin pursed his lips at them. "A fine gift, indeed. But you are not known to us."

Clare didn't even stammer. "My uncle, the right honorable governor of Lochair, sends me in his stead. He regrets that he couldn't attend, but I'm 'ere to make up for it."

Merwin glanced back at Merna. "I did not know that Ionan had a niece."

Merna shrugged, pouting because—for once—all attention wasn't on her. "Strange that you would not know that. 'Tis common knowledge."

Orlianna restrained a laugh. Merna bought into Clare's tall tales just to preserve her pride. They were all proud—standing upon a pedestal, elevating themselves above everyone else. Three rulers, so different, yet so alike. Merwin, Merna, Maeve—they all had something in common.

When someone stood up against them, they eliminated that person.

The list of casualties had grown longer than Cahair's trading laws. Harrison's name burned at the top of the list. But now, Orlianna was beginning to wonder if Maeve was responsible for even more than was already evident. Lachlan's death seemed too conveniently timed. And Galcobhar, too?

She pressed down on the dagger beneath her linen robes. It was time for vengeance.

The folds of Merwin's neck bunched as he nodded. "Thank you for your gift, Lady Eirann. Bring her forward."

Clare's heels clicked on the marble as she prodded Orlianna again. "Get on, you."

Orlianna stumbled toward the thrones.

"Here." Clare tilted her head back, locking eyes with Merwin. "May she benefit you in every way you deserve."

Merna released a violent gasp. She jumped up from her throne, pointing. "I know who you are!"

Orlianna stole a sideways glance at Clare.

Clare stood still, but her eyes had grown wide, her chest throbbing beneath the indigo robes.

"Guards!" Merna jerked her hands towards the soldiers who stood at attention on either side of the platform. "Seize them both!"

"Sister—" Maeve stood.

Merna waved an arm. "I tell you, this is that dratted little snake who has poisoned my son's mind!"

"Sit down." Maeve crossed her arms.

"I will not sit down!" Merna's voice rose to a shriek. "Your assembly has been breached. Who knows who this alleged *servant* she has brought is." She glanced around desperately. "Guards!"

The guards advanced toward Orlianna and Clare, spears pointed.

The crowd pressed backward into pillars, walls, giving the fracas some space.

Orlianna stepped back, bumping into Clare. She caught Clare's eye, raising both eyebrows in a desperate plea for a backup plan— any plan. She tried to spot Arliss and Orlando, but they had vanished into the crowd.

She glanced back at the approaching guards. And in that moment, she looked up at the pedestal.

It happened too quickly for her to look away. Maeve met her gaze. The gray eyes flooded with shock, almost fear. The silver bracelets jingled all down her wrists as she, too, pointed.

"Seize them!" Maeve commanded. "It is Orlianna! Seize her!"

Orlianna gritted her teeth. She was being slapped with a reputation as disturber of everyone's peace.

Clare hissed into her ear, "What should we do?"

"No use in disguises anymore." Orlianna clawed at her wimple.

"Let us be ourselves."

She tore off the restrictive fabric, threw off the scratchy cloak. Beneath, the maroon dress she'd borrowed from Clare fit a bit too tightly on her body. Her blood pulsed through her arms against the laced green sleeves. But it was better than that hideous disguise she'd been touting.

All that mattered was the dagger. She drew it, holding it tip-out by her side.

"Stop them!" Merna clutched her silk skirts.

Clare threw off her cloak, drawing two short swords. She spun into the quartet of guards, gilded hair flying.

The crowd erupted into shocked gasps and interjections.

Orlianna strode past the fray and toward the thrones.

Arliss stood on tiptoes, elbowing her way through the crowd. People smothered her on every side, pushing back in fear of the fighting by the thrones. But Arliss wasn't afraid. She just needed to get to Orlianna.

Orlando stepped in front of her and plowed a path through the masses for her. He was silent, his expression tight.

She drew her bow from beneath her cloak. No sense in secrecy now. What cover they'd had was blown.

"Out of the way!" She drew her arrow and pointed it into the crowd. "Make way!"

People suddenly started parting for them.

Arliss kept moving, threading her way around the pillars. Orlando was on the carpeted aisle now, taking slow steps. She reached him and jabbed her right elbow into his arm.

"Let's go!" she urged. Orlianna advanced toward the throne—armed but alone. Maeve had descended the pedestal and was trying to calm the frenzied crowd, to no avail.

But Orlando would not move.

Arliss jabbed him again with her draw arm. "We have to help

her."

He stared, eyes glazed. "I can't."

"What are you talking about?"

"She's about to kill my father."

"The only thing Merwin did for you was bring you into existence. He is no father."

He glared at her, teeth bared. "You sound just like Orlianna."

"Because she's right!"

"So you hate me, too? Just like her?" He placed a bolt on his crossbow. "I'm done with you all. You speak words of forgiveness, but in your hearts, you're all afraid of me. You're just waiting for me to stab you in the back. And here you are, ready to do just that."

Arliss's chest burned. "Merwin is *not* you."

Orlando advanced down the carpet, crossbow ready.

Arliss paced after him. "Stop this! This isn't who you are."

"Yes, it is."

"No! You're lying to yourself. You are a child of God, a knight of Reinhold. You're not the murderer Thane made you to be."

He kept going. "If you heard what happened in the catacombs, you know that's not true."

Orlianna mounted all three steps up the pedestal in one stride. She brandished the dagger at Merwin. He stood alone, both royal ladies having descended to calm the crowd.

"Where is the sphere?" she demanded.

Merwin fumbled in his robes for a concealed weapon. "I—I don't have it."

"Murderer! You know where it is!"

He drew a short sword. "I'd kill again and again if only to ensure you never sit on a throne as queen of any country! Ikarra is weak—welcoming Reinhold, intermarrying with Anmór. A realm of half-bloods and weak rulers!"

He swept the sword at her.

She stepped back, and he stumbled forward, slashing air. She reached up and locked her arms around his sword arm, nearly popping his shoulder out of joint. The blade spun to the floor.

She shoved him back into his throne, panting. "You know this dagger?"

His eyes went wide as he placed his hands on his paunchy stomach. "It once belonged to me."

She licked her lips. "It can be yours again."

She drew back the dagger to thrust it home.

Time slowed to a trickle for Arliss as she pounded after Orlando.

He raised his crossbow, aiming for Orlianna.

Maeve spotted him and Arliss at the same time, her mouth twitching open and shut. She jerked her head back at the thrones and saw what was happening. Grabbing her skirts, she rushed toward the platform.

But Arliss knew she wouldn't reach it in time.

Orlando's finger tightened around the trigger.

Arliss rushed at him, arrow still drawn but pointed at the ground. She threw herself into him, grappling for his arms while still holding her bow.

He struggled. The trigger clicked. The bolt flew wildly into the far back corner of the room.

Orlianna stabbed deep. The dagger submerged in Merwin's flesh, sinking into the fat all the way up the handle.

He collapsed on the floor in front of his throne. Blood gushed down the front of his already-dark robe as his stomach closed over the dagger.

Merna's shriek drowned out every other noise in the room. She stumbled toward the thrones, collapsing against the steps. She clawed her way across the platform.

"No!" she bellowed. "*No!*"

Orlianna stepped back, adrenaline spiking her bloodstream. She could breath freely again. Harrison was avenged.

It vaguely registered in her reeling brain that Arliss was shouting her name.

Then the spear butted into her temple and her world went black.

CHAPTER THIRTY-FIVE:
SHACKLES

A STEADY, PULSING RATTLE SHOOK ARLISS FULLY AWAKE. SHE BLINKED, feeling numbed by the vibration that beat its way into her bloodstream. She'd fallen asleep sitting up against cold metal. Her right shoulder, wedged in the corner of the shiny surface, felt limp as a crogall's tentacle.

She blinked again, and the light that streamed in the windows stung her eyes.

The windows of a train car.

She sat up, her limp arm flopping in her lap. It was an ugly train car, far uglier than the one she'd ridden in Anmór last year. This one was bare sheet metal, the rickety bolts rattling with every roll down the tracks.

She ran her left hand down the leather seat. Dry. Cracked. Feather stuffing puffing out of the crevices.

"You're awake."

Arliss glanced across the train car. Orlando sat in the opposite corner, burgundy cloak gathered tight about him. She shifted her weight. "Where are we going?"

His hood hid his eyes. "Does it matter at this point?"

"Not if we don't know." She raised an eyebrow. He might act defeated, but she wasn't going to give up just yet. They had a bloody lot of reasons to keep going. At least, she felt they were there somewhere—deep in the reaches of her mind.

She leaned her head back into the metal and closed her eyes, recalling the maps of Ikarra she had studied while on Orlianna's ship. The old parchments, scratched and lined by quill pen, had marked the train stations. Anmór had half a dozen, but the northern realm of Ikarra had but two: one just west of Cahair, the other in North Havens, a key trading and fishing city.

So if they were in Ikarra, it would be easy to narrow it down.

But supposing they were in Anmór?

Not likely. Maeve would want to cart them to Ikarra as quickly as possible and lock them in the deepest dungeon she could find. Speaking of which, where were Orlianna and Clare? In an adjoining car? She could only hope.

She stood and nearly tripped on her wobbly legs. The train rattled beneath her. Pressing her palm against the window, she stepped forward.

She tripped, knees slamming into the steel. Her palms caught her from breaking her nose.

"You're shackled in."

Arliss jerked her right foot, and the chain rattled. "I can see that."

It still afforded her a few paces' movement from the corner seat. She pushed herself up, wincing at the pain that jabbed into her forearm. The crogall's bite wasn't going away anytime soon. She stood and leaned as close to the window as she could get.

The landscape outside was a prologue to the sea. White birds soared past. Grassy marshlands spread out their endless fingers, while the gray mountains formed a backdrop.

She fixed her eyes on the distant line of mountains. Her eyebrows twisted, deepening the headache that had been lurking in her forehead. The sun shone straight into her eyes. That meant the mountains lay southwest. And another line of mountains beyond that…even further south.

She inhaled tightly. They were in Ikarra. And already far beyond the mountain-lined bay of Cahair.

That meant one thing: they were headed to North Havens.

She swallowed. Maeve wanted them as far from Cahair as possible. Which meant she was planning something far more terrible and shocking than anything that had come before.

The entire trip from Anmór passed in a confusing blur for Orlianna. Her mind floated in a fog, searching for answers to questions she hadn't yet asked. But now the train slowed, jerking her and Clare forward.

She met Clare's grim stare. The landscape outside was a grayish green blur the color of dead grass. But she did not have to look; she knew just where she was by the sharp scents that pierced her nose. Fish. Salt. Vanilla.

The conflicting scents of North Havens.

The windows outside were suddenly dark. The train screeched to a halt. Orlianna leaned back into the metal to counterbalance the momentum.

"Where are—" Clare began.

"North Havens."

Clare lowered her head. "So far north?"

"It's a major city, but Maeve must want us as far from everything else as possible." Orlianna let air trickle into her lungs. "She won't risk us ruining things any further."

Clare nodded. "And by the time we could escape, news will've traveled of Merwin's death. Everyone will be afraid of us."

"Escape?" Orlianna echoed, her hollow voice bouncing off the metal walls. "There is no escape."

The door to the car slid open. Four guards—Ikarran, unlike the Anmórian rogues who'd shoved them along so far—entered. Helmets of green-tinted metal hid everything but their eyes. They jerked the two ladies up, bound their arms to their sides, then unlocked the ankle shackles.

One guard leaned close to Orlianna as he prodded her down the steps to the train platform. "Forgive me, princess."

"The wrong is not yours." She gasped for air that wouldn't come. Loyalty, even in this circumstance? It was too much to ask for.

The train station was tall, arched, edged elaborately in bronze, swirling designs. Tinted glass gave a green, underwater look to the whole place. Yellow light flooded in on either side of the open-ended building.

The guards led them to the right, toward the adjacent building. Even through the darkened glass Orlianna could see a royal assembly; and beyond that, carriages lined up outside.

Someone bumped her shoulder. Arliss—also guided by an Ikarran guard—nodded a hallo.

Orlianna whittled her voice to a breathy hiss. "Imprisoned in my own country. Maeve truly has won."

"You assassinated someone. In most places, that's a crime."

"I killed a criminal and a villain."

Arliss licked her cracked lips. "You've read the words of the Bible: 'vengeance is mine, I will repay'?"

"And what do you think God is going to do—come down in human form to kill Merwin himself?" She restrained herself from shouting. "God did that once, but it was a one-time sort of thing."

"It wasn't your place to kill him."

They were almost to the station building. Orlianna's cheeks burned at Arliss's slicing criticism.

"How do you think God accomplishes his will, then? Is it not through his creatures?"

"Of course." Arliss's eyes traveled down from Orlianna's face to her chest and went wide. "But murder in cold blood for a good reason is still murder in cold blood."

What was Arliss staring at? Orlianna glanced down at her own breasts. She nearly choked. The square neckline of the borrowed gown cut angularly across her pale skin.

And for the first time in as long as she could recall, that skin was bare—exposed.

No pendant lay against her collarbone. No chain noosed around her neck.

Two guards ahead of them pulled open the double glass doors. The party within was colorful, elegant. And of course, Maeve stood at their head, handing money to two hansom-drivers. She turned to face the four prisoners, a deeply satisfied smirk spreading across her face.

Arliss leaned close to Orlianna. "She's taken all our gifts."

Maeve was backed by a trio of bulky warriors, but she didn't need even that protection. Around her neck hung the glittering pendant of Reinhold. She motioned the guards forward as she waved the drivers away. "Take them away."

Orlianna's senses blurred into pain; deep, deep pain in her heart that seared its way through her limbs; the ropes around her wrists chewed into her. If Maeve had the pendant in her grasp, they were all as good as dead.

The prison cell was walled with cold stone hewn roughly into rock—a mountain, or some sort of ridge. They'd been blindfolded for the carriage ride and also for the last leg of their journey, which had been a bumpy jaunt across undulating waters.

Orlando lay back on the bed in the corner of the dark cell. A river? The sea? He had no idea. The thick air that followed the thin light beneath the door smelled salty. But any river in North Havens would be saltwater, not fresh, so that proved nothing.

He tilted his head over on the thin mattress and inspected his prison mates. The four beds sat in the cell's four corners. Orlianna lay opposite him, rolled over with her back to him. Arliss and Clare sat facing each other against the other wall, conversing quietly.

"You don't suppose there's any way out?" Clare was saying.

Arliss sighed. "I heard one of the guards speaking kindly to Orlianna. But at this point, they're all too afraid of Maeve to *do* anything."

Orlando rolled back over and faced the black wall. There was no *doing* anything, for any of them. Didn't Arliss see that?

She kept musing. "If Philip finds out where we are…"

Orlando sat up quickly. "He will never find that out. Don't you see? We are *captured*. Which means we are likely to be *executed*.

And if you think Maeve will slip one word of our location, you know nothing about royal espionage."

Clare's nose flared. "Don't talk to me about royal espionage, you half-bred backstabber. I know exactly who you are."

"Do you? I don't think anyone does." He clenched his fists on the mattress.

"You tried to murder Orlianna."

"She *did* murder my father."

Clare shrugged. "A criminal in his own right."

"And by that you're implying that I'm a criminal."

"Technically we're all criminals now."

"Technically," Orlando leaned forward, "you fought against us in the battle on the Tuáma Fields, which makes me question why you're suddenly on our side."

Clare rolled her eyes. "Obviously someone wasn't payin' attention to what really happened there."

"Quiet!" Arliss stood, sweeping a glance around the room. "This is just what Maeve wants. She wants to turn us against each other. It's easier to have us kill each other off than for her to kill us herself."

Orlianna laughed bitterly, still facing the wall.

Orlando shook his head. What did she have to laugh about, at this point?

The Ikarran princess turned over and rose from the bed, stepping toward the center of the shadowy cell. She clapped her hands to emphasize each word. "How dumb are we?"

Orlando cocked his head. "I'm sorry, I don't follow."

"You really think Maeve will just kill us off?" Orlianna shook her head, eyes wide. "*No.* Oh, no. She will parade us around, a spectacle to show people just what will happen to those who oppose her. And *then*, my friends, she will slaughter us and let our blood stain the streets of Ikarra, a reminder of the failure of everyone who stands up against her."

The shadows held their peace. Quiet reigned for a moment.

"Ikarra is lost," Orlianna lamented. "In the end, no matter how bravely we fought, we have lost. Good has lost."

Arliss stepped over to Orlianna. In the dark, their two figures were like elegant statues of queens of old. She reached out, brushed Orlianna's tangled hair from her face, and lifted her chin. "Good never loses in the end."

"How can you say that, even now?"

"Because I have seen evil rise and move in for the kill. I have seen every enemy against me succeed in their plans—often more than even they anticipated. But they have not succeeded in destroying me. They have not smothered the light." Arliss faced Orlando. "The light shines in the darkness, and it is not overcome."

Orlando looked up. "She's right."

Arliss's eyebrows curved. She seemed surprised that he so readily agreed with her.

But how could he not? They had all been tedious companions, but they were *good* to him in a way that no one else had ever been.

Especially Arliss. She had shown him what it meant to be a friend, a family. She had taught him the meaning of clan.

He stood. "Clan, it means family. And though we here represent three different clans, we are still one family. And we can fight together until every drop of our blood is spent."

Clare rose with the others. "I agree. And I'm sorry, Orlando. I shouldn't have spoken against you."

"You're right to speak against me." Orlando locked eyes with Orlianna. "I've done so many unforgivable things. I can barely look at myself with honesty, so how can any of you?"

Arliss drew herself to her full height as she repeated his earlier words to her. "It's not about how others view you. It's about how you view yourself."

"Maybe." He tilted his head back and forth. "Or maybe it's both. I forgive, because I am forgiven."

Somehow in the conversation they had all drawn closer. Now they stood in a tight circle. Orlando reached his arms around the three—all now like sisters to him. Even Orlianna didn't resist his touch.

He exhaled. "Let's forgive each other. And no matter what happens, let us fight together as one."

The door to the cell scratched open, letting a few more drops of light inside.

Maeve stood in the door way, silhouetted by the sunlight that drifted down the stone hallway behind her. "I desire an audience with Arliss. Alone"

"I suppose you have guesses as to why I imprisoned you all the way out here."

Arliss kept silent, staring at the tumultuous ocean that surrounded the rock island. Across the inlet lay the elegant city of North Havens, looking like something from a storybook with its high spires and arching roofs. Spring wildflowers crowned the sloping shores.

Maeve tilted her head at Arliss for a response.

She trudged over the uneven rock. "Bringing us so far from Cahair and from Anmór? It's a smart move."

"You are wise to think that. But in truth, I wanted to show you something."

"What?"

Maeve folded her arms, the long sleeves of her brown dress draping about her. She glanced behind her at the two guards who trailed a few paces behind. A sharp glare and a flip of her hand, and they stopped, frozen.

She led Arliss up rock formations crusted with barnacles. Wild seagrass sprung out of crevices, waving its wild sprigs in an attempt to grow on such a barren landscape—an island prison in the middle of the ocean.

Finally they reached the pinnacle of the mountain-island. Below them, the prison—carved into the rock itself—thrust its arched entrances out at intervals. The guards' stocky barracks tower blocked half their view of North Havens now.

But the sea beyond—it spread out forever and forever again, reaching endlessly into the sky.

Maeve pointed out at the blue. "I wanted to show you *this*."

Arliss caught her breath. She'd never imagined so much clear, endless blue in her life. A world of sapphire rippled out from this port. It drifted lazily down to Anmór in the south. Straight across lay Reinhold, hidden by leagues of fog.

And north…

Maeve followed Arliss's line of sight. "Ah, the mysterious north. It beckons to you, too?"

Arliss nodded, though she didn't know why.

"Our people came from the north, long ago. The three clans fled oppression and began life anew in these rich realms," Maeve said. "But I fear things have gone sour."

"Indeed." Arliss squinted, trying to make out just where the sea met the sky. "Instead of coming together, we have fallen apart."

"It only takes one great ruler to save an empire from collapse."

"This is about more than one empire."

Maeve gave an admissive lift of her eyebrows. "But it doesn't have to be."

Arliss faced Maeve. She'd heard enough of this jabber about three clans becoming one. It would never happen. Imagine if she, Ríon, and Orlianna were all royalty of the same kingdom?

She nearly laughed aloud. That would never work, not in ten lifetimes.

"In all your wisdom, you are mistaken, Lady Maeve." Arliss assumed a superior tone. "The three clans are too individual and unique. If the story of the realms is like a song, then we are the three notes of a chord. And no matter how you blare your one note, you cannot change the beauty of contrast."

Maeve stepped back, elevating herself onto a higher clump of rock. "You are so foolish! Blind! Conceited! Thinking that you could challenge me? That *you* could be a queen?" She glanced around wildly. "Where is your power? Where is your strength? Where are your armies?"

Arliss looked down at the rock. Three of her closest friends lay imprisoned within. But they were not dead. Yet.

And she had so many other friends across the realms.

She stared defiantly up at Maeve. "They will come. And you will see how right I was. You will watch your lies crumble about you."

Maeve's chest shuddered, and Arliss thought she had caught a chill from the sea winds that whipped about them. But then her trembling caught sound and spun it into laughter. Hideous laughter. It bellowed from Maeve's open mouth, echoed off the rocks, carried along the winds across the sea.

Arliss stood, every laugh stabbing her through. This was arrogant confidence so certain it made her blood run cold.

"Oh, my dear, poor child." Maeve stopped laughing. "Do you not see that I have won? I have your pendant, crown, and sphere. Your life is in my very hands. Anmór is ready to bow beneath me. And Reinhold will be easily enough extinguished."

"What about the vial, and the sword which opens it?" Arliss shouted back, digging her heels into the rock. And the ring—she hadn't even mentioned that. "What about Ilayda, my parents, and Ríon?"

Maeve's gray eyes opened a touch wider.

"What about Philip?"

"Philip?" The gold lacing across the front of Maeve's gown went taut. "His fate will be yours. Once I fulfill my goals, I shall find him and slaughter him for you to see. And you will weep for how deeply you have failed."

Arliss sank down on the rock. The image flashed into her brain before she could stop it: Philip's bloodied head resting in her lap, his dead body stretched out on these very rocks.

Above her, Maeve towered, growing to giant size. She seemed to block out the sun's light until there was no day, no horizon.

Arliss clutched at the rocks, and the image vanished. She trembled up at Maeve, tears dripping from her eyes. "The truth will win in the end. I will win in the end."

Forehead wrinkling, Maeve leaned down and glared at Arliss

beneath her thin eyebrows. "You speak well, princess. But there is nothing in your words but air. They are words spoken like the queen you will never be."

Maeve stalked toward the edge of the crag, holding her skirts to descend. She motioned for the guards to come up to her.

Arliss called hoarsely after her, "If I were to become queen of Reinhold, would my voice matter? Would you listen to me?"

Maeve froze, back to her. "Yes. But that will never happen."

"How are you so sure?" Arliss stood as the guards reached her. They grabbed her wrists, ready to drag her back to her cell.

Maeve didn't look back again. "Because the moon is full, and it is about to rise."

As the guards shoved her down the rugged hill, Arliss strained for one last glimpse of the north. The sun had begun to sink behind the shore city, and in the east, fog creeped in with growing tendrils. It was a fog that separated her from everything she'd ever called home. And in the north—who knew what world lay beyond the farthest reaches of Ikarra and Reinhold? Somewhere, they ended. And there the oceans began.

Where, then, did the oceans end? In the mythical realm of Eire from which the three clans had originated?

She couldn't say. It was too distant. The fog caught the sunlight and burned it into her eyes, forcing her to look away.

The fog could not, however, obscure what Maeve had said.

Nor could it hide the many hints she had let slip.

CHAPTER THIRTY-SIX: GO NORTH

Ilayda gripped the steering stick with sore fingers. Her forearm burned from holding the bird steady for so long. But she couldn't let go. Not even if she wanted to, really. Her fist seemed glued to the stick.

Erik lay on his back on the platform at her right, his arm rested upon the narrow wooden trunk Elowyn had sent, his eyes slitted open just enough that she knew he wasn't asleep. He'd asked her to take the stick for a little while just so he could get some rest. And, after a little turbulence, she'd settled in for a smooth flight.

But something was changing. A harsh wind that smelled like flaming ice rushed through the bird from behind.

The bird dropped, and Ilayda worked life into her sore fingers, trying to even the contraption out. But the wind toyed with the aircraft body, forcing it lower.

Erik opened his eyes. "You got it?"

She bit her lip. "I…think so."

"So you don't have it." He sat up and kneeled beside her. "Here, let me have a go."

Rolling her eyes, she gave up control of the stick and sat back, arms crossed.

He glanced around, sniffing. "Do you smell that?"

She inhaled. "Smells sweet." She wrinkled her nose. "But also…not."

"Vanilla and fish." He reached for the lever that controlled the rudder. "And judging by that sunset, we're farther north than I expected."

Ilayda exhaled against her arms. They might be almost back to Ikarra right now. Would they find Arliss and the rest alive? Dead? Fighting? Imprisoned? She had no clue.

It all depended on what moves Maeve had made. The woman was patient. She'd obviously been behind Thane for some time. But everything seemed so right. The stage was set for the last act of her grand play.

She cracked the tension out of her neck. "Do you think we're *too* far north?"

"I'd rather reckon us too far north and end up beyond Cahair than too far south and end up in Anmór."

He had a point: Anmór was a nightmarish place. Yet there were villains in other places too.

"But if Maeve has taken over Ikarra—"

"Then they'll need us more than ever."

She clenched her jaw, trying to steel herself with his level of resolve. It was there, somewhere deep inside. But hard as she tried, she couldn't make this easy. A flight across the ocean should have been fun. The arrow knives that were sheathed within her boots should have been exciting.

Fear still wound its way through her bloodstream.

Erik grabbed her arm. "Look—there!"

The foggy clouds parted below them, revealing leagues of indigo ocean. And in the middle of that ocean, a dark pentagonal shape. The closer they flew, the more rough and jagged it looked, almost like a mountain rising out of the sea.

And beyond that rose the skyline of an impressive city— beautiful, bright, but certainly not Cahair.

Philip buttoned the tight jerkin as he walked down the dark alley of Cahair's second cantar, keeping a wary eye on his surroundings. Ríon had said to meet him here, in between the church and the blue apartments, right as the sun sank behind the castle. If he craned his neck, the citrus bite of the sun's dying breath stretched across the sky behind the silhouette of Maeve's tower.

It was time. But where was Ríon?

Philip backed up against something that looked and smelled like a rotten coffin. Supposing Ríon had been delayed—or even caught. Coming back without new intelligence would be better than not coming back at all.

He took a deep breath and instantly regretted it. The fishy odor of rotting garbage gouged his nostrils again. He crept to the other side of the alley and tried again—this time breathing with his mouth open.

A shadow shifted across the main road—by the riverway near Rose's tea room. He could barely glimpse it from his obscured vantage point.

He knelt on the rough stone, reaching for his long knife. He patted down his leg. He had quite the stash of weaponry from the day's work. Maybe just a dagger—quieter, stealthier?

The sheath of his sword scraped the ground like an obnoxious old friend. Yes, perhaps it would be better to stick with the familiar in case of an attack.

The shadowy figure glanced both ways down the quiet street, then dashed across to the alley opening.

Philip's muscles hardened, freezing over, hand on the pommel of his sword.

The shadow halted. Hard breathing. Desperate for air, but still restrained. The breathing of a spy. And it may have only been air, but it still had that uncanny Anmórian twang to it.

Philip stood, relaxing. "You made it."

Ríon pointed his knife straight at Philip.

Philip raised his hands. "It's just me, idiot."

"Oh." Ríon quickly sheathed the knife, pulled it out again, then re-sheathed it. "I'm just—I don't know. Jumpy. More than usual."

"What's made you jumpy?"

Ríon moved closer, and his voice sounded hoarse. "Haven't you heard the news? It's all over the city!"

Philip snorted. "May I remind you, I've spent the day looting through junk piles and scouring open-air markets for weapons." And it had been productive. He rubbed the leather etching of the fingerless gloves he'd come up with. Snug, but movable. Orlando would be proud.

He glanced up at Ríon, waiting for the news. The moonlight caught Ríon's eyes and flickered in the corners, betraying his tears.

Philip's heart drummed faster. Something must had happened to Clare. Or even…

"My father's dead," Ríon managed.

"Dead?" Philip leaned back, stunned. Was Merwin's murder something of Maeve's doing? Everything seemed to be. "By whose hand?"

"Orlianna's."

Philip felt like he'd been punched in the stomach. Orlianna would not have killed without incitement—provocation. And she had plenty reason to, after Merwin had killed Harrison. But this still gave an excuse for Maeve to label her and all her company as outlaws.

"I'm sorry, Ríon."

"He was a bad man, and a worse father." Ríon pursed his lips. "But that's not all. Finín has learned some intelligence that will bring you great interest."

The spark in Ríon's moist eyes was encouraging. Philip nodded for him to go on.

"There are royal prisoners being kept here in Cahair. The rumors are they're in the guard building next to Lord Domnall's house." Ríon lifted his eyebrows. "There's some hope for us yet."

"I don't follow you."

"You see? Orlianna, Arliss, Orlando, and Clare all intruded on Maeve's celebration in Anmór. And they were all captured. Maeve won't pass up this opportunity to display her power."

Philip's nostrils flared. "We have to rescue them." He started down the alley toward the first cantar. He'd find that blasted

Domnall's house and rip the guard building to shreds with his bare hands if he had to.

"Wait." Rion rushed after him. "We don't even know if it's them."

"It doesn't matter."

"If you're caught, Maeve'll throw you on the pile with the rest."

"Then we'll die together." Philip reached the end of the alley and glanced out into the street. Relatively quiet. Most of the tall, narrow houses were dark. As long as they kept their weapons beneath their cloaks, they wouldn't be suspect.

Domnall's house was as tall and imposing as he was: four stories, iron staircase leading up to a second-floor entrance, gardens that bloomed verdantly even in the moonlight. But his windows were dark.

The windows of the adjacent guardhouse, however, were not.

It was everything Domnall's house was not: a squatty two stories of crumbling brick. Beyond it Philip could see for a good length—grassy field, sandy shorelines, the ruined tower at the end of the peninsula. The dead midnight sky hid every star beneath a sheet of cloud, but the waxing moon glowed through the blur.

On the top floor, shadows moved behind thick curtains. Philip could have sworn he saw Domnall's silhouette.

Philip leaned over to Rion as they lingered in the shadows between two of the spaced lampposts. He pointed at the guardhouse. "It looks like you could storm it and level the building with just a dozen men."

"Looks are deceiving, I'll bet." Rion cracked his knuckles. "But you're right, it is old. One of the oldest buildings in Cahair—two hundred years, by the look of it. Domnall's house, on the other hand, was built by his father when Maeve was queen."

"The *first* time." Philip moved toward the treacherous lantern-light.

Ríon followed. "As king of Anmór, I'll never look at her as queen."

Philip kept walking but gave Ríon a glance. "*As king?*"

"My father's death means the throne passes to me."

"But Merna—"

"Anmór isn't like Ikarra. A woman can't rule without a king."

Philip shrugged. "Your mother doesn't care that much about following established laws."

Ríon stared at the guardhouse. Two guards patrolled the outside but hadn't spotted them yet. His chest heaved. "Clare is in there."

Philip caught the back of Ríon's jerkin. "We can't just go knocking on the front door. Who knows what all we'd find inside."

"Then what do *you* suggest?"

Philip turned back toward Domnall's house. "Let's see if there's a back entrance."

There was. The door at the back of the guardhouse was nothing more than a few rotting, rain-sodden boards. Lazy carpentry. Philip wrenched the door out of the frame pretty easily and set it on the grass.

He glanced back at Ríon, nodding. They advanced into the darkness.

Chinks in the brick walls let in fragments of light that flickered off dull blades. There weren't any prisoners down here. It was more of a cellar. A primitive armory.

Seemed a strange place to keep Arliss, considering she was one of the most valuable royal prisoners in the realms at this point. And if Orlando, Orlianna, and Clare were *all* here…

It didn't sit well with Philip's growling, empty stomach. Not at all. Something was afoot—something of Maeve's doing.

Footsteps creaked above them. And a raised voice.

Domnall's voice.

Philip held his finger to his lips and edged toward the far corner of the room, where light from above fell down a flight of rickety stairs.

"Where are they?" Domnall was shouting as his boots clamped

across the boards. "I'm sick of this nonsense."

"I don't know, you idiot."

Philip started as the female voice spoke. Could it be—

Domnall stomped. Cell bars rattled. "Neither Prince Ríon nor that Philip chap have been seen since the battle. You're a spy. You know where they are."

"I don't."

Philip edged to the base of the stairs. The upper story was the prison. Empty cells lined the fraction of the room he could see. From here, he could just glimpse the edge of Domnall's cape as he motioned to an unseen attendant.

"Very well," Domnall said.

A guard stepped from the corner with a spear and handed it to Domnall, blunt end out.

The butt of the spear hit someone's flesh.

A pained groan echoed from the far cell.

"No!" The female speaker wasn't Arliss. But Philip couldn't quite place the voice. "Domnall, we know *nothing*."

"Well, perhaps it would be some small interest to *you* to know that Orlianna has been captured, along with Arliss, Orlando, and Clare." Domnall savored his captive's gasp. "But there's so much more you'll never know. Your aunt was a meddling fool, trying to spy under Maeve's nose. She got caught up with one of those Reinholdians, too—a man named Eamon. Looks like your fate will be the same as hers."

Rose. Philip tested out the stairs. They were far too creaky to attempt without instantly revealing him and Ríon.

Rose's voice shook. "My aunt wasn't captured. She…"

"Vanished? Fool! There are no accidents here. Not even the one that killed Mícheál's parents."

Philip froze, nearly as stunned as the upstairs captives probably were. Maeve continued to show her hand throughout all their stories.

Domnall turned on his heel. "I'll leave you to think on whether or not you'd like to tell me anything else."

Two guards trailed Domnall. The front door of the guardhouse slammed behind them.

The other two guards stayed behind.

Philip jerked his head at Ríon. "Let's take them."

He rushed up the stairs and into the sparse room, a hallway lined with empty cells.

The other two guards ran at him from the end of the hall.

Ríon joined him from behind.

Philip glanced at the sword of Reinhold in his palm, sighed, and sheathed it. He wasn't going to kill these men. They were good Ikarran soldiers who were just following orders.

But he also wasn't going to let them stand between him and his friends.

The guards split—one rushing at Ríon, the other throwing himself at Philip.

The solid force of a warrior's body hit Philip head-on. The guy was unarmed, and looked like he was about ready to turn in for the day. But that didn't mean he wasn't threatening. His short-sleeved tunic showed off a body rippling with experience.

Philip tried to summon to mind everything he'd heard Orlando teaching Arliss. At the time, he had ignored it.

The guard grabbed Philip's wrist and jerked it back, hooking his other arm beneath his biceps. Pain stabbed down Philip's arm. The lever the guard had created could break his arm in half in one moment.

He spun toward the guard, reaching around for a hold on his neck. He clawed across the mouth—clenched teeth snapping at him—and hooked his arm around the far side of his opponent's neck.

The guard tried to break Philip's arm, but there wasn't enough tension any more.

Philip jammed his knee into his chest.

The warrior backed up, reanalyzing him.

No—he wouldn't let this fight slow down, not now. Philip spun toward him with a kick that lashed across his face.

Spitting blood, the guard grabbed Philip's raised leg and gave a good jerk.

Philip crashed to the floor, face grinding into the stone. Blood mingled with saliva in his mouth, tasting like rusted iron. He rolled, dodging another blow.

He glanced straight up. A tapestry hung by the door—the brocade fabric hanging nearly to the floor. Philip squinted at the carven mounts. He knew this kind of basic carpentry. There were no screws, just a dab of mortar keeping the thing in the wall.

The guard leaned over, his panting breaths blasting into Philip's face. "You're outdone, outlaw."

Still lying on the floor, Philip reached up and gripped the fringes of the tapestry. "I may be an outlaw now. But I'm never outdone."

He jerked—hard. The bracket burst from the wall, chunks of mortar exploding in a miniature dust storm. The wood bracket smashed into the guard's forehead.

He dropped to his knees, grabbing his head in pain. Philip was behind him in an instant, pulling the tapestry tight around his neck—almost tight enough to choke him. He leaned close. "Where is Arliss being held?"

"I don't…know what…you're talking about."

"Stop lying." Philip tightened the noose. "I know you've got royal prisoners here."

"Not the prisoners that're royal, you dolt." The guard coughed. "Prisoners of royalty."

"Who else is of interest to the crown right now?"

"Everyone."

Philip released the tapestry and crushed his fist into the guard's temple, and he fell forward, unconscious. Ríon's opponent lay in the same manner.

Philip jumped up, pulled a torch from its bracket by the door, and rushed toward where Rose gripped the bars of her cell. The torchlight revealed her dingy clothing and confining cell. Her glossy shoulder-length hair and sharp eyebrows.

"I'm glad you found us."

He stepped toward the bars. "Are you hurt?"

She shook her head. "I'm fine. But Mícheál's not doing well." She nodded to the cell two down at Philip's right.

He flashed the light in that direction. Mícheál lay on a pallet, facing the door. His eyes were open but burning with feverish pain. A red gash split across his forehead.

Rose sighed. "I was afraid we wouldn't get out until it was too late."

Philip gave the bars a good shake. They were a lot more solid than the tapestry bracket. "You're not out yet. And chances are Domnall's household will have heard the racket and come running. We don't have much time."

"Nor do we have keys," Ríon added.

Rose squinted upward, eyebrows lowered in thought. "Do you have a bow an arrow?"

"No."

Ríon reached down for his fallen opponent. "Yes, actually." He held up a standard Ikarran longbow.

"Hurry." Philip passed the bow and an arrow through the bars to Rose. "What exactly are you doing?"

She placed the arrow on the string and tested the weight. "I may not be as good as Arliss—" she pointed the arrow through the bars and aimed at Mícheál's cell. "—but I can handle a bow."

Before Philip could release the dozens of confused protests in his mouth, Rose released her arrow.

It stuck perfectly in the keyhole to Mícheál's cell. The lock clicked, and the door swung open.

Rose smirked in satisfaction.

Philip stared, surprised. "All right, then. And how will we get *you* out?"

Grunting, Mícheál rose and stepped out of his cell. His forehead wrinkled with pain and dried blood, but he gave Rose a sharp nod. She speared the bow between her cell bars and into his palm.

He tugged the arrow from his keyhole and set it to the string.

One shot, and Rose pushed the door to her cell open.

She tossed her hair behind her head. "What now?"

"It's time we end this." Philip drew his sword and pointed it toward the ceiling. The torch he held in his other hand flickered on the spotless blade. He stared at it, entranced by the fires of war it seemed to hold.

Maybe, just maybe, those fires were about to burn out for good.

"What's your *plan*, though?" Mícheál leaned against the wall.

"Stop Maeve."

Ríon gnawed on his lip. "That's an objective, not a plan." He dropped his voice to a mutter. "No plan on earth will do us much good now."

"He's right," Mícheál agreed. "Maeve has the people of Ikarra twisted around her finger. She's forced Merna into submission. All that's left is—" He sighed and met Rose's gaze.

Philip also looked to Rose.

She combed her fingers through her hair, pulling it over one shoulder. "I know we all have a lot to tell each other. But there's something you need to know, Philip."

He waited, still gripping his sword. Whatever she was about to say, it wasn't going to talk him out of facing Maeve and fighting her forces until his last drop of blood.

She continued. "I'm good at pretending I'm asleep. Good at listening to all the guards' gossip. I discovered a lot of things while imprisoned. There's a price on all our heads—especially you, Arliss, Orlando, and Orlianna. Maeve would give anything to have you all imprisoned."

"She's almost got her wish."

"True." Rose sucked in her cheeks. "But you're still free. And while you're free, you have to free the others."

Philip squeezed his sword hilt. "We don't even know where they are."

"Maybe we do." Rose's eyebrow twitched upward. "But more on that in a moment. What matters now is that Maeve is about to make the last grand move in her game."

"Which is?"

"Isn't it obvious by now?" Mícheál asked.

Philip shot him an irritated glance, then recoiled his expression. Mícheál was right. All of Maeve's actions were threads in a tapestry, working to form one ultimate image. The kindness shown to the Reinholdian guests, the attempts to stop the war, her exertion over the rigdál mór, her self-coronation. The party in Anmór, the imprisonment of the rebels. A union with Anmór. All that was left was…

"In three days, Maeve will crown herself queen of the realms."

Philip's spine tingled. "Surely no one will agree to that. There are enough loyalists—enough to rise up and stop her."

"Fear silences even the noblest of tongues." Rose crossed her arms. "Without a leader, no one will act."

They needed a leader.

And a battle plan.

But they had neither.

Rose stepped toward him and placed her hand over his on the hilt of his sword. "We *have* to find Arliss."

"And leave Cahair to its doom?" He exhaled. "Why Arliss?"

"Because Arliss is the only one with alliances in all three realms. Maeve knows this, and she's terrified. *Terrified.* You realize this, don't you?"

"I do. But I'm not sure Arliss does."

"She's going to have to." Rose drew a strand of leather from her pocket and knotted it around her loosely gathered hair. She waited, hazel eyes expectant for his response.

Philip sheathed his sword. "Where do we find her?"

She grinned. "Follow me."

She headed for the door of the guardhouse. She paused over one of the fallen guards, stooped, and unfastened his leather vambraces. Once these were around her forearms, she also snitched the poor fellow's long knife.

Philip nodded at Mícheál and Ríon. "Both of you—take anything that will aid us." As the other two stocked themselves up, he rushed after Rose. "How can you be so sure where Arliss is?"

She reached the door and peeked out into the dark street. The beginning of a rainshower had turned the stone pavement slick and shiny.

"I've lived in Ikarra all my life. I know every road and river." Rose pointed to the north. "There is only one place Maeve would keep Arliss."

BO BURNETTE/430

CHAPTER THIRTY-SEVEN:
WORLDS APART

THE SCRATCH OF BOOTS AGAINST ROUGH STONE RASPED THROUGH THE bars of the cell, alerting Orlianna of the guards' return long before they arrived.

She sat up on her cot, wedged in the far corner of the room. She wanted to hear every word Maeve had said to Arliss. Her grandmother wouldn't have wasted time here unless she had something important to say.

But it stung, somehow, in the pit of her chest, that Maeve had held council with Arliss and not with herself. She was Maeve's granddaughter, was she not? The leader of this burgeoning rebellion?

Did Maeve truly not consider her a threat?

Or could she simply not face her own granddaughter?

Keys jangled in the lock. The cell door scratched open, hinges whining from years of disuse. Two guards released Arliss's arms and shoved her into the room. Arliss stumbled over to her cot.

One of the guards held a torch which revealed the symbol of the dragon on his red tabard. Anmórian guards. Maeve likely didn't trust even the harshest of Ikarrans to keep their own princess in custody.

The torchlight flickered, revealing the silvery figure who stood behind the guards.

Orlianna stood quickly. "Maeve…"

The guard started to slide the door shut.

She strode forward, catching the bars. "Grandmother, wait!"

Maeve turned. The light outside had faded to dying blood, and the passageway was dim but for the lone torch. Maeve's eyes were pure silver shining orange in the firelight.

Orlianna pressed her face to the chill of the bars. "Will you not even speak to me?"

"What have I to speak to you about?"

"Plenty." Orlianna pushed back against the strength of the guard who tried to force the door closed. "I am your granddaughter. I am the heir to the throne. By our laws, I should be queen."

Maeve pursed her lips. "The people have chosen me over you."

"Holding a sword to everyone's neck and *then* asking their opinion isn't much of a choice."

Maeve stepped toward the cell. "I am giving them peace and tranquility. In the days that come this land will see riches such as it has never imagined. What can you give them?"

"Love," Orlianna said. "I would sacrifice my life for my people. And you? Once, I might have said you would have. But I see now that you think only of yourself."

Maeve did not contradict her. She just stood there, holding Orlianna's gaze.

Orlianna refused to glance away or even blink.

But in the corners of her vision, she could not help but notice the pendant—*her* pendant—hanging from Maeve's neck. The powers of the Lasairbláth bottled within were still unknown. It terrified her for such a weapon to be in such hands.

Yet without Orlando's ring to open it, the pendant was useless.

Maeve smiled. "My alliances are bringing a strength that Ikarra has never known. The people will grow strong—eating and drinking and being merrier than they have ever been. That could never happen under a weak, broken ruler like you."

Orlianna set her jaw, absorbing the insults. "How have you come to this?"

Maeve hesitated. Then she broke Orlianna's stare, turned, and left. The guards locked the door and departed behind her.

Orlianna grasped the iron bars. Maeve was wrong about many

things. Most exceptionally, she was wrong about Orlianna's weakness.

She *was* broken. It was true. But now that she could admit it to herself, she was stronger than ever.

Arliss stretched out on the cot, staring at the rough rock ceiling. The stub of a candle was melting away on the rickety table beside her, but it offered a glimpse of her three companions. All sitting on the edges of their beds. Staring at her. Waiting.

She exhaled, the weight of her body dragging down through the bed. Her heart felt like it was being slowly turned to stone. Each pulse became more and more painful as the confusion evaporated the hope from her bloodstream.

"What did she say?" Orlianna finally ventured from the corner directly across from her.

Arliss turned her head on the lumpy mattress to face Orlianna. "Too many things to think about."

"Surely there was something."

Arliss faced upward again, trying to piece together the conversation. Maeve had wanted to tell her how horrible her situation was: imprisoned, her gifts taken, Philip missing. But she had shown her something, too.

"The north," Arliss said. "She showed me the direction from which the clans came."

"But why?"

"I think she wanted to make a point. Our clans came here for peace and unity. Right now, we have wars and schisms."

"And she's the only one who can fix things?" Clare scoffed.

"It's not true." Orlando moved restlessly on his cot. "Surely she knows how dangerous you are, Arliss? How dangerous we all are?"

Arliss sat up. "Are we really, though? Right now—imprisoned and separated—we are nothing."

"*If* we were liberated," Orlianna murmured, "If help came from

Reinhold, if we recovered the gifts, would she consider us dangerous then?"

Clare shook her head. "That's a lot of *ifs*."

"Of course she would," Arliss answered Orlianna. "But those things are beyond hope now."

She lay back on the cot, fixing her eyes on the rock ceiling, letting her vision blur into the distant nothingness of a drifting daydream. She was done talking about this. The talk with Maeve should have given her strength and refined her focus. But what focus did she have in this place? There was no goal, no battle plan, that could save them. They were prisoners.

The candle coughed, almost dying.

Arliss blinked slowly, tears dripping from the corners of her eyes and wetting the cot. She had failed. All the reasons she had come to Ikarra—all had collapsed.

Stop the war from happening? She had become one of its chief fighters, and a spearhead in a rebellion.

Preserve the unity of the clans? She had found herself divided between even close friends.

And as for the other matter…

Her mother's last requests before her departure ran through her head. *We know now from Ríon that Merna was not the only one involved in Thane's villainy. Perhaps he supported himself, but I suspect something darker.* So much wisdom! If only her mother had known the full truth. But she didn't know, even now. Even if Ilayda and Erik had reached Reinhold, they had left Ikarra before the revelations about Maeve.

I want you to find out the truth about Thane—about our whole story. For my sake.

Arliss lungs swelled with constrained breaths. The task her mother prescribed sounded simple—like finding the missing piece of a chess game. But it had turned out not to be a piece, but the board itself.

And not just for mine, but for Eamon's.

She had failed them all. She should have accepted—no,

begged—for the throne before she departed. Instead, she had turned her nose up at her father's advisements.

It wouldn't have helped things. She hadn't been ready then, any more than she was now.

Tears sealed her eyes shut. It was hopeless. Every time she took leadership, death and destruction followed. Maybe she *needed* to be queen to incite fear in Maeve's heart. But she—imprisoned, defeated—was no queen to anyone.

The candle flickered out.

Arliss was back in the castle of Reinhold. Not the bare foundation that was being laid when she left, but the castle that Thane had destroyed. This was the castle as it had been long, long ago, in her childhood.

She stepped barefoot across the cold stone floor. The world outside the window was dark and starry, but a fire within blocked out the bitter blackness. Shelves lined the walls. The reading stand stood by the window, but with no book upon it.

She caught her breath. This was the library—but almost before she could remember. This was before they had laid down the rich rug, and when her father's chair was on the other side of the room rather than in its familiar spot by the hearth.

High, musical laughter reverberated in her ears, beautiful but almost ghostly.

Arliss turned to see who was so merry.

A golden-haired girl, no more than eight, scampered into the library. She rushed to the nearest bookcase and climbed onto the second shelf so she could reach higher. Her fingers grabbed at the spine of a large leatherbound volume. It pulled free, and she jumped down off the bookcase.

A tall woman entered the room, her head tilted forward in reproach, but her lips pursed playfully. "Silly wee princess! What shall I do with you?"

The girl hugged the book to her chest. "A story! Please, mother."

Elowyn reached down and grabbed girl and book into her arms. "Very well. But only one. It is late, and if your father finds you still awake when he returns from his hunt—"

"One is enough." The girl's sapphire eyes sparkled with hints of green.

Elowyn sat in Kenton's chair, her arms cradling her daughter as she rested the book on their laps. And she told the story. Arliss stood by the fire, watching them at a distance. She mouthed the words to the story she'd heard so many times.

"But the queen, an innately skilled archer, could make the shot. There, poised on top of the tower, she readied her arrow. The arrow for this shot was no ordinary arrow." Elowyn paused dramatically. "It was a fiery arrow."

Arliss smiled, resting her chin on her fist as she waited for the climactic ending.

But Elowyn said no more. She ushered the little girl to her feet, then stood herself, clamping the book shut. She strode past older Arliss—not seeing her—and returned it to its shelf.

Arliss slid her hand down the shelf toward her mother's. "But…the ending of the story?"

Elowyn glanced at her. "It is not yet written."

"Yes, it is!" Arliss grabbed the book back out. "I have read it myself."

"You do not know how the story goes." Elowyn turned. "You have forgotten it."

Forgotten? How could she forget the story that had fueled her imagination—and given her the strength to save her people?

"You must finish the story, mother." Arliss turned, motioning to her younger self. But the child was gone.

She and Elowyn were alone in the library.

Kenton's chair had moved, too, and the rug now covered the floor. Elowyn was suddenly seated, and she sorted through a pile of papers. She cast many of them on the floor, but the stack never grew smaller.

Arliss jerked the huge book open and placed it on her mother's lap. "Look!"

She gasped in surprise. Where the ending had once been inscribed, the pages were now blank.

"I cannot write it for you," Elowyn said. "You must become yourself."

"I am myself!" Arliss shoved the book away.

"Are you?" Elowyn asked sternly.

"Of course." Arliss stood, biting down frustration. "I am Princess Arliss of Reinhold."

Elowyn stared at her, and as she did, a lone tear dripped down her cheek. Then she stood. And at once, the castle crumbled around them. Arliss felt painfully weightless for a moment as she stood on the air. The stone melted away—wafting like smoke on the wind.

Arliss blinked through the cloud of ashes.

Elowyn kneeled not far from her. Her usually deep eyes were blank, glazed over. Beside her, a stone marker stuck up through fresh dirt. "Death wields its greatest weapon—war."

Arliss stepped toward her. "What are you talking about?"

"Death wields its greatest weapon—*war.*"

Arliss tried to reach the tombstone, but her steps brought her nowhere. "Who has died?"

A desperate fear burned in her chest. She struggled to walk, but an invisible force tugged her back. She knew whose name must be written on the tombstone. He had almost been taken from her so many times before. She had thought him dead at the Battle of the Tuáma Fields, and now...

No, her heart screamed.

"Death wields its greatest weapon—war." Elowyn fell on her face by the grave, repeating the words again and again. But they faded into the air.

The west wind's arms grabbed Arliss and pulled her through the sky, away from the castle's ruins. It threw her down in the fields outside the city, on the very spot where Eamon's grave lay.

Arliss brushed ashes from her slit skirt, then looked toward the city.

She blinked, disbelieving her eyes. This, the capital city of Reinhold? It was magnificent. The castle alone spanned the entire hill that had once contained the whole city. Towers and turrets and walls and gardens spanned the height of the tiered hill. And all around the hill in every direction stretched the new city's streets.

It still retained a shadow of the original design: one lone tower on the flat hilltop. But this tower was greater and grander than anything Arliss had imagined could exist in Reinhold.

"It's a beauty, isn't it?"

She whirled to face the speaker, even though she knew the voice well. "Eamon?"

He smiled as he stepped toward her, arms crossed behind his back. "My dear Arliss."

She stumbled into his arms, hugging his muscled frame close. His huge arms surrounded her, cloaking her in safety. She let her breaths grow deep and full again.

"I need your help," she found herself saying. "I have failed you. I've failed everyone."

"Not yet. It isn't over yet."

"Soon it will be."

"Dear Arliss, how can you of all people lose hope?" He brushed her hair behind her ear. "Your faith is strong. Do not forsake it."

"I seek God's guidance, but he is silent."

Eamon scrutinized her. "You are wrong on both accounts."

She hung her head.

He touched her chin and pulled it back up. "The moon is full, and it is about to rise. Do not be afraid. Trust the Creator. Trust your friends. And be who you were always meant to be."

"I am *myself.*" Arliss clasped his hand. "I am Princess Arliss of Reinhold!"

"No." He stepped back, and the wild grasses encircled his legs. "You are so much more."

The winds grabbed her again and hurled her across the plains—

across the seas—across the world. She could smell saltwater, hear the call of gulls.

And at once, Arliss awakened from her dream. She sat up straight on her cot. Her three companions were asleep. Judging by the blackness outside, it was the deep heart of midnight.

So what had awakened her?

She jerked her head toward the cell door. There it came again— a faint tapping. It certainly hadn't come from one of her slumbering comrades.

She clenched the wrinkled sheet, breathing quickly. If it was a guard, maybe she could trick him. She could act like she was dying of thirst, get him to bring her water. Then when he opened the door—

She let the ratted sheet slip down to the cot. If she acted fast enough, it might work. Then they could swim for the shore and run until they found Philip. Because after the dream, all she needed to know was that he was still alive.

The pattering came again, and with it a soft, padding tread. Two guards—and both trying to be quiet. *That* was truly unusual.

Then another sound rattled the midnight air. Even if her companions had been awake, they might not have noticed it. But Arliss had grown up all her life hearing this sound: during royal assemblies, during arithmetic class with Lady Elisabeth, on hikes through the woods.

It was the systematic crackle of someone's spine popping into place.

She leapt from the cot and grabbed the cold bars of the cell, squinting into the darkness.

"Ilayda?" She said it so confidently it almost wasn't a question.

From the shadows, Ilayda stepped, her purple sleeves drooping down her arms as she placed her hands over Arliss's from the other side of the bars. Erik stood right behind her, a satisfied smirk creasing the corners of his tired eyes.

Arliss stood speechless.

Ilayda rubbed her lips together, reveling in Arliss's surprise.

Arliss found air for her lungs and drank it in. "But how—"

Ilayda held up her hand. "There will be time later. Right now we have to get you out of here." She popped her neck again for good measure. "Silly princess."

CHAPTER THIRTY-EIGHT: FIND HIM

"However did you find us?"

Orlianna had awakened at the sound of a key grating in the lock. Now, as Ilayda embraced Arliss and Erik watched from outside, tapping his foot, Orlianna was pulling herself together far faster than Orlando was.

She strode directly across the dank cell and shook him. "Wake up. Now."

He squinted. "What?"

She gripped his biceps and tugged him up. "We're leaving."

He staggered drunkenly, rubbing both eyes with one hand. "How…"

Orlianna looked to Erik and Ilayda. It was a fair question—and one that still wasn't answered. How, in the name of all that was still good and true in the world, was this even happening?

Erik cast a glance over his shoulder. "Look, we have as many questions as you do. But now is not the time for confabulation."

"Nicely done," Orlianna murmured.

Arliss stepped through the door with Ilayda. "Enough of you two and your big words. There's a prison to break out of."

Erik put a finger to his lips. "And we're not out of it yet. The guardhouse will be alerted if you don't drop your voice." He turned toward the dark hallway.

Arliss rolled her eyes.

"Indeed." Orlianna brushed the folds from her dress.

Erik pointed at her. "You, too."

Orlianna huffed, but she followed him out of the cell. Air from outside forced an involuntary chill up her spine. She was still wearing the borrowed dress from the party in Anmór, and it wasn't the thickest material. Nor was it in the best shape. None of them were, physically.

But inside, her mind flowed like an ocean. All they needed was to escape this wretched prison.

Erik tiptoed down the rugged hallway in the lead, Ilayda and Arliss behind him. Orlianna followed them. Orlando and Clare dragged along in the rear.

Orlianna glanced over her shoulder and motioned for Orlando to walk beside her.

"Eh?"

"We're about to be free." She flattened her footsteps silently into the unevenly hewn stone.

His eyes, blank with sleep, sharpened their focus. "In one way, I suppose. But I can never undo I've done."

"You have forgiven yourself?"

"I'm trying to. But it's hard when—" He glanced at her, then quickly away.

She stared at the starlit sky which widened as they neared the open doors of the prison. He couldn't forgive himself fully, because she hadn't yet forgiven him. Not in her heart. And—just as from the moment they had first met—he could see straight into her heart.

His voice shook. "Do you forgive me?"

She stopped walking. "I'm trying to."

Orlando half-smiled.

When they looked up, two of the Anmórian guards appeared in the doorway, blocking out the stars with the emblem of the moon on their dark tabards.

Arliss instinctively reached for her side, but of course her quiver wasn't there. She had nothing.

The guards lunged at her and Erik with their swords, forcing them back down the hallway. Metal hissed as Erik drew his sword, ready to protect them. But he would be no match for two trained warriors in this situation, and they both knew it.

Ilayda reached quietly into her boots and pulled out two identical weapons—the arrow knives.

One of the guards pointed his sword at Arliss. "How did you get out?"

Arliss stood tall. They only had three weapons among them. But perhaps rhetoric could rescue them. "That's exactly what I was trying to figure out."

"Don't speak smartly to me, lass."

"Honestly, I'm not speaking smartly." Arliss shrugged. "I hardly ever do."

The guard snarled, swiping his sword at them.

Arliss stepped back, bumping into Ilayda. Arliss caught her eye and jerked her head backward.

Ilayda arched her eyebrows. She wasn't catching on.

Arliss's chest tightened. She darted a glance at her former cell, nodded at Ilayda, and mouthed "trap."

Ilayda edged backwards.

Arliss faced the guards. "Surely you realize you cannot defeat us?"

Both guards laughed. "You talk too much, prisoner."

"And you move too slowly, guard."

She grabbed Erik's free hand and pulled him back down the hallway with her. Ilayda, Orlianna, and Clare had already retreated—turning down the left corridor at the end of the hall. The guards pounded into the rocky prison, shouting.

Arliss pulled Erik's ear close. "*Hide.*"

He darted into the corridor to the right.

She backed up against the cell door and glanced around, feigning a little more terror than already pulsed through her veins. She felt for the bars behind her and gave a little tug. The door was still unlocked.

The guards advanced from either side, ready to grab her wrists.

She jumped forward, swinging the door with her. Iron smashed across the first guard's forehead, knocking him to the floor.

The second guard raised his sword for a cut. Arliss dropped, rolling free of his blade.

Orlando burst from the shadows, spinning at the guard with a high kick that splayed him backward—right into Erik's long arms.

Erik jammed him in the side of the head with his sword's pommel. As the guard crumpled, he pulled the sword from his hand.

"We left a longboat moored on the west side of the island." Erik tossed the guard's sword to Orlando. "We must make haste—the tide is coming in."

Orlando sniffed at the weapon. "Not my choice."

Orlianna wrenched it from his hand and started for the door. "I'll take it."

Arliss hurried in front of her. "I'm in the lead here."

"*What?*" Orlianna's voice had tinges of both anger and amusement.

Arliss waited until they were all out of the prison. The night air was full of the ocean's vivacity, and it made her lungs feel less deflated. Straight across from them, a few lights still kept North Havens alive at midnight beyond the rolling beaches. Left— south—the shoreline disappeared into misty darkness.

And on the rocks behind and above them, the guardhouse was getting noisy. They must've heard the commotion.

Arliss faced her company—meeting Orlianna's fiery green eyes. "You have to let me lead us."

"But—" Orlianna began.

Arliss shook her head. "I came to Ikarra to bring peace to the three realms. And—" She found it hard to breathe as she finally admitted the truth aloud. "—I'm the one who Maeve is really against. You know this, Orlianna. She's not afraid of anyone else."

Orlianna glanced upward. "She *is* if…"

"If Arliss is leading them," Orlando finished.

Clare spoke quietly. "We all know Arliss well. We all trust her. She won't lead us astray."

"Very well." Orlianna assented. "And where are you leading us?"

Arliss faced south. "To Cahair. To find Philip. And to stop Maeve." She pointed up at the sky. "The moon is full, and it is about to rise."

Ilayda suddenly gasped. "About the moon—"

Chaos struck and silenced her words. A wave crashed on the rocky shore that stretched a few paces from Arliss's feet, spattering her with saltwater. Two longboats she hadn't yet noticed crunched against the rock.

And the entire guardhouse emptied itself and rushed over rock and stone toward them.

Ilayda's muscles went icy and stiff at the sight of the dozen guards scrambling, shouting, across the mountain-island. The ominous darkness of the sky and ocean closed in around her. Her lungs tightened against the salt air.

She forced herself to breathe. They'd come this far to find Arliss. She wasn't going to let fear turn her into a statue.

She shoved both the arrow knives back in her boot sheaths, turning sharply on her heel. Her boots crunched against the sandblown stone. Behind her, Erik and Orlianna had swords at ready, with Arliss, Clare, and Orlando preparing their fists for a fight.

They all looked quite brave.

But there was only one *logical* way to act. Ilayda tossed her head and headed straight for the longboats.

Arliss called after her, "Where are you going?"

"Away from here!" She didn't turn around.

"Ilayda!"

She reached the water's edge. Violent waves crashed around from the other side of the island. She swiveled to glance back up the crags at Arliss. "I suggest you all join me!"

That got Erik's attention. He spotted her in the dark, and in that dark, she could see his eyes getting wide. He said nothing, but his lips formed her name.

The guards were halfway between the guardhouse (on the far edge of this side of the island) and the longboats.

Ilayda felt for the edge of their longboat—and the wooden casket stored inside. "Come on!"

Arliss threw her glances back, forth. Then she scrambled down the craggy descent to Ilayda. "All of you, follow me!"

Ilayda smirked to herself. Follow *me*, rather. And so they did. Erik and Clare ran to join her, with Orlando and Orlianna finally turning at the last moment. The guards spread out as they neared, fanning out to encompass the escaped prisoners.

Erik knelt by their boat, holding it steady and indicating for her to enter.

She stepped in, and the boat still rocked a little on the rough water. She pressed her hand on his shoulder for support.

He looked up, catching her eye for just long enough.

She sat in the far end of the boat.

Clare jumped in, almost tripping, and sat across from her. She lifted an oar.

Arliss climbed into the other boat, Orlando and Orlianna right behind her. She grabbed an oar and stabbed it into the rocky shore, shoving off.

Erik did the same.

The guards reached the water's edge just as the boats left. One of them threw himself at Ilayda's boat, grabbing the side of the boat. It dragged him through the icy water.

His weight jerked the boat downward, tossing Ilayda an inch up off her seat. She slammed down again, and a splash of what felt like ice hit her across the face.

Erik tugged his oar through the waves, trying to speed fast enough that the water would rip the guard away. But the guard held on, hauling himself over the side.

"Erik—" Ilayda began.

Then Clare raised her oar and walloped the guard in the side of the head.

Crying out, he slipped from the side of the boat.

Some of the other guards were swimming out, but they couldn't keep up with the boats. The rest of them dashed for the guardhouse. Which meant…

Ilayda gulped. There were more boats. Probably sailboats. They'd be overtaken. Unless they evaded them in the darkness. Unless…

She looked at Arliss, whose boat still speared ahead parallel to theirs, only an arms' length away. "We have to split up."

Arliss panted. "There's been enough of that. I can't bear it any longer."

"In a group, we'll all be captured." Ilayda reached for the long, narrow casket they'd brought from Reinhold. "It's the only way. We split up, and meet back up once we've found Philip."

"In Cahair." Arliss's words were almost lost to the wind.

"You know he's there?"

"I can only hope. But I have to go to Cahair to stop Maeve—no matter where Philip is." Arliss glanced up, a realization running into her eyes. "Oh dear. So much has happened since you left. I guess you don't even know about—"

"I know all about Maeve," Ilayda said. "How do you plan to stop her?"

Arliss seemed almost unable to speak. She blinked, and Ilayda knew the brain behind those eyes was whirling with confusion in an attempt to set so many stories and revelations straight. "I'm not sure. But I know we can. It will come to me. God has always shown us a way before."

Ilayda lifted the casket and slid it through the salty air until it propped on the sides of both longboats, spanning the space between. "Perhaps this will help."

A white sail flashed on the horizon, speeding from the island prison.

Ilayda addressed Erik. "You heard what we just said? We must split up."

Erik kept his gaze steady, as he changed their course—heading back to the barren northern shores, where they had landed the bird. The longboats split farther apart.

Arliss gripped the casket on her own boat. "What is this?"

Ilayda shouted across the explosion of waves. "It's from your mother!"

And at once, Arliss was out of earshot. She, Orlando, and Orlianna drifted away south. As their own boat jerked northward, Ilayda felt like she was being ripped apart.

Arliss sat in the prow, cradling the casket in her arms. The new wood, smooth as paper under her palms, looked *and* smelled like Reinhold. But she couldn't open it yet—not here, not on the water. Whatever Elowyn had sent, it would be too important to risk it being ruined.

Across from her, Orlando and Orlianna rowed tirelessly, never asking her to help.

She *couldn't* have. Her head ached just from the thoughts that exploded inside it. Hunger had knotted her stomach and made her body raw and sensitive. She felt that, any moment, she might vomit over the side of the boat.

She shifted her weight, but it didn't help much. Ilayda and Erik were back in Ikarra—sent by her mother with a gift for her. And they knew about Maeve's treachery.

But how—how had they returned so quickly? And without any aid? Ilayda had said nothing of Kenton and his armada of ships. Then again, there hadn't been time to say much of anything.

And how, how beyond asking, had they learned about Maeve? No matter how she puzzled it over, no matter how hard she clenched the casket, it made no sense. Erik and Ilayda had left before the battle. That meant that, while Maeve had demonstrated her obstinate opinions about unity and her subtle opposition to Orlianna, she had still been pretending to be loyal to Ikarra and helpful to Reinhold.

The longboat jumped a sudden wave, and specks of water smacked her cheek. She wiped her face and suddenly remembered to breathe. Maybe the answers were in this casket.

Orlando finally ventured the first words any of them had spoken since they parted from Ilayda. "Now what?"

Arliss tore her gaze away from the wood and looked at the coastline. The rising sun revealed sloping green cliffs that rose all along the coast in the distance. These shores were wild and uncultivated, and they reminded her of Reinhold more than anything she'd seen here yet.

Orlianna bit her lip. "We can only stay along the coast so long before we get to settlements. They lie all along these shores until you reach Cahair's bay."

"And the tide will come in," Arliss found herself remarking. "This boat'll be crushed against the cliffs."

Orlianna squinted pensively. "We need to find a covert landing spot. And then—"

"Philip." Orlando spoke the name that pounded constantly in Arliss's mind. "Because if we find him, we find Ríon, too. And I feel they will both know more about what Maeve and Merna are planning."

Orlianna shivered. "I don't really want to face your brother right now."

Orlando glanced away. "I suppose *none* of us really want to face each other right now."

The sun emerged from the ocean's horizon, a rich citrus fruit being drawn from a dark pool. The sphere of light grew, taking over the whole sky as it turned shades of crimson, orange, gold.

Orlianna rested her oar a moment, reaching up to her neck. Her fingers moved agitatedly around the bare skin. "So, we join with Philip. And after that?"

Arliss hugged the casket close and faced the line of cliffs. "First, we have to find him."

CHAPTER THIRTY-NINE: TREASON

PHILIP KNELT IN THE SLICK GRASSES AT THE TOP OF the knoll. The sun had barely risen all the way, and now it shone down on his left shoulder—sending rays of light that bounced into his eyes from the not-too-distant sea.

He squinted at the glaring horizon. The ocean couldn't be more than a mile off. Just a quick climb over this knoll and the next, then the shoreline. If they could pillage a boat from the next settlement they passed, maybe they could head out to sea and reach North Havens that way.

Mícheál joined him—standing, but eyeing Philip's crouching position. He followed his gaze out to the ocean. "By water?"

"It's safer than land."

"Is it?"

Still crouching, Philip turned his head up, splaying his hands in the cool grass. "You've seen the guard presence. They're rushing through Ikarra—everywhere. Every settlement seems more dangerous to pass close to. Every wood seems more haunted."

"And you think the seas are safer?"

Philip stared. The incident with the crogall on the journey here seemed like ages ago, but it still hung in his mind. The seas weren't safer, it was true.

But they were unknown. And the unknown always seemed safer than known danger.

He exhaled. "What's important now is that we find Arliss."

Mícheál squinted. "We won't find her if we get killed."

Philip's whole body tensed, and he snatched a fistful of grass, readying to stand. "Why do you have to question *everything* I say and do?"

"Because," Ríon answered as he reached them, "It's all questionable."

"Go easy on him, boys." Rose hauled herself to the top of the knoll. "He's led us this far."

"Sure." Mícheál started back down the hill.

Rose grabbed his arm. "Mícheál!"

He leaned in close to her. "Who are the trained spies here? *Us.* Who's lived in these realms all our lives? *Us.*"

"Technically just me, if we're talking about Ikarra." Rose smirked.

"Fine, then." Mícheál shrugged. "*You* lead us. I want to find Arliss, too. But I swear, I'm not getting us all killed."

Philip stood, fists almost clenched at his sides. "Arliss would do it for us."

The salt breeze tore across the knoll, spraying flecks of sand in their faces from the cliffs beyond. Philip looked left, down the other side of the knoll. Pools of water gathered in the valleys. The forested land was dark and uneven.

He relaxed his fingers. "We can give it a try, but—"

Mícheál tackled him to the ground, and Philip got a mouthful of seagrass.

He spat, rolling, trying to force him off.

Mícheál held on with surprising strength. "Hush, you imbecile."

Philip spat out the last blade of salty grass. "What is your problem?"

"Shh," Rose hissed.

Philip glanced up. She and Ríon had dropped, too, and they were all looking toward the sea—toward the opposite knoll. Mícheál wasn't fighting him. He was trying to save his life. Philip relaxed and slid free.

A figure hid across from them in the shadow of the knoll. A few moments more, and the sun would be shining straight down on the person—and on *them.*

"A guard," Mícheál said.

"A scout." Rose edged backward. "We have to move before we're spotted."

Philip squinted at the scout. Darkly hooded, back towards them, he couldn't make out much. The individual leaned around the knoll's mossy edge and waved to someone.

Philip jumped to a crouch and crawled swiftly back down the hill they had just ascended. "Come on!"

Once the hilltop hid their flight, they all stood and quickened their run. Philip outpaced them all—because, he realized, they were holding back.

He slowed, turning. "Coming?"

"Where are you going?" Rose panted.

He pointed into the nearing green shadow which was the forest. "There."

She shared a glance with Mícheál. "But—"

"He's right." Mícheál started running again, coming alongside Philip. "We have to take cover."

As they reached the fringes of the forest, a noise—or noises— exploded from just over the knoll they'd just been on. Stamps. Shouts. Whinnies. There must've been a dozen horsemen.

Philip and Mícheál were the last ones into the dark treeline. As the branches swallowed Philip and made him invisible, the first rider appeared atop the hill.

"They've seen us."

Arliss half-ignored Orlando's comment as she crouched beneath the overhanging rocks coated in stringy heather. They'd climbed this far, up from the seashore where they'd ditched their boat. Up the cliffs, over the knolls.

And now—

"We're halfway to Cahair." Orlianna pointed at the forest which lay a bowshot away. "That forest is all that separates us."

Hugging the wooden casket to her chest, Arliss stared at the murky green line of trees that tangled its way heavenward in the distance. It wasn't welcoming. But neither was the whinny and gallop of the approaching guards.

Orlando knelt. He pressed his gloved hand into the rock formation above Arliss's head. "I'm telling you, they've seen us."

"There's no way." Arliss's fingers tensed around the box. "We've been so careful. And this is the first time we've seen them."

Orlianna crouched low, hand on the pommel of the broadsword she'd stolen from the prison. "I knew it was only a matter of time before Maeve sent her soldiers on us," she muttered. "It makes sense that she would send her best."

Orlando reached over and pressed his hand to her lips.

Orlianna's eyes went wide with a mix of emotion, but her ears twitched, realizing the purpose to his sudden action.

Arliss froze. The noises on the knoll above them had ceased.

Then they began again. Footsteps pounding the grassy stone. Horses beating rhythm through the ground. The cry of a charge.

"*Go.*" Orlando shoved her right—north.

Arliss stood—knees still bent—staying hidden within the ridge's shadow. "Back the way we've come?"

"They won't expect it. We hide and continue once they're gone."

"But the forest—"

"Go." Orlando stepped in front of her. Orlianna hurried beside him.

Arliss followed, hugging the casket as she went. But she couldn't help stealing one last glance toward the forest: the path they should have been taking at this moment. The path that led straight to Maeve, to the confrontation that would end this once and for all.

And what she saw made her freeze.

She would have known him anywhere—even from the back. His athletic silhouette, framed by a blue jerkin, was unmistakable to her eyes. His tawny hair hanging around his head in rich shades of brown. His steadfast footing.

Philip dashed across the rocky plain and into the forest.

And right behind him, a young man in the distinctive garb of an Ikarran guard was pursuing.

Arliss's heart slammed up into her throat. She gasped for air, squeezing the wooden box against her ribcage. "Philip."

Orlianna turned. "Truly? Where?"

Arliss gripped the box close, wishing desperately that she had a bow and arrow. "In there."

She ran for the woods as the rampage of horseman bounded down the hillside after her.

Philip's legs throbbed, aching from the hike—and now this sprint through the forest. Thick trees pressed in close as he ran, their branches stretching toward him like claws. And though this land was thickly forested, it was still stony and uneven. The ground hammered pain up the soles of his feet.

Just ahead, Rose's hair whipped around behind her. Ríon ran alongside her, arms pumping, edging forward. His sweaty shoulder-length locks flapped, too.

Philip cast a glance at Mícheál beside him, then jerked his neck around to look over his shoulder.

The forest was moving. Branches waved, disturbed by the trees behind them. Colors and shadows flitted toward them from the edge of the wood.

The guards had entered the forest.

He sucked in the green, living air and urged energy into his raw muscles. The guards wouldn't be able to bring the horses this deep into the forest—the trees were too close together. But trained soldiers had endurance to match any of them.

They had to get clear—evade notice. Right now, that could mean anything. It might even mean splitting up.

Because Arliss was dozen of miles away from him, imprisoned in a cell on some rock island. And he couldn't bear the thought of that—or the fact that he was running *away* instead of toward her right now.

Philip!

Her voice reverberated in his brain, screaming his name.

He shook his head and tried to run faster, but his legs felt filled with acid. How long had it been since he'd truly rested—truly slept? Days? A week?

Now he was hallucinating.

Mícheál's pack bounced against his back, so he cinched the strap tighter across the chest of the jerkin he'd stolen from the Cahairian prison. He was keeping a steady pace, but he winced every few moments. The wound on his forehead must've been bothering him. "What do we do?"

Philip glanced back again. Their pursuers were gaining, but still obscured by a good hundred paces of trees.

He halted, turning and planting his feet.

Mícheál also stopped, head cocked in confusion.

It took Rose a moment to realize they'd stopped, but when she saw, she rushed back to them, panting. A twig had wrapped itself in her hair. "What're we doing?"

Ríon finally noticed he was running alone. He glared back at everyone else, then ambled back. "Well?"

Philip drew his sword and held it in block position. "We can't outrun them."

Mícheál nodded, his jaw set. "So we fight?"

Rose's pale arms tensed beneath her leather vambraces. She gripped her long knife. "For Arliss?"

Philip held her gaze, seeing there the realization that he felt in his heart: that they had to do whatever they could for Arliss, no matter what happened. Arliss knew how to unite everyone's stories, pull the three clans together. She could control the gifts and bargain with them. She could draw together her cloud of witnesses. She could battle the lies with the truth.

And Rose knew, like him, that Arliss *could* stop Maeve.

He nodded. "For Arliss."

He faced the oncoming guards as the first three of them broke free of the thick woods.

One was a male—average height, athletic build, with sandy blond hair and a burgundy cloak.

Philip lowered his sword.

The next was a stunning woman wearing a ragged maroon dress and wielding a massive sword. Her hair was deep, deep red and her eyes radiant green.

Philip's sword arm went limp.

And the third: waves of hair tangled around her shoulders, simple traveling dress in shreds, clutching a narrow wooden box. Eyes as blue as the summer seas. Hair rich and pure as golden wheat. Face regal and perceptive as her mother's. Bearing strong and proud as her father's.

Philip let his sword tip sink into the dirt as Arliss threw herself into his arms.

Arliss dropped the casket to the forest floor. She let the tangling forest melt around her as she pressed herself into *him*, his strength enveloping her, his scent driving the shallow breaths from her nostrils: the smell of leather and sweat and sweet grass.

He was here. Alive.

So was she.

He wasn't running off in pursuit of fleeing enemies.

She wasn't dashing off to escape a collapsing catacomb.

They were together. And together they would stay. She felt herself whispering the words, forcing them up her dry esophagus. "No matter what happens, I will not be parted from you. Not until this is over."

He stroked her hair down, smoothing it out like he always did. "Never."

"Arliss—" Rose's voice was a comfort. Still a new friend, technically, but in this time of horror and uncertainty, Arliss considered her like a sister.

Arliss exhaled, stepping back from Philip. Rose, Mícheál, Ríon! They were all here. She wanted to hold them all close to her to assure herself she wasn't dreaming.

"Arliss…" Rose said it again, and this time the note of concern in her voice cracked a notch higher.

Following Rose's eyeline, Arliss swiveled to look into the woods she'd already come through.

The Ikarran guards—all on foot—were almost upon them.

Her heart panicked, telling her to run. But she would get nowhere. And none of the rest of them were even trying to run. Except for Orlando and herself, they were all fortunate enough to have weapons, and swords and bows and knives now pointed into the oncoming infantry.

Arliss swallowed. She hadn't enjoyed killing Anmórian warriors. But they were invaders, assassins. This was different. These were Ikarrans: honest soldiers who probably didn't understand everything that was going on. And even if they did, did they have a choice?

And in the fraction of a second before the guards reached them, Arliss's heartbeat slowed. Her hands no longer itched for a bow and arrow. There had been so much killing. Her soul felt dark, heavy, grimy from the thought of it.

The leader of the troop burst through the line of trees before his men. He froze, sword upraised, staring at the line of weapons facing him. Once his men arrived, they'd be outnumbered. But right now, he could be killed before he took another step.

Arliss stepped forward between her friends and the Ikarran guard.

He raised his sword, posture tense but eyes flicking back and forth beneath thick brows. Arliss recognized him—the handsome Ikarran captain from the North Havens who had escorted her and Orlianna from the train.

Orlianna, too, recognized him and stood straight, still pointing the long sword like an accusation.

Arliss spread out her empty palms. "I do not want to fight."

His eyebrows knotted. "Then why have your friends drawn weapons on me?"

Arliss rotated, silently pleading with each person to lower their weapons. But the bewildered stare on Philip's face, the derisive twist in Ríon's lip, told her it was ridiculous to them.

Tree branches crashed all around. And before she could speak again, the other twenty guards reached them and surrounded them. Some of them advanced, as if waiting for a command from their captain to move in.

"Please." Arliss faced him again. "What's your name?"

"Captain Finbar." He stroked the front of his tabard—a deeper shade of green than that of a common soldier.

"Well, Captain Finbar." She tilted her head back. "I remember you. You escorted us in the North Havens from a train to a carriage. And at the time, you begged forgiveness of Princess Orlianna."

"Aye. And what naught is it to you?"

She edged closer. "I think you had a reason. I think you're still loyal to Orlianna, and that if she could regain power, you would follow her over the hideous witch who now sits on Ikarra's throne."

One guard gasped as if he'd been shot. "You can't speak in that manner! It's illegal."

Arliss tossed her head at him. "Good luck trying to place laws on my tongue."

"He's right." Finbar finbar ran his hand down his tabard again. "New laws have been flooding from Cahair like the river itself. 'Tis treason to speak that way against Queen Maeve."

Queen Maeve. It grated in Arliss's ears.

"Are you or are you not loyal to Princess Orlianna?" she demanded.

Finbar stared over her shoulder, calculating. He looked excited, almost enthusiastic; but a line of mistrust crossed his forehead.

Frustration burned in her forehead. She gestured to her companions. "Drop your weapons! Every one of you!"

The wind whistled through the forest.

"There has been so much killing already! If Ikarrans begin slaying their countrymen, when will it end? When will the corpses pile high enough?"

A breeze gasped over her and died out.

All her companions sheathed or dropped their weapons.

Then, to her surprise, so did all the Ikarran guards. Swords thunked onto the mossy ground, some clanking as they hit stone.

Finbar delicately gripped the blade of his sword with his left and and held the weapon at arm's length in Orlianna's direction. He knelt as she stepped forward. "My lady. Forgive me, again."

"It isn't your fault." Orlianna accepted the blade. "You were just doing what you knew best. But your princess has returned—" she raised the blade, pressing her palm into the shimmering steel. "—and she comes with strength and power."

Arliss stepped back into the crowd of guards and friends, slowly realizing the gravity of what had happened.

They had an entire contingent of guards at their disposal. But, as of now, no one knew about it. Not even Maeve. And in two days, Maeve was going to do something in Cahair that topped everything that had come before. They needed a way in. Alive. Unnoticed.

"Let's find a bigger clearing, get a fire going!" Finbar ordered.

As hands were shaken around her, swords resheathed and information exchanged, Arliss breathed deeply and stared up the tall trunks that pillared the clearing. Their branches netted together like fingers, offering a webbed view of the blue sky above.

Show me the way, God.

She let the breath fill the empty places in her lungs.

An answer came: *I have already shown it to you.*

I know. The thought was in her head already. *I just have to put the pieces together. But how?*

Again the wind spoke in her soul: *The pieces are putting themselves together. The Lord will fight for you. You need only watch.*

She wrinkled her brow. *Am I to stand and do nothing, then?*

The wind tingled like laughter in her ears. *You will fight like the warioress you are.*

She looked back down at the trees and people around her. She tried to grasp for the invisible voice, but it was gone again. She sighed. The pieces were already fitting together? But how? She'd only gotten fragments of Maeve's plan, much less constructed a plan of her own.

The moon was full, and it was about to rise.

Orlianna was coming back to herself—the leader of her people.

Ilayda and Erik were in Ikarra again.

She and Philip were reunited.

They were allied with a squad of Ikarran guards.

Two days. The gifts, not all within her grasp. Her father—who knew where? The dream. Eamon speaking to her. Her mother, urging her to find out the truth about Thane. And she had, but what good had it done? And two futures—the one, with her city rebuilt in grandeur; the other, with a story full of blank pages.

And at once, it clicked in her mind. Goosebumps prickled her skin all over. She could have shouted or danced for joy. She sort of did: grabbing Philip's arm and spinning him toward her.

"What?" He had been examining the wooden casket.

"It's come to me," she panted. "I know what we have to do."

CHAPTER FORTY: BURGUNDY BURNS

PHILIP STARED AT THE DYING FLAME THAT BURNED IN THE middle of the campfire's remains. Each moment the sunrise reached between the trees and across the forest floor, it rendered the fire even weaker.

Sitting on the wide tree stump, he gripped his knees. Finbar's company was departing in the distance, beginning the trek to Cahair. To his right, Orlando and Orlianna packed up camp. Rose and Mícheál were making a perimeter, keeping watch for unfriendly guards.

And Arliss was marching back to him from her bath. She'd insisted on going alone to the river despite his protests, and now she walked with a swagger—face gleaming and hair dripping wet.

She reached him, rounded the stump, and fingered the back of his neck. "Ready?"

He tapped his foot. "I feel like we should have gone over the plan once again."

Her fingers tensed at the nape of his neck. "It'll be fine. Finbar knows what he's doing. He has the easiest part, really."

"And what about your part?" He stared at the squad of troops as the last of their green uniforms vanished between the trees.

"I know I have to face Maeve. I have to tell her who I am and what I intend to do."

"She'll never take you seriously."

"Your confidence is inspiring." Arliss swung around on her heel and crouched by the fire, where she'd left the wooden casket—

unopened. "But I told you, it's coming to me. And I think there are answers in here."

He leaned over, stomach tensing. "What is it?"

She sat on the ground, resting the box on her lap. "My mother sent it with Ilayda and Erik."

Philip bit his lips together at the mention of his cousin. He felt like they were still worlds apart. He reached for the box to shove his thoughts away, rubbed his hand down wood so smooth it was almost slick.

He peered at it. Something eerily familiar ran through his fingers as he examined the box's craftsmanship.

"It's a fine box," Arliss commented.

"Of course it is," he laughed. "*I* made it."

She jerked her head back, surprised.

He explained, "Your mother asked for it before we left. I think she meant to give it to you before, but decided against it."

Arliss slid the lid out of its track, revealing the length of the box's contents.

"*Oh.*" Arliss caught her breath. "It's beautiful."

Philip's cheeks burned red as he freed the smile that heated his face.

She lifted the bow from the box. Unstrung, it still curved elegantly at the edges, the mahogany stain giving it a sharp contrast to the gray birches that pillared the forest around them. She fisted the wood and ran her hand up and down it. "My last bow...I told you about the incident with the crogall, didn't I?"

Philip nodded. "Briefly, over the campfire last night."

"Well, it met its end. That was a good bow. But this—" She lost grip on her words.

But he'd seen the bow before. He'd *made* it, for goodness' sake. He peered into the bottom of the box, where a splash of fire spread. "What else is in there?"

Orlando and Orlianna had joined them by now, both looking over Arliss's shoulder.

Arliss pulled out a garment of fiery red fabric. It was just like the outfit her mother had made for her for the trip to Anmór the year before—practical dress with a slitted skirt and leather vest—but this one was red as fire. The moment Philip looked at it, he recalled a dress Arliss had worn a long time ago. The dress she'd worn to come rescue him from Thane.

She gave him a knowing smile.

"Look!" Orlando pointed.

Arliss glanced down into the box again, her smile melting at the shock in Orlando's voice.

Philip squinted at what Arliss pulled out next.

Papers. Letters, from the looks of the elegant ink across the pages. Lots and lots of them. Arliss thumbed through the yellowing pages, her brow getting tighter and tighter. Then her face relaxed. Her blue eyes went shot with emotion: first fear, then understanding, then pure excitement.

"Here it is." She thrust the letters at Philip. "My mother's given it to us."

"Given what to us?" He tried to read the scrawling script.

"The way to bring Maeve down." Arliss jumped up, clutching the red dress. "This is the correspondence between Maeve and Thane."

Philip's jaw went limp. "But—"

Orlianna snatched the letters from him. She scanned them quickly. "These letters will prove to the Ikarran people what a backstabbing fraud she is. If we can use the gifts to leverage a bargain…"

"The battle will be over before it is fought." Arliss ran for the cover of thicker trees. "I'm going to change."

Philip stood, dusting moss off his knees. His sword hung a little slack, so he jerked the belt tight. He wasn't comfortable with writing off the fight. Not until this was all over.

Orlando ran his hand along the inside of his cloak as he stared at the letters written by Maeve to his former master. Thane was dead, but his legacy was living on—largely because it was not his own. He had only ever been a pawn in Maeve's game.

And so had he, Orlando.

That was over for good. But all of them going up against Maeve—publicly denouncing her—meant facing another of his former masters.

Merna. She was like a hideous shadow to everything Maeve did.

And now he'd have to face them both.

Orlianna handed the papers back to Philip, her green eyes sharp and curious.

Philip nodded. "Kill the fire. We need to get moving." He turned and walked after Arliss.

"Any water left in your flask?" Orlianna asked Orlando. "You can refill it when we pass the stream."

Orlando pulled the flask from beneath his cloak. The ratty burgundy fabric rubbed the back of his hand, and he paused.

She stared at him, waiting.

He let the flask drop to hang by his side again.

"What's the matter?"

"Nothing." He reached for the clasp that held the fraying piece of woolen fabric to his body. "I'm going to kill more than just the fire."

"What?"

He jerked the cloak over his head and held it inches over the fire. "I've hidden beneath this thing for too long."

She nodded in approval. "I told you before—your eyes look nicer without it."

"It was always a part of me, like a second skin. But that old life is beyond me. I'm a new man now. And I want more people to see that than just..." He stared into her eyes. "You."

She reached for his hand and grasped it.

He dropped the burgundy cloak into the fire and stared. The fabric caught flame and burned, until nothing was left but charred wool and ash.

Ilayda was glad when they left behind their smoldering campfire and got on the road again. Well, not really the road. They were staying off the beaten paths as much as possible, because guards had been on their backs since they split from Arliss in North Havens.

She followed Erik. He seemed to have embroidered the maps of Ikarra into his memory. He was guiding them just as well as if he was in Reinhold.

Clare tried to make conversation—about what they would do once they reached Cahair, about what Philip and Ríon might already be doing. But Ilayda only heard the sound of her words. Her mind was elsewhere.

Deep in her soul, an impression was stamped from afar. An impression of Arliss.

Arliss had, indeed, found Philip.

More than that, they were headed to Cahair.

To bring down the regime of the moon.

Ilayda gulped, and the arrow knives sheathed in her boots sent tingles up her legs.

They were all going to do battle one last time.

BO BURNETTE/468

BO BURNETTE/468

CHAPTER FORTY-ONE: REALIZATIONS

As the trees thinned, Arliss found Rose standing on a grassy ledge that overlooked the bowl-like land below. The road cut through that valley—straight along the coast to Cahair. She could see it, a glimmering mound of emerald in the distance. The ruined tower stuck out most prominently, obsidian stone reflecting the sun's brilliance.

"How will we get there?" Rose must have heard her near-silent approach.

Arliss stood beside Rose and crossed her arms across her chest. "We can't march straight up. We have to find a secret way in."

"Philip told you about Merwin's death?" Rose tilted her head to look at Arliss. "You know that after what happened in Anmór, every road and river will be heavily guarded. Maeve won't risk it happening again."

The other four members of their company exited the forest behind them. Arliss looked over her shoulder and caught Philip's eye. He winked at her.

A fierce wind gushed up from the valley and whipped the slits of Arliss's dress. Anticipation sparkled through her arms and down to the tips of her fingers—fingers that gripped her new bow as if it were pure gold. "I don't know. But we'll find a way."

Rose kept her gaze steady. "It won't be easy."

Orlianna strode forth. "You do realize you have the most elite team of warriors and spies in the realms at your disposal?"

Arliss took a quick survey. Orlianna, talented weapons fighter and skilled aircraft pilot. Philip, swordsman and tactician. Orlando, expert spy and martial artist. Rose and Mícheál, lethal archers and spies.

And herself: archeress, huntress, princess.

And—soon—so much more.

She strung her bow around her chest and started to descend the slope. They were going to face Maeve as she proclaimed herself queen. She would cast the spell of the gifts they still had possession of—the ring, the sword, hopefully the vial—around Maeve and draw back the reins of her bargain. She would throw Thane's letters in her face and let her reputation melt around her.

Maeve wasn't the only one with a royal proclamation.

Maeve was not the only one ready to be queen.

The air in Cahair had never felt so dense with secrets and sorcery. Orlianna breathed in the realization that her city had become something evil, wicked. But not irredeemable.

She stayed in the lead beside Arliss and Philip as they approached the ruined tower from the barren northern beaches. Every step she made brought her closer to danger. Cahair was enemy territory now—the stronghold of Queen Maeve of Ikarra.

Soon to be Queen Maeve of the World.

Orlianna tried to manage a laugh, but it got caught in her throat and made its way out as a cough. Something none of them had discussed was how to really *take down* Maeve. Yes, they had factored so many things into the plan: rallying the loyal Ikarrans to their side, using the remaining gifts (ring, sword, and vial) to bargain with Maeve, showing the Anmórians how they were being bewitched.

But when the time came for them to deal with Maeve herself? She couldn't be left alive. That much was clear. But who would deal the death blow?

Orlianna imaged herself running a sword through her

grandmother's abdomen. Throwing her from a great height. Firing an arrow into her heart.

All the images clenched her stomach.

She quickened her pace, the heels of her boots chewing chunks out of the sands. The beach was quiet, deserted. That meant Finbar had done his work. His guards—not Maeve's—would be patrolling the mouth of the bay.

Philip jogged to catch up with her. "This will be the easy part."

Orlianna stared out at the misty ocean. "None of this will be easy."

Philip glanced at her. "You okay?"

"I'm unsure." She focused on the sand. "This city has always been my home. Now, I'm an invader. A stranger."

Arliss joined them. "No. You're a queen coming to inherit her throne."

Orlianna smiled at her, but she couldn't restrain the tinge of grief—the spark of realization—that burned in her heart. She stared beyond Arliss at the ruined tower. The tower that had guarded these lands from time beyond. The tower that still held one of the aircraft on its spiraling floors.

Arliss thought she was aiding Orlianna in overtaking the throne of Ikarra. But even without the pendant's weight on her chest, Orlianna could feel the truth of her destiny deep inside.

This battle would, indeed, end in Maeve's death.

And it would also end in her own.

The news from Orlando's brief reconnaissance venture brought back nothing but bad news. Philip paced along the open-sided middle floor of the ruined tower, fighting to keep his composure as Orlando related everything he'd observed in Cahair.

"The city is absolutely crawling with guards." Orlando spread his tense hands wide. "Checkpoints at every main intersection and at the entrances to public places. A lot of businesses are probably closed down."

Philip glanced at Rose. She looked away, leaning into Mícheál for support. She knew as well as anyone that Maeve would target their places first, considering how brashly they stood against her at her first coronation.

And they'd also fled from a royal prison.

Jumped from it by none other than himself. Philip ran his hand through the hair that drooped over his forehead and let his fingers sit there. Everyone in their company had a price on their heads.

"What about the castle?" Orlianna questioned.

"Barricaded." The sun through the gaps in the walls sparked fire in Orlando's eyes. "They won't let anyone near it. You can't enter the library, much less the bridge. But—"

Arliss leaned forward from one of the spans of stone wall.

Philip's fingers froze in his hair. "What did you see?"

"Boats. Lots of them. Shipping things from the riverway to the castle. Since the crogall destroyed the funicular, the only transportation is by boat."

Philip imagined dark figures floating across the river to join Maeve in her darkening castle. Merna. Domnall.

"Who was going to the castle?"

"I think you mean *what*." Orlando shattered Philip's notions. "Cargo. All kinds. Food, decorations, candles. I only got glimpses of it. But I've seen enough of this kind of rot before. It means only one thing."

Orlianna's lips parted sardonically. "Maeve is throwing a party."

Philip dropped his hand from his hair. His brain start whirring. Party. Decorations. Guests. Merna, probably. Parties in Ikarra. They'd been to a party at the castle before. Not just a party. A ball. Feasting. A toast to unity.

"And you're sure you weren't discovered?" Philip finally addressed Orlando.

"Utterly."

Arliss spun to stare out at the city far below and beyond them. "Maybe we could—"

Philip cleared his throat, politely cutting her off. "I have a thought. Our alliance with Finbar will make it possible—though not easy—to get into this party. But we need to find out more about it. What is it, when is it. And for that we need someone who is close enough to Maeve to know her secrets but loyal enough to us to help us."

"But *who?*" Arliss smacked the blue marble in frustration. "Who in this city is going to help us?"

Philip caught Orlianna's eye as they both said the name.

"Garrick."

CHAPTER FORTY-TWO:
OLD ALLIANCES

With the aid of cover from Finbar's guards along the streets, Orlianna led the company around the outside of the city boundary to Garrick's house. Grasses brushed up Orlianna's dingy skirts and tickled her knees.

Noise throbbed from the heart of the city. She glanced up at the barrier wall which spanned the houses of this end of the first cantar. They were nearly half a mile from the coast, but her father had been a careful king. Lachlan had ordered this barrier built to protect in case of floods.

Now, it was keeping her hidden from her own city.

Jutting above the wall, Maeve's tower stabbed the naked blue skyline. A reminder of who really controlled Ikarra. A reminder of where this quest would end.

The dividing wall ended abruptly as the back of Garrick's house shot up to her left, his barn on the right. The backside of the young lord's mansion clearly wanted a new coat of paint. Unlike the bluebird-colored front, this end was scathed and peeling.

Orlianna edged around the corner of the barrier wall, waving the others forward to join her. She could see all the way down the main road of the second cantar: past all the riverway shops to the church at the end of the road. The library past that. Over the river on its isolated island of stone, her castle.

Guards swarmed everywhere in between.

She'd never seen so many in her life. And some of them were most assuredly *not* Ikarran. But she couldn't tell the Anmórians apart at first glance. Because the green Ikarran tabards and red Anmórian ones had been ditched.

In their place: shimmering silver, with the emblem of the moon on the chest.

Orlianna's blood chilled. She shoved away from the gate.

Arliss was right beside her. "We just walk up to the front door?"

Orlianna hurried across the gap—where they might be visible to some—and threw herself against the back of the house. Her shoulders pressed into the stone foundation which rose a good six feet from ground level.

"What are we doing?" Arliss whispered.

"Drop the suspicion, if you will," Orlianna hissed. "I'm the one who's lived here all my life."

She leaned forward and caught Orlando's eye. He still stood with the others in the shadows behind the barrier wall.

She dipped her chin.

He sprinted across the bare span of field to them.

Then Philip.

Rose.

Mícheál.

Ríon.

Orlianna tapped her head back against the stone. They were quite the troupe. Staying hidden wasn't going to be easy.

She faced the stone foundation, tracing its mortared crevices. It was here…somewhere. She hadn't used it in years. But surely he hadn't filled it in.

The heat of everyone else's stares mingled with the sun on the back of her head. She swept her hair over her shoulder in frustration and cast an irritated glance at her audience.

Arliss, who had leaned close, backed up.

Orlianna shoved at the wall, trying to find an uneven spot. But it wasn't there. Nowhere did the stones give. Nowhere was that familiar click—

Click.

She grinned. Just like when she'd been a child and had sneaked in here to play with Garrick during royal councils without either of their fathers knowing it. Now, both their fathers were dead, and she'd long forgotten what childhood looked like.

But now she felt it—the hope of life, the thrill of impossibility—with that one click beneath her fingers.

A whole section of stone slid back and swung around on a hinge, revealing the passage into the lower floor of the house.

Orlianna stepped into the basement armory and let the others file in quietly behind her. Garrick had an impressive arsenal. He was particularly proud of his collection of Anmórian crossbows. Swords, bows, and all manner of accessories racked the walls of the dim room.

Garrick's mother and sisters still lived in his mansion, but this room was all his own. His private little cave. Opposite the secret entrance, the empty doorway let light flood in from the sunny front foyer.

But a silhouette blocked that light. A lean man with blockish boots and a sharp-shouldered tabard.

Her heart pulsed—once, twice.

Without hesitation, he grabbed a sword from its rack on the wall and swung it toward her.

She jerked her stolen sword from its sheath and batted his blow away. He spun, recoiling, then slashed down from over his shoulder. Easily blocked—Harrison had taught them both better.

This was just like the old days, wasn't it? She and Garrick sparring. And just like in the old days, she was going to beat him.

The darkness flickered as the rest of her company drew their weapons or reached to draw them from the walls.

Orlianna blocked Garrick's cut, forcing his arm backwards. He stumbled. She sliced up into his blade. Another step back.

He slashed angrily at her. She ducked just in time, gasping. That one could have taken her head. Had he not recognized her by now?

She swung her sword into his as he followed through, then slammed into his exposed chest. He tottered.

Rose jabbed her bow behind his ankle.

He tripped backward, his rear slamming into the floor. He winced.

Rose looked prim. "You deserved that."

Garrick rubbed his rear and glanced up at her. "Rose?"

"Yes?"

He gaped at Orlianna. His bearded jaw swung open and closed like a bad hinge, and his typically dashing face looked incredibly unattractive.

Orlianna couldn't help but smirk with amusement. "Surprised to see me free, armed, and in Cahair?"

"That's not a strong enough word for it." He scanned the group. "Arliss—Philip—Mícheál." He squinted at Ríon. "What the devil's going on?"

She pointed her sword at his chest. "What I want to know is, what's going on *here*? What's Maeve doing?"

He leaned his chin back, practically inviting her to hold the tip of her blade to it. She did. Still he said nothing.

Rose plucked her bowstring. "You may be our former comrade and spy, but I won't hesitate to use harsher methods."

Garrick tossed his head at her. "I'm not afraid of you."

"What about of me?" Orlianna let the sword touch his neck a bit harder.

His nose wrinkled. "What do you want?"

"Tell me what Maeve is doing."

"And betray her trust?"

"Or else betray mine."

"But I have sworn allegiance to her."

"She is not worth following."

"She is the queen."

Orlianna hurled the weapon to the ground. It clattered on the stone, spinning across the floor dangerously close to Philip's ankles. "She is not, and will never be, the queen!"

Garrick cautiously eased to his feet.

Orlianna calmed her breathing. "Garrick, you are one of my oldest friends. And if I know you, you will still be loyal to me. You will follow me no matter what, even if it means going against Maeve. And I know you have information that could help us."

"Help you do *what?*"

"Bring down her regime. End this nonsense about one combined clan. Restore relations with Anmór—" she motioned to Ríon "—and Reinhold."

Garrick stepped closer, the suspicion in his eyes melting. "Tomorrow night, Maeve is holding a grand ball at the castle to celebrate her becoming queen of the realms."

Orlianna sucked in her breath. Not just any party. *A ball.* It was so unexpected, but made so much sense. Ikarrans loved balls. They loved dancing and the rush of the crowd. And Maeve knew better than anyone how to manipulate a crowd.

"So all that means," Arliss mused, "Is that we have to sneak into this ball and interrupt it at an opportune moment."

"Or get ourselves invited."

"I can help get you in, perhaps." Garrick paced. "But there's something else." His eyes twinkled beneath auburn brows. "It's a masquerade."

Arliss gave Philip a curious glance. Probably Reinholdians had never heard of a masquerade ball.

But Orlianna felt a surge of joy—possibility—filling her tense chest. Maeve was practically inviting them to go undercover. This didn't make their plan any less dangerous. But it made it viable.

Rose gave a starting gasp. "*Oh.*"

Orlianna rubbed her aching temples. "What is it?"

"Oh…" Rose stared up at the ceiling. "I had an idea in my mind. To speak. But…I forgot."

Orlianna didn't care. She repeated the phrase over and over in her head.

A masquerade ball.

Masquerade.

Ball.

A grin spread across Rose's face. "Oh, I remember now. The big closet upstairs, Garrick? The one I always wanted to steal a dress out of?"

Garrick squinted one eye at her. "I think you *did* steal a dress out of it."

Rose waved her hand at him. "We're going to take a lot more before we're through. Don't you see? We'll need outfits for this ball. Your clothes—and your sisters'—will be perfect."

Garrick shrugged, but he could not hide his smile. "No more faffing about, then. We've only got one day to get you all decked out."

He motioned for them all to exit into the foyer. Before Orlianna could leave, though, he barred his arm across the doorway. She tensed.

"Wait." Garrick paused. "There's something you should see, before anything else."

"I thought you'd want to see where they buried him."

Orlianna stepped through the arched iron gateway, trying to absorb both the beauty and the stark coldness of the place. A gate of wrought iron circled the grave: an elaborate stone that marked the center of the area. The dirt around it was fresh brown, sprinkled with a dusting of dead grasses. Benches sat around the edges of the tomb—as if anyone would want to linger in this place.

Anyone, except for her. She fell to her knees in front of the tombstone.

The letters that carved *Harrison* into the stone were simple, just as he would have wanted. The benches, too, were rough-hewn rock. But with the shoreline visible just beyond, and Cahair rising behind them, the place looked almost mystically beautiful. The swirling designs of the iron caught the misty remains of the sunset and held them captive.

"He knew what he was fighting for." She gasped out an exhalation, barely keeping herself from slipping over the edge of tears. "He knew what kind of world he wanted to live in."

Garrick stood beside her, arms crossed. "He'd be proud of you."

She brushed her hair behind her ear and looked up at him for an explanation.

He knelt beside her, keeping a few feet of distance. "You're fighting for what is right, even when so few are. I didn't want to believe the rumors about Maeve. She gave me so many reasons to disown you as my princess. But now——"

He held her gaze, his hand stretched toward her face.

She inhaled. They both knew that whatever spark he had wanted to ignite between them was long gone. If she was ever to love someone, it would have been Orlando. But here, on the verge of battle, the thought of romance was laughable.

So when he pressed his warm palm to her cold cheek, it was nothing more than the touch of a friend. "I see you are the only one I could ever follow."

She smiled, her tense abdomen relaxing. She glanced back at the tombstone. "I need him now more than ever."

"We all do." Garrick dropped his hand from her cheek and placed a hand on his hip. His eyes flitted cautiously toward her. "I'm sorry. I knew you'd be gutted if I brought you out here. But you needed to see."

She rose, brushing the seagrass off her dress—a simple green frock borrowed from Garrick's supplies. "Thank you."

She turned back to Cahair. Seen from a distance, the skyline was still a familiar comfort: the enormous ruined tower, the bare peninsula, the undulating harbor, the apartments of the first cantar, the glass library glimmering, the riverway, the castle.

And over the river the Tuáma Fields, on the far edges of which this grave lay.

The sun had sunk into the sky beyond the fields, giving the atmosphere the color of a deep bruise. Striated layers of purple and gray sliced across the evening sky. And at the bottom of it all…

Orlianna peered across the fields. A dark mass lined the horizon and crawled steadily eastward. She'd seen this before.

She tapped Garrick's arm to rouse him from a daydream. She

pointed west. "Look."

He jumped up beside her, grasping his chin, rubbing his goatee. His head lunged forward and back several times like a bobbing chicken. "What the bloody…" He faced her. "It's guests. On their way to the ball."

"Those don't look like ball guests. That looks like an army."

"It is."

She reached for one of the iron poles to steady herself. She knew all along that the confrontation with Maeve would culminate in battle. But it seemed that Maeve had also somehow anticipated this. Merna herself probably rode somewhere in the approaching blackness.

"We have to tell the others." Garrick strode through the iron gates. "Anmór has returned to the Tuáma Fields."

"But this time," Orlianna mused, "They were invited."

CHAPTER FORTY-THREE: MASQUERADE

ORLANDO HAD SPENT THE MORNING UP IN GARRICK'S EMPTY ATTIC. Staring through the tall window. Waiting. Arms crossed across tight, shallow breaths.

The castle seemed to grow larger with every passing moment.

The light was shifting now. The sun had passed its pinnacle in the sky and leaned toward the castle in a sky so utterly blue and cloudless it seemed almost unreal. And, if he squinted, he could just make out the faint outline of the full moon in the skies across the harbor.

He turned and headed for the spiraling stairs. It was nearly time.

Downstairs, he found Arliss putting the final touches to her outfit. As usual, she looked stunning, but a touch unrefined. A strapless silk overlay layered the long-sleeved red dress with its many slits, hiding the fact that she was dressed more for battle than ball. Her hair: braided loosely, strands framing her face.

He bounded down the last few steps. "Ready for this?"

"Not at all." She fingered the velvet lining of a black cape. "But I'm doing it all the same."

"Do you really think you can defeat her?"

Arliss swung the cape around her shoulders and let her hands rest there, the cape unfastened. She glanced at the polished floor. "I don't know. I guess I don't think anyone will really follow me."

"They will." He looked behind her into the adjoining room, where Philip and the rest were readying their outfits. "The question is, what will you do when they follow you?"

She hesitated. She hadn't thought of the true implications of that yet.

Afternoon light flooded down the hall from the huge windows in the front of the house. Rose and Mícheál were laughing with Philip as they readied. Garrick clanked about in the armory below.

A horn sounded from the castle: regal, pompous. A little menacing.

Arliss fastened the cloak around her shoulders. "Maeve has destroyed so many things I love. If she has her way, we will all bow to her slavery. I can't let that happen."

"So you'll be the queen?"

She opened her mouth to speak, closed it, bit her lip. Then she strode across into the room opposite where everyone else was.

"Arliss?" he called after her.

She turned, her face twisted somewhere between rage and anguish.

He tugged off the fingerless glove from his left hand. The ring of Reinhold—simple, gleaming—shone bright in the rich light. He eased it off his finger and held it out in his palm. "It's time I give this to you. I know you'll need it to bargain with Maeve."

She started to reach for it, then pulled her hand back and fisted it over her heart. "Keep it. You have your own battle with her. And we're going to fight it together—all of us." She disappeared through the wide doorway.

Ríon swung around the doorframe on his heel, arms crossed over his chest. He cocked his head back against the doorway.

Orlando replaced the ring on his hand and let his fingers curl. He must have been listening to the whole conversation.

"She's right," Ríon said.

"About what?" Orlando already knew the answer. He just wanted to let his half-brother feel like he was leading the conversation. Might help the poor fellow.

"Your fight is against Maeve. Not Merna."

Orlando relaxed his hand. They both shared Merwin as a father—and both understood that neither of them felt very much at his death. But Merna was different. To him, she had been an enslaving master. But she was Ríon's *mother.*

"I was Merna's tool." Ríon adjusted the buckles on the front of his doublet. "I realize that now. She wanted me as a successor. She never wanted that for you. But Maeve…she fears you."

"What's there for her to be afraid of?"

Ríon shrugged. "Oh, just that you're the half-heir to the Anmórian throne, you were closer to Thane than anyone else, you know half of Merna's secrets, and…" He gave his eyebrows a seductive lift. "You're tight with her granddaughter."

It was true. All of it.

For once, he was glad to admit Ríon was right.

He took a shaky step forward. "Look, Ríon, I want you to know—before we jump into this whole mess—"

His throat cinched up. What did one say to a lifelong enemy who turned out to be a brother?

"I know what you're feeling." Ríon leaned forward from the wall. "I hated you. You were always working for the baddies. Then all of the sudden, you were in the right, and I wasn't. And I hated you even more for it."

Orlando grasped his shoulder. "Can we learn how to at least be friends?"

"We're more than that." Ríon reached around Orlando's neck, pulling him close. "We're brothers."

Orlando buried his face in Ríon's dark locks and squinted back the tears that burned inside his eyelids. "Speaking of Maeve's granddaughter, where is she?"

Ríon relaxed his embrace and stepped back. He pulled from his pocket an ornate black mask with glittering gems. Once over his eyes, it obscured his facial expressions. He pointed into the room Arliss had just entered. "In there."

Orlianna massaged her temples, but nothing would settle her

sprinting heart rate. She dropped her tense shoulders and stopped trying. From this point on, the adrenaline that intoxicated her bloodstream would be fuel.

She smoothed out her outfit's base. A simple black dress so fitted it was almost constricting, but for the soft fabric. A deep-set square neckline meant the dress would stay hidden beneath her true ball gown.

She picked up the pile of yellow silk just as Arliss entered the room.

"Ready?"

Orlianna snapped the dress like a whip to rid the wrinkles. "Rather."

Arliss placed her hands on her hips. "You're going to fight in *that?*"

"It's perfectly fine." Orlianna cast a defensive glance back down at the black dress. "And we have no guarantee it will come to fighting."

"You're not a fool. You know what has to happen."

Orlianna turned, still clutching the yellow dress, and faced the floor-length mirror. "Yes. But it terrifies me all the same."

In the mirror, Arliss's reflection reached down the side of her silk overlay and drew her long knife. It flashed light into the mirror and back.

Orlianna glared over her shoulder. "What're you doing?"

Arliss knelt behind her. "Stay still."

Before Orlianna could move, the sound of shredding cloth tore through the room's peaceful stillness. She jerked, smacking Arliss across the face with her shin.

"Heaven and earth! What are you doing?"

Arliss held onto the dress's hem. "Hold…still." She stabbed between Orlianna's knees and cut all the way down to the base of the dress.

That was when Orlando entered the room.

Orlianna reached down and shoved Arliss back by her forehead. "Your alterations are unneeded"

Arliss ignored her. "Just two more slits, that's all."

She grabbed Arliss's knife forearm and pulled her up. "I'll make do just fine."

Eyebrows twisted like ropes, Orlando sauntered over. "Last-minute alterations?"

"At least," Orlianna muttered, but she couldn't help but smile at Arliss's practicality. Slits would give her much greater range of motion, even if the cutting was a little jagged.

Orlando nodded. "It's mid-afternoon already. We'd better get going."

Orlianna gave him a glance-over. Sans the burgundy cloak, he looked as he had the entire quest, since Reinhold. "And what, sir, are you wearing to the ball?"

"That's none of your business." He turned on his heel, his lip curling smugly.

She placed her hands on her hips. He was still his saucy self. Yet she decided that, with some work here and there, she might actually tolerate him. Human beings had never much been her expertise. But he was someone she could build a life with.

She shook her head, and the red tresses tangled around her shoulders. Odds were, by the time the sun rose tomorrow, they'd both be dead.

He turned to leave, but stopped. "And what are you wearing?"

She stepped into the yellow gown and pulled it up, letting the silk glide over the black underdress. It covered it completely, the full skirt cascading down around her heels, the snug bodice encasing her racing heart. She thrust her arms through the satin sleeves and let them settle on the edges of her shoulders.

Arliss clapped. "You look splendid."

Orlianna bent down and picked up the ornate, feathered mask from the floor. She held it over her eyes and tied it behind her head. "What do you think, Orlando?"

His jaw twitched. Then he promptly left the room.

Orlianna turned back to the mirror once more. She *did* cut a stunning figure, after all. But the ball would be full of lords and ladies so decked out in silks and satins the place would be absolutely slippery.

And there was something—a small something, but in her mind very large—entirely wrong about her outfit. It was the blank span of skin between her neckline and collarbone.

The place where her pendant should have hung.

Arliss tried to remind herself that she was wearing a mask as she took Philip's assisting hand down from Garrick's carriage. It felt as if *surely* the ball guests streaming toward the bridge around her all saw straight through her.

Garrick was known for having many friends, so there was nothing suspicious about him exiting the carriage with seven attendants. The carriage had enabled them to pass down the road of the relatively quiet second cantar unnoticed. All the people of Cahair were currently in one of three places: at the ball, headed to the ball, or moping at a tavern and waiting for the latest gossip to spill in.

The glass library at the foot of the bridge was awake with orange light as the sunset fell behind it. It shone like a dying star, drowning out the castle that rose behind it.

Philip's tug on her hand reminded her that they had to keep moving.

They blended with the crowd, not trying to stay together. She hadn't wanted this, but the rest of them—especially Orlando—had forced her to see the sense of this. Split up, ambling around the party, they would have far less chance of being recognized. And if one of them was recognized, the rest would stay hidden.

Philip disappeared in the crowd as they passed the library. The loss of his touch left her fingertips chilled.

The sheer noise suddenly crushed her like a wave and deafened her ears. Swish of silk, clap of feet against stone. Chatter, jubilee. Music droning from the castle.

A voice whispered in her ear, "You'll never be alone. Our allies are all over the castle."

She found a tall woman in a ravishing yellow gown. Her hair was knotted in a bun and hidden beneath a black veil, but the mask couldn't hide the emerald eyes.

"Be vigilant," Orlianna hissed. "It will be hard to tell friend from enemy."

"It's always been hard."

Arliss's voice was lost in the crowd with Orlianna.

As they reached the bridge, Orlianna's words materialized. Guards bracketed the bridge in pairs, one on each side all the way up and over. She recognized one of the first pair as being from Finbar's company. But his face was the only sign. When they first allied with Finbar, his guards wore the distinct mark of the North Havens. Cahairian guards had their own.

But now, each guard wore the silver tabard of the moon.

Arliss swallowed as she stepped onto the white stone of the bridge. Everyone had a mask. A disguise. A oneness that made them all no one, that turned them into a unified mob of guests rushing to a party.

But she had read books of Ikarran traditions during the voyage here. And she knew that, at a masquerade, all the masks were eventually lifted. Before the night was over, everyone would know who everyone else was.

And that included Maeve.

BO BURNETTE/490

CHAPTER FORTY-FOUR: THE LAST BALL

PHILIP STARED AT THE WRECKAGE OF THE FUNICULAR TRACK AS he stepped off the bridge onto the castle's rocky island. Arliss had related to him the incident with the crogall, but he hadn't realized what kind of damage the creature had done. An attempt had clearly been made to patch up the track, but it would have to be rebuilt to be usable. The beams were cracked into splintered firewood. The iron—twisted like wire.

Long, flat boats crawled across the river to his right. The most distinguished guests were coming that way—from the riverway.

The rest of them had to trek up the mountain.

The guards at the end of the bridge ushered Philip and three others to follow the path others were already climbing. "Enjoy your evening," one of the guards said with a welcoming nod.

Philip knew his mask hid the crinkle in his eyes. "Oh, I will."

He stepped around the jagged remnants of the conductor's booth. Sharp glass refracted the sunset's rays and sliced into his eyes. He blinked, edging around the structure. Now something became clear that he hadn't noticed during his whole time in Ikarra: the funicular had not always been the way to ascend the hill.

Above, gowned-and-caped guests stumbled upward on a natural staircase. He placed his foot on the first flattish place and started climbing. The dying strains of ocean waves rolled up against the base of the rocks below, spitting a pitiful gurgle up at him.

The higher he got, the brighter everything became. The castle was decked out in lights, and the glass walls of the ballroom revealed the flickering interior. And the music—it beckoned to him, made his sore feet feel like dancing the way he once had, before life had become dark and dangerous.

He bounded the last few steps onto the top of the mountain. He'd find Arliss somewhere in this mob. And they would enjoy at least one dance before this was over.

A trio of guards accosted him at the door. Unlike the ones further down, these were masked just like all the guests. They kept their expressionless disguises on, and allowed Philip to do the same. But they scanned him up and down, patted down the front and back of his green jerkin, and poked at a lumpy spot where his brown pants disappeared into tailored boots.

"Kindly remove your boot, sir," the guard ordered in a voice that was two shades not friendly enough.

Philip tugged the snug footwear off. He had nothing to hide. But he couldn't help but glance back down the craggy hill at the stream of guests behind him. He knew Arliss had stowed a knife somewhere in her outfit. But knowing Arliss, she would stow it somewhere they'd be sure not to check—provided they had any shred of honor in their prying hands.

The guard grunted approvingly and cast the boot back at Philip. "Enjoy the ball, sir."

Philip stuffed his foot back in, mounted the stairs to the open doors, and immersed himself into the grandest ball the three realms had ever seen.

Dazzling. That was the word that burned its way through Arliss's blinking eyelids and into the back of her head as she drifted through the ballroom, the crowd dissipating around her.

She'd spent a hefty time of her stay at the castle here in this vast room. But not until now had she truly been struck by its *vastness.* The welcome ball had been a small affair: one long table, two dozen guests, a few chandeliers lit here and there, the surrounding balconies dim.

The ballroom around her seemed a different place entirely.

Six blazing chandeliers burned like dying stars, suspended from a vaulted ceiling that flashed white light in her eyes. She looked down, but coming down to earth didn't help. Lamps on golden poles—the lamp portion resembling an Anmórian design Arliss knew all too well—stood between each floor-length window.

And all at once she was in the center of the room, spinning around, letting the folds of her overlay swish around her heels, absorbing the beauty.

Why did the darkest moments have to also be the brightest ones? When could she ever be free to savor life, to chase down the adventures, grasping them by their tails, holding on for dear life as they whisked her away? Did every ball have to end in battle?

She stepped slowly to the edges of the room, away from where most people's eyes would naturally land. The rainbow of colors around her melted together, blurred.

She was sixteen again—descending the steps to the ballroom of Reinhold. That room had been a hovel compared to this. She saw it rise around her: pale stone walls, everyone dressed in what would hardly pass for the simplest attire in Cahair.

She tried to recall how that ball had looked, how it had felt, how it tasted. But all her senses could comprehend was the dazzling brightness, the burning vibration at the bottom of her stomach, and the bitter taste at the back of her tongue.

She swallowed. This was nothing like that ball from so long ago.

Behind her, someone cleared his throat.

She whirled, her spinning skirt swishing against the fellow's legs. His wore fancy boots: neatly tailored, with folded edges and tasteful brass buckles. She knew them well. She'd picked them out for him this morning.

She glanced up at his face. Something of a beard spread down his cheeks and over his chin. She wrinkled her forehead. Did she like this new growth? She wasn't sure. It would have to grow on her.

But it mattered not. Because behind that dark mask lurked the most handsome, enigmatic pair of eyes she had ever known. Greenish-blue, flecked with brown, ringed with yellow.

Philip bowed deeply, extending a hand. "My lady."

She offered her own hand, and he brushed his lips against it. "A fine mask you have there."

He tilted his head to the side. "A mask can only do so much. It can only last so long."

A horn sounded from the staircase at the back of the ballroom. They both turned, along with the rest of the guests, fixing their attention on the shimmering figure who descended the steps and halted on the middle landing.

"Welcome!" Maeve spread her arms wide, the dripping silver sleeves swaying beneath her elbows. "Tonight is a night of celebration. For tonight, for the first time, our clans have come together truly as one—no fighting, no political debates. This is neither a battle nor a rigdál mór. We have had enough!"

A rousing round of applause rushed forward from the crowd. Arliss forced herself to clap—once, twice—and it made her stomach jerk itself into a knot.

"We come here to dance!" Maeve signaled to the musicians who crowded the balconies, flanked by guards. She smiled, but Arliss wondered what expression she hid behind the gray mask. "Let the grand march begin!"

The fiddles began a lilting introduction. A rich cello began to form a counterpoint. The pluck of a harp resounded with swift arpeggiations.

Philip turned back to her, still gripping her hand. "May I have this dance, my lady?"

She caught her breath as he pulled her into the string of couples lining up. "Of course."

They joined the line in the middle of the room, directly beneath the flickering cast of one of the chandeliers. Arliss leaned out to the right, trying to see past the line of couples in front of them, but it was difficult to make out what was going on. *The grand march,*

Maeve had said. Must have been one of the many Ikarran customs lost in the Reinholdians' flight to the Isle of Light so long ago.

When they reached the end of the line—at the base of the staircase—couples paused before drifting left or right. They circled around to the back of the line again.

Arliss craned her neck to follow them. The couples were rejoining the line at the far back of the room, this time with two couples joined in a row. Four hands stepped slowly forward.

Philip squeezed her hand. They were only four couples from the front of the line now. Maeve had descended to the base of the stairs, where she nodded graciously at each passing couple.

Arliss stared at the back of the dress of the lady in front of her. She hadn't expected to come this close to Maeve before the planned reveal. What if she saw right through them?

She squinted at the golden-brown curls that graced the lady in front of her. There was something strangely familiar about the subtle backward tilt of her head, as if saucy thoughts were tugging it back.

The couple reached the base of the stairs. The man bowed deeply, the lady curtseying, before stepping right. That meant she and Philip would go left.

Arliss forced herself to inhale. She glided forward and caught the lady's glance, cast back at her through the gap in her mask as she passed.

Clare.

Arliss released a tiny gasp. It was Ríon and Clare, both of them, together.

She and Philip came to the end of the stairs and paused. Philip bowed. After a moment's hesitation, she curtseyed, spreading out her overlay.

Maeve rested her hands over her belt with its jangling celestial charms. "Welcome to the ball. Enjoy the celebration!"

Arliss rose, her skirt's layers smoothing out. Should they just walk away? Or thank their hostess? Inform her that they planned to incite a revolt against her within the hour?

She decided on a simple, monotonic "Thank you."

Philip guided her to the left to behind the cycle over again.

Maeve's voice rang after her. "Young lady, wait!"

Arliss's heart forgot how to beat. Her neck went taut as a bowstring. Chills stabbed like needles up her back. She turned slowly.

Maeve smiled. "You have a charming mask."

Arliss dipped in a half-curtsey. "As do you, my lady."

She turned and strode with Philip to the back of the line before anything else could happen.

Thoughts whirled in her mind like the ocean at high tide. For one thing, Clare was here—alive and ready to help them. But the last time she'd seen Clare, she was in a boat with Erik and Ilayda. And Erik and Ilayda were nowhere to be seen. Unless they were here in disguise.

She couldn't help a glance around. How would she know? She could dance with every man in the room and not find Erik.

But the subtext burning in both Maeve's words *and* hers? It was almost more than she could bear. Maeve had singled her out with a compliment that almost certainly had a double meaning. Did Maeve recognize her? If so, why was she continuing as if nothing was ado?

And her response…

She smirked to herself at her own cleverness. She'd kept her wits enough to shoot an answer back right away. And more than that, she'd addressed Maeve as *my lady*, even though the correct title should have been *queen*.

Arliss let the strength of Philip's hand settle her nerves. Maeve was not queen of all three realms.

Not yet.

Chapter Forty-Five:
The Full Moon

Orlando's tense arms relaxed as the second dance ended, and he tried to fight it. The fact that they'd made it through the grand march *and* first dance without being noticed meant nothing. If anything, he needed to be warier from here on.

An involuntary ripple—almost like a shudder—spasmed through the muscles of his upper body. He gripped Orlianna tighter, leading her off the dance floor through the maze of dispersing couples.

She leaned her mouth close to his ear. "We can't dance every dance together. That will look terribly suspicious."

He caught her eye. "But you do wish we could dance every dance together?"

Beneath the mask, her expression was unreadable. "Perhaps."

She slipped her hand from his and lost herself in the crowd.

Orlando took a pivoting view of the ballroom. Above him, all around the balcony, strings plucked and warbled as musicians adjusted, preparing for the next dance. Gentlemen bashfully approached the women they wanted to dance with. A fiddler up on the balcony opposite him repeatedly twisted one of his tuning pegs. Food and drink decked the tables in the corners of the rooms.

His stomach groaned, and he glanced away. He refused to taste the slightest bit of Maeve's delicacies. Ten to one they were probably poisoned or drugged.

"A waltz!" Maeve had returned to the top of the staircase, a safe vantage point from where the entire room could hear her.

Couples streamed onto the dance floor. Ikarra was famous for its waltzes, in which dancers changed partners every two rounds.

Orlando glanced around quickly. It would look strange if he didn't dance. But with whom? Half of these guests were Anmórian nobility, some of whom he'd done spy work for in his past. Surely they'd recognize him with his arm around their waist and his face a foot from theirs.

A strong yet soft hand held his from behind. "Dance with me."

He resisted the urge to lock her arms in his and snap her bones. He'd almost done it so many times before. She was too good at sneaking up on him. And it was hard to kill the old urge that insisted she was his enemy.

The music began a drifting introduction that pulled him toward the dance floor.

"Come on," Clare said. "We don't have much time."

Two rounds. Two rounds of repetitive steps, unnecessary spinning, and whispered conversation. It would have to suffice for whatever intelligence Clare had to tell him.

He began the moment they joined the line of couples. "How did you get here?"

"It's a long story. If I live to tell it, it'll be worth hearing. But our time is limited. Maeve plans to make her announcement after this dance."

"Who found that out?"

"Fiach and Finín," she whispered. "They're in the room— somewhere. Our allies are everywhere."

Orlando was barely taller than her—just enough for him to peer over her head and scan the room. "And our enemies."

"Don't be afraid." Clare's hand trembled in his. "God is always at work. You know that, don't you?"

"I do." His dry throat allowed only a raspy whisper. He spun her away from him.

The foresty green of her dress, overlaid with a pattern of twisting vines, brushed against his legs as she spun back in. The second round was almost over. He would soon pass her off to the next partner.

He rushed out one last question. "What made Ríon change? Was it you?"

"No." Her lips parted, her chest suddenly breathing hard. She reached for his cheek—as if thanking him for something. "It was you."

Him? His brother had rejected Merna for *him*?

"I tried and tried," Clare confessed. "But seeing how you stood with Arliss and Orlianna, even when no one else would…seeing the way you faced Merna, it gave him courage to do the same."

The round ended. The music swirled, crescendoing.

He passed Clare to her next partner. And he received his next.

Merna.

His stomach hurled itself up into his lungs, making the back of his throat taste like vomit. She wore a typical gown of chartreuse silk, but this one was trimmed in purple satin. Her mask was entirely purple sequins.

He swallowed. She wasn't hiding. This was someone who wanted to be found.

He forced himself to dance through the rounds stiffly. Even the lower half of his face could reveal no emotion. He repeated Ríon's words to himself over and again. Merna *had* wronged him. But she wasn't the one who had used Thane, and thus used him, from the beginning. She deserved a downfall as great as anyone did.

But his real fight was not with her.

Philip had begun the dance with an unknown partner (he guessed Ikarran, based on the snatches of her voice he caught over the strands of music), but after two rounds of redundant waltz steps, he found Arliss's waist once again.

Her lips twisted. "We meet again."

He pressed his palm against the small of her back, intertwined his fingers with hers, and closed the space between them. He waltzed slowly, leaning into the heat of her breaths with closed eyes. Was this to be the last dance they ever had together? The thought made his heart feel heavy, full to bursting with the rush of his own blood.

He opened his eyes. Their foreheads were touching, and her blue eyes burned straight into his, through the two masks.

"One last dance before we die?" She spoke his thoughts.

He pressed his head deeper into hers. "And it all comes to naught. Even if you do this, if you assume the role of queen of Reinhold—Maeve can still destroy us all."

"Maybe. Maybe not." She tightened her arm around his back. "We came to Ikarra for a reason. My mother knew that, I think."

"For what reason?" A blackness drained Philip's strength, filling his blood. The life he had wanted to build back in Reinhold was gone. He was about to spill it out on the floors of a foreign land, far from home, far from the life he had wanted for himself—for *them.*

Arliss leaned back and locked eyes with him. "Our friendships with Orlianna, Rose, and Mícheál. The discovery of the truth about Thane. Seeing Gally one last time. Flying. Is that not worth it?"

He opened his mouth and closed it, unable to form words.

She pressed her cheek to his. "Is not *this* worth everything we have been through?"

Hope enlivened his body once again.

His lips searched for hers.

She reached up and pressed her fingers onto his mouth. "It's not time." She smiled halfway. "Not yet."

The music ended sharply.

Up on the stairs, Maeve made signals to various people. Guards repositioned themselves, musicians set down their instruments. Merna ascended to the middle landing, along with Lord Domnall. The guests drew themselves into a sort of order. A curious hush crept over everyone.

Philip fixed his eyes on Maeve. Arliss still gripped his hand.

Maeve descended the stairs with surety, halting a few steps above the landing. "And now, friends and visitors, comes the reason why you are all here."

Orlianna stood in the middle of the room, her eyes fixed on Maeve. This would be it. The moment Maeve rose in all her glory to subdue the three clans.

She had already subdued them. And not with a sweeping battle, but a simple ball. She had lulled them to sleep with song and dance. Now all that remained was for the good hearts in this room to stay silent—frozen by fear.

Maeve stood at the edge of the landing with Merna and Domnall on the steps below her. She smiled. "Ah. Such beauty and tranquility. To think that, not one week prior, we were hacking at each other like barbarians."

The crowd didn't so much as mutter.

"That time is over. The tense councils and bloody conflicts are a thing of the past. We have sought and found a true solution." Maeve adjusted the crown on her head, and Orlianna's stomach clenched. "The sacrifices along the way have been difficult, though some have been necessary."

Merna gave a little nod, the corners of her mouth turned down.

Orlianna fought the urge to shove through the crown and run up the steps. Maeve's implications were all too clear. How could she lump Merwin's assassination into the same category as Harrison's death?

She licked her lips. Because to Maeve, both deaths had been necessary to accomplish her goals.

Maeve placed a hand on Merna's shoulder. "Rebels have tried to rise against us, and may still. But the time has come for a united kingdom between Ikarra and Anmór. That is why I have invited you all here: to witness the coronation of the first queen of that united kingdom."

Now the crowd found its voice. A gasping whisper whooshed through the room's swishing silks. Up on the balcony, a hollow clatter resounded as a fiddler dropped his instrument. The whisper turned into a sharply divided murmur: half warm assent, the other half cutting suspicion.

Maeve raised her hands, and the crowd mostly silenced. Her power over them was evident—almost unnatural—and Orlianna both envied and loathed her for it. "There will be time for discussion later. And the transition will not happen overnight. I will be assisted by my sister, who will be duchess of the lands formerly called Anmór, and by Lord Domnall, now duke of the area of Ikarra. We will ensure that things are done fairly and in accordance with ancient customs."

The dissenting noises dissipated.

Orlianna edged her way forward between two ballooning dresses.

A man spoke up from the crowd. "What about Reinhold?"

Maeve's eyes must have widened beneath the mask. She glanced around quickly for the speaker. "Reinhold?" She resumed her composed posture. "Ah, Reinhold. Yes, those lands will be incorporated later. For now we must focus on the more pressing issues on this side of the ocean."

Domnall gave a generous sweep of his hand to the guests. "I think they mean, the people of Reinhold."

"I can see what they mean." Maeve pursed her lips at him furiously. "I simply do not see what the question is. Reinhold's only connection to us is their warmongering and rebellion. They incited the Battle of the Tuáma Fields, plotted Merwin's assassination, and have opposed the unity of the clans at every turn."

Another voice—Rose's, not very well disguised—rang out. "Is it true that the Reinholdians escaped your imprisonment?"

Maeve smoothed out her silver bodice. "It is not."

Blatant lies now? This was almost too much to be borne. But it was not surprising.

"What about Orlianna?" This voice came from the balcony.

Maeve glanced about in frustration, trying to regain her control over the crowd. "Orlianna is no longer a threat. Her fate will be decided by a tribunal once the transition is complete."

Heat throbbing through her limbs, Orlianna slipped forward through the crowd.

"*She* never wanted this united kingdom," Maeve said. "She wished for us to remain separate, always fighting. For unless we all come together as one clan, we will never have peace."

Orlianna reached the front of the crowd. The bodice of the black underdress strained beneath the yellow gown above.

The crowd seemed satiated, but still tense.

The man who had called out first spoke again. "Where is Orlianna being kept?"

Maeve began to reply, but her voice dissolved into air.

For Orlianna stepped away from the guests and stood between the crowd and the staircase, pulling herself to her full height. She reached up, lifted the mask from her face. Then she cracked the mask in half and threw it on the marble floor.

"Orlianna is in your midst."

BO BURNETTE/504

BO BURNETTE/504

CHAPTER FORTY-SIX:
THE CLOAK OF ARLISS

ORLIANNA DRANK IN AIR THICK WITH TENSION. THE BALLROOM'S FLICKERING candlelight seemed suddenly sapped of its warmth. Guards advanced around the crowd of guests, drawing their weapons. She guessed that some of the guests would be drawing weapons, too, by now—if they had them.

As for Maeve, the tension in her body was unmistakable. Clenched fists rested by legs so straight, posture so erect, she seemed almost a statue.

Orlianna glanced left and right at the approaching guards, daring them to come any closer.

The one on the left halted. He lowered his sword.

The right-hand guard kept coming, sword pointed straight at her.

Still she held her ground. She stared up the magnificent stairs at her grandmother, forcing Maeve to look the situation straight in the eye. If Maeve killed her now—in front of all these witnesses, without even hearing one word—she would instantly look like the villain she really was.

But perhaps it would be worth it. Perhaps Orlianna's death was worth the price.

The guard was almost upon her.

She set her teeth, biting together so hard her jaw numbed.

"Wait!" Maeve threw up a hand, and the guard stopped. "Let her speak."

Orlianna cast an imperious glance at the guard and approached the bottom step.

Domnall drew a concealed sword. "Don't you even dare come not one step closer!"

"So I might, perhaps, even dare to come *two* steps closer?" She cocked her head as he seethed. "This castle is my home. I should be free to walk these steps as I choose."

"This is not your home," Maeve rasped.

"Is it not?" Orlianna faced the guests, keeping Domnall and his sword in her peripheral vision. "My home, and my people. I am their princess." She whirled back to Maeve. "And rightfully their queen."

"There is no queen of Ikarra, not anymore. Before you interrupted, we were beginning to celebrate a new queenship—the queen of the united kingdom."

"United?" Orlianna laughed bitterly. "Oh, grandmother, if only you could hear the lines that cut through this crowd. Ikarran and Anmórian. Royalty and nobility. Male and female. You think you have pulled everyone together? You are only cutting them further apart."

"Be silent, you murderer." Merna lunged her neck forward. "Your say in this matter is over."

"This is not about my say." Orlianna stepped back. She had to choose every word as carefully as if her life depended upon it. Because it did. Her life, and so many others'. "This is about the voice of all three realms. You have squelched two voices and ignored a third. I am here to set things aright."

Maeve said nothing. The questions about the Reinholdians and their imprisonment had shown the people were curious and even vindictive about the fate of the smaller clan. She couldn't contradict Orlianna even if she wanted to.

Orlianna looked up at the chandelier-crowded ceiling and threw her voice through the vast room. "I call for a rigdál mór!"

Maeve stayed still, but Orlianna thought she rolled her eyes behind her mask. "Very well, then. Let us have it. Here. Now. I am the judge. Plead your case."

Orlianna paused. This was not how the plan was supposed to go. She needed the others to reveal themselves and help her. And they had hoped for Ilayda to show up—and with her, the vial. She now didn't have a piece of the bargain she hoped to construct.

A young woman in deep green satin stepped forward behind Orlianna, holding a leatherbound book. Clare. "I think this will help."

Orlianna fingered her shiny skirts, smiling.

Clare opened the book, propping it on her forearm as she thumbed the pages. "Here the words are: '*There must be monarchs from all three clans present to hold a rigdál mór.*' All three." She slammed the book shut and shot Maeve a deadpan stare. "I don't know, but I think this might be relevant."

"A decision that affects all three realms must include all of them," Orlianna affirmed. "As you yourself just said, we must follow ancient customs."

Maeve looked like she wanted to fly at Orlianna and rip her tongue out. But she controlled her fury and gave a haughty, affected glance about the room. "Everyone here knows I would be the last person to deny ancient customs. So be it—let the Reinholdian monarch come forth! We will welcome them with due council."

Taut silence prevailed.

"Show me your Reinholdian monarch! There is none."

Orlianna glanced around. Orlando lurked at the far right edge of the room, waiting. Philip was close behind her, a few rows back. And of course, Garrick would be around somewhere. But what about—

A regal figure in a dark cloak parted the crowd and strode forward, coming to stand beside Orlianna at the bottom of the stairs. The hooded cloak hid her identity from everyone else. But Orlianna knew.

Orlianna gestured to the cloaked figure. "I present to you the Queen of Fire."

Merna looked disgusted. "Enough games. Will no one silence

that flame-headed brat?"

"Peace." Maeve held up a hand, but her attention was fixed on the newcomer. "We do not know this Queen of Fire, nor do we recognize her authority!"

"You will recognize *me*!"

Arliss threw off the cloak, ripped off her mask, spread her arms wide. Her golden hair streaming behind her, she stood tall, the sleeves of the red underdress dripping beneath her elbows. She ascended the steps toward Maeve.

"And who do you think you are?" Maeve demanded. Her chest pitched up and down at a frantic rate.

Who was she? What a question! Maeve had known from the beginning, before Arliss herself had known, just who she was destined to be. But now the realization of who she had become had filled Arliss's heart with a sense of urgency, a drive that forced her up the staircase.

"I am Queen Arliss of Reinhold." Arliss raised her voice as she climbed the steps. "I have no crown, because you stole it from me. I have no land, because I am far from home. You have scattered my friends, assaulted my home, and murdered my uncles."

She was only three steps from the landing. Domnall barred her way with his sword. Merna sank back behind Maeve.

Arliss stopped. "I have come to stop you from destroying the three clans."

Tension so pressurized the room Arliss was sure the glass walls would burst. Blood throbbed in her eardrums, making it hard to focus. But she kept her attention on Maeve, waiting to see what her next move would be. Maeve could summon guards to kill her. But that would be cold murder. It would turn most of the guests against her at once.

The tightness in Arliss's chest was constricting. The brown overlay was cutting off her circulation. The knife hidden in her bodice pressed against her side. Her fingertips itched, and she curled them. They itched more for a bow than anything. A solid arrow to fire through Maeve's heart.

Arliss remembered to breathe.

And suddenly Maeve laughed. Not her usual mocking chuckle. This was a high, rollicking cackle—and it reverberated off the ceiling, threaded through the chandeliers, echoed in Arliss's ears. It entered the silent instruments on the balcony and made them come alive.

The laugh drew up memories from Arliss's subconscious like water from a well: Thane guffawing when she drank the bitter wine, Merna sniggering at her ignorance during that fateful party in Anmór. This laugh was all of those and more.

Maeve's lips closed at last. "You are no queen. Not one to challenge me."

"Maybe you should deliver your sentence once you have seen the evidence." Arliss turned to the crowd, deciding to test how much sway *she* had over them. "Am I not right, honored guests? Does not every clan, every person, have the right to at least be heard?"

Thunderous applause answered her.

She leaned back. She hadn't expected such support.

Maeve smiled and tossed her hand. "I agree. Let us judge whether you are a true monarch of Reinhold. From there we can discuss the matter of a rigdál mór at a later date. For now, we must attend to the business at hand: the coronation for the united kingdom."

"Of just two kingdoms."

"No." Maeve held up a hand with curled fingers. "As I said, Reinhold will be incorporated later on."

"The *lands* of Reinhold. That's what you said. But not until every last one of us lies dead."

Maeve spat. "That's ridiculous."

"Is it?" Arliss hitched up her overlay and reached into the pockets of the red dress, pulling out the folded letters. She unfolded the yellowed paper and turned to the crowd. "I am here today to talk about one person—a man who has, unbeknownst to some of you, had an impact on every person in this room."

Behind her, Maeve drew in her breath as if she was choking.

"His name was Thane."

This drew more response from the crowd than she'd expected.

"That greedy warmonger?"

"I thought he was a trader for Anmór."

"Didn't he mysteriously disappear?"

"I heard he's half-Reinholdian."

Arliss held up a hand, but the crowd kept on muttering. She shrugged down the stairs to Orlianna.

Orlianna turned on the crowd. "QUIET!"

At once, she could have heard a sequin hit the floor.

And Arliss began her tale. She told of how the clan of Reinhold had settled on the Isle of Light, then fled because of the volcano. She relayed Thane's disappearance and then shocking resurgence twelve years later. She told of the fiery arrow and the man in the burgundy cloak—calling Orlando up to testify. With Philip's witness, she told about her voyage to explore the Isle, a voyage that had taken her to Anmór.

She spent extra time on the parts about Anmór, considering her audience was nearly half Anmórian. They needed to know the truth. While she spoke, she stole glances at Merna. She said nothing to contradict Arliss, but her face faded to a ghostly white.

Fire burned in Arliss's lungs as she recounted the battle for Reinhold, the fall of the old city, the death of Thane. She praised Orlando's heroism. A few people clapped while Orlando glanced down sheepishly.

Then Orlianna entered the story: a wild new figure with red hair, summoning them across the seas to Ikarra.

Arliss paused her story. She didn't realize until she spoke it how powerful it was. How many threads connected in ways she hadn't considered. It deserved to be told better than this condensed proclamation. It should be…written down.

She pivoted, one side to the crowd and one to Maeve. "I came to Ikarra hoping to find the truth about Thane. I realized that Merna could not have been his only benefactor. He was too secret, too disconnected." She thumbed through the stack of letters. "These letters came from the ruins of Thane's fortress in Reinhold. In it, he kept correspondence with this mysterious ally, someone he calls 'the moon.' And I have found out who the moon is."

Beneath her black mask, Maeve's skin couldn't have been paler.

Arliss pointed straight at her. "Her! This woman you are about to let crown herself as queen over you is the one who has been manipulating every event in the three realms."

"That's preposterous!" Domnall exploded.

"Is it, Lord Domnall?" Arliss smacked the papers against her palm. "Don't you recall the Council of Lords right after Ríon attacked the ruined tower? I brought up Thane then, and Maeve claimed ignorance."

"Because she *is* ignorant." Merna's voice was unnaturally shrill. "As am I. I never had any involvement with this… *Thane* fellow. You're mad. You're drunk. You're a warmonger. Away with you, away—"

"Shut up." Maeve cut her off.

Arliss took a bold step onto the landing and faced Maeve, only a few paces between them. "These are letters written to Thane in your own hand. Do you deny it?"

Maeve spat her words through her teeth. "I deny nothing."

Arliss narrowed her eyes. "Then you're a bloody liar."

This drew a collective gasp from the crowd.

Arliss held the letters up in the air. "Have I shocked you? Bloody good for me, I say! No one has been more shocked than I. One day, Ikarra and Anmór are mere fairytales. The next, they're at war with me. I call Maeve a bloody liar because she *is*. You are welcome to peruse these letters. I have others in safekeeping. You can read everything—*every bloody thing*. Maeve's love affair with Thane, her plans to make him lord over Reinhold, the ways she desired to exploit my land's resources. It *is* bloody, because every word is written in blood—the blood of every person Maeve has destroyed in her path. My uncles, Nathanael and Eamon. Scores of Anmórian mercenaries. Harrison. Thane himself! Every letter of her story is written in red, dripping with blood!"

She finished the speech and gasped for air, filling her sore lungs.

For once, Maeve stood speechless.

Arliss drew enough breath to add one more thing before Maeve found her silver tongue. "I speak especially to the people of Ikarra right now. In these letters, one thing is terribly clear. She never thought of you, those who are technically her people."

Maeve staggered forward. "That's a lie…"

Arliss descended a few steps. "Maeve has always known what kind of world she wanted to create. And you, people of Ikarra, have no place in her world."

The crowd couldn't move. But Orlianna, Orlando, Philip, Ríon, Clare, Rose, and Mícheál were all ready. They waited.

Arliss looked at Maeve. "Take off the mask. Admit who you really are."

Maeve pulled her mask from her face. She cast it over the edge of the handrail. It clicked on the ground somewhere in the hall behind the ballroom.

She stared down at the gleaming white landing. Then she slowly raised her head to glare at Arliss.

She flicked her wrists toward the balconies. "Guards!"

The balcony guards were all on Maeve's side, because they rushed to the top of the staircase, awaiting a command. Domnall readied his blade.

Maeve withdrew with Merna to the top of the stairs. She gestured at Arliss and at her company at the base of the stairs. "Put them all down. But leave the Reinholdian princess for me."

Arliss looked back at Philip. He nodded at her as if to say, *I am with you.* They had lined up: Philip, Orlianna, Orlando, Clare, Ríon, Rose, Mícheál. Garrick, too, had appeared from the crowd and thrown off his mask. Now he was pleading with individuals in the crowd.

And Arliss saw the crowd begin to split in two: separating like a gaping wound, leaving a bare space of marble floor in the middle. People were shouting threats. Grabbing at each other's skirts and capes.

Half of them supported Orlianna and Arliss—the side of the old Ikarra, the side of Reinhold.

The rest of them were on the side of the moon.

Heat burning in her chest, Arliss rushed up after Maeve, reaching inside the right side of her bodice. She pulled out the knife and gripped it tightly.

Domnall rushed down at her, sword drawn.

And so began the battle between the three clans.

CHAPTER FORTY-SEVEN: DARKNESS AND LIGHT

ALL PHILIP COULD SEE WAS EVERYTHING THAT WAS WRONG WITH Arliss's plan of attack—or lack thereof. She was rushing up against a stronger enemy practically unarmed. Her opponent had the upper ground. And she hadn't once turned to give orders to her comrades.

His fingers itched for a sword. He saw one—in the fist of a guard who rushed at him from the side of the room. The guard's face flushed red. He slashed at Philip.

Philip ducked under the cut. Jamming his elbow in the man's ribs, he forced his weight into his side. The guard tripped, limbs splaying out on the lower steps. His chin cracked against the marble.

Philip tore the sword from his grasp. He motioned to Orlando. "Come on!"

Orlando had his typical twin knives—where in his outfit he'd hidden them, Philip didn't know and didn't want to know. He pounded up the staircase behind Philip.

Arliss had dodged Domnall and now engaged a guard at the top of the stairs.

And Maeve and Merna? They'd disappeared entirely, probably back into the castle's winding chambers.

Domnall stalked down toward Philip. "You Reinholdian brats have wreaked enough havoc. No more."

Philip planted his feet and nodded to Orlando. They could take him. If they moved right—

A hand gripped Philip's shoulder. He pivoted, swinging his sword.

And he looked straight into Orlianna's green eyes.

"Lads," she said, her other hand on Orlando's shoulder, "Let me handle this from here. Get the people to safety." She hitched her skirt up and tossed her hand toward the confused, squabbling crowd.

Philip leaned toward her, teeth clenched. "Orlianna, you can't make me do this."

"I'm not the only one here taking up the role of queen." She forced her way easily between the two of them. "Now help me empty this castle."

Domnall waited, licking his lips. But the flick of his eyes betrayed his fear.

Philip glared hard at Domnall, then turned down the stairs with Orlando and Clare. The crowd argued—some quarrels turning violent—and he knew that he would be the best one to break it up. But he still wanted to do some real fighting.

And emptying the castle meant turning out the two menaces who had just disappeared into its halls and passageways.

Jogging toward the guests, he called to Orlianna, "Don't you face Maeve without me!"

"I wouldn't dream of it!" Orlianna shouted.

Clare's hair tangled as she ran. "And let it be known—Merna is mine!"

Philip halted, holding his sword up in the most non-threatening position he could as he walked into the mob. He'd never considered who would deal with Maeve, if it came down to it. Who would face her. Who would kill her.

They all had a reason to. But it hadn't even been discussed among them. They'd only gotten as far as revealing Maeve, bargaining with her. And that had gone well, hadn't it?

Clare pulled the double doors open. Night wind rushed in.

"Listen, everyone!" Philip spoke with a volume that made his lungs stretch. "Tonight's events have been troubling. But we cannot give way to fear and chaos! We will exit safely and quickly. Come on!"

Some followed Clare's lead.

Others stayed still. "What about the battle?"

"Battle?" He wrinkled his brow. Arliss, Ríon, and Orlianna skirmished with a handful of guards. Merna had a troupe of warriors encamped in the fields. But no one had yet spoken of an outright *battle*.

"Yes, battle," one man echoed. "It's ragin' in the city right as we speak."

Philip lowered his sword, striding for the double doors. He rushed onto the rocky hilltop with Clare and Orlando behind. The sun had fallen, leaving darkness over the river that surrounded the castle. But the city exploded with light and noise. Down and to the left, the stretch of the riverway glinted with reflected firelight.

He sucked in his breath. Word had gotten out already, then. Maeve had been presented as a fraud. Finbar's guards were in the thick of it.

Philip took a heavy step. "We have to get down there, now."

Clare stepped ahead of him. "Orlando and I will hurry ahead. Go back and help Ríon. And Orlianna. And Arliss."

Arliss spun around the railing at the top of the stairs, twirling free of an oncoming guard. He rushed past her, unable to stop his momentum.

That was all she needed. She jammed her knife into the underside of his left knee. Screaming, he dropped to his knees, wildly slashing his sword.

She hit the floor. Her cheek pressed into the cold marble. The blade sheared the air inches above her head.

She rolled toward the railing. The crowd below was a mess. But there wasn't any real fighting going on yet that she could see. Orlianna had drawn Domnall and several of the guards off the stairs. She and Ríon were making quick work of them.

Still on his knees, the wounded guard lunged at her with his sword.

She sat up, slamming her back into the balustrades. The guard leaned too far forward. The pain in his knee must have been too much, because he fell forward and lost his grip on his sword.

"Thanks." Arliss grasped the hilt and stood. "And I'm sorry."

He only snarled.

The balcony stretched down the upper sides of the ballroom to the right and left. She could see across to the left balcony, still lined with musicians and some guards. Arliss took the right-hand balcony. She rushed around the corner—

—and straight into a pair of guards. Both their tunics bulged with muscle. The silver masks on their smooth faces made them seem somehow inhuman.

She swung her sword up toward them, barely able to manage it with one hand. It was like fighting with a living creature that refused to obey.

The guards' lips twisted with mockery. Then they both cut down on her sword at once. The force jerked the blade from her grasp.

She ducked, slipping between them. Her silk overlay slid her like water down the balcony. She bumped into an overturned cello and came to a halt.

Below her, Philip—who must've been outside—rushed back into the ballroom. He scanned the room. Searching for her.

She scrambled up, knife in hand. The guards closed in on either side of the balcony, their swords barring the space between them. She was cornered. No escape—and no chance of following Maeve through the twisting corridors of the private chambers.

"Arliss!" Philip's voice rang out clear amidst the hubbub.

Her hand settled on the railing. She stared down at him, casting rapid glances at the approaching guards. "Yes?"

"Jump!" He held up his arms. "I'll catch you."

Her breathing sped its tempo. It was a long fall—probably twenty feet. If he didn't catch her…

One of the burly guards burst forward, shouting.

She jerked herself over the railing and jumped.

Pressure knotted around her chest. She sucked in air and found she couldn't release it. Her shoulder blades compressed together.

The guard had grabbed her by the back of her silk overlay. And she was hanging in midair, looking down at Philip's horrified eyes.

She twisted her left arm behind her head, stabbing through air with her knife. But she couldn't get enough range of motion. The overlay cinched tight around her bodice.

She kicked, and the slits of the red dress showed beneath the overlay. This was the dress her mother had sent. And though her mother was far away, she probably knew some of what Arliss was getting into.

Arliss judged the distance between herself and Philip. If he stayed still, it would work.

She slid the blade down her bodice between the two dresses. And she slashed through the overlay—all the way down. Silk ripped.

She fell—her stomach hurtling into her ribcage for a sickening second.

Philip's arms broke her momentum. He squeezed her close, then set her on her feet. "You all right?"

"Yeah." She started for the double doors, where Orlando was ushering the guests out. "Let's go."

"The battle's already begun." He was alongside her. "This may get uglier than we expected."

"Battles always get ugly."

He motioned for her to exit the castle first. "I've got a special feeling about this one."

She descended the steps and strode across the uneven surface of the island mountaintop. Two things startled her. First, how utterly dark it was. Night had fallen long ago during the ball, and the change from the candlelight indoors made her blink. Residual flashes of light blinded her everywhere she looked.

But second, she marveled at how *light* it actually was. The city was alive. But that wasn't all. She stared heavenward. The sky was starless, hidden by bright storm clouds. Clouds illumined by the biggest full moon Arliss had ever seen.

The moon was full, and it was rising.

Shouts rumbled from the castle. People tripped over each other in a rush to get out. Garrick threaded his way through their midst, urging the guests to get off the castle island via the rocky staircase.

Soon everyone was out. All descended the way they had come.

Orlando jogged over, and the rest of the company soon lined up beside them. The double doors to the ballroom clanged shut, hiding whatever had caused the stir. Someone was coming.

"Domnall?" Arliss asked.

Orlianna sheathed the one claw knife she still had and rubbed her palms. "He's got his pride hurt, at least."

"So what's the noise about?"

Rose fixed her eyes on the doors. "Who do you think?"

Arliss leaned forward, glancing right and left. Most of them were here. Philip. Orlianna. Garrick. Ríon. Rose. Mícheál. In the city, Clare and Orlando were joining the fray.

A pang of heat stuck in the back of her heart. She didn't know where Erik and Ilayda were. But Clare believed they were alive. That was what mattered.

The castle doors trembled.

The storm clouds above groaned.

Mícheál raised his bow, giving her a little nod. "We're with you, Arliss."

"All of us," Rose added. "We'll do whatever you command."

Arliss glanced to Orlianna for support, for instructions. This was Orlianna's city. She should be leading them, guiding them. Why did everyone suddenly look to *her*?

"She's right," Orlianna said. "I await your orders, Arliss."

Arliss breathed in the air—a swirling blend of cool and warm that made her nose itch. She'd cast off her fear and guilt. She *was* a queen. Why, then, was it still so hard?

She gripped the bow her mother had sent her—hard, harder, until her hand became one with the wood. The shouts in the city below were growing. The winds stirred the battle up like an oar in raging seas.

She stepped back from the line of comrades and toward the natural rock staircase. "We need to get off this island, now. Maeve and Merna won't wait forever. The real fight is in the city."

She descended the stairs. Everyone else followed.

Garrick slipped in front of her, jogging downward. "I'm going to find Orlando and Clare! They're down there in the mix of it."

Arliss cocked her head back at Orlianna. "Joining him?"

"Not at present. There are other matters that need my attention." Orlianna's eyes glittered in the darkness. "Mind if I borrow your fiancée for a bit?"

"What for?"

"This battle needs to be fought on more than one front."

Arliss stared upward, swallowing. She meant the birds—the two that were presumably still hidden in Garrick's barn. The time had come for their use. "I agree."

Rose was right behind her. She leaned forward to talk in Arliss's ear as the staircase wound down to the base of the bridge. "I know you're in charge and all, but I figure you wouldn't mind some suggestions."

Arliss lifted an eyebrow at her. "Yes?"

"Mícheál and I should thread through the entire city, communicating with every spy Maeve hasn't yet rooted out. If we can get the people to rise up against her…"

Arliss nodded. "It's a good plan."

The slabs of umber stone vanished abruptly into the bridge's base. Water spattered up into Arliss's eyes from the river as she jumped up onto the pale structure.

Down here, on ground level, she no longer had a panoramic view of the city. But what she could see—beyond the library, through buildings and lampposts and scattered trees—looked ten times more shocking than it had been from high up.

When they reached the end of the bridge and everyone dispersed, Arliss turned to look back up at the castle.

The double doors swung open, and a line of Maeve's guards rushed out onto the hilltop. At their head, Maeve rode on a dappled gray charger. The smooth curves of her plated armor caught the moonlight and made her look like a human star.

Then the clouds above ripped open. The first drop of the storm hit Arliss's forehead. It took a moment for her to process that the icy shard wasn't rain, nor was it a late snow.

It was a hailstone.

CHAPTER FORTY-EIGHT:
OUTNUMBERED

ORLANDO LEVIED HIS TWIN KNIVES—DRIPPING WITH BLOOD—AT THE next opponent. The endless ranks of guards in silver tabards never stopped. They swarmed around him and Clare, flooding the main road of the first cantar.

He recognized some. They'd been spies, soldiers, palace guards in Anmór.

Here, they were all set on one thing: bringing about Maeve's regime.

He ducked a sweeping cut from the nearest guard, tumbled underneath his arms, and plunged a knife into his chest. The guard's sword clattered to the cobblestones moments before he did.

"Orlando!" Clare's voice cracked. She was a few feet away, struggling against two opponents at once.

He wiped one of his knives clean on his breeches. His fingers found the fallen sword. The handle was just like the ones Thane had trained him on.

Sword in one hand and knife in the other, he rushed to aid Clare.

She was backed up against the rear side of the circular church. Each blow from her opponents' swords forced her closer to the deep wood. Down the street, her fight was mirrored a dozen times over: a shimmering guard fighting a colorful rebel. Some of them guests in flamboyant party clothes. Some guards from Finbar's—or another faithful—company.

Orlando swept his sword up into one of Clare's unsuspecting assaulters. He took a step back, his balance ajar.

This was all Clare needed to finish off her other opponent—a female guard with a double-sided knife. Clare grabbed her knife hand and forced it back, twisting the guard's forearm behind her back.

Orlando blocked his enemy's upward cut, holding his blade down. He gritted his teeth. His muscles flamed as he forced the blade lower—tucked his tip beneath the crossguard—and, with a jerk, snapped the sword from his opponent's hands. It whirled through the air and stuck in the dirt in the middle of the church's manicured gardens.

His opponent raised his fists.

Orlando had his knife in his hand, but he didn't need it for this. He rammed his knuckles into the man's face.

"Ready?" Clare demanded.

He grabbed at his man's arm and cast her a glance. What—did she think they had some sort of preconceived cue?

Then he saw how she had her opponent's arm in a tight lock. And he had the same. He gave her a tight nod.

They swung their foes toward each other. Bone crunched. The two guards' backs smacked together before both hit the ground, groaning.

Clare nodded approvingly. "You're not half-bad."

He smirked. "I wish I could say the same for you."

He strode past her, around the church, toward the stretch of road that overlooked the harbor. Impenetrable fog had settled on the bay. Even the Anmórian ships anchored there were practically invisible. The storm clouds obscured everything but the moonlight.

Something cold pricked his neck.

He whirled to face Clare. "Cut it out!"

"What?" She raised her hands, which were full of weapon. She hadn't touched him.

The chill struck again. And again. Frozen pebbles, icy diamonds, raining down on him from above. The storm had begun. It rattled the cobblestone street and thickened the mist over the harbor.

He gazed toward the castle. There was fighting in both cantars, but he couldn't get his mind off the castle. Maeve and Merna were both in there, last they knew. And Orlianna and Arliss and the rest still hadn't joined them.

Clare read his look. "Something's happened. Ríon would have come by now."

Orlando started jogging. They dashed past the street that cut right down the riverway. He ignored the flashes of steel in his peripheral vision. The library sat right ahead. He kept his eyes on it.

Then figures reached the top of the arching bridge and ran down it toward them. Garrick. Arliss. Rose. Mícheál. Ríon. Philip.

Orlianna—who was in the process of tearing off her yellow ball gown. She let it wilt onto the cobblestones. Now, in the black dress, she became one with the night.

Orlando slowed down as he neared them. The rush of his pulse relaxed a little. This was quite the team. They'd sort this whole thing out, all right.

Then a dozen more figures appeared on the bridge. These were neither friends nor allies. These were Maeve's private guard.

He halted, ready for communication from the others. But they rushed past him, around him, as if already on preassigned missions of their own. Well, wasn't that grand of them all? Leaving him and Clare alone while they made their own plans.

He grabbed Orlianna's arm as she rushed by him. "What're you doing?"

"Just the usual," she said. "Flying about."

He let go of her arm. "Be careful."

She turned back and laughed as she and Philip streaked down the road that led to Garrick's mansion. "Not one chance!"

Guilt wrenched at Arliss from every side, ripping her heart in a dozen different directions. She wanted to help them all. She wanted to follow Rose and Mícheál through the city, inspiring those who could fight and rescuing those who could not. She wanted to join Orlianna and Philip on the birds, waging war on Maeve's armies from above.

She glanced over her shoulder at the glass library as she sped toward the riverway. More than anything, it was hard to leave Orlando, Clare, and Ríon facing Maeve's private force alone. They were outnumbered four to one.

But Finbar's guards would be there to reinforce them soon. And the private guards weren't the real target, anyway. The real target was the one they were protecting—or rather, covering for.

She had probably hoped to avoid being spotted, but Arliss had seen Maeve descend the far side of the island on her white charger. The horse had stumbled down the steep rock to the edge of the island that faced the Tuáma Fields.

Arliss sucked in cool night air and willed herself to keep going. Orlianna and Philip had gone down the main road of the second cantar.

She took a different route: the stony lane that dipped into the river itself. All the riverway's lamps were flickering. But unlike the rest of the city, this road was empty and held only ghostly echoes of the battle around her.

Over the river to her left, a flash of white bounded across the river and kept going. Maeve was riding into the center of the fields.

Arliss gritted her teeth. The army in the fields—the one that Orlianna and Garrick had spotted. Maeve was bringing them orders.

Arliss set an arrow to her bow. If that number of enemy soldiers marched through Cahair's streets, her own people would be wiped out within half an hour. She had no such reinforcements to counter Maeve.

She tried not to think about home, about her parents, but her eyes had already glanced back toward the eastern horizon. They should have come. Erik and Ilayda had summoned them, hadn't they? Where was her father's fleet? Her mother's courage?

She passed Rose's tearoom—boarded up by Maeve's guards. Her bitterness crescendoed into pure terror. Supposing her parents *had* attempted to come to their aid—and never reached Ikarra. There could still be swarms of crogall lurking in any of the realms' oceans.

The fleet of Reinhold might even now be floating firewood.

She raised her bow and pointed the arrow at Maeve—a distant white speck. It was too far a shot from here, but it reminded her of what she had to do. She picked up her pace and sped down the riverway, leaving Rose's tearoom behind her.

An old sensation of adventurousness rose in her chest. It felt like autumn wind in her lungs and tasted like the tang of wild citrus.

She reached the point where the riverway's smooth stone walkway dropped off into mushy riverbank. The river itself curved away to the left, around the castle. A few of the castle windows still blinked like cat's eyes. Someone was still in there. Merna.

The last lamp in the riverway hung from an iron stuck in a brick wall. Arliss quickly traded the arrow she'd nocked for a different arrow, one she always kept in her quiver. An arrow wrapped in oil-soaked cloth.

She unlatched the lamp's rusty clasp and let the little glass-paned door swing open. The flame within withdrew from the arrow she stabbed into it. It coughed smoke, almost dying.

Then it resurrected on the tip of the arrow. She pulled the shaft free. Flames licked the air. The hail had slowed for the moment. Arliss prayed it would stay that way.

With a longing glance back at Garrick's barn, she stepped out onto the wet bank and strode out into the Tuáma Fields. She had imagined, as she lit the arrow, that the dark mass in the distance was growing. Now she knew she wasn't imagining. Maeve rode at the head of the infantry, guiding them across the black fields.

The soldiers rushed forward around Maeve's horse until she was in the middle of them, shouting at them, goading them on. The tramp of feet multiplied over and over until it was a thunder that mingled with the rumblings above.

Arliss raised her bow and drew the fiery arrow back.

She was just one woman, but she was facing an army of a hundred.

CHAPTER FORTY-NINE:
REINHOLD ARISES

PHILIP HAULED HIMSELF UP THE LADDER INTO THE OPEN UPPER story of Garrick's barn. The birds were still here, all right. Orlianna hurried, severing the ropes that held the aircraft down.

He made toward the craft she'd already freed and crouched on the platform, making sure everything was tight. "There's still one up in the ruins, right?"

She sliced through another rope. "I thought it would be safe there." Sheathing her knife, she quickly gathered her hair and knotted it behind her head. "But nothing is safe."

He bounded off the platform and over to her. "You can't believe that."

She started the engine. "You can't tell me what to do."

He jumped over the tail of her bird and leaned down to look her in the eye. "Orlianna, you've taught me a lot while we've been here. And I'm grateful for it. But maybe you could let yourself learn something for once."

She stood, reminding him that she was as tall as he. "What might that be?"

"That you're going to live." He stared as deep into her green eyes as he could. "Because you really do have something to live for."

She reached for the neckline of her dress. "If there was ever a time to use that pendant, it would be now."

On the open side of the barn, the Tuáma Fields lay dark, as if a heavy blanket were thrown over them.

He squinted, then jogged over to the gaping launch space and stared out over the fields. A crawling mass of soldiers turned them black.

Orlianna froze, but she'd seen them, too. "Without reinforcements, without the pendant, without numbers and magic and everything Maeve has that *we* don't—" she huffed "—we'll never win."

A fiery flash emerged from the riverbank across from the castle, flitting steadily toward Maeve like a flaming bird.

Philip ran back to his bird. "Quick, we've got to help her!"

"Who?"

"Arliss." Philip scanned the room for something flammable. "She's down there. Alone."

"Then we haven't a second to spare." Orlianna settled onto her bird. Her lips moved into something like a smile. "Let's fight, Sir Philip."

A bucket of oil hung beneath an unlit torch on the wall. Philip pulled it down and set it on his platform.

"What're you doing?"

He turned to her, grinning. "Who doesn't love playing with fire?"

Arliss moved slowly enough that the flame didn't flicker out, but fast enough that the tingle in her legs quieted. The army had seen her by now. They must have. She was wielding a flaming arrow in a field of utter darkness.

They raged forward across the field where so much death had been dealt in the previous battle, heedless of the graves they trampled.

She stared heavenward, ignoring the fear that reached its tangled vines around her heart. What did God see, when he looked down on her? Did he watch—waiting to see what she would do? Or was it His hand that moved her, even now?

The stars stabbed needles of light through the black canopy.

Together, they formed an orchestra of light.

She focused on the surrounding horizon. Anything but Maeve and the approaching warriors. The castle loomed dark and ominous in the night. It had to be around midnight by now. The creeping layer of fog that had settled on the bay now stretched around the river, almost uncannily. Almost as if it was controlled. Manipulated.

She shook her head. Maeve's powers weren't *that* great.

Were they?

The line of warriors broke into a charge. Their taunts reached her even here. They may have been in Anmórian, but she knew their meaning.

You are just a woman. A girl, really. One girl with one fiery arrow against the forces of the greatest queen the realms have ever known. You are alone. Forsaken.

Something whispered in the air high above her head. A breeze ruffled her hair. She pulled the arrow as close as she could without setting herself on fire.

The birds were in flight.

Philip flew directly overhead, descending toward the oncoming warriors. Orlianna circled her aircraft, forming a tight perimeter around the warriors. They kept coming on, but their faces turned skyward.

Maeve jerked her horse forward, away from the mass. Something had triggered this reaction. Arliss squinted. Something like rain fell over the field. More hail?

But no icy pebbles shattered themselves over Cahair. This was coming *from the birds themselves.* Arliss grinned upward. Orlianna and Philip saw her plan, and they were helping her with it. Oil. They doused it all over the army and the ground on which they walked.

She raised her bow and readied the shot, her stance wide. Her right foot squished into the dampness from river-water which had seeped into her boot. The grasses under her feet were new and green. But dead thatch still piled the fields.

Dead *and* flammable.

The oil-soaked soldiers shouted at each other. Confusion cut through them like a sword.

Arliss drew the arrow to her mouth and let her fingers release. The arrow sped, whirling, burning, straight into the oiled field. The night was still and starlit for a fraction of a moment.

Light exploded. The trail of fire sped around the warriors, engulfing them in flames. They scattered, some rolling on the ground to smother their blazing uniforms.

In the midst of it, Maeve jerked her charger right and left, dodging her own men. The horse whinnied, terrified. Every time Maeve bounded free of the fire, a new flame burst up beside her.

The fire stretched so close that Arliss could feel the heat of it against her chilled fingers.

Overhead, Philip and Orlianna swooped toward the city. Some commotion must have drawn them. Why else would they leave her alone with—

Maeve cantered free of the fire at last, and at once she was ten paces from Arliss, sitting proudly on her horse. Her face burned with anger, even in the midnight.

Arliss fought the urge to turn around. The foggy city behind her had exploded with sounds—shouts, cries, clashes. Her friends needed her.

Maeve prodded her horse forward. "So here you are: Arliss, *queen* of Reinhold. And you amount to nothing. You are alone."

Arliss glanced back toward the city. "I am not alone."

"Blind, too." Maeve remarked. "But it matters not. I will not let you die alone, isolated from view."

"You plan to kill me?"

Maeve arched her back, staring into the fog. She stroked the pendant where it hung on her chest. "Killing you has never been high on my list."

"But *I* have been, haven't I?"

"Yes." Maeve's gray eyes glazed over with memory. "You have haunted my dreams for a long time, Arliss. Back when Thane first wrote to me of his spying upon you. My dreams were nightmares. Because, you see, I saw you not as you were then, but…"

"What I am now?"

Maeve's gaze snapped back to the present and to Arliss's face. "I knew how dangerous you would become. But also how useful you could be. So I set about to destroy everything closest to you."

Raging sorrow burned from Arliss's heart and through every vein. She could feel the brush of Nathanael's lips on her forehead. The dying strength of Eamon's hand. The heat of her city, crumbling around her.

She nocked an arrow.

Maeve raised her hidden left hand, and Arliss saw the sphere for the first time. So small—yet such a deadly weapon. Maeve snarled. "There is only one more person for me to destroy, I suppose. The one thing that will really break you."

"No." Arliss held the bow steady, but she couldn't shoot. Maeve would blast her with deadly fire the moment she did. She'd never be able to save him then.

"*Yes.*" Maeve tightened the reins with her right hand and reeled around, heading toward the foggy river. "And when he's dead…"

Smoke from the fire coughed into Arliss's eyes, and she blinked. "I will kill you before you touch him!"

Maeve halted her horse as mist swirled around its hooves. "Your words are nothing to me. You are no queen to me. I am the only true, crowned queen in this battle."

Arliss began to reply. But her tongue knotted up and choked the back of her throat. She stared, openmouthed, at the horseman—or rather, woman—who emerged from the mist by the circling river.

"No, Maeve!" the newcomer called out with a loud, certain voice. "You are not."

Maeve's eyes went horribly wide. She somehow recognized who this was, and what she meant. A jerk of her reins and a dig of her heels, and she sped past Arliss—heading down the peninsula toward the ruined tower.

Arliss rushed forward to the elegant woman on the tan destrier.

"Mother!"

Elowyn held out a hand for Arliss to mount behind her. "Hello, Arliss."

Arliss's head was exploding with questions—conundrums—stories. But her mother didn't give her time to do anything but hold on tight. She forced the horse into a rollicking canter back toward the city.

With one arm around Elowyn's waist, Arliss let her bow dangle down the other side of the horse. Wind whipped her mother's hair back into her eyes, further obscuring the misty harbor.

The wisps of gray fog unfurled, parting before them as they reached the harbor proper. The horse's hooves clattered across flat paving-stones.

Arliss caught her breath. The signs of battle were strewn all along the harbor. Fallen soldiers, some still holding onto life. Streaks of blood darkening the reddish stones. People still crowded the wide stairs and walkway out to the harbor, but the fighting had paused. Everyone stared out into the murky bay.

"What's going on?" Arliss demanded, though she felt she knew. It was just hard to believe.

"Hold on," Elowyn ordered. The horse bounded down the steps and to the edge of the elevated docks. Guards threw themselves to the side to avoid being trampled.

"Mother," Arliss squeezed her arm around Elowyn's waist, "Please. Explain yourself."

Elowyn tugged the horse to a halt and gestured to the mist. "You called for us, didn't you?"

Orlianna eased the steering stick down, guiding her bird beside Philip's. Something had happened in the city—something dreadful enough to attract everyone's attention. Only an important death, or the arrival of reinforcements for one side, could have brought this kind of commotion.

Orlando's death would be an occasion, wouldn't it? Enough to shock people like this, at least. He was known to many Anmórians, and rumors about him had spread through Cahair during his stay.

She gripped the stick so hard her knuckles went white. No need to torture herself with these kind of thoughts. Orlando was fine. He'd survive this battle, she was sure of it.

"Look!" Philip's shout was almost lost to the wind. He brought his bird even lower.

Orlianna jerked her bird up to avoid the object that appeared at the nose.

Something like a tree trunk stuck up through the fog, stabbing the night sky and almost scraping her wing. The billowing sheet that ballooned from it turned almost invisible in the mist. But as the fog cleared, Orlianna circled, staring down the familiar shape.

A mast. A crow's nest. Rigging, sails. A wide deck.

The wind soared up toward her, catching her wings and carrying her along. She turned the bird around for another look at the ship. As she did, the wind cleared some of the fog and sent the ship's flag flying.

Philip gave an exuberant shout above her. His bird pitched through the sky.

Sheer triumph filled her chest like a sunbeam.

The flag of Reinhold streamed out from the ship.

Kenton's ship.

BO BURNETTE/536

Chapter Fifty: Reinforcements

IN THE MIDDLE OF THE CHAOS SWIRLING AROUND HER, ARLISS stood secure in what felt like home. The reek of death, the tart whiff of the brewing storm clouds, vanished from her nostrils as she buried her face in her father's chest. The wind hissing in her ears quieted. The throbbing pain in her arm—the one the crogall had hurt—subsided to a dull ache.

She welcomed Kenton's strong embrace in a way she never had before: longingly, desperately, realizing just what her father meant to her. Despite his imperfections, he'd built them a life that surpassed every towering apartment in Cahair.

She gasped against his chest. An unfastened buckle on his jerkin scraped her cheek. "I've missed home."

"I've missed *you*." He squeezed her. "But now's not the time to be missing things. Let us fight this battle."

"We've *been* fighting it." She turned back to the deck and took it all in.

Further down the docks (closer to the castle) floated an Anmórian ship. Guests from the party packed the vessel, frantically searching for safety belowdecks. Missiles and stray arrows from the city battle flitted dangerously near. The deck crawled with sailors readying to make headway out of the bay and back to their capital.

But there were two problems. First, Kenton's three ships formed a line that blockaded them into the bay.

And second, they weren't pulling up anchor and ramming into the Reinholdian armada like they could—and really should—have.

They waited, keeping their anchor dropped.

"Anmórians?" Kenton squinted at the dragon flag, the incredulity in his voice almost amusing.

Arliss nodded, her gaze shifting to the castle. "They're waiting for someone."

"Maeve?" Kenton asked.

She met his eyes—their strong blue like the sky in the mountains. So he knew about Maeve. Of course he knew. Everyone knew now. But it still felt so strange—having her two worlds collide. The one she'd always known, where everything was sure; and the one full of surprises and twists that sometimes left her feeling sick.

"No," she said. "Maeve fled on her horse toward the ruined tower."

Go after her.

Arliss swallowed. Of course she needed to go after her. But how did she explain all of this to her parents? Why she had to abandon their ship just to find and face Maeve?

Go.

She thumbed through her stash of arrows. "I think Merna's still in the castle. The ship won't leave without her."

"Maybe if we draw it out." The voice that spoke these words was new—but also familiar.

Arliss turned. "Brallaghan!"

"Arliss." He kept one hand on his sword, the other behind his back.

She strode toward him and pulled him to her in a hug. He was one of her oldest, truest friends. In this situation, the past conflict between them meant nothing. He was practically family.

After a moment of stiffness, he embraced her as well.

Elowyn paced the deck, palms pressed against her temples. "Perhaps we could draw Merna out? Or at least engage her ship and pull it away?"

"We can't have her escape." Kenton grasped Arliss's shoulder. "Where's everyone else? They're in the city, are they not?" He hesitated. "Assuming they are all still—"

"Everyone's still alive. I think." Arliss realized he didn't know who had made it this far, if his last word came from Erik and Ilayda *before* the first battle. "Ríon, Clare, and Orlando are leading the fighting in the city. Philip and Orlianna just took flight on the birds."

"Birds?" Brallaghan peered skyward.

"I'll explain later." Arliss waved her hand. "And I'm here—trying to do what I can to fix all this."

"And where's Ilayda?" Brallaghan asked.

Arliss turned slowly. "I—I don't know."

At first all Ilayda could see was fire.

Heat and smoke wafted up from the Tuáma Fields. It only broadened as she and Erik galloped closer. She caught glimpses of the city beyond. The castle started to materialize out of the haze, a dark mountain framed against a hopeless sky. It wasn't aflame. Nor was the city, as far as she could tell.

But there was fire—and that meant battle. And it usually meant another thing, in her experience.

Arliss. Arliss and fire went together like a sword and sheath.

Erik urged his mount ahead. "We've got to hurry."

She leaned over the mane of her borrowed mount, willing it to go faster. They'd been loaned these horses by some friendly villagers farther north, and though she thanked them for their kindness, she wished she could have been given something a touch faster. A charger, or a destrier. Not a common work horse.

An open patch of gray field lay between the flames and the castle moat. They sped through the gap, the fire licking dangerously close.

Ilayda glanced through the flames as they passed. She saw bodies—dark shapes fallen all around. She shuddered to think that some of them could be her friends.

Erik slowed slightly, cantering alongside the curving river. The clatter of his horse's hooves echoed down the empty riverway road. But this must have been the only quiet lane in Cahair. All around Ilayda, confusing noises exploded like a hurricane.

The alleys between the riverway stores flitted past, giving her fleeting glimpses of the battle raging through the streets. The wind had carried smoke from the fields and threaded it down the second cantar, covering everything in a dismal haze.

Please, don't let us be too late. Please.

The riverway ended. To their left, the street stretched down the lengths of the docks. To the right, the bridge led over to the castle island.

And in both places, things were happening that made Ilayda's mouth drop open.

Four ships sailed in the bay. One was clearly Anmórian: the flag and ornate scrolled edging betrayed it. But the other three were simple and frustratingly familiar. Ilayda squinted at the line they formed across the bay.

Her heart jumped. It couldn't be.

Erik reached over for her arm. "It's King Kenton. He's come!"

She glanced over at him, gasping for joy. Then she saw beyond him—up to the castle perched on top of the rocky island. Her thrill melted. "Look."

Erik pivoted in his saddle.

A group of heavily-armed guards had emerged from the castle. Behind them strode a hideous personage whom Ilayda recognized instantly. Who else would dare to wear a chartreuse silk dress *and* gilded plate armor during such a battle?

"Merna." Erik jerked at his reins. "We have to hide."

"You mean fight." Ilayda stayed put.

He tilted his head, indicating for her to follow. "Not until we know what's going on and where our friends are." He cantered toward the glass library at the edge of the bay. "Come on."

She followed, resisting the urge to look back at Merna descending the rocks far behind her.

Orlando cleared his throat and spat on the road. His saliva tasted like blood, probably because that's what it mostly was at this point. His fingers had gripped his knives so long they felt stuck in place.

He flipped his opponent over his head, snapping their arm in the process.

The guard landed on a shrub in front of the Mícheál's tavern, moaning but motionless.

Orlando paused, heaving. He'd fought and fought through the city, covering for Clare and Rose and just about anyone he could. Rose and Mícheál had swayed many hiding Ikarrans off the fence—onto their side. Garrick and Finbar led swaths of troops down the streets.

Still, it wouldn't be enough. Not as outnumbered as they were.

A new enemy rushed at him, pike raised.

Orlando ducked as the pike swept over him. His knives were practically useless. The pike put too much distance between him and his opponent. He sheathed the knives. Tumbled beneath another of the guard's mad slashes.

He leapt to his feet and grasped the pike with both hands. He and his opponent held it there in the air between them. Orlando gritted his teeth, his muscles burning like fire.

But this guy—obviously Anmórian—was taller than he was, and stronger, too. He forced the head of the pike closer to the left side of Orlando's body. The forked end pierced the air dangerously close to his neck.

"You're not Ikarran," the guard spat. "Traitor."

Orlando felt his left arm giving out. "If Maeve…wins this fight…there will be no Anmór. No Ikarra."

"I can live with that."

An arrow whistled past Orlando's right ear and stuck in his opponent's heart.

Orlando wrenched the pike out of the fallen man's hands and

spun it to face the newcomer.

Mícheál. He jumped from the doorstep of his tavern, two full quivers slung over his shoulder.

"Thanks."

"No problem." Mícheál started down the road—back toward the bay. "Come on. We just got word that Domnall has turned the stave church into a base camp. He's barricaded himself off."

Orlando rushed after him. "Probably planning a second wave of attack."

"That's what we thought."

A noise like a hurricane blew down the second cantar from the bay. Orlando halted. Grabbed Mícheál's arm.

"Do you hear that?"

"Hear what?"

"Listen."

It was a shout. A battle cry. From here, it almost sounded ghostly. But as it grew louder, Orlando finally discerned the words, and his heart soared. This cry was coming from the true Ikarrans.

The ships of Reinhold are here. The ships of Reinhold are here.

The wind rippled above him. He looked up into the starlit sky.

A dark, winged shape flitted between him and the moon.

Orlianna. Headed for the bay, too.

He broke into a run, tossing his head back at Mícheál. "Have fun with Domnall."

The vial thumped against Ilayda's leg inside her pocket as she hurried across the library's map of a floor. The far wall was one huge glass curve, and from it she would be able to see out on the rest of the city.

She pressed on the hard shape in her pocket. She hadn't had much use for the vial thus far. With battle already raging, though, she'd need it soon enough.

Erik burst through the doors behind her, barring them behind him. He glanced around. "We need to barricade them with something."

Ilayda scoured the walls of shelves and the scattered reading desks and chairs. "Why?"

"Merna's guards are almost to the bridge. I'm afraid they saw us."

"Oh, joy." Ilayda edged toward the windows, arms crossed over her chest. The smoky haze had cleared a little. She now had a view of what was happening all down the harbor, the bay, the city streets.

And everything she saw made her flesh prickle.

He kept talking. "Maybe we should get back outside. Get back on the horses and make a run for it. We might at least find out where Arliss is."

She reached for the glass. It stung her hand with a bitter chill. "*Look.*"

Erik glanced up from the floor behind her. His posture went stiff. He joined her by the window, his breath fogging the glass. "Oh."

The blood, the fighting that strewed the streets with wreckage was only a border to the chaos that swept over the battle from the sky and blockaded it by sea. Orlianna's birds were in the air—their swift shapes flitting back and forth in the night sky. And in the bay—so close to the library's windows that Ilayda felt she could touch it—an Anmórian ship waited expectantly.

But it could not leave if it wanted to. Three Reinholdian ships blocked its passage.

Ilayda pressed her other hand to the window and stared down. The ground below the library cut straight down into the raucous ocean. Waves tumbled black against the rocks in the darkness.

"We have to help them." She tilted her head forward. "Maeve is somewhere in all this mess."

Mess. That's what it was. Nothing more than the final thread in a tapestry Maeve had begun weaving long ago.

Ilayda sighed. Everything had led her to this moment, hadn't it?

Letting Arliss drag her along on that fateful first adventure when they first faced Thane. Running along on the second voyage, that time because of a foolish feeling she thought was true love. And now…

She glanced over at Erik, and, as he wasn't looking at her, she let her gaze linger.

His chest rose and fell—breaths tightly restrained—as he stared through the glass. She caught her breath. He was afraid, too, just like she was. She smiled. It was almost comforting to know that she was not alone.

He realized all at once that she was staring at him. His breathing steadied, and he shrugged. "I suppose this is the end."

She dropped her hands from the glass. "I can't think of a better person to die beside."

The corners of his mouth curled. His eyes penetrated her as always. He peered closely, as if noticing something about her for the first time. "You love me."

The truth burned in her chest as the words came out. But it felt good all the same.

"I always have."

CHAPTER FIFTY-ONE: SHATTERED

Every fight Orlando passed beckoned to him. He wanted to help them all—finish off every one of their enemies. But there wasn't time. From the end of the harbor, he'd seen the dark insectile mass crawling from the castle.

He poured every bit of his strength into his aching legs. No matter what, Merna couldn't get out of this city. If she returned to Anmór and sent reinforcements…

The victory would be hopeless. Even now it was dangling by a thread.

He rushed past two dueling Cahairian guards, unsure of which was his ally and which was on Maeve's side. Up and down the city streets, the story was the same. Orlianna's rebels were doing a valiant job, but without a clear leader, their organization was scattered. The question was, where were Maeve's troops getting their orders?

The back of his neck prickled as a cool wind drifted over him. Still pounding across the cobblestones, he looked over his shoulder.

At the edge of the peninsula, the ruined tower was silhouetted in the navy inklings of a sunrise. And atop that tower gleamed a pillar of silver and gray, illuminated by the moonlight.

Orlando gulped and kept running toward the bridge. From up there, Maeve could see everything—and signal orders to everything. Once they dealt with Merna, Maeve had to be faced at last.

The glass library shimmered beside him as he left the second cantar.

A chariot swerved out of the main thoroughfare and onto the harbor road, almost toppling over. One of its wheels lifted off the ground. It clattered down again as the chariot jerked to a halt.

"Hop on." Ríon ordered. He wasn't smiling, but the crinkle in the corners of his eyes told he was quite pleased with himself.

Orlando hauled himself onto the chariot behind him and Clare. "Where'd you get it?"

"Pinched it." Ríon snapped the reins.

"You saw Merna, then?"

Clare had her eyes fixed on the castle. "I'd think so."

The fire that gushed somewhere behind her eyes was deathly focused. Clare wanted only one more thing out of this battle: to finish Merna off. And rightly so.

Ríon halted the chariot at the base of the bridge. Merna and her guards had reached the top of the arch.

Orlando, Clare, and Ríon dismounted, weapons in hand.

Merna pointed down at them. Her guards pounded down the white stone toward them as she remained atop the bridge.

All at once, Orlando found himself and Clare thick in fight with the most elite Anmórian warriors he'd seen. But Ríon wasn't with them.

He had rushed up the bridge to face his mother.

Ilayda rushed down the library's front steps, not pausing to analyze the scene on the bridge. No time. Orlando and the others were in trouble—heavily outnumbered.

She drew the arrow knives from her boots. It was time to put them to use.

Erik jogged after her. "Ilayda!"

"Come on!" She jerked her head and felt her vertebrae crackle.

Orlando and Clare fought back-to-back, assaulted by a swarm of Merna's guards. Ríon was higher up, battling the two bodyguards who held him back from Merna. One of them wielded a double-pointed spear, whirling it against Ríon's sword.

Ilayda burst forward, edging around Clare's fight. She barely avoided getting her head taken off by a wild cut.

Ríon grabbed the legs of one of his opponents and flipped him over the side of the bridge. That left just the guard with the spear. The length and weight of the weapon made it hard for Ríon to get at him. He just couldn't reach him.

Erik had his longbow and knife in the same hand, going back and forth helping Orlando and Clare. Ilayda swallowed. She needed that bow.

Ríon grunted. His opponent was beating down on him with the spear. His sword wasn't going to take much more.

"Erik!" Ilayda raised an arrow knife.

His perceptive eyes saw past her to what she was trying to do. He opened his draw hand and held it out. "Throw it!"

She hurled the knife at him.

His palm closed around the long, skinny handle.

A hideous crunch resounded behind her. She turned, readying her remaining knife. Ríon stood empty-handed. His sword lay at his feet—twisted into a mangled curl of steel.

The bodyguard readied his spear for a plunge.

The arrow knife whizzed past Ilayda's ear and stuck straight in the bodyguard's heart. He collapsed. The spear slipped from his hands, clattering to the stone.

It rolled slowly, coming to rest at Merna's feet.

Ilayda saw it coming, but she was powerless to stop it. Her feet could not move fast enough.

Merna lifted the spear and thrust it into Ríon's unprotected back.

Clare screamed.

Ilayda staggered forward, her knees weak. She had to help him. She fumbled in her pocket for the vial. If someone else could cover for her…she could heal him…

Merna's eyes flicked up triumphantly from where Ríon groaned on the ground. She bared her teeth at Ilayda. "I have won."

"No." Ilayda held the knife in one hand, the vial in the other. "You will never win."

Merna swung the spear like a club. It slammed into Ilayda, crushing into the arm that held the vial.

Fractals of pain exploded through her arm. She rammed into the solid side of the bridge, her head knocking against the stone. For a moment she fought against unconsciousness. But the sound of shattering glass forced her to stay awake.

The vial hit the bridge and shattered into a thousand pieces.

Ilayda tried to scream. She tried to crawl forward, but she couldn't move her right arm. It had to be broken. Her ear pressed into the stone, she could hear the clash of the fight still raging at the bottom of the bridge.

Clare's boots appeared in front of her eyes, crunching down glass shards.

Ilayda forced her head up.

Clare approached Merna, who was now weaponless. Glaring at Merna, she knelt by Ríon. The spear still stuck out of him. She quickly pulled it out, and he gasped in pain. Blood covered the back of his tunic. His legs were motionless.

She stared at him—the one she loved, dying, beyond her control. When she spoke, her words were cracked. "How could you do this to your own son?"

"He stood in my way," Merna said, "As do you."

Ilayda's arm burned as she tried to heave herself up. She *had* to help. But she couldn't. Her body refused to budge.

Clare's face twisted with emotion. "How can you be such a monster? Can you feel nothing? You've killed your own son. This is *wrong*."

"There is no right or wrong in war." Merna seemed to be struggling to breathe. "You should know that as well as anyone."

"You know that isn't true." Still kneeling, Clare gripped the spear. "You alone have killed so many. So have I. But I'm done killing. There is only one more."

Clare plunged the clean end of the spear into Merna.

Orlianna's fingers trembled around the stick. She forced herself to keep the bird under control as she rounded the castle, staring down at the scene below.

Her heart burned with a hollow emptiness. Ríon hadn't truly been her comrade until two days ago. This stung nonetheless.

But Merna was dead.

Her lungs inflated again. There was only one more battle to be fought, now. And the outcome of that confrontation would determine the fate of the entire war.

Maeve had ridden off for the seaside ruins. She pulled the lever that controlled the flap and redirected the plane a little left— straight for the ruined tower. Clouds wisped through her and filled her nose with cold air.

She passed right by Philip. A gusting east wind blew in their faces, forcing both aircraft back. She squinted through the wind. "I'm going for Maeve."

His brown locks whipped against his forehead. "I'm coming with you!"

"Good!" The wind relented, and she forced the bird forward. "And find Arliss!"

Ilayda's chest pressed into the harsh stone of the bridge. She rolled onto her left side, and her broken right arm flopped against her. Sparks of pain shot through her bones.

A few feet away, Clare knelt over Ríon, silently crying, muttering to him. His legs had to be paralyzed. He was losing more and more blood by the second. There was nothing now that could save him—Ilayda knew that much.

A light behind her speared through the storm clouds and hit the shattered glass, refracting the beam into a million pieces. But one spot shone brighter than all.

She reached for it, her palm closing carefully around the silver cap. Hope rose in her heart, soaring higher than she could contain.

She dragged the silver piece closer. It was the cap to the vial—the part that the sword of Reinhold should have unlocked. The rest of the vial had been shattered, the healing liquid spilled down the bridge.

But inside the cap pooled a few droplets of purplish cordial.

A gasp burst from her lips. She forced herself up, crawling at first, then standing, her arm hanging useless at her side. Her hand shook, nearly dropping the cap.

Tears streaked Clare's face. Her lips moved, but she couldn't find the words.

Erik and Orlando rushed up the bridge. Erik moved toward Ilayda to make sure she was all right, but Orlando halted—frozen. He stared at Ríon in disbelief.

Ilayda leaned down and held the cap out to Clare. "There may be enough to save him."

Clare's lip trembled, her eyes flicking between hope and despair.

Above, Orlianna and Philip's birds cut through the brightening sky, down the peninsula, toward the ruined tower.

Orlando's voice was shaky. "You-know-who is up there."

Erik grasped his bow. "What are we waiting on?"

Ilayda looked back at Clare, hesitating. Should she stay with her? What if Ríon didn't make it? What if Clare had to watch him die, alone?

Clare nodded at her as if she'd read her mind. She took the capful of the vial's remnant. "Go—end this." Her voice dropped to a hoarse gasp. "Kill Maeve."

The movements atop the tower told Arliss that Maeve had seen her sister's death and was in great distress. She, too, had seen it from her perch in the crow's nest of the ship.

Her throat tightened. It had been hard to tell what else had happened on the bridge, but she had seen Ríon fall and not rise again.

Noise—dark, guttural sounds—erupted from the tower.

Arliss pressed her palms into the mast. Maeve had summoned some new horror. What kind of beast could make these noises? Hideous, bellowing, but almost like…language.

Her body clenched. Like the Anmórian tongue.

It was. *Ionsaí! Scriosann!* She knew where she'd hear those words before. And she knew these words came from Maeve's own mouth, magnified and echoed by her own sorcery.

Crogaill, ionsaí! Crogaill, ionsaí! Lig an abhainn sreabhadh le fuil!

Arliss stared down at the deck below her where her parents and Brallaghan were. She glanced back at the bridge, where Clare and Ríon remained. She looked up. Through the clouds, Orlianna's bird flew forward. To her left, Orlando rattled down the harbor on a chariot. Not far behind him, Erik and Ilayda galloped for the peninsula.

None of them realized the danger they were in. None of them— except perhaps Orlando or Orlianna—knew the meaning of Maeve's incantations.

Crogall, attack! Crogall, attack!
Let the river run with blood.

CHAPTER FIFTY-TWO:
THE JUMP

ARLISS'S FEET HIT THE DECK AND SHE STARTED FOR THE starboard side. Her fingers closed over the edge of the slick wood. She peered into the foggy mouth of the bay.

Kenton stood tall. "What do you see?"

"Something's coming." She looked up at him. "I can't explain it, but it's horrible, and it could crush this ship into pieces. You can't pierce its hide—only the tentacles. We faced one of them on the voyage here."

"The crogall," Elowyn intoned behind her.

Arliss turned. How did her mother know?

"Erik told me," Elowyn explained. "We must secure the ship."

Arliss opened her mouth. "I—I can't stay on the ship."

Kenton frowned. "Whyever not?"

"The rest of them—they need me. Philip needs me." Arliss pointed upward toward the distant tower. "Maeve must be stopped."

Kenton pushed away from the side, striding toward where Brallaghan manned the wheel. He raised his hands and his voice to be heard by the whole ship—in fact, he could probably be heard by the adjoining ship as well.

"Prepare for an attack! All hands on deck! Archers at ready!"

The very sound of Kenton's voice made people start moving. Obeying. Readying themselves. But nothing could make them ready for the tentacled creature that rammed into the side of their boat.

Arliss saw the crogall coming and threw herself down. The ship rocked over to the port side, and she rolled across the deck.

Her father reached down and stopped her momentum, pulling her up.

The ship rocked back and forth. She steadied herself against the mast, staring up its piercing trunk. Layers of clouds stacked the sky above, obscuring most of the crow's nest.

She grasped her father's muscled forearm. "I have to get up there."

"I can't…" His voice ended in a tense gasp.

She leaned close to him, holding onto him as hard as she could, fearing he would leave her just as much as he feared her abandoning ship. "Trust me."

He stepped away from the mast. "I do trust you."

With a nod to her mother—Elowyn was hard at work knotting down the sails—Arliss grasped the rope ladder that stretched down the mast. She climbed.

A tan shape sheared through the clouds above her. Orlianna's bird, more than likely.

She climbed faster. The ropes gnawed into her hands. The air grew bitterly cold with the whip of the wind. And all the time, the crogall jerked the ship back and forth until her stomach sagged with nausea.

"Philip," she whispered his name into the wind.

Philip's arms were on fire. The wind fought him: forcing his bird lower, blasting in his face until he nearly came to a halt.

He wrenched the stick forward. What was with this weather? Orlianna was already headed down the peninsula toward the ruins. At this rate, it'd take him ages to catch up with her.

Three masts jabbed up through the rolling fog before him. The Reinholdian ships.

He pulled back on the stick. Last he'd seen Arliss, she'd been speeding toward these ships with her mother. She might be on them right now.

Then again, she might not have boarded. She wanted to defeat Maeve more than any of them. She could have asked her mother for the horse and ridden straight to the tower.

Philip.

He craned his neck, but the clouds certainly hadn't spoken to him. Had he heard an audible voice? Or had it just been in his head?

"Philip!"

It came again. Definitely audible this time, but wispy—almost lost in the mist.

A harsh wind beat down on his wings from above. The bird plummeted, and he stopped fighting it. The winds were erratic things. But right now they seemed to be directed at him, focusing in an almost divine organization.

"Philip!" The voice rang clear, but that might just have been the way his head heard it. One thing he knew: it was Arliss.

"Arliss!" He felt like a fool shouting down into the fog. "I'm coming."

Arliss pulled herself onto the wood decking that surrounded the tiny crow's nest. She stood in a cloudy, gray world. The crogall's vicious hiss, the squelch of its tentacles, the distant clash of steel, the rumble of hooves; they were all dulled by the thickness of the mist.

Her boots stuck over the edge of the railing. She swayed back, holding her balance there. She could barely make out her father on the deck below. The whole crew joined in the battle against the crogall.

She stared outward, blocking the Reinholdian ships from her mind. She couldn't help them. Not now. Her father understood that. Worrying about their fates would only distract her from her mission.

Arliss.

She glanced around, ears twitching. Philip was near her. He was close.

Jump.

She stared heavenward. This was insane. If she jumped, she'd be throwing herself from a ridiculous height either to be crushed into the deck, swallowed by a crogall, or drowned. Or all three.

Jump. Now.

She pulled her hair behind her shoulders, spanned her arms out beside her like wings. She closed her eyes. Filled her lungs.

She jumped.

At first Philip thought something had cut the wings from the bird. It jerked down, plummeting toward the crogall that swirled the waters below.

Then it leveled out. The body of the aircraft bumped forward through the air currents, finally finding its way.

He leaned far over the front of the platform. His weight should have tilted it forward, but something counterbalanced him. He stuck his head upside down and peered under the platform.

Arliss hung from the far back, clutching fiercely to the edge. The wind tore away her words, but he could read her lips better than anyone. "For Reinhold?"

"For Reinhold." He slid back up and guided the bird forward.

On the peninsula, Orlando clattered over the hilly land on a chariot. A ways behind him, Erik and Ilayda galloped on horses. But Orlianna was nowhere to be seen. Her bird must have reached the launching level of the aircraft tower.

Like a candle being lit, a flash of red hair appeared atop the gray tower.

Philip swallowed. Orlianna was facing Maeve alone.

Ilayda reined her horse into the lead, rounding the library and heading down the main road that cut right by the docks. Orlando's chariot had already outstripped them and now rumbled down the peninsula toward the tower. She and Erik had to get there. They had to help Arliss.

A horse whinnied near her—but definitely not hers or Erik's. She looked back.

Two of Maeve's guards were in pursuit on horseback.

She struggled to work the reins with one hand. Her broken arm Erik had fixed up in a makeshift sling. These guards *wouldn't* reach the tower. Not if she had any say in it.

Erik had seen them, too. "We need to—"

"Split up. Go!" She jerked her horse down the riverway road before he could say anything.

She trotted past apartments and taverns, dodging debris from the battle-scarred district. Adrenaline pulsed through her body. Taking charge like this felt weird and made her heart do uncomfortable things. But if Erik was willing to follow her orders, she had to be doing something right.

A cry shot down the road behind her. One of the horsemen had followed.

A crossbow bolt ripped through the air beside her.

Her brain spun. She jerked the reins right at the last moment and darted down the alleyway beside Mícheál's tavern.

The moment she burst down the adjoining road, she knew something was wrong. Down at the head of the street, the doors of the stave church were wide open. The cacophony of battle echoed within.

Worse, Erik's horse stamped outside, riderless.

She galloped down the road, reined her mount to a halt, and swung off—the cleanest dismount she'd ever managed. She rushed into the church.

The scene inside made her whole body ice over.

Domnall had turned the church into a bunker for Maeve's guards. A lot of them. Fresh. Armed. Ready for a final assault that would sweep the city from end to end.

Domnall himself stood straight down the aisle from Ilayda. He held Rose, his sword against her neck. To the left, a guard had Mícheál cornered against a pew, disarmed.

And up by the table of communion, a hulking guard had Erik in a choke hold. His bow lay on the wood floor several paces away.

Ilayda drew an arrow knife with her good arm. "Release them!"

"Aren't you that timid Reinholdian girl they sent back to fetch help?" Domnall snorted a laugh. "And where is that help now?"

Ilayda pointed the knife at the door. "Three Reinholdian ships sit in the bay as we speak." She stalked down the green carpeted aisle. "And I am not some timid girl, you silly lord."

Rose caught her eye. She glanced up at the balcony.

Ilayda looked, but saw nothing. She decided to gamble a few more words against Domnall. "I've come for my friends."

This was a bit of an overstatement. She hardly knew Rose and Mícheál. They were more Arliss's friends than hers. But if Arliss loved them, so did she.

And above it all, there was Erik. Finally admitting her love for him somehow made everything else fuller.

Domnall dipped the sword closer against the hollow of Rose's neck. "Not another step, or I slit her throat. All their throats."

A shadow shifted on the balcony. Ilayda looked again.

She tried to restrain from gasping with joy. *Garrick.* He'd entered through a doorway on the balcony and now edged around a story above Domnall.

Ilayda caught Rose's eyes. She couldn't mouth anything. Couldn't give away Garrick's presence. Domnall would read her lips.

But he couldn't read Rose's.

Rose mouthed: "Garrick?"

The tension made it easy for Ilayda to let her head tremble a bit. A nod.

Domnall swept his hand around the room to his battalion of soldiers. "You do not stand any chance. I don't want to kill you. But if you force my hand…"

Ilayda opened her mouth. But Rose mouthed, "Let me."

Very well. Ilayda hung her head, trying to fake a defeated posture.

Rose leaned her head back against Domnall's chest to free her esophagus. "If I could have a few words, your lordness?"

"Make it quick." Domnall moved the blade from her neck an inch or two.

Rose cleared her throat. "I have to say, I'm a little disappointed in you all. I don't know all of you. But some of you guys are soldiers and spies for Orlianna. Or were, I guess. Before you turned your back on her and started working for that *witch* and her overcompensated minions."

Domnall's face twitched.

"So I just have one thing to say: why? Why have you come to this? Are you making this choice because you think it's right? Or because it's the easiest path?" Rose trembled, staring at the sword blade that could decapitate her in a moment. "When the dust clears from this battle, I want life to move on. I want to rebuild *Cahair*, the capital of *Ikarra*. I want to live and love and discover and create. I want to get married and travel to Anmór and Reinhold and North Havens and have lots of…you know, good times."

Even at sword point, Mícheál grinned.

"So if you want to kill us, kill us. But know you're killing Ikarra, too." Rose held her head high. "Oh, and if you get rid of Orlianna and Garrick, I don't know who's going to pay your salaries."

The church went as silent as during prayer on a Sabbath. Ilayda took shallow breaths.

"Who says any nothing about Garrick?" Domnall sneered.

Garrick dropped from the balcony, pouncing on Domnall like a cat. The shield he held clocked Domnall in the head. Rose slipped out from the sword as Domnall collapsed, unconscious.

Garrick raised the shield. "I'm with Orlianna. Now who's with me?"

The church echoed with battle cries, full of fire, full of life.

Rose caught Ilayda's arm. "I'm needed here. But…"

Ilayda nodded. "We're going to Arliss."

Rose hugged her—the first time she'd done so. She didn't seem like the touchy type. "I hope you make it out of this alive."

"You, too."

Ilayda took Erik's hand onto the horse behind him. They vaulted straight toward the ruined tower.

Chapter Fifty-Three: Unity

Orlianna stood as close to the edge of the top of the tower as she dared—the back of her heels almost hanging over the side. She froze there, letting herself become a statue but for her hair. It whipped in the wind like a flame that refused to go out.

She stared out at the bloodstained horizon. This was no ordinary sunrise. The morning was fighting against the night, holding onto the last shreds of darkness. Red fingers of light reached up and tainted the gray sky all around her.

For once, she wanted to linger and admire the view. It was worthy of being remembered, of being painted and preserved for all time. This moment was one that could last forever.

Yet the silver figure who stood opposite her erased the beauty of the moment. She turned the sky into what it truly was: a mirror to the battle below.

Maeve showcased the sphere with her palms. "I always knew this moment would come."

Orlianna closed her eyes, but she saw more red. More blood.

"The moment when you would stand against me," Maeve continued. "When you would fight me."

Blood raced through her veins, picking up speed. The fire of battle coughed itself to life. Words appeared in her brain, and she savored them, realizing what they could mean.

Fight. Destroy. Kill.

"I have not come to fight you." She opened her eyes and took a shaky breath. Then she stepped toward her grandmother. "You—

you are my grandmother."

Maeve held the sphere in front of her. It had Arliss's crown wrapped around it already, ready to spit fire. "Then why are you trying to bring me down?"

"Because what you're doing will reduce our world to rubble."

"You're doing a bloody good job of that on your own." Maeve swept her hand toward the city. Flames still burned in the fields. Smoke blanketed the streets. The bay was a mess of crogall, ships, and thrashing waves.

"I will not take the blame for your sins."

"My *sins*?" Maeve's voice turned shrill. "When you are the rebel, the outlaw, the one who has murdered an innocent king?"

Her, an outlaw? Merwin, an innocent king? Orlianna's blood boiled. *Enough.*

"We are *alone*, grandmother!" she shouted. "You don't have to pretend! Enough of your lies! Take off the disguise!"

Maeve dropped her voice. "Do not call me *grandmother*. I am nothing to you."

"But you are..." Orlianna desperately clung to every good memory from her childhood. "You taught me how to...to read the stars and the weather. You bought me that telescope from Anmór—it's still in my bedchamber! You taught me how to write speeches and how to navigate a world where so many despised me simply for my womanhood. You told me to strive for perfection— to strive for queenship."

"My mistake." Maeve bared her teeth. "Everything I taught you, hoping you would join me, you have used against me."

Orlianna froze as her memories shattered, the joy draining from them. But they showed her two things more clearly than ever. First, that Maeve had always been a villainess, a manipulating sorceress who used others.

But the realization that made her pull herself to her full height was stronger than that. Even if Maeve had been a horrible person and a deceptive grandmother, she had done one thing: she had turned Orlianna into a strong woman.

She advanced across the flat stone. "You know I can defeat you."

Maeve's face remained unchanged. She ran her finger beneath the pendant's chain. "Is that so?"

"Yes." Orlianna kept moving. Philip's bird advanced in the distance. "Because I have true friends on my side. They will do anything and sacrifice everything. No matter how hard you try, you can't blot out the light. We will hold onto the light and fight for the good, because that's what lasts."

"*Good.*" Maeve flipped the pendant on her chest.

"You told me once that good and bad were merely matters of perspective. You were wrong. It isn't about who wins. It is about who *loves.*" Orlianna kept speaking before Maeve could cut her off. "And I do not mean sentimental, garish love. I mean love that is strong—fierce—and triumphant over your desperate hate."

Maeve reached behind her neck for the pendant clasp. "I could set this aflame now and kill you all." She held up the sphere. "I could end it all."

"You could have done it before now. But you didn't."

"Until now, I didn't have you all together." Maeve glanced down the peninsula, up at the skies, then back at Orlianna. "Now, I do."

Her heartbeat pulsing, Orlianna took a step. Maeve was going to do it. She was going to light the pendant and reveal its power. She was going to destroy…everything. Even Cahair itself might share in the destruction.

So she had no choice. This woman who stood in front of her was no longer her grandmother. She had said so herself. She was a monster, a witch. And she had to be stopped.

Orlianna drew her claw knife and dashed toward Maeve.

Maeve put both hands on the sphere and twisted.

A beam of fire burst out toward Orlianna.

The pounding of his footsteps bounced off the walls of the cavernous tower and echoed in Orlando's ears. He ran up staircase after staircase, rounding his way up the levels. The higher he got, the more light flicked in from the widening openings.

A rushing wind met him when he reached the level where the remaining bird was docked: waiting, facing the completely open side of the tower, ready to be shot out. Behind it lay Orlianna's bird.

He drew his knives. She was already facing Maeve—alone.

A dark shape rushed through the sky toward the opening. Orlando threw himself to the side and rolled against the wall just in time.

Philip jerked his bird to a halt. The platform scraped against the greenish-blue stone, spinning the bird to a halt. The pointed ends of the wings jabbed dangerously near the other bird's stretched canvas.

Arliss jumped off the back, Philip the front. "Orlianna?"

He was already on the stairs to the top. "This way."

Arliss crossed the room to join him.

Philip started forward.

Just before he reached the top of the stairs and the opening that cut up into the sky, Orlando shouted down, "Secure those birds! With this wind, they might rip each other to shreds."

Philip nodded and started to tie them down.

The wind hurled itself at Orlando, blinding him a moment. He forced his eyelids open as he emerged on the sheer, naked top of the tower.

What he saw made him want to vomit. But the sick feeling quickly gave way to burning anger that snaked through his arms and melded his knives with his hands.

Orlianna lay at the edge of the tower opposite him, barely moving. Wisps of smoke curled around the singed slits of her skirt. Advancing toward her, Maeve held the sphere—ready to fire again.

"No!" Orlando threw himself at Maeve just as she twisted the crown.

The sphere clicked.

He rammed into her, forcing her off balance. She staggered to the side, flailing, dangerously near the edge.

The blast of fire hurtled over the side of the tower. The fireball hit the sandy grasses below. They ignited.

Maeve regained her balance and glared at him. She fired again.

He ducked. The blast went over his head, again falling to the ground.

Arliss emerged from below, an arrow already nocked. She aimed it at Maeve. "Don't give me a reason to shoot this!"

Maeve readied the sphere. "You don't need one."

"Neither do you." Arliss jerked her chin at the sphere. Then she noticed Orlianna lying on the ground. "Oh—"

Orlianna rolled onto her side, wincing. Red burns ran down what Orlando could see of her legs. Not the worst he'd seen, but definitely the most painful. If he had the stores of herbs and medicines he'd once collected, he could dilute the pain.

Now, he could only watch her suffer.

Arliss edged closer to him as Maeve held the sphere out. She leaned over to him and whispered in his ear. "I have some Lasairbláth in my jerkin. Cover for me."

She carried that stuff everywhere, didn't she? He stepped toward Maeve.

"No whispering among yourselves!" Maeve snapped. "You can hide nothing from me."

Arliss knelt by Orlianna.

Orlando advanced, scraping his knives together. They hissed in metallic unison. "Then let us have out with it! Since you know everything about everyone, speak it! Rub it in our tedious faces. Summon your strength and power and kill us."

Maeve's lips curled. "Do you *really* want to know the things I know? I know the answers to questions no one has dared to ask."

Arliss glanced up from pressing Lasairbláth into Orlianna's burns. "What questions?"

Maeve smirked, seeing she had their attention. "Like why I ever helped Thane in the first place."

"Simple." Orlando shrugged. "You wanted to take over the

realms as easily and bloodlessly as possible. He was reckless and powerful—and expendable."

"There is more to that story than you might guess." Maeve's eyebrows rippled. "More to every story. Even yours. Have you never wondered what happened to your mother—your *real* mother? Whether she's still alive?"

This tore at a string in his heart he'd never dared to pluck. His mother was hardly even a memory. He'd practically forgotten what she looked like.

And Maeve *knew.* If they killed her, all these secrets would die as well.

Maeve savored their shocked expressions. She rattled off a list. "Has anyone considered that Clare has Reinholdian heritage? She's distantly related to you, Arliss. Could even lay claim to the throne! Or does no one wonder why Galcobhar died when he did, just when he was the one person with as much knowledge of the gifts as me?"

Arliss gasped. "How could you?"

"Did you never ask why Thane waited to attack until he did? Why he let Reinhold grow strong? How Thane and I corresponded so efficiently and covertly? Merna never knew half of what went on." Maeve seemed to have summoned greater height, greater volume of voice. "I have you all under my grasp— all those who have nearly brought my plans to shambles. And so you will die. First you, Orlando. Then Orlianna. Then Philip."

As if on cue, Philip emerged from the stairs.

Maeve smiled coldly at him. "And then, as my creatures destroy her parents' ships, I will kill Arliss."

Orlando couldn't hold himself back. He slashed toward Maeve.

The blast of fire hit him and knocked the breath from his chest even before the searing pain came.

Arliss watched Orlando fall on his back. He hit the stone with a crack that made her wince, but he kept moving—rolling to smother the flames. Then he forced himself to his feet. He and Philip charged Maeve, who had produced a short sword from her belt.

Arliss took her hands from Orlianna's burned leg. "I have to help them."

Orlianna swallowed, gritting her teeth. She held a hand out. "We both do."

Arliss gripped Orlianna's hand and pulled them both up. She left her bow lying on the ground—it wouldn't be much use in a close fight. And a close fight was what they had to have.

She turned to Orlianna. "Keep her from using the sphere. It's our only chance."

"I'm going to do more than just defend myself." Orlianna still had her claw knife on her left hand. "I'm getting my pendant back."

Orlianna crossed the tower toward Maeve, who struggled to keep both Philip and Orlando at bay while still holding the sphere. The pendant hung free around her neck, swinging like a pendulum as she wielded the short sword.

She muttered something and slashed at Orlando's knives. One of them ripped from his hand and spun through the air, disappearing over the side of the tower. But her mutterings must have been the power behind her attack. He staggered back as if he'd been kicked in the stomach.

Orlianna raised her fists—one clawed, the other bare. "Maeve, stop!"

She kept fighting—this time managing to click the sphere while defending herself from Philip's cut. Philip threw himself to the floor as a bolt of fire shot over him.

Maeve fired again. Philip dodged the force of the fiery explosion, but his outer jerkin still caught fire. The navy fabric flamed against his attempts to smother it.

Orlianna narrowed her eyes. Sure as anything, that sphere's contents wouldn't last forever. And despite her sorcery—Maeve's shuddering lips couldn't mean *fear*, could they?—her grandmother was old. Sometimes it was easy to forget, considering her spryness, but she was no match for four expert fighters in the prime of youth.

She pointed her claws at Maeve. "Are you afraid to shoot me again?" She licked her lips. It was time to goad Maeve into shooting this thing and depleting it. "Afraid to harm your precious *granddaughter?*"

Maeve's eyes flashed. She put both hands to the sphere, arms shaking.

Fire ignited from within the sphere's heart. It exploded forward from the front. But the shot wasn't aimed at Orlianna's heart. It was aimed lower.

Orlianna dropped, her hands splayed to catch herself. Time slowed as she realized Maeve's cleverness. They'd all ducked before, and she'd overshot. Now she was catching on.

She readied to feel the heat torching her face.

It never came.

Her face smacked the stone. She shook away the burst of pain and glanced up to see what had stopped the fire.

Orlando stood between her and Maeve. His hand was outstretched—but empty. His other knife had been blasted away. He was defenseless.

She rose, a scream welling up in her throat. But she couldn't do anything.

Maeve clicked the crown again. The sphere erupted.

Orlando fell backward, winded, weaponless, flaming.

Orlianna flexed the fingers of her free hand. This was it. She'd rip the pendant from Maeve's neck if she had to. They had to have *something*, some upper hand.

She charged Maeve, dodging Orlando and Philip's flaming forms. Arliss knelt, trying to help Orlando, who was almost too hurt to move. But Orlianna pressed on. This had to end.

She reached out for Maeve's swelling throat. Her fingers closed around the pendant and she jerked it over Maeve's head, jumping back.

That's when the next blast hit her in the chest.

Her lungs forced their contents out. Her vision tunneled, dimming. The fire around her seemed suddenly hazy; the distant ocean, crisp and real.

The burning bite of fire on her arm ripped her mind from unconsciousness.

Arliss rolled Orlando onto his back again, shaking his shoulders. His clothing was charred, his hands badly burned, but he wasn't permanently damaged. "Can you get up?"

His eyes were closed, but his lips cracked open. "I—"

Behind her, Maeve laughed deeply.

Arliss glared at the marble stone below her knees, her shoulders shaking. Her back was toward Maeve—exposed, practically inviting a shot. That was all it would take. Finish her off. Turn the girl with the fiery arrow into a flame herself.

Orlando moaned, and his jaw went slack. He'd gone unconscious from pain.

Arliss spun, grabbing her bow and standing in one fluid movement.

The situation spread across the square tower was an ugly one. Orlianna lay like Orlando—on the far edge, wounded and rolling somewhere near unconsciousness. Philip was closer to her, and he'd pushed himself to his knees, but the lines slashed across his forehead betrayed the pain he was stomaching.

And of course, Maeve stood unscathed. Shimmering, silhouetted by the sun trickling like blood through gray clouds.

And at once Arliss felt like she'd been crushed by an impossible weight. This woman—this *moon*, as she called herself—had been manipulating her from the beginning. The time she'd spent as

Thane's prisoner had only provided Maeve with information. The victory she thought she'd gained when Thane was killed? A false joy, like a hollow tree ready to collapse with its own weight. Thane had killed Eamon and Nathanael, yes. And she'd blamed herself for it, thinking she could have stopped it.

But could she? If Thane was only a piece in Maeve's game, was she anything less?

"It was you," Arliss finally gasped. "It was always you."

Maeve nodded. "Everything has been part of my plan. And now—" she gave the sphere a little jiggle "—there is only one thing left to do. Feels like there's enough left in here for one more shot."

Arliss reached for her quiver. The battle had depleted her stores. She had just one shaft left. The one type of arrow she always saved: with a tip wrapped in linen.

"And you're wrong, Arliss. This isn't all my doing." Maeve traced the intricate design of Arliss's crown where it wound around the sphere. "It's yours."

"What do you mean?" Arliss drew her arrow out, not bothering to hide it. She couldn't hide anything on this bare, wind-whipped tower.

"I'm not killing you because you stand in my way—though you do. I am killing you because you are the one who started this fire." Maeve's fingers curled, tensed. "Face reality, my dear girl. You could never have been a queen like me."

The sphere clicked without warning and ejected a blast of fire straight at Arliss.

And before Arliss could react—nock her arrow—do anything—Philip forced himself to his feet and took the blow.

It hit him square in the chest. He gasped, straining. Then he fell forward at Arliss's feet, squelching the flame. He lay there below her, unmoving.

She dropped to her knees, feeling down his back. "No…no, Philip, no." She rolled him over, tugging his shoulders up onto her knees. His head hung limp on her lap.

Her entire body shook. The blood in her veins felt at once like both fire and ice. She wanted to scream as loud as she could, to cry every drop of water from her body, to throw herself from this accursed tower and be done with the pain that tore at her heart.

Maeve stepped closer, heels clicking on the marble. "I knew he'd take it for you."

Arliss glared up. "They are my friends—my soul! *You are ripping it out!*"

"It was the only way to break you." Maeve said in a cold voice. "I discovered that long ago. Kill him, and you'd be as good as dead."

"He's *not* dead." She held his face and stared at his closed eyes. "Philip, wake up. Come on."

He said nothing.

She pressed her hand to his muscular chest. It was still. She pressed harder, refusing to believe that there was no more life in his body.

His chest shuddered upward slightly in response.

A spark of relief ignited in her chest. She stood shakily and nocked her arrow, facing Maeve. Then she glanced wildly around at the sights: the raging ocean swirling with sunrise, Cahair behind her covered in smoke, her father's ships still battling one of the crogall. The other two beasts were swimming back down the bay toward the tower, drawn to the flame created by Maeve's wayward blasts.

The battle still raged on. Crogall against Reinholdian ships. Reinholdian ships versus the Anmórian vessel. The Anmórian sailors defending against rebel archers on shore. The rebel archers battling Maeve's guards.

"Is this what you wanted—more bloodshed?" Arliss shouted louder than she ever had. "Look around you! Ikarrans and Anmórians spilling each others' blood. Is this what becomes of your truce between the clans? You wanted unity. This is *your* unity!"

Maeve's eyes traced the panoramic horizon.

"You can blame this on me until we are all dead at your feet, but you're bloody wrong. You say you want peace, but you cause only war."

"*You* caused the war," Maeve said. "If not for your underhanded actions, we could have had unity. But now I am left to pick up the pieces of my plans."

"You can thank Orlianna, I suppose, for bringing us to Ikarra in the first place."

Maeve's sharp laugh almost sounded like a cough. "You fool! I *let* Orlianna bring you. Do you really think she was able to keep it a secret from me? I could have stopped her. But I let her go, because I wanted two things: To see you and meet you. Yet also, to have you dead."

Just one more way in which Maeve was behind everything she did, everywhere she went. Arliss tightened her grip on the bow her mother had sent her. It still felt unfamiliar in her hand, but she hoped it would shoot true.

Maeve stared into the distance. "We were so close to being unified."

"No," Arliss said. "We're too individual, we clans. We could never be one and the same, only separate parts of a unified whole. Somehow, in all your thoughts, you failed to see that."

Maeve held the sphere up. After using it on Philip, it probably wouldn't fire again. But judging by her calm disposition, it might. "I have failed in nothing. My triumph lies at your feet."

Arliss stared down at the bodies of Philip, Orlando, and Orlianna.

"And you—" Maeve smiled "—are next."

Arliss raised her bow.

Maeve twisted the crown. She shot.

Arliss stayed still. The sphere flickered, coughed to life, and spat out its final blow—not even a fireball, just a tongue of flame that snaked through the air between them. The heat hovered dangerously near Arliss's knuckles.

But it touched only one thing: the fabric-wrapped tip of her arrow.

Maeve twisted the crown over and over, but nothing happened. Her gray eyes went terribly wide. She dropped the metal ball, and it rolled to the edge of the tower and disappeared.

Arliss pointed the fiery arrow at Maeve. "Do not move."

Maeve glanced toward Orlianna—whose burned right hand clutched the pendant. "You're going to kill me?"

"I know what you're trying to do." Arliss arched her eyebrows. "If you drop that pendant into the fire below us, you'll kill us all."

Maeve glanced at Orlianna again, as if judging the distance.

Arliss struggled to breathe. Philip's sword lay close enough for Maeve to grab it. If Arliss missed her shot, she'd be unarmed. Maeve could drop the pendant, and who *knew* what would happen then.

"We can still stop this," Arliss pleaded. "We can end this battle and rebuild what you've broken. God does his best work from the ashes."

Maeve stared at the three fallen—all beginning to stir. Once they regained consciousness, she would be outnumbered. "My world does not have room for you, or your friends, or your God."

"This is not your world." Arliss drew her bow fully, the flame flicking close to her grip hand. "This is not your story. It is mine— the story of a princess with a fiery arrow, just trying to find her way in a world that becomes stranger at every turn. Like every legend, it's almost too impossible to believe."

Maeve stood tall, chin lifted with scorn.

"But this legend began with a fiery arrow. And it will end with one."

Arliss breathed. Her fingers relaxed.

The fiery arrow hit Maeve in the heart.

CHAPTER FIFTY-FOUR: FAREWELL

ARLISS COLLAPSED ON HER KNEES, HER BOW TUMBLING FROM HER hands to hit the stone. She felt for Philip's chest—now beginning to heave with real breaths again—just to have something solid to hold onto. Pattering noises—footsteps—echoed up from the opening to the lower floors of the tower. Someone was coming.

But she didn't feel threatened. She didn't feel afraid. For the first time in as long as she could remember, she could breathe freely without her lungs screaming, without her heart aching.

Maeve was dead.

Pierced in the heart by the fiery arrow, she had staggered back and fallen over the edge of the tower—into the fire now raging below.

The footsteps loudened until they rose up the staircase to the top of the tower. Ilayda and Erik emerged, glancing around, bewildered.

Arliss cradled Philip in her lap again. Not far from her, Orlianna had sat up, her eyes glazed over as she stared off the edge of the tower where Maeve had fallen. Orlando, too, had managed to roll over and blink hazily.

Ilayda gaped. "What—what happened?"

Arliss started to answer, but Orlianna cut her off.

"Maeve is dead." Beneath a tangle of red hair that drifted across her face, her eyes had become bright and bold again. "The scourge of the realms is gone."

Ilayda rushed to Orlando, kneeling beside him. "Are you all

right?"

He forced himself to sit up, clenching his eyes shut. He laughed bitterly. "I'll live." He let Ilayda help him to his feet.

Arliss half-smiled, but glanced down at Philip. His lips moved, trying to form words. He seemed caught between sleep and waking.

She leaned down and pressed her forehead to his. "Wake."

Her words took effect like magic. His eyelashes brushed hers. He reached up and slipped his hand behind her neck, squeezing. Then he rolled over and stood, pulling her up with him.

She threaded her arms around him. He'd saved her life. Not like it was the first time. But his bravery—his selflessness—never ceased to make her heart feel like it had wings that itched to fly.

"Maeve's gone." She breathed into his chest. "It's over."

Erik strode over to Orlianna, offering his hand. "This battle isn't over." He pulled her to her feet.

Orlianna unclenched her fist and fastened the necklace around her neck, arranging the pendant in its usual place against her heart. She then strode forward to the side of the tower that faced Cahair. "Quite right. It's not."

Arliss stepped back from Philip and looked toward Cahair, her heart sinking. Battle still burned in the city. Her parents still fought with every drop of blood in their bodies.

And the tower shook, surrounded by smoke. It had been easy to ignore during the confrontation with Maeve. But as she joined Orlianna by the edge and stared down, she faced the truth.

Two of the crogall swam in the shallows by the tower's front porch, hurling their tentacles toward the doors, rattling the foundations. All around the rest of the tower—where there were dry, sandy grasses—the fire from the sphere burned higher and higher.

And rushing up the hilly peninsula toward them came a mass of Maeve's guards. Whether coming unknowingly to help their queen or to avenge her, they were coming, and there were a lot of them.

Arliss realized everyone had come to stand by the edge. They all faced the battle, each forehead knotted with focus as they tried to come up with a solution.

She sighed sharply. There was nothing, nothing that didn't risk the lives of everyone she loved.

"All of you, get on the birds." Orlianna grasped the pendant. "I know what must be done."

"What?" Ilayda asked.

Arliss caught Orlianna's eye and held it. No. She couldn't do this. It was suicide. It was madness.

Orlianna dipped her chin, eyes pleading. "You have to let me, Arliss."

"You can't!" Arliss insisted. "You're the queen of Ikarra!"

"That's why I must do it."

Ilayda placed her hands on her hips. "Do *what?*"

Orlando's voice was unsteady. "Use the pendant."

Philip sucked in his breath. "That thing will destroy—"

"Everything in a mile radius, at least. It's the only way to kill the crogall and the rest of Maeve's forces." Orlianna glanced around the group. "You have to understand."

Arliss looked to Philip for support, but his face was set. He knew as well as she did that Orlianna was right.

Orlando suddenly exploded, fists curling. "I'm not getting on a bird and flying to safety while you kill yourself!"

"Orlando—" Orlianna reached for him.

"There has to be another way! We'll all fly out of here together…we can drop the pendant into the fire *from* one of the birds."

"*Orlando.*" The strength of her voice silenced him. "That could never work. What if we missed? What if we couldn't fly away in time?"

"Then I would die with you!"

She closed the distance between them, hooking her outstretched hand around his neck. "I promised myself you would survive this battle. Don't make this harder for me than it has to be."

He opened his mouth to speak, but a rasping sob was all that came out.

She embraced him. "I have peace that this is God's will. Let me do this, for you. For all of us." She stroked his sandy hair as if he was a child. "Go back to Reinhold. Live your life."

"What life is it without you?"

To this Orlianna could not respond. But when she stepped away from Orlando, she held his ring in her hand.

Arliss stood behind them, her hands hanging at her sides. Tears pooled behind her eyes, and her face twitched as she tried to hold them back. This was goodbye, then. After all they'd been through, this was the end of her time with Orlianna.

Orlianna turned to Ilayda next. "Take care of Arliss for me, won't you? Heaven knows she needs it."

Ilayda looked close to bursting into tears, but she kept her voice steady as she hugged Orlianna. "I will."

Erik was next. He stood tall—face resolute and stolid as ever. But the shimmer in the corners of his eyes betrayed him.

Arliss bit her lips. She didn't think the worse of him for it. A glance at the others showed that they were *all* crying.

Orlianna held Erik's stiff arm. "You are one of the bravest men I've ever known."

He bowed slightly, not even trying to speak.

Orlianna turned slowly to Philip, her brows drawing together. "Oh, Philip." She threw her arms around him. "There's not a man like you in the three realms."

"There's not a woman like you," he managed, "in the world."

Now there was only one more goodbye: Arliss herself. Orlianna smoothed out her ragged skirt. She smiled, and her green eyes were so *peaceful*—all the hatred and horror drained from them at last. She was not just resigned to her fate. She welcomed it with open arms.

Arliss had to smile. "I can hardly bring myself to say goodbye."

Orlianna shrugged. "Let us not say goodbye, only farewell. We will meet again on other shores."

And Arliss hugged her, treasuring her last moment with this

person who had been so much. A guide. A teacher. A friend. A comrade.

A sister.

Orlianna stood alone on the ruined tower, watching the two birds drift into the east. She'd barely been able to make eye contact with Orlando as he climbed onto the platform with Erik and Ilayda. And her arms had physically ached when she pulled the lever to hurl the bird into the air.

She exhaled. They were free. They'd all survived the battle. And now—when she dropped this thing—Ikarra would be free, too.

There would be scars. Rebuilding the things that had been broken. But they would endure, even without her. Garrick would step up and lead them. She was sure of it.

She squinted into the rising sun and let its heat thaw her frozen muscles. Arliss and Philip's bird was almost blotted out by the light. The one with Erik, Ilayda, and Orlando hung back, weighed down as it was.

But the third bird hadn't been usable. Its wing was torn from the harsh battle and landing. It lay, useless, on the level below her.

She reached for the pendant. The cool metal seemed to hum with life against her fingers. It was time.

With a swift jerk, she snapped the chain. She twisted the ring around the cap. She dangled the pendant at arm's length over the edge of the tower.

In a few moments, this tower would explode, engulfed in flames. The crogall would be nothing but fragments of bloody tentacles. The shoreline of Cahair would be altered forever.

And she—Orlianna, queen of Ikarra—would be gone.

She'd never feared death. Death had always stolen the people she loved long before their time. He was not a friend, of course, but certainly more than an acquaintance. She knew Death well from his many visits. William. Her mother. Her father. Harrison. Even

Maeve.

But somehow she was suddenly afraid. A deep, slicing regret flooded from her heart through her bloodstream.

Why? Why this sudden weakness? She fought to relax her fingers and drop the pendant.

But she couldn't. Death was no longer an inviting thought. It was not yet her time.

Not yet her time because, for the first time in her life, she had something to live for.

She took one last look at the pendant's swirling silver petal designs and the deep purplish contents within. She breathed out, turning to face Cahair. And she released the pendant.

Arliss looked back at Cahair just as the tip of the peninsula exploded with fiery light. It rippled outward from the tower, undulating the waters and ripping through the land. The tower itself appeared to be sinking into the sands as it crumbled, chunks of stone falling like hail.

Her throat tightened. She'd done it, then. The pendant's power was shaking the earth to its core.

And Orlianna was gone.

The ripples touched their bird. Arliss reached up to warn Philip, but the blasting wind reached first.

The right wing tore clean off. The bird spun, almost flinging Arliss off. She grappled for a hold on the platform. They were flying at a ridiculous speed—due south.

Ocean and sky spun around her until she was almost sick.

Cold water shocked her body as it hit her. The rotating bird hurled her and Philip off, her body still spinning as if the oceans were a whirlpool.

The sun disappeared. The water around her was ice, freezing her in place. She started to sink.

An even bigger shadow overtook her. Warm arms surrounded

her—so this was what dying felt like?—and she felt herself rising, soaring, rushing upward.

When her vision cleared and she blinked back the saltwater, she was lying on her father's ship.

Brallaghan met Arliss at the door to the state room cabin. He reached out to stop her from depressing the door handle and bursting in.

"Take a deep breath." He looked at her, his eyes deep with pain. "He's not going to make it much longer."

She shoved him aside and forced the door open. Brallaghan couldn't be right. Kenton was fine. Anyone would be shaken after *that* battle. But a little medicine and rest…

The sight inside the state room made her thoughts silence. She floated forward through the dim room, barely feeling the polished floor beneath her feet. It just…couldn't be.

Elowyn sat in a carven chair beside the four-poster bed where Kenton lay. She sat upright as ever, gripping his hand. She turned to face Arliss. "Good. I knew you'd make it in time."

She crossed to the bed, realizing how precious each moment was. "We landed in the ocean." Her memory of the last few hours had turned hazy. "The crew pulled us out. How did you escape?"

Elowyn looked at Kenton, whose eyes were closed. "The explosion triggered the river, the tides. We set out to sea at full sail."

Gray light cut through the window behind the bed and gave the room a cloudy atmosphere. Arliss stood on the other side of the bed and took Kenton's other hand. The lines in his forehead carved deeper, and he shifted.

"Arliss." Strength pulsed through his palm into hers.

She knelt slightly. "Father, I'm here."

He smiled, eyes still closed. He'd been changed into a fresh shirt—thin and blue—but Arliss could see his wounds through it.

There were too many to count. His hands were raw, and the front of his shirt revealed a nasty gash across his chest.

The door opened and clicked quietly shut. Philip entered, treading silently. He stood by Arliss.

Kenton opened his eyes. "My children. God is good to let me say goodbye to you."

"This isn't goodbye." Arliss leaned forward. "I won't let you die."

"That isn't a choice any of us get to make," Kenton coughed.

Arliss tucked her hair behind her ear, brushing a tear aside with it. "How will I keep going? We can't lose you. You're the king of Reinhold."

He released Elowyn's hand and took Arliss's in both of his. "Reinhold is ready for a new leader. *You* are ready."

Philip's hand against her back was all that kept her on her feet. Her diaphragm shuddered, fighting every breath.

Kenton held his hand out toward Elowyn. Solemnly, she lifted his crown from the bedside table and placed it on his palm.

"Come closer," he whispered.

Arliss leaned over, offering her bare head. Tears dripped from her eyes and wet Kenton's bedcover. The pale morning light stung her eyes.

A sudden weight rested on her head, forcing her tangled waves of hair to lie flat.

She glanced up into her father's eyes.

He was smiling. "You are now, truly, Queen Arliss of Reinhold."

She stood, her legs finding strength again. She smiled down at him, and he at her. But something was different. The ridges across his forehead flattened. His sunburned cheeks paled. His sharp blue eyes stared, dull and unfocused.

He was gone.

She stood, staring at him. He'd been her rock since childhood. He had shaped her into the woman—the queen—she was today. And now she had to try to stand on her own.

But she wasn't alone.

She collapsed into Philip's arms as the sobs racked her body, ripping through her bones. For a long moment, he held her, letting her soak his tunic with her tears.

Elowyn's voice came out steady, deeper than normal. "The rest must know."

Arliss nodded. Philip led her to the door of the state room and opened it. They stepped out onto the deck.

The crew's faces were grim—tense. Ilayda and Erik stood close by, waiting. The sea rolled on beyond them, ignoring their troubles, simply carrying the ship home.

Philip spoke for Arliss. She was glad. She couldn't have made a speech now if her life depended upon it.

"The king is dead."

The crew hushed. Ilayda closed her eyes to hold back tears. Erik pulled her close.

Arliss looked to her mother. For once, Elowyn's steady visage looked ready to crack. Tears flooded her cheeks. Her jaw shuddered. Arliss reached for her, wishing with everything in her that she could wipe the pain from her mother's face.

But the same pain burned in her own heart.

Philip paused to give the crew time for shock. Disbelief. Sorrow. "In his final moments, King Kenton helped the realms defeat the greatest evil we have ever known. Now, he has passed the crown on to his successor—Arliss."

The crowd hushed as they noticed the crown on Arliss's head.

Philip motioned to her. "The queen of Reinhold has come! All hail Queen Arliss of Reinhold!"

The crew—Erik and Ilayda the loudest—responded, "All hail Queen Arliss!" A ripple spread over them all as they knelt, honoring her.

Arliss's heart was full to bursting with so many emotions that she could neither speak nor move. She simply stood and breathed the salt air.

Philip turned from the crowd and faced her. "Well, you're the queen now."

She swallowed. "Yes."

"Then, my queen—" he ran his hands through her hair and pulled head closer "—I must ask if I may kiss you."

"You may—" she closed her eyes "—my king."

Their lips met. She leaned into his warmth. It wasn't what she'd expected. Not the soft, comfortable thing she had always imagined.

He'd been through a battle. His lips were dry, cracked, and bloody.

But so were hers.

CHAPTER FIFTY-FIVE: THE CHRONICLES

ORLANDO KNELT ATOP THE CLIFFS OF AÍLL, WATCHING EVERY WAVE roll in. He should have been helping them unload the ship. But he couldn't control himself. If he so much as looked Arliss— or any of them—in the eye, he'd lose it.

No, he was better off up here, with his lungs full of clean ocean air. He watched the other two ships coming into view. After two week's journey and spreading apart, they'd been a little behind, but they were finally dropping anchor.

Boots crunched the sandy clifftop behind him.

He closed his eyes and listened to the steady trudge. Light footsteps, but with a decent amount of weight behind them. Philip's.

He opened his eyes and stared at the last ship. It was sending out the first longboats with the wounded, rushing them to treatment in Cladach—the seaside city.

Philip knelt beside him. "Hard to believe we're back home, isn't it?"

"There are harder things to believe," Orlando said bitterly.

Philip cocked his head, but still Orlando refused to make eye contact. "It does feel impossible, doesn't it? She felt so…immortal. Legendary."

"And now she's *gone.*" Orlando's voice grated away into silence. He quieted. It was no use trying to say anything else.

Philip clasped his shoulder. "Remember the day we met her? She and Arliss walked straight up the hill between the cliffs. We were right here, waiting for them."

Orlando forced his breath through clenched teeth. This wasn't helping him. It was just dragging back up every memory of her—hurting him, taunting him. This was what he'd endure forever, it seemed. Waiting here on these lonely cliffs, staring into the west, remembering everything she had been to him.

New footsteps scraped up toward them nearby. Arliss rounded the edge of the clifftops, scrambling toward them. The edges of her dress dripped water, and her face was spattered with sand. She still wore the crown, but it somehow didn't work with her disheveled appearance.

She was panting like she'd run all the way uphill. "Philip…Orlando…"

Philip jumped to his feet. "What is it?"

Arliss looked at Orlando, her lips quivering as she tried to form the words. "Come down to the bay. There's—a friend I want you to meet."

Philip hesitated, confused.

But Orlando rose, his legs shaking. She'd said these words before on that day so long ago, when he'd met *her* in this very place. There was only one thing she could mean by them now.

He ran across the cliffs, around the curve, down the steep decline. Gravelly sand flew all around him from the divots his heels were carving.

He stumbled. He didn't care. Nothing mattered but running, closing the distance between himself and her.

Orlianna stood by the water, crimson hair waving in the wind. She began to run as well. "Orlando!"

"Orlianna!" His legs threatened to give out beneath him. "Orlianna!"

They collided, spinning, embracing, kissing.

"How—" he panted.

"The last bird…I flew it out."

"But it was—"

"Broken, I know. But it lasted me long enough to land on the deck of the ship, and…"

He lifted her up, spinning her around, practically dancing. It didn't matter how she was alive. She was alive. And they were together.

And together they would stay, forever.

Orlianna forced him to look into her eyes as the beach breeze swirled around them. "I know it's a bit sudden to ask this, but I'm going to anyway. Ríon survived—paralyzed from the waist down. Once he recovers, he's going to marry Clare and rule Anmór. Arliss and Philip will do the same for Reinhold. And while I *can* rule Ikarra alone…"

"You don't want to?" he finished.

She nodded, green eyes shimmering.

"I suppose I'll marry you, if you make me." He smirked. "But trust me. It's not just that you don't want to do it alone. You can't."

She opened her mouth to say something, then closed it, lips pursed. They both knew he was right.

He looked up at Arliss and Philip, standing together on the clifftops, hand in hand. Arliss was beaming. Behind them, the sun rose in a clear sky, red fingers fanning out all around.

Orlando exhaled. A new day. A second chance.

And the sun was only just beginning to rise.

FIVE MONTHS LATER

Arliss crossed the southern bridge from the hill, watching the sunlight play with the moat below her. The wind that whispered in her ears felt like spring, but deeper, darker. More mature. And the colors of the distant forest betrayed the truth: it was autumn.

She savored a lungful of her favorite season and strode off the bridge. The glass library in front of her was gleaming, every pane of glass reflecting the sunlight. Tendrils of cloud crept across the sky, shielding her just slightly from the glare.

She smiled, fingering the handle of the teacup she carried. Perfect lighting to write by.

A quick glance behind her showed that her city was waking up. Once the entire village had fit on the hill. Now just the castle spread over the hill's tiers. Smoke drifted from the chimney in the right-hand kitchens. Ilayda must have been up already—rather unusual—and she must have been cooking breakfast as well—doubly strange.

Bridges spread out like compass points at the base of the hill, arching over the moat. East went between the market and the church, with the homes around them. West stretched down the craftsmen's road. North led to—nothing, yet. But Erik was already talking about using it to develop and fly aircraft.

And south—the bridge she'd just crossed—led to this round glass library. It reminded her of the one in Cahair, but it had its own character. And most of its towering shelves stood empty, waiting for years to fill them with stories.

She ascended the rough-hewn steps and pressed the brass handle. The door swung in, and so did she.

Lines of dark bookcases stretched on either side, all so tall there were ladders to help reach the top shelves. The empty spaces and sides were plastered with maps—portraits—sketches. Memories.

And a bright aisle cut between the two sides to the wide window on the other side of the building.

"You finally made it." Philip turned from the desk that touched the glass and overlooked the plains.

Arliss rushed down the aisle toward him as fast as she could without sloshing her tea. "I had to stop by Rose and Mícheál's. I won't be much good without some tea."

"Quite true." He grinned—cheeks dimpling even under his scruffy beard—and motioned to the desk. "I've made it ready for you."

She stepped forward. A stack of blank paper centered the mahogany desk. Beside it, a quill stuck upright in its inkwell. Two more inkwells—their lids screwed shut—waited for their companion to run dry. A tray of fresh bread lay on the left hand side with a lump of melting butter.

She stared out the curving window. The golden plains of Reinhold were as bright as ever. She turned to Philip.

"It's perfect."

"The least I could do." He bowed at the waist, shrugging modestly. He lifted an eyebrow. "I suppose I'll take my leave now?"

She nodded. Once the library doors clicked shut, she sat in the velvet-seated chair and reached for the pen.

Her hand froze. The blank page curled up at the edges, waiting for her.

But where did she begin? Who did she tell about first? Her parents—Kenton and Elowyn, first rulers of Reinhold? Or perhaps Nathanael, or maybe Eamon. She could begin with any of them, all of them.

Ilayda.

Erik.

Rose.

Mícheál.

Ríon.

Clare.

Orlando.

Orlianna.

Even Philip.

She took a deep breath, stared out the window at the golden fields one more time. Holding the teacup to her lips, she let the warm liquid slide down her throat. She swirled the inkwell once.

Then she lifted her pen and began to write.

BO BURNETTE/590

Acknowledgements

It's impossible to condense my feelings on the seven-year adventure which has been *The Reinhold Chronicles* into words. I've grown and changed so much—as a writer and just as a human being—because of these characters and their stories. And though I may be closing the pages on Arliss's story, I know these characters will always be with me, largely due to the real-life people who have influenced these tales.

Thanks is due to so many people:

My parents, the most supportive I could ask for.

My sisters: Kendall, who designed the arrow you've seen hundreds of times throughout this book; Courtney, who inspired me to add one more scene to this already-monstrous book; Kelley, to whom I've been divulging plot details since the beginning; and Susanna, who has read each book more times than I think anyone else ever will.

Fiona McLaren, my amazing editor—thanks for stepping in so seamlessly for this final book and understanding my characters as well as I do.

Chrissy from Damonza—I still can't get over these covers.

To everyone who helped get this book into its final form—beta readers, reviewers, proofreaders, and all those who helped with the book trailer—thank you. Thanks especially to Corley and Kelsey, who helped me cut fifty pages from the initial draft. (And of course, thanks once again for the map, Kels. You're the best.)

And thanks above all to God, who blessed my life with these stories. I give them back to him, and to you all, in hopes that they will bless you as well.

Authors love hearing how their writings impacted their readers. If you enjoyed the book, would you please consider writing a review on Amazon and Goodreads?

Bo Burnette lives and breathes stories, finds adventures everywhere, and survives mainly on coffee and tea. He has several books with his name on their covers, most notably World War II biography *Denver and the Doolittle Raid*, middle-grade mystery *The*

Lighthouse Thief, and the short story "Finding Viola."

His *The Reinhold Chronicles* trilogy of medieval adventure stories includes *The Fiery Arrow, The Realms Beyond,* and *The Three Thrones.* Bo makes his home in the state of Georgia, halfway between the soaring mountains and the rolling sea.

Bo Burnette/594

The opening chapter of *The Reinhold Chronicles* trilogy

Arliss, the sixteen-year-old princess of Reinhold, despises the class boundaries which plague her city on a hill. When her father the king forbids her friendship with the young peasant swordsman Philip, Arliss sets off on a quest to the heart of the land Reinhold, only to discover an evil more threatening and ancient than she could imagine.

"I could hear the music again, and somehow it seemed louder than before."

Every day, Miss Erikson hears mysterious music coming from behind a locked door at the Lang School of Fine Arts. When the strict Mrs. Borg demands she leave the door alone, Miss Erikson's curiosity propels her to uncover the secrets of the ever-closed door. As she pursues the source of the inexplicable music, she must finally face the grief of the past she has long tried to ignore. (A 3,000-word short story)

A historic lighthouse. A suspect thief. An intolerable cousin.

The Fourth of July is always a big holiday on Saint Simons Island. But this year, while coping with a visit from his contrary cousin, 14-year-old Ethan discovers strange happenings at the historic lighthouse. Soon he is caught up in an unexpected adventure and a quest to save his beloved lighthouse.

A story of bravery, cunning, and sacrifice during World War II.

The 1942 Doolittle Raid on Japan—America's first strike after the Pearl Harbor attack—is now accessible to all ages in this lavishly photo-illustrated book.